Advance Praise for *When Javi Dumped Mari*

"*When Javi Dumped Mari* is Mia Sosa at her absolute best! Friends to lovers, with a little second-chance romance sprinkled in, the sexual tension and laugh-out-loud humor will have you turning the pages and sighing in satisfaction at the end."
—Farrah Rochon, *New York Times* bestselling author of *Pardon My Frenchie*

"The most fun that I've had reading a book in a long time. Mia Sosa expertly strikes the balance of crafting a story that makes you laugh out loud and also pulls at your heartstrings."
—Kristina Forest, *USA Today* bestselling author of *The Love Lyric*

"Mia Sosa is the reigning queen of the modern rom-com, mixing hilarity with heat and so much emotional wisdom when it comes to families, work, and love. Each time she releases a book, it's an event for me and a cause for great celebration, because she's the master of feel-good romance."
—Olivia Dade, *USA Today* bestselling author of *At First Spite*

"Mia Sosa is the undisputed queen of the unputdownable romance. The yearning is divine, the tension is delicious, and the chemistry is explosive—*When Javi Dumped Mari* is friends-to-lovers perfection. Sosa has delivered her signature combination of wit, heat, and heart, and I can't stop talking about this completely devourable book." —Denise Williams, author of *Just Our Luck*

"*When Javi Dumped Mari* is everything I want from a friends-to-lovers romance! Full of swoons and tension and steam and so many laugh-out-loud moments, no one does humor and heart and heat like Mia Sosa! If you love *My Best Friend's Wedding*, but have always wanted it to have an HEA, this is the book for you!"
—Naina Kumar, *USA Today* bestselling author of *Flirting With Disaster*

"A funny, thought-provoking, and delightful friends-to-lovers romantic comedy full of heart and sizzling chemistry. Mia Sosa never misses!" —Farah Heron, author of *Accidentally Engaged* and *Just Playing House*

"With *When Javi Dumped Mari*, Sosa pens a sublime romance that leaps off the page with humor, heart, and heat. Her ability to craft the perfect rom-com is the best I've ever seen."

—Tracey Livesay, author of the American Royalty series

"A sexy, banter-filled, humorous ride that rom-com lovers are sure to adore. This book kept me on the edge of my seat until the very last page." —Gabriella Gamez, *USA Today* bestselling author of *The Next Best Fling*

"[Mia Sosa's] hot and swoony romances are always ones that we know we're gonna obsess over as soon as we pick them up. So it's not too surprising to see that her next one hits the same just from the first page." —*Cosmopolitan*

"Another absolute banger from the queen of laugh-out-loud rom-coms. There is simply no one else writing rom-coms that deliver so many laughs with equally delicious tension, chemistry, and sizzle. Mia Sosa does not miss, and this banter-filled homage to *When Harry Met Sally* might be her best yet."

—Adriana Herrera, *USA Today* bestselling author of *A Tropical Rebel Gets the Duke*

"Mia Sosa gives us all the rom, com, and yearning you could ask for in this endlessly entertaining, chemistry-filled journey between two best friends. Layered with surprises and a tension-packed dual timeline, *When Javi Dumped Mari* is friends-to-lovers gold!"

—Lauren Kung Jessen, author of *Yin Yang Love Song*

"I want to live inside a Mia Sosa romantic comedy! Full of so many hilarious moments that are sandwiched between careful emotional development. Bold, funny, and dynamic, Mia Sosa has written another banger!" —Danica Nava, *USA Today* bestselling author of *The Truth According to Ember*

"*When Javi Dumped Mari* has it all. It's funny and sexy, and delivers an incredibly satisfying happily ever after. The perfect homage to the one that got away."
—Neely Tubati Alexander, author of *Courtroom Drama*

"With *When Javi Dumped Mari*, Mia Sosa adds yet another sexy, fun, and satisfying romance to her oeuvre. I savored it from beginning to end."
—Rachel Runya Katz, author of *Whenever You're Ready*

"Full of chemistry, humor, yearning, heat, and raw emotion, Mia Sosa has written an addictive friends-to-lovers romance. The will-they-won't-they drama had me hanging by a thread! Every page was infused with delicious tension; there are scenes in this book that are going to live rent free in my head, and I'm not mad about it."
—Aurora Palit, author of *Sunshine and Spice* and *Honey and Heat*

"Full of heart and hijinks, *When Javi Dumped Mari* is Mia Sosa at her most delightful. I wish she'd write *my* love story!"
—Adib Khorram, *USA Today* bestselling author of *I'll Have What He's Having*

"A welcome return from Sosa in a rom-com homage to *When Harry Met Sally* and *My Best Friend's Wedding*. Press into the hands of readers who love romances with past and present timelines."
—*Library Journal*

"*When Javi Dumped Mari* is the friends-to-lovers romance of my dreams! Voicey and playful, sharp and sexy, this is Mia Sosa at her absolute best!"

—Christina Lauren, *New York Times* bestselling author of *The Soulmate Equation*

"The Queen of Rom-Coms does it again! *When Javi Dumped Mari* is chock-full of the sorts of outrageous hijinks only Mia Sosa could pull off, along with the signature steaminess her readers know and love. Blending humor, spice, and drama, Sosa once again delivers romantic-comedy gold."

—Alexis Daria, bestselling author of *You Had Me at Hola*

When JAVI Dumped MARI

BY MIA SOSA

The Wedding Crasher
The Worst Best Man

LOVE ON CUE

Acting on Impulse
Pretending He's Mine
Crashing into Her

SUITS UNDONE

Unbuttoning the CEO
One Night with the CEO
Getting Dirty with the CEO

When JAVI Dumped MARI

– A Novel –

MIA SOSA

G. P. Putnam's Sons
New York

PUTNAM
— EST. 1838 —

G. P. PUTNAM'S SONS
Publishers Since 1838
an imprint of Penguin Random House LLC
1745 Broadway, New York, NY 10019
penguinrandomhouse.com

Copyright © 2025 by Mia Sosa
Penguin Random House values and supports copyright. Copyright fuels creativity, encourages diverse voices, promotes free speech, and creates a vibrant culture. Thank you for buying an authorized edition of this book and for complying with copyright laws by not reproducing, scanning, or distributing any part of it in any form without permission. You are supporting writers and allowing Penguin Random House to continue to publish books for every reader. Please note that no part of this book may be used or reproduced in any manner for the purpose of training artificial intelligence technologies or systems.

Book design by Laura K. Corless
Interior art: dandelion with heart seeds © shaineast/Shutterstock.com

Library of Congress Cataloging-in-Publication Data

Names: Sosa, Mia, author.
Title: When Javi dumped Mari: a novel / Mia Sosa.
Description: New York: G. P. Putnam's Sons, 2025.
Identifiers: LCCN 2024050374 (print) | LCCN 2024050375 (ebook) |
ISBN 9798217044306 (trade paperback) | ISBN 9798217044313 (epub)
Subjects: LCGFT: Romance fiction. | Novels.
Classification: LCC PS3619.O84 W54 2025 (print) | LCC PS3619.O84 (ebook) |
DDC 813/.6—dc23/eng/20241223
LC record available at https://lccn.loc.gov/2024050374
LC ebook record available at https://lccn.loc.gov/2024050375

Printed in the United States of America
1st Printing

The authorized representative in the EU for product safety and compliance is
Penguin Random House Ireland, Morrison Chambers, 32 Nassau Street,
Dublin D02 YH68, Ireland, https://eu-contact.penguin.ie.

For V, my partner and best friend.
It was always you.

*Love without friendship is like a kite,
aloft only when the winds are favorable.
Friendship is what gives love its wings.*

—Sherry Thomas,
Ravishing the Heiress

When JAVI Dumped MARI

PART ONE

The Seed

CHAPTER 1

Javi

Now

I'm not the kind of person who fidgets, but tonight I can't stop messing with every object on this table. The pepper shaker isn't close enough to the saltshaker. The candle centerpiece should be shifted three centimeters to the right. The tiny ripples in the cream linen tablecloth need to be smoothed out too. Now that I think about it, where are those little sugar packets for our after-dinner coffee? Mari loves her café con un montón de azúcar like no one else I know.

And where's my best friend anyway?

I glance at my watch, then loosen my tie as I scan the small group of people lingering near the host station. Maybe I shouldn't have dressed up for the occasion. Not that this is a special occasion exactly, but to me, it's a big deal, so I figured I'd look the part of a guy who's going places. Overkill? Perhaps. Still, Mari's going to be floored when I tell her about the recent changes in my life: a spot to call home that isn't a glorified frat house; excellent career prospects on the horizon; a therapist to help me process years of suppressed emotions. These are huge personal milestones—all of them long overdue and meant to show Mari that I'm on my way to becoming a worthy partner. Mari would probably say I have a lot of nerve being impatient now; given how long it's taken me to get my shit together, she'd be a thousand percent correct.

I survey the dining room, my attention snagging on a man who's tapping a spoon against his wineglass. He stands, presumably to address his guests, and because this stranger's business isn't mine—a phrase Mari jokingly imprinted on my brain years ago—I look away.

The absence of a suitable distraction means I can no longer ignore my clammy palms and bouncing knees. Annoyed by my own restlessness, I reread our latest text exchange.

> ME: we still on for 7 at Bella Trattoria?
>
> MARI: Definitely
>
> ME: can't wait to see you
>
> MARI: Same :-)

Mari's never stood me up, so I'm not worried that she won't show. She probably got held up at work. I'll just send her a quick text to be sure she's on her way.

> ME: everything okay?
>
> ME: not a problem if you need a rain check

I'd hate to miss out on the opportunity to see Mari tonight, but I don't want to place any undue pressure on her. Besides, if I have anything to say about it—and Mari's suggested on numerous occasions that I do—we'll have plenty of time to spend together while I'm here in California.

The moment I take a sip of water, someone settles a hand on my shoulder and squeezes. I look behind me, and there she is: the woman who's captured my heart in a vise.

Mari rounds our table and slips into her seat, then takes a deep, steadying breath. "Hey, sorry to make you wait. I had to run to the restroom."

She gives me a weak smile, places her hands in her lap, and centers all of her attention on the bifold card promoting the restaurant's cocktail specials.

No kiss on the cheek. No hug. No eye contact, for that matter. Her placid expression suggests she isn't particularly upset, but she also doesn't seem to be herself. I'll find out what's up in the next few minutes. Neither of us has much patience for bullshit. In the meantime, I can't help but stare at her, taking in her glowy tan skin; the gorgeous curly hair skimming her shoulders; the full, glossy lips that always captivate me when she's talking.

"It's good to see you, M," I say, shifting in my seat. "You look beautiful."

She blushes, her gaze slowly lifting to mine. It's the first sign of the Mari I'm used to. The one who never quite knows how to take a compliment.

"Oh, stop. I'm the same ol' me. But you? You look fantastic, Javi." Waggling her brows, she adds, "Que gato."

We quietly eye each other, matching smiles on our faces, and my spirits lift. We're good. *Of course* we're good. Now that my mind's at ease, I can't contain myself any longer and blurt out, "I have good news!"

Giving Mari a secretive grin, I reach into the messenger bag at my feet and grab the rough draft of the musical script she's been urging me to finish for *years*. It's done. Finally done. Well, the bones of it. And yeah, there's still a ton of work to do before it's ready for showtime—the music and half of the lyrics, for starters—but this is a symbolic end to the rut I've been in, and I'm in a celebratory mood.

The brightness in her eyes dims, and her shoulders slump, immediately putting me on high alert. "I have news too," she says less enthusiastically.

I let the libretto slip from my hand. It lands at the bottom of my bag, the faint thump of its pages making me flinch. The book can wait. Because she didn't say her news was good, and my antenna when it comes to Mari couldn't be more fine-tuned.

"You first," I say, peering at her closely.

She reaches for her water glass and takes a long sip, then leans forward, as though she has something urgent to say. "Listen, I'm sorry I didn't give you a heads-up sooner, but I brought someone with me. He's parking the car."

I relax into my seat and blow out a slow breath. Jesus, is that all? A random date I can handle. These men are never worthy of her anyway. "I thought you were going on a romance hiatus? That's what you told me in the fall."

"It ended," she says, her face as blank as an untouched canvas. "Didn't get a chance to tell you."

I casually park an elbow on my chair's armrest. "So, who is he? Another former classmate from law school?" I chuckle. "Damn, that guy was a pendejo to rival all pendejos."

Mari twists her lips into a half smile and playfully rolls her eyes. "Don't remind me. He's married now, and I pray for his partner daily." Straightening her shoulders, she adds, "But seriously, this new guy's great, and I *really* hope you like him. His name is Alex Cordero. We, uh . . . we work together at the firm."

The passing mention of her father's entertainment law firm irks me. It's just another tool Luiz Campos uses to exert control over his daughter. She'd be better off someplace else, where her talents aren't wasted, but her career choices are just that—hers—and I tend to give a wide berth to any subject that relates to her dad.

Wait. A frisson of alarm runs down my spine when I focus on what she said about her date: *But seriously, this new guy's great.* By agreement, *I'm* supposed to be the judge of that. I mean, considering we've been gatekeeping each other's relationships the past two years, that's *literally* my job. And as for Mari, I have yet to meet someone who passes muster. Hell, *I* don't even pass muster, but I'm willing to live trying.

I lean forward conspiratorially. "Still, I'm here to do my duty as your best friend. Tell me what you need, an interrogation or a shakedown?"

Most people are subjected to interrogations; shakedowns are reserved for individuals who've already raised a few red flags. Either way, this guy will be a blip in Mari's history once I'm done with him.

"Neither," Mari says. "Just do me a favor and get to know him organically, okay? No third degree. No snarky remarks. I want you to give Alex a fair chance."

Well, damn. She's never imposed any stipulations on my assessment before. Is she into this Alex guy? Does she want me to rubber-stamp what she already knows? In all the time we've been vetting each other's dates, our mandate has been unfailingly clear: approve or disapprove. Except Mari's essentially telling me she won't be swayed by my opinion—as if it's too late for me to do anything. I'm fucking stumped by this change in the status quo, but I eventually gather enough wits to respond. "Sure, sure. Whatever you need."

Mari briefly closes her eyes and exhales, then glances at the restaurant's revolving door.

"Is everything okay?" I ask, unsure what to make of her mood. She seems . . . off. And she seems especially off considering it's just us. Mari and Javi. Javi and Mari. She can tell me anything. She *has* to know this by now.

Mari reaches over the stretch of distance between us and places her right hand on mine. "You mean so much to me, Javi. Please don't ever forget that. I . . ."

Okay, what the fuck, heart? Chill. I breathe through my nose and massage the left side of my chest, hoping to calm my quickening pulse. Is there something else? Is she moving out of the country? I narrow my eyes and study her face more closely. Is she sick? What the hell is going on? "Whatever it is, Mari, just tell me. I want to be there for you. We'll get through it together."

She looks past me, and her whole face lights up as she rises to her feet. "Here he is now."

I turn in the direction she's facing, my jaw dropping as I watch Alex make his entrance. And I'm *not* exaggerating when I describe it as an entrance. The guy's straightening his cuff links, his topcoat flapping behind him like a superhero's cape while the people in his wake pretend they're not staring at this prime specimen. He's Latine, *maybe*, and tall. Really tall. I mean, I'm no short king, and this guy probably has four inches on me. To add insult to injury, he also comes equipped with hazel eyes, a chiseled jaw, and—I glance at the floor around him—huge feet. He's the fucking Beyoncé of men. Okay, fellas, no need to get in formation. It's a wrap.

Alex folds Mari into a warm embrace. "Sorry to keep you waiting, princesa," he says, his lips grazing her temple. Then he looks down at me, flashing a big, confident smile. "And here's the man of the hour. Glad we're finally meeting in person, Javier. Marisol's told me so much about you."

Mari and I exchange an awkward glance before I jump up and shake his hand. "I wish I could say the same."

Alex grins, completely unaffected by my tepid greeting. "There's plenty of time for us to get to know each other before the wedding."

I frown at him, my brain struggling to comprehend the words coming out of this stranger's mouth. "What wedding?"

Alex's gaze swings between Mari and me, and then he tips his head back, not a strand of his chestnut brown hair out of place. "You didn't tell him, Marisol?"

Mari clears her throat, her eyes blinking at warp speed. "I was working up to it when you arrived."

"Ah, got it," Alex says affably. "Well, then, this is the perfect time for a toast, isn't it?" He raises a finger in the air, and our server, a white kid with floppy hair, rushes over. To the server, Alex says, "My fiancée and I would like your best bottle of champagne. This is a celebration!"

"This is an Italian restaurant," the server replies in an even tone, his brow lifted.

Alex puffs out his chest. "Your best Prosecco, then. The bubblier, the better."

"Right away, sir," the server says before dashing away.

I'm itching to call him back, because this isn't a celebration at all; as far as I'm concerned, it's a catastrophe, and none of this is making any sense.

I look between Mari and this Alex guy as they share a furtive smile. Wait, wait, wait. Hold up. Am I being played right now? The tightness in my chest unfurls. Damn, I can't believe I almost fell for it. I throw my head back and wag an index finger at my devious best friend. "Okay, okay, I'll admit you almost had me there. Seriously, though"—I jerk my thumb in the man's direction, not even sure if Alex is his real name—"is he an actor? I mean, you've done some wild shit in the interest of pranking me, but this is next level."

I tap the guy on the shoulder. "'Princesa' was a nice touch, by the way."

Beside him, Mari winces. "This isn't a prank, Javi. Alex is my fiancé."

I stare at her, then at him, then back at her, my chest tightening all over again as tiny pinpricks pierce my body from head to toe. My ears are burning too. Worse, I'm feeling unsteady on my feet, so I collapse onto my chair. "You're getting . . . married?"

"I am," she says, taking a seat and pulling Alex down with her. "I mean, *we* are." She laughs at herself, nervously flashing the gigantic engagement ring she's obviously been hiding since she arrived. Damn, it's a wonder she doesn't sink to the floor from the weight of that thing. "Um, *Alex* and I are," she pointlessly clarifies. "In six weeks."

"In six weeks," I repeat, my mouth going dry.

"The eighteenth of May, to be exact," she says, nodding. "And I was hoping you'd be my man of honor."

Fuck me. Fuck Alex. And fuck the stupid-ass Tesla he probably owns.

"What the hell is a man of honor anyway?"

"It just means you have a special place in the bride's life," Mari explains.

Shit. Did I say that out loud? How do I play this off? *Think, Javi, think.* "Oh no, I wasn't asking. It's actually a song."

Alex tilts his head, his eyebrows snapping together. "There's a song about a man of honor?"

I clear my throat. "Yeah, it goes, 'And what'—clap—'the hell'—

clap—'is a man of honor?'—clap. It's a military chant. You know, when they're running or marching. Left, right, left . . . Saw it in a movie once."

"Riiight," Alex says, stretching out the word.

Yeah, I'd be skeptical too. Chacho, this is a mess.

Mari shakes her head as if to clear it. "Anyway, I want you to stand beside me when we take our vows."

The irony of this statement pummels my chest like a battering ram. Still, the lie flows from my lips so easily I almost believe it myself. "Nothing would make me happier. I'm touched."

In reality, though, I'm a carcass being pecked to shreds by vultures at the side of the road. (Sue me, I've always been dramatic.) One thing's for sure: This is *not* how the night was supposed to go. I had declarations to share, explanations to give, promises to make; now I'm just processing the trash fire before my eyes.

As I try to regroup and decide my next steps, I catalog every interaction between Mari and me, trying to pinpoint the moment when I should have seen this coming, the same two questions cycling through my brain: One, how did we get here? And two, what the hell am I going to do about it?

CHAPTER 2

Mari

Now

Javi looks good. *Really* good. Objectively speaking, that is.

The vintage chandeliers above us highlight the bridge of his strong nose, his enviably high cheekbones, the smoothness of his medium-brown skin. He's licking his lips as he studies the menu, accentuating the well-defined contours of his Cupid's bow. His thick eyebrows stand apart from the rest of his features, the one attribute that isn't meticulously groomed. Nearly twelve years and he still hasn't figured out how to tame them; okay, maybe I *am* biased, but that nod to imperfection only adds to his appeal.

God, this is all new to me. Is it okay to admire a handsome man who isn't my fiancé, or am I the asshole? Wait, what am I thinking? *Of course* I can appreciate that Javi's criminally fine. So long as that's where the admiration train ends—and it does. Because I've moved on. In fact, any lingering doubts about my ability to put my feelings for Javi to rest have been silenced by this evening's experiment. My heart didn't race the moment I saw him, nor did butterflies flutter in my belly.

Sweet Jesus, I'm finally free.

I smile up at Alex and brush my shoulder against him, more confident than ever that he's my person. Judging by Javi's rigid posture and the tightness in his expression, he isn't similarly convinced. Well, that's not my problem. Contrary to whatever Javi might believe, this engagement isn't an impulse or a rebound. It's a manifestation of the mature love I've always dreamed of. Steady. Dependable. *Grown.*

The server's reappearance breaks the tension, our uneasy trio watching with overly rapt attention as he presents the bottle of Prosecco to Alex and prepares to pop the cork. A casual observer could rationally assume we're expecting to be tested on the specifics of the process.

"Okay with you?" Alex asks us.

I nod. "Fine with me, but Javi doesn't drink wine."

Alex looks over at Javi. "For sobriety reasons? Health?"

"Neither. It's a preference."

"Ah," Alex says. "Would you like to order something else? For the toast?"

"No, thanks," Javi says, shaking his head. "I'll just stick with water."

I'm so invested in these two liking each other that I'm surveying their actions through a microscope, mentally high-fiving them for merely being civil. On a normal day, Javi and I would jump at any opportunity to poke fun at each other, to laugh together. Not today. Everyone's on their best behavior, and apparently our best behavior is stale as hell.

Alex and I raise our flutes. With his eyes fixed on the area behind us, Javi follows suit, positioning his water goblet in front of his face like a shield.

"To Mari," Alex says, his eyes glowing with affection, "the woman who has made me the happiest man on earth."

Javi's gaze flicks to the ceiling before he adds, "I'm wishing you both the very best as you embark on this"—he clears his throat—"next chapter of your lives. Congratulations."

"Thank you," Alex and I say in unison as we all clink glasses.

I study Javi, my perusal drifting to his broad shoulders, highlighted by the exquisite fit of his navy blazer. The tie's a surprise, especially because he once said they always make him feel like he's cosplaying a middle-aged man. Then it hits me: He's dressed up for a reason. "Oh, wait a minute," I say, snapping my fingers. "Earlier you said you had good news. Tell us what it is, so we can drink to that too."

"It's nothing," Javi says, waving his hand dismissively.

"If it's good news, it can't be nothing. Spill."

He studies me carefully, as if my reaction to whatever he's about to say needs to be stored in his mental archive. "I finished the libretto for *The Mailroom*. The skeleton of it, I should say. And I took Jeremy up on his offer to stay with him while I write the rest of the lyrics."

My heart swells. He's been working on that musical for years, and he's finally made some progress. This is exactly what I wanted for him. Precisely what I urged him to do the last time we saw each other.

"Javi. That's amazing news, and *definitely* not nothing. It's a breakthrough."

"It is," he says, beaming at me.

"You'll be in California," I say, stating the obvious while trying to absorb the implications of his temporary relocation. Javi will be here. In my hometown. We can see each other more often. Get together for lunch when I'm not working.

"For the next six months," he confirms. "Maybe less, depending on how things go." Before I can pepper him with questions, he glances at Alex and freezes, as if he's just now remembering my fiancé is here with us. Blowing out a short breath, Javi shifts in his seat and leans forward. "Well, enough about what I'm up to. I need to know more about this"—he points back and forth between Alex and me, feigning nonchalance—"and how it came about."

Alex chuckles, his long fingers gliding over the stem of his wineglass. "I don't know that there's much to say. I mean, you've known her a lot longer than I have, so you also know how amazing she is. Marisol's everything. I'd been circling around her for more than a year. One day, I just decided to shoot my shot." Alex looks over at me and rests his free hand on mine. "To my surprise, she was open to it. And when it's right, it's right, so here we are."

"So here you are," Javi agrees, though I *swear* there's a hint of mockery in his tone. He studies us, a pensive expression on his face. "This was when? Six months ago?"

"Give or take," Alex says, nodding, then looking to me for confirmation.

"Yeah, something like that," I say, scanning the dining room. "Shouldn't we have ordered by now?"

As if on cue, a different server than the one who brought us the wine (Umberto, he informs us) appears at our table, runs through the specials, and asks if we have any questions. When we tell him we're ready to order, he looks to me first.

"I'll have the—"

"Seafood risotto," Javi finishes with a grin.

I laugh. "Am I that predictable?"

"C'mon now, you're on a personal mission to try the risotto dish at every Italian restaurant you go to."

"True, true," I say, playfully covering my face with the menu.

"And you, sir?" Umberto asks Alex.

"The branzino, please. With asparagus, no cheese."

"Do you have a food allergy we should know about?"

"None at all." Alex pats his stomach. "Just watching my figure."

"Ah, I see," Umberto says flatly before shifting to face Javi. "What about you, sir?"

"I'll have the lasagna," Javi says, staring at Alex, who's staring right back at him. "*All* the cheese, please."

Umberto's wide smile transforms his face, revealing laugh lines that tell me he's no stranger to joyous times. "Very good, sir." Then he collects our menus and abandons us to fend for ourselves in Awkwardville.

I tap my finger on the table, racking my brain for a topic that can bridge the distance between these men. To my relief, Alex fills the silence.

"So, Javier," he says, wearing a serious expression. "I just want to be up front about something: I'm not trying to replace you. Or erase you. Or box you out. I understand how much you mean to Marisol, and I don't intend to get in the way of that. Her happiness is my priority."

I lean into Alex, smiling up at him. *This* is why Alex is my perfect match. He *chose* me. He *wants* to be with me. As my therapist often says, I deserve someone who's prepared to love me without reservation; Alex is the only man in my life who qualifies. He's bright, ambitious, kind. And sure, he's handsome, but he doesn't expect his looks to do the heavy lifting. It also doesn't hurt that my father's estimation of me went up several notches when Alex and I announced our engagement.

Javi nods, a blank expression on his face. "Mari's happiness has always been my priority too, so I'm sure we'll get along just fine."

He doesn't say "for her sake," but his flat affect all but shouts it.

This is what I get for not telling Javi about Alex sooner, and I only have myself to blame. Javi deserved to know that I was dating someone, deserved to know that the relationship was progressing to the point that marriage was a possibility. If I'm being honest, though, I needed distance from him at the time, and yes, maybe a small part of me worried that Javi would veto Alex on the spot. Whatever the reason, it's clear that not confiding in Javi was a misstep, and I'm prepared to own it.

"So what about you two?" Alex asks, his gaze trained on Javi. "How'd this dynamic duo happen?"

Javi narrows his eyes at me, his mouth twisted into a smirk. "You didn't tell him about your shady past, Marisol?"

Oh, we're going there?

I incline my head and give Javi a faint smile, granting him permission to talk about our origin story while also telegraphing that I know what he's up to. "We were teenagers. I was a different person back then. Definitely my mother's child."

"And now?" Javi asks, jutting his chin.

"And now I'm my father's child too," I say, giving him a half shrug.

There's no question that I'm a tamer version of the girl I was in college. Back then, I pushed buttons. Raised hell when I felt someone had been treated unfairly. Kissed a lot of frogs. But life isn't a never-ending party; at some point, we need to take it seriously and start adulting.

Alex looks between us, his lips slightly parted. "So who's going to tell me how you two met?"

I set my elbows on the table, rest my hands under my chin, and stare at Javi pointedly. "The floor is yours, my friend."

CHAPTER 3

Javi

Eleven Years and Seven Months Before the Wedding

A tall and shapely burglar is lurking near the entrance to my dorm.

I should wash off the sweat from my morning run and head to class, but I'm nosy by nature, and after a year on this boring campus, even an attempted crime seems interesting. I fish out my phone, intending to call school security, but something—intuition, maybe—stops me. I might be jumping to conclusions. To be fair to them, the person's just standing there. To be fair to me, they seem suspicious as hell in their look-at-me-I'm-about-to-steal uniform: black skinny jeans, a pair of dark sunglasses, and a fitted black sweatshirt with the hood pulled so tightly over their head it covers most of their face. Isn't the point of that getup to blend into your surroundings at night? How's that supposed to help when it's dawn?

Which makes me wonder if I'm misreading the situation. Since I'd rather be right than rash, I decide to observe them for a minute or two.

The person's alternating between peering across the damp lawn and checking their watch. Likely waiting. For someone or something. They're probably a scout, but even if not, they're *definitely* suspect. Suddenly they're frantically gesturing with their hands, and that's when I notice an SUV idling in the student parking lot across the quadrangle. I bet that's the getaway vehicle.

Seconds later, Petey, the junior who delivers the school's newspaper, pulls up in his Camry. The burglar ducks behind a hedge of bushes just as Petey passes them. Unaware he's being watched, Petey drops a stack of papers on the building's redbrick steps, then slips back into his car and drives away.

The burglar jumps up, scrambles to a tree, and crouches in waiting. What an amateur. And what the hell is the goal? Are they trying to slip inside the dorm? Before I can make a solid guess, the person scurries to the building and lunges for the stack of newspapers. Hmm, not at all what I expected. And absolutely my cue to scare the living shit out of them.

I sneak across the street and tiptoe behind them. "Hey, one of those papers is mine!"

The thief startles, the stack of papers crashing to the ground. "Merda!"

The curse word throws me, as does the silvery voice, but I recover quickly. "It's *mierda*," I say. "Not only are you bad at stealing, but you're also terrible at Spanish."

"It's *merda*, asshole," she growls, "because I'm *not* speaking Spanish."

"And just like that, you've given me enough to pick you out of a lineup."

"Ugh, get lost," she says, bending to pick up the stack. "This is serious business, and none of it is yours."

"Give me my paper, and I'll pretend I never saw you."

"Get out of my way, and I'll pretend you're not nosy as fuck."

Undeterred, I hold out my hand. "Paper."

"Sorry," she says, cradling the stack like a baby. "No one gets the paper today."

"Why not?"

"Because it's sexist trash, and we're trying to make a point."

"Who's 'we'?"

"The female students at this school."

Well, that confirms who I'm dealing with. And honestly, I'm sympathetic to the cause, would even consider joining it, but the last thing I need is another person using and dropping me like my brothers did, so I go with "Don't care. I want to read it."

"Ah, you're worried about missing your horoscope, aren't you? No problem, I can tell you what it is."

"This'll be good," I mutter, rolling my eyes.

She takes a big step forward, invading my personal space, and lifts her chin in challenge. "Remember: Not every curiosity needs to be satisfied. You'll escape certain death if you mind your business today."

I look down at my nemesis, standing my ground despite how twitchy I feel being so close to her. "Cute. And useless as hell because you don't know my sign. Now give me my copy."

"No."

"Why not fight fire with fire?" I ask. "Write something that *isn't* sexist trash."

"Not my job. Besides, Dylan Gardner's column is a disgrace, and they shouldn't be pedaling his bullshit in the first place. It gives the guy credibility he doesn't deserve."

"That might be true, but you're just going to piss off everyone, including me."

She gives me a slow smile, and my knees wobble, which obviously has *nothing* to do with her and *everything* to do with the aftereffects of my morning run. "Well, we want their attention," she says, "so mission accomplished, then."

I stare at her lips and lose my train of thought. What was I going to say? As I fumble for words, she hightails it toward the SUV in the lot. Within seconds, she and her accomplice are gone.

What the *hell* was that?

And why is my heart thudding?

* * *

I slip into my usual seat near the door to the lecture hall seconds before Professor Amar strolls to the front of the room. Amar's a hard-ass, and if this civil liberties class weren't a requirement for my political science degree, I would skip it altogether. He's brilliant, though; I'll give him that.

The stadium-style seating allows me to scrutinize everyone. In the middle are the jocks, wearing their team jackets in case there's any doubt where they fit in the social hierarchy. None of them has a laptop or tablet in sight, probably because they, too, are only here to fulfill a requirement. Up front and to the right are the poli sci ass-kissers clamoring for the professor's attention. One of them, Lance, monopolizes most of the discussions. Worse, he's an elitist dick who wants everyone to know his mother's an ambassador to Belgium or some shit. A group of women who habitually shuffle off together to use the restroom take up most of the seats on the left. Which leaves the balance of the room occupied by people like me. Individuals. Loners. We don't need to attend class as a group activity, and we're perfectly fine navigating college on our own. Seriously, I'm not here to make friends. No, I'm here in the middle of some random Philadelphia suburb because it's the farthest place from my family that would give me a full scholarship.

"Sometimes life and pedagogy intersect in a way that's truly inspiring," Professor Amar tells us.

A few hands shoot up, and Amar grimaces.

"Pedagogy refers to *how* we teach," he adds. "The art and practice of imparting knowledge."

The hands disappear.

Damn, we're only a month into the semester, and this class is already torturing me.

"You see, my dear scholars," he continues, "an interesting situation occurred this morning, and it directly relates to what we've been learning in class. As I understand it, a group of students took it upon themselves to seize more than six thousand copies of the *Belmont Gazette*, our school's newspaper, arguing that one of its columnists was misogynistic and sexist and made approximately half of the student population feel unsafe and uncomfortable."

I sit up, intrigued by where the discussion is headed, especially given my encounter with the paper swiper just a few hours ago.

"That's what I've been saying," one of the male jocks shouts, pretending to shiver in fear. "Men feel threatened on this campus."

His buddies laugh while the rest of the class bristles.

"Silence," Professor Amar says. "No more outbursts or you'll get an automatic zero on next week's quiz."

That shuts up *everyone*.

"My *point*," Professor Amar explains, "is that this conduct implicates one of our most prized civil liberties: freedom of speech. But *whose* liberties are impacted? In an effort to curtail the sleuthing and finger pointing, the president's office has issued a statement indicating that none of the people responsible will be punished. Instead, Belmont College will use this incident as an opportunity for dialogue and to examine whether the column at issue *should* be protected. So, is it censorship, rightful protest, or plain old theft? I'm interested in hearing—"

The door to the lecture hall flies open, and a girl stumbles inside. "Merda!" She stops short and scans the room, likely noticing all eyes are on her. "Uh, so sorry, didn't mean to interrupt!"

Professor Amar's eyes narrow at the newcomer. As do mine. Because I recognize that voice—and now I have a face to attach to it.

Well, well, well, if it isn't the paper swiper in the flesh.

She lets out an embarrassed chuckle. "Truly, I apologize. I, uh, tripped."

"I'd love for you to trip on my dick," one of the jocks shouts.

Professor Amar's head snaps in the guy's direction. "Get out of my class. And see me during office hours."

The guy wisely chooses not to plead his case and storms up the stairs toward the exit, passing our latest arrival on the way.

"That would be like tripping on a twig," she says to him, smirking as she sweeps her gaze from his face to his crotch.

Heat stains the jock's cheeks, but he doesn't respond.

Damn, not all heroes wear capes; some of them wear burglar uniforms, though what she's wearing now—a royal-blue T-shirt, a pair of jeans that molds to her figure, and the whitest all-white Adidas I've ever seen—is a definite upgrade. She's gorgeous. Sun-kissed brown skin. The front of her hair done up in braids while thick, luscious curls fall around her shoulders. And she has the most striking brown eyes I've ever seen. I squirm in my seat, drawing her attention.

She does a double take when she notices me, then grins like the Cheshire cat before she drops into the spot next to mine. Christ. She smells good too. A peaches-and-vanilla combo that wafts around her and wraps itself around me. I shut my eyes. It's *that* intoxicating.

"Fancy meeting you here," she says, leaning over to whisper in my ear. "Had no idea we were in the same class."

"Do I know you?"

"Oh, c'mon," she says. "We both know you recognized me as soon as I walked in the door."

I decide to fess up. Honestly, she's entertaining. "I'm surprised you're even acknowledging me."

"Didn't you hear? We're off the hook. No jail time for me."

"The court of public opinion could be a different story, though."

"You'd rat me out?" She pretends to wipe a tear from her eye. "I'm crushed."

Professor Amar clears his throat. "It's one thing to be late. It's another thing to disrupt the class when you enter. But it's downright disrespectful to chatter while I'm lecturing."

My neighbor glances my way, then gulps. "Apologies. It won't happen again."

Professor Amar nods. "What's your name?"

"Marisol Campos."

"Well, since you're in the mood to talk, Ms. Campos, how about you give me your thoughts on what happened this morning."

"*This morning?*" she asks, her eyes widening.

"Yes," Professor Amar says. Then, as if Marisol's grubby handprints aren't all over the scene of the crime, he brings her up to speed, clearly deciding she deserves to be in the hot seat today. I couldn't agree more.

"So, thoughts?" the professor prompts.

"Well," she begins, sitting up and tapping a finger across her lips as she makes a big show of pondering the issue, "I'd say the better course would be to fight fire with fire. Why not take the columnist to task and write your own scathing takedown of his ridiculous views?"

My jaw drops. Did she just use *my words* to get her ass out of the hot seat?

"I mean, wouldn't it make sense to get the court of public opinion on your side?" she asks. "Taking the newspapers is only going to piss everyone off."

Then she turns and winks at me.

Narrowing my eyes at her, I mouth, *Un-fucking-believable.*

"You there," Professor Amar says. "Looks like you want to say something."

"Psst, he's talking to you," Marisol says, undisguised glee in her voice.

I whip my head in Professor Amar's direction. "Sir?"

"Care to share your thoughts, Mr. . . . ?"

"It's Javier."

"Mr. Javier?"

Christ, this is excruciating. "No, Javier Báez, sir."

"Okay, got it. So, Mr. Báez, looks to me like you're champing at the bit to add to the discussion."

"Indeed," Marisol says, staring at me with wide-eyed innocence, her elbows propped on the desk and her chin resting on her hands.

Okay, fine, two can play this petty game. "Well, the way I see it, nonviolent protest is at the heart of our democracy. No one was hurt, and now the university's paying attention. And I wonder why anyone's even humoring this columnist. I mean, if half of the student population feels harassed by his views, shouldn't the school do something about that? Even if the answer is to challenge this guy's ideas, he has the backing of the school's paper behind him. That gives him an unfair advantage and credibility that isn't warranted. Also, I've seen the comments on IG. Because I was uh . . . interested to see what provoked all this, and it turns out the president's office probably wants to sweep this under the rug because some of the newspaper's staff was in on it too, which means the call was coming from *inside* the house. Plus, this guy's views are fucked up—"

"Language, Mr. Báez," Professor Amar warns.

"Sorry, sir. What I meant to say is his views are . . . reprehensible. I've read them. He doesn't think the school should support women's athletics, questions whether date rape is even a thing. If this were a speaker on campus, we'd be protesting his presence on the green twenty-four-seven. Seriously, it sends a message to the women of the school that they don't matter as people."

"Wow," Marisol says loud enough for everyone to hear. "Where were *you* this morning when those papers were stolen?"

Everyone laughs, including Professor Amar. And *especially* Marisol.

What a chaos demon. I'm sitting next to one of the culprits, and she's implicating me. I may not be guilty of stealing the student newspaper, but I might very well be guilty of murder soon.

"Okay, okay," Professor Amar says, chuckling as he jots something down on a legal pad, "let's table this discussion for next week's class. We're going to talk about viewpoint discrimination, and this will be the perfect segue. For now, though, it's pop quiz time!"

We all groan and grumble as we pass around the quiz sheets.

Twenty minutes later, I pick up my book bag and move to turn in my quiz. Before I leave the row, I look at Marisol. "That little performance was uncool."

She scoffs and rolls her eyes. "Considering the hard time you gave me this morning, I'd say it was well deserved. Especially if you believed everything you said in that monologue. Sounds to me like you messed with me for shits and giggles."

Dammit. She's right. But I'm not waving the flag. She's too powerful as it is. "Whatever, Marisol. Have a nice life."

"You do the same," she says with a smug smile.

Outside the classroom, I'm barely able to make my way through the crowd. Because seemingly every woman in the class is trying to speak with me.

"You were amazing!" one says.

"That was legendary!" another adds.

"Finally, someone who understands," a fellow poli sci major gushes, tearing off a piece of paper with her number on it. "Maybe you'd like to join my study group?"

Marisol weaves through the throng, narrowing her eyes as she registers that I'm the source of the commotion. We lock eyes as we pass each other, and then she looks back at me and scowls.

I can't resist needling her, so I give her a ridiculous wink. In truth, this many eyes on me is making my skin crawl, but I'd never give her the satisfaction of knowing I'm self-conscious. "Thanks for being my wingman. Had no idea that little speech was going to make me a minor celebrity. Well deserved, wouldn't you say?"

She gives me a once-over and laughs. "Well, since I'm your wingman, it's only right that I tell you something."

"What?"

She cups her hands against her mouth and, with as much intensity as if she were yelling "Fire!" in a crowded movie theater, shouts, "Your fly's open!"

I look down at my crotch and immediately see that she's right.

God, I can already tell Marisol Campos is going to be a pain in my ass.

Tuesday, October 15, 2013

WhatsApp Voice Message

Marisol, it's your mother. Tio Ivo put WhatsApp on my phone, so now I can leave you voice messages whenever I need to remind you that I exist. Call me when you have time. I want to know everything. How's school? Your friends? What happened with the newspaper thing? Did it work? [*whispers in Portuguese to someone in the background*] Sorry, filha. Your uncle Ivo is talking in my ear. Anyway, is your father leaving you alone? If I need to speak with him, I will. I'm going to Cabo Frio with Vovó for a week. You can call me whenever. Okay, I think that's all for now. Call me, sweetheart. Tchau. Tchau. Tchau.

CHAPTER 4

Mari

Eleven Years and Seven Months Before the Wedding

After listening to my mother's latest voice message, I blow out an amused breath. Even though she relocated to another continent, she still expects daily updates on my life. And now she's on WhatsApp. Jesus, take the phone.

"Earth to Mari, are you listening to me?"

Katy Maldonado jumps in front of me and waves in my face.

I sidestep her and set about arranging the stickers and flyers for the Fall Club Fair on the folding table. "I heard you the first time. Be approachable. Be friendly. Be informative. Not a problem, I've got this."

We're standing on a busy stretch of Centennial Walk, a brick-paved path that serves as Belmont's main thoroughfare. If you need to be anywhere on campus, you're likely traveling along Centennial. And if you want to be harassed by a student group looking for new members—say, the Latin American Student Association—the Walk is where that will happen.

"You'd better," she says, straightening the stickers as if I hadn't just done that.

This girl is uber high-strung, and if she weren't the LASA president, we'd never say a word to each other.

She slings the strap of her thousand-pound backpack over her shoulder, nearly tumbling to the ground from its weight. "I need to get to class."

No, Katy, what you need is some weed and the kind of random hookup that will leave you bowlegged for a week.

"Don't worry about this," I say, trying to calm her nerves. "I've got it covered. I'm VP for a reason, you know."

She gives me her patented "bitch, please" side-eye, then says, "Yes, and we all know the reason: You won a popularity contest."

What. A. Viper. She hovers and hisses, and then when you least expect it, she strikes, using her sharp teeth to sink her venom into your bloodstream in milliseconds. Katy wants me to give up my position, because she thinks I didn't earn it, so she pushes my buttons, hoping I'll implode from the frustration. Not going to happen, Katy. Sticks and stones may break my bones, but if my father's words never hurt me, yours certainly won't either.

When she fails to get the reaction she wanted, Katy fakes a smile. "Be sure to stay the entire hour. No one's going to relieve you before then, and we don't want to leave the table unattended. Oh, make sure to talk up the holiday ice cream social. And don't forget to tell them we'll have pizza at our first meeting."

"Absolutely, will do. But you better get a move on, Kay. You're going to be late for class."

She gives me a frosty look (Katy hates that I gave her nickname a nickname), then flounces away in a cloud of hubris.

Finally.

Now I can focus on reeling in a few new club members. And we need them. Desperately. Only student groups with at least twenty-five members receive school funding, making outreach efforts like this club fair essential to LASA's continued existence. But I'm working with terrible odds. Belmont's a relatively small liberal arts college, and Latinx students represent just six percent of the student population. That number drops significantly once you subtract the Latinx-on-the-admission-application-only cohort and the folks who have no interest in building a community inside Belmont's walls. So here I am, holding a platter of freshly baked chocolate chip cookies (individually wrapped, of course), a playlist of music by Latin artists on repeat (Pitbull never says no to a collab, apparently), while I guard a table displaying Latinx-themed stickers (because college students *love* decorating their laptops). Yes, I might be doing too much, but my father has set his sights on sending me to law school, and I can't very well make that happen if I'm vice president of a defunct student group. Plus, organizations like these matter. For me. For every Black or brown student navigating through spaces with people who don't look like them. So I'm not letting LASA go down without a fight.

Half an hour later, I grudgingly accept that the cookies are the main draw. Or perhaps it's the skinny jeans, because honestly, my ass looks amazing in them, and these boys have nothing but sex on the brain. Whatever the reason, there's a small crowd of people wiping crumbs off their faces as they (not so intently) listen to my pitch on why they should join the group.

After I name all the Ben & Jerry's flavors they can expect to try at the holiday party, someone in the back clears their throat. "Can we dispense with the pleasantries?"

I frown as I stand on my toes to get a look at the heckler, not appreciating the confrontational tone they've taken for no apparent reason. Although I can't see who's addressing me, I engage with them nonetheless. "What do you mean?"

The person shuffles forward, a few students stepping out of their path.

Ugh, it's the guy who was trying to get on my nerves in class last week. Juan? No, Junior. Wait, now I remember: *Javier*. There's just something about him that burrows under my skin and festers every time I see him. He seems, I don't know, above it all? As if he can't be bothered to hide his disdain for his classmates—or people in general. I'd usually try to improve upon someone's negative first impression of me, but I suspect there'd be no point with this guy. Most boys at Belmont walk around in a cloud of cheap cologne they purchased at Walgreens; Javier walks around in a cloud of contempt. It's a shame, too, because he could make a living off those high cheekbones and dark almond-shaped eyes. That fact deepens my displeasure at seeing him here.

"What I mean is," he says, "if someone wants to join LASA, they should know what they're getting themselves into. For instance, are we Hispanic or Latinx? Because I, for one, see no reason to refer to myself as Hispanic; that's tying me to the colonizer."

A few people nod; others speak softly among themselves.

"And how about prejudice and colorism in our community?" he asks, pacing as if he's an instructor in a classroom instead of a student on a walkway. "Are we just going to sweep that under the rug? I can't tell you the number of times a fellow Latino expressed surprise when I spoke Spanish. All I'm saying is, any organization worth its salt is going to tackle the important stuff, not waste my time feeding me Ben & Jerry's."

That last comment elicits a few snickers—just as he intended.

Well, shit. He's not playing around. Little does he know I'm here for it.

I give Javier my bubbliest smile. "Thank you. This is *precisely* the energy our organization needs. Because all of these issues *are* important, and wouldn't it be great if we had a safe space to discuss them? The thing is, LASA is what we make of it. What we need are people like *you* to join us and help us develop meaningful programming to tackle the hard questions. Prejudice in our community? I can write a dissertation on that topic from my personal experiences alone. And what terms we use to identify ourselves is no small matter. I'm Brazilian American, so 'Hispanic' doesn't even apply to me. But you know what? We can talk about all this, and even have a bowl of ice cream while we do it. Maybe then we can think about building connections instead of focusing on the negatives." I hold out a pen to him. "So what do you say, *friend*? Are you ready to sign up and be a part of the change?"

Javier blinks at me. I'm not entirely sure he absorbed a single thing I said.

"What?" he asks.

"Be a part of LASA," I say, waving the pen. "Join us and bring all your amazing ideas with you. I mean, you're good at identifying problems. Are you capable of coming up with solutions too?"

He blinks some more, his maddeningly exquisite jaw clenched, then scans the crowd that gathered to watch our exchange. Seconds later, his face relaxes, as if he's just realized the corner he talked himself into and isn't all that mad about it, and then he chuckles. It's truly a thing of beauty to watch, this reluctant surrender. With a sigh, he gingerly plucks the pen from my fingers.

"You're probably going to regret this," he says softly enough that no one else is likely to hear him.

I immediately imagine Javier whispering dirty nothings in my ear, then mentally smack my brain for going rogue. Recovering quickly, I smile at the dozen or so people lined up behind him. "Actually, I don't think I will. You're an ass . . . et already."

When he's done adding his name to the sign-up sheet, he straightens and readjusts the strap of his backpack. "Make sure there's vanilla at the holiday social. It's my favorite."

I step back and eye him from head to toe. "Pegged you as a vanilla type the first time I spotted you."

His eyes narrow. "Cute."

"I know."

"Bye, Marisol."

"It's Mari."

"Marisol it is, then," he says before strolling away.

Ugh. Javier's insufferable. And ridiculously handsome. Which probably means I'll be dating and dumping him within a week.

* * *

"I'm telling you, watching those two yesterday was hot," my best friend, Sasha, tells our third roomie, Brittany, fanning herself. "It rooted me to the spot, so I ended up being late for class. Seriously, you had to be there to get the full effect of the hotness."

"I *was* there, and she's exaggerating," I say, rolling my eyes. "Also, stop saying 'hot.' It's annoying."

"Annoying is you telling me how to use my words. I learned them all by myself and I'll put them in a sentence however I want."

Brittany shakes her head at us, her wavy brown hair styled in the same way as her current obsession, Lorde. The fixation's so bad that Sasha and I had to ban her from playing "Royals" on repeat. Just last week, she forced us to study the video like a final exam so we could help her re-create the singer's winged eyeliner look.

"You two are a mess," she tells us, pouting her nude lips (also a nod to Lorde).

Sasha snatches a strip of bacon off my plate and winks at a guy across the dining hall. "Some might even say a *hot* mess." She sticks her tongue out at me.

"Okay, so what's the deal with this guy?" Brittany asks as she squirts mayonnaise on her scrambled eggs. "Do you two have history or something?"

She's a dainty thing with the oddest habits. I love her fiercely.

Sasha grimaces. "Ew, that's gross, Brittany. You're no longer invited to the cookout."

"Who's hosting a cookout?" Brittany asks, furrowing her brow. "No one told me."

Sasha groans and stares up at the ceiling. "It's the metaphorical cookout thrown by Black people, sweetie. It means you're 'in.' But if you keep doing shit like that"—she points to Brittany's tray—"we're going to kick you out."

"Maybe she shouldn't be 'in' if we need to do this much explaining," I say.

"You're both assholes," Brittany says. "I *earned* the right to be at this cookout. *You*." She points an accusatory finger at Sasha. "Have you forgotten the *hours* I spent taking out your braids last year? And *you*." She points a sausage link at me. "Yesterday you described me as the least problematic white person you know."

"To be fair, she doesn't know tons of white people," Sasha says.

Brittany drops the sausage and crosses her arms over her chest. "Bite me."

"See, now you're just begging to be disinvited," I say, trying to keep a straight face.

Sasha's the first to break, her loud snort causing me to giggle. Brittany follows not long after, completing the usual domino effect. This is our trio, inseparable since we met in our pre-freshman advisory group last year. We bicker, we banter, we bitch. But it's all in good fun. And know this: If someone messes with one of us, we're *all* throwing hands.

Brittany composes herself, then narrows her eyes at me. "It's obvious you don't want to talk about *him*, but I'm not letting you off that easy. So, explain."

Sasha takes a long sip of orange juice and waits for me to do just that.

"Okay, okay, he and I had a run-in when I was swiping the newspapers last week. Javier wanted his copy, and I told him no."

"Did you notice how *hot* he was then?" Sasha asks cheerfully.

"He's not *that* hot, okay? He's broody and a know-it-all."

"And now he's a member of LASA," Sasha observes.

"Well, that remains to be seen. I'm not sure he'll show up."

Brittany gives me a knowing smile. "But you want him to."

"I couldn't care less."

Actually, I *could* care less. I *wish* I cared less. But something about the guy has captured my attention and won't let go. I'm unreasonably irritated by this turn of events.

"So do what you always do," Sasha suggests. "Scratch the itch, then keep it moving."

"Or," Brittany chimes in, batting her eyes, "you could make an actual effort with this guy, discover he's more than just a typical bonehead, and maybe even fall in love."

Sasha and I stare at each other, and then I say, "I think I'll just go ahead and scratch that itch, thank you."

Believe it or not, my own mother would wholeheartedly approve of this plan. She met my dad in college, turned her world *and* her future upside down to remain with him in the United States, and twenty years later skedaddled back to Brazil because she no longer wanted to be here—with my father, really, but a pesky side effect is that she isn't here with me either. It took me a while to get to this point, but I'm at peace with her decision now that I understand she stayed in this country as long as she did for my sake.

As far as I can tell, my mother got swept up in my father's hurricane, and I was the baby doll left behind in the rubble in her rush to get to safety. He didn't abuse her, physically or mentally, but he became a different person than the one she married, and she worried that she wouldn't recognize herself if she stayed. So my mother's advice about my time at Belmont boils down to this: Discover your passion and have fun. Whereas my father's advice can be summed up in his parting words when he dropped me off my first year: "Don't fuck around on my dime." My mother, a journalist herself, gave me the idea about swiping the *Gazette* as a nonviolent means of protest. My father would drag me back to Cali if he had any inkling I was involved. Yeah, it's easy to see why my parents' marriage didn't last.

Sasha stands and stretches, her lavender sweatpants hanging off her enviably curvy hips.

"Where are you going?" I ask, looking up at her.

"Grimy Neal is headed to the waffle station. I'm going to get in there before he puts his grubby hands on everything." She narrows her eyes, then pretends to retch. "Ugh, he just picked his nose."

I shudder. "Ooh, quick, can you make me—"

Someone slides onto my bench and jostles me, throwing their arm over my shoulder. "Well, if it isn't my favorite hottie."

"I'm never using the word 'hot' again," Sasha mutters as she sits back down, apparently deciding the waffles can wait.

"Get off me, Spencer," I say, shrugging his arm away while mean-mugging his entire entourage.

Brittany glares at him. "You can't just put your hands on her without asking, jerk." She's not one for confrontation, but violating someone's personal space is a pet peeve, especially when one of us is being harassed.

Spencer throws up his hands in surrender. "Chillax, Britt. I was just saying hi."

"You only need to open your mouth to do that," she replies. "Now leave."

Spencer ignores her and settles his dazzling blue eyes on my chest. "Give me a chance, Mari. One date. That's all I'm asking for."

"A single date, Spencer? How romantic. At least you're up front about your intentions. One and done, am I right?"

His friends laugh as they shove each other like buffoons.

"Oh, c'mon," Spencer says, swinging his gaze from my chest to my face and giving me puppy-dog eyes. "Don't be like that. Everyone knows if one of us is going to ghost, it's definitely you."

Well, he isn't wrong; that's kind of my thing. "You're right, Spence. So why don't we skip to the end and just pretend I've already ghosted you."

"Take the L and go," one of Spencer's friends shouts.

"Fine," he says, rising from the bench with a smirk. "You'll cave eventually. Every girl does."

"Bye, Spence," Sasha says, waving him off like the pest that he is.

After he and his toadies drift away in a cloud of Drakkar Noir, I drop my chin and let out a deep sigh. "Maybe I should give up dating altogether. Boys are exhausting."

"And yet we can't quit them," Sasha observes, her shoulders slumped in defeat.

"Speak for yourselves," Brittany quips. "Girls are exhausting too, but at least they're not *that*."

Sasha nods. "Yeah, there's gotta be better than that to look forward to."

I remain silent, mostly because Javier's face immediately popped into my brain, and I'm giving said brain a good internal talking-to: *No, we're not going there. That one's trouble. Please stick to the rivers and the flakes that you're used to.*

CHAPTER 5

Javi

Eleven Years and Seven Months Before the Wedding

What am I doing here? Spending a Wednesday evening at some Latin American student group meeting just isn't my vibe. At all. I mean, I love my people, but we are *not* the same. Puerto Ricans from New York. Cubans from Miami. Chicanos from East L.A. *Not* the same. Which isn't a bad thing. It's just a thing some of us forget. And sometimes we simply don't mesh the way other folks might expect us to. Plus, a rolling stone gathers no moss and all that. So joining a student group is *not* on my to-do list. Still, I talked a lot of shit the other day, and I need to back it up. One meeting. That's what I'll give her. And they'd better give us pizza like they promised.

To my surprise, Marisol Campos is nowhere to be found. (Not that I was looking.) Instead, a short redhead commands the room, introducing herself as if she alone is responsible for the group. That can't be right. Marisol doesn't strike me as a foot soldier.

"As your president," this Katy Maldonado person says, "I'm here to bring your vision for LASA to fruition. We already have a holiday ice cream social on the schedule, but we need to make an impact. Think bigger. Get noticed. So if you have ideas about what we should be focusing on this semester, I'd love to hear them."

A guy up front timidly raises his hand.

"Yes?" Katy says, looking at him expectantly.

"Um, I thought there was going to be pizza."

She stares at him for a few seconds, barely holding in a sneer. "Right. I've got someone on that. Should be here any minute." She claps once, then circles the room. "Anyone? Thoughts? Suggestions?"

Everyone stares at the floor. This isn't what we signed up for. I, for one, assumed we'd be working with a template of some kind, not inventing their entire programming. Thankfully, a commotion at the door saves us from answering, and soon after, Marisol charges inside, a stack of pizza boxes in her arms and a plastic grocery bag dangling from the fingers of her right hand.

Before I can even stand, three guys swoop in to help. Worse, they're fawning over her as if she kneaded the dough herself. It's embarrassing to watch.

"Marisol will set up the pizzas in the back while we continue discussing your ideas," Katy announces, her tone underscoring that she doesn't appreciate the interruption.

First, we weren't discussing any ideas, *Katy*.

And second, why are you acting as though Marisol's your lackey?

Third, why am I suddenly protective of the girl who's done nothing but annoy me since I met her?

I track Marisol's movements as she crosses to the rear of the room and instructs her admirers on where to place the boxes. They return to their chairs like they're coming back from the battlefield, leaving Marisol to set up the food alone. It's not fair for one person to do all the work, so I quietly join her, stacking the napkins and plastic cups while she removes the top half of each box.

Our gazes meet, and then she mouths, *Thank you.*

I understand why people gravitate to her. She's sure of herself. Funny. Impossible to ignore. And it doesn't hurt that her lips are lush and glossy all the time. Or that her dark brown eyes can captivate you with a single glance. Marisol shines just by existing. In other words, *she's heartbreak in human form.* Which is why I like bumping heads with her. Our friction reminds me not to get sucked into her orbit.

"Pizza's ready!" Marisol says, startling me out of my thoughts.

People jump up from their seats, but Katy stops them with an outstretched arm. "Hang on, hang on, let's hold off until we've finished our discussion."

"No one has good ideas when their stomach's grumbling, Kay," Marisol counters. "Let's feed them. Besides, we can talk as we eat."

With thirty sets of eyes staring her down, Katy relents, and then everyone swarms the table.

"So, where were we?" Marisol asks, holding a slice of pepperoni pizza. The New Yorker in me shudders when she doesn't even fold it before she takes a bite.

"I was trying to make a plan for this semester," Katy says.

"Well, to start, we need a fundraiser to support our community service banquet in the spring," Marisol says. "It's our opportunity to celebrate the high school students who participate in our tutoring program, and we're hoping to award a few scholarships. The school gives us some funds, but we need to bridge the gap to the

WHEN JAVI DUMPED MARI

tune of two thousand dollars. If we don't, we'll be serving everyone tater tots and giving the kids gift certificates to McDonald's. Maybe we can toss around ideas about that?"

In less than two minutes, Marisol has given us the focus we needed. And she's championing a cause with substance. Not that I'm trying to hype her up—or embarrassed about the snarky comments I made during the club fair.

"A bake sale?" someone suggests from the back.

"We won't earn enough money to make a dent in our budget," Katy says. "And I don't want LASA to be responsible for any food safety issues."

"What about a kissing booth?" a guy asks, after which he cocks his brow and smooches his lips, unintentionally emphasizing how bad his idea is.

Katy scrunches up her face in disgust. "Not on my watch. That's gross and unsanitary."

"A car wash?" another person proposes. "We could play Latin music and make it a party."

"Not enough people have a car on campus, though," the person next to me says.

"Ooh!" Marisol exclaims. "Let's skip the car wash and just throw a party in Camden Hall. We can charge admission."

Katy blows out a breath and rolls her eyes, her reaction probably as much about the messenger as it is about the message. "But then we'd have to pay for the room rental, a DJ, refreshments, maybe security too. I'm not sure we would even turn a profit."

I should remain quiet. The last thing I want is to make myself the subject of attention. But the thing I hate *the most* is wasting time, and we're spinning our wheels here, so I reluctantly add my two cents. "Okay, this might seem a little unconventional, but a student association at Rice sponsored a date auction a few weeks ago. Video of the event made the rounds on Instagram. One person bid five hundred dollars for a date."

"I saw that!" someone adds.

"Holy shit," another person says.

"So LASA could do the same thing," I continue. "You'd have to work out all the specifics—maybe make the winning bidders choose from certain preapproved dates like dinner, bowling, whatever—and then all you'd need to do is design a flyer, advertise the auction, and reserve a place to hold it."

Katy nods enthusiastically. "Meaning, most of what we raise would be profit!"

"We'd need people to volunteer to go on these dates, though," Marisol says. "Do we have enough members who'd be willing to do that?"

"The people going on the dates don't have to be members," I point out. "They just need to be willing to offer their time for the cause."

Marisol's eyebrows snap together. "Yeah, I get that, but it would seem odd if LASA members aren't up there too."

"Sure, of course," I say, shrugging. "Whoever wants to do it is welcome to."

"Would *you* do it, Javier?" she asks, a sly grin on her face. "To support the incredible high schoolers hoping to get accepted to Belmont someday?"

"Oh my God, yes!" Katy says. "I'd try to win a date with you myself!"

Shit. *This* is what I was afraid of. I never should have said anything. Now they're all staring at me. Worse, the attention I'm getting here is only a fraction of what I'd experience if I had to smile at an audience as people bid on a date with me. "Um, sorry, I can't."

"Why not?" Marisol asks, needling me for fun. "It's just a simple date."

I stare down at my clammy hands. *Think, Javi, think.* "Because I have a girlfriend," I blurt out, raising my head and peering at Marisol so she doesn't detect the lie. "I don't think she'd be cool with it."

A staring standoff ensues between Marisol and me. After a long, uncomfortable moment, she narrows her eyes. "What's your girlfriend's name? Is she a student here?"

I struggle for a name, my gaze darting all over the room until it lands on the two-liter bottle of Fanta on the back table. Too obvious. "No, she doesn't go here, and her name's . . . *Fantasia*."

Marisol's eyes widen. "Like the singer?"

"Who?" I ask, rubbing the back of my neck.

"You know, the woman who won *American Idol*," she prods.

"Sure, sure, yeah, like her."

Marisol pokes the inside of her cheek, then says, "She wouldn't even let you do it for a fundraiser? Goodness, tell your girlfriend to lighten up."

This figment of my imagination is serving her purpose right now, so I'm not telling her shit. "Sorry, everyone. You'll have to look somewhere else."

The guy next to me says, "Marisol, *you* should do it. We'd make the money we need in ten minutes."

As people murmur their agreement, Marisol stacks her hands on top of each other, props them under her chin, and bats her eyelashes. "Oh, you better believe I'm doing it! Who's joining me?"

A girl in the back row shoots up her hand. "My boyfriend's on the lacrosse team. I'll get him to ask a few of his teammates."

"Perfect," Marisol says. "This is going to be lit!"

A couple of guys bump fists and give each other dap. One of

them jokes that he's going to work overtime to win a date with Marisol. Something about that bothers me, even though there's no reason it should.

"What an excellent idea!" Katy exclaims, staring at me all starry-eyed. "Would you be willing to help us organize it?"

"Um, I hadn't really planned on—"

"Great," Katy says, bulldozing right over my attempt to say no. "Thanks so much for volunteering. Marisol is the head of our fundraising committee, so you'll report directly to her. How does that sound?"

"That sounds wonderful," Marisol says, throwing me a devilish wink.

Well, there you have it: My first mistake was coming here. My second was opening my impatient mouth. The snag is, if I try to extricate myself from the situation, I'll look like an asshole *and* leave Marisol in the lurch. I give zero fucks about the former and absolutely *hate* that I care about the latter. I guess it can't hurt to help out until the auction—just to keep an eye on things and make sure it doesn't go off the rails. I mean, the event *was* my suggestion, so it's only right that I see it to its conclusion. "Yeah, fine, that'll work."

"Fantastic!" Katy says more enthusiastically than necessary before turning away.

Marisol wanders over to me and taps the toe of my shoe with hers. Looking down at me with a smug expression, she says, "I guess we're going to be working together, me and you. How's that for a plot twist?" She spins on her heels, takes several steps, then adds over her shoulder, "Oh, and welcome to LASA."

I scowl at her, fold my cheese slice in half, and bite it as if it did me wrong.

Pain in the ass? Confirmed.

(But weirdly, I like it.)

* * *

Spending a Saturday morning helping Marisol Campos put up posters and flyers all over campus didn't make this year's to-do list either. And yet here we are.

The *good* news is that Marisol is a worker bee who's thrown all her energy into promoting LASA's date auction. The *bad* news is that our task requires one of us to hold the ad while the other person does the stapling, which means we've been invading each other's personal space since we started a half hour ago. The *worst* news is that whatever perfume Marisol wears smells like vanilla and caramel, a combination that reminds me of flan, my favorite dessert in the world. Yeah, my brain is going places it *really* shouldn't.

Wearing a wrinkled T-shirt with a photo of Rihanna throwing up her middle finger and gray sweatpants that seem seconds away from falling to her ankles, Marisol jumps onto the ramp in front of Myers Hall and scans the building's freestanding community bulletin board in search of a good spot.

"Hold on to my legs so I don't bust my ass," she tells me. "I can staple it myself."

That's how I end up with my arms wrapped around her thighs and her butt in my face as she stretches to attach the paper to the board.

I huff out a breath. "I'm five inches taller than you. I could just do this for you."

"Nope, I'm fully capable of doing it," she says over her shoulder. "Just stand there and look pretty."

I pinch her leg, and she yelps. The soft giggle that follows makes me smile.

When she's done, she accepts my hand and hops down onto the pavement. "Let's do this one too," she says, pointing to a bulletin board in front of the dorm reserved for international students.

We silently scan the board for the best available space.

"Ooh, International House is hosting a food festival next month," Mari exclaims, bouncing on the balls of her feet. "Empanadas, asado, arepas, yuca. Yum. I love how no matter what Latin American food I eat, it always feels like *us*. I'm definitely buying a ticket to this."

"You're Brazilian American, right?" I ask, a flush of warmth going up my neck when I remember why I already know the answer.

"Yup," she says, popping her lips. "I mentioned that last week when you were trying to annoy me at the club fair."

"I was just doing due diligence about LASA," I counter.

"Even if I did believe that you were"—she makes air quotes—"'*just* doing due diligence about LASA'—I *don't* believe that, by the way—you were also trying to annoy me. Can we at least agree on that?"

"We can," I say, sheepishly.

She smiles, then motions for me to come closer. "Psst, let me tell you a secret."

I lean forward, bending slightly so she can whisper in my ear.

"If the shoe were on the other foot," she says, her soft lips ghosting over my ear and a few wisps of her hair grazing my neck, "I would have done the same thing."

I literally shiver. That's what being near her does to me. It's unsettling. I'd like to think I have control over my own body, but when Marisol's around, it does what it wants—and what it wants is to sink into her touch. But that isn't all. I like her voice; it's soft, a little husky, and there's a lyrical quality to it that my musically inclined brain gravitates to. The unguarded way she speaks captivates me too; she just says what's on her mind, a refreshing trait to someone like me—namely, someone who's always curbing their thoughts so they don't sound like an asshole.

Apparently I'm the only one affected by our closeness, because she moves back to the task at hand, standing on the tips of her toes so she can tap the board. "Let's put one of the posters here. This time, I'll hold and you staple. I can't reach up there anyway."

Get it together, Javi. This crush is definitely one-sided.

Helping her position the poster, I say, "So, your parents, are they both Brazilian?"

She nods. "Yeah. I'm second gen on my father's side. He was born and raised here. My mother was born in São Paulo. They met at USC."

"Where are your parents now?" I ask.

"My dad's still in California. He's a lawyer there. My mother lives in Brazil."

She says this in a flat tone that doesn't mesh with her bubbly personality. I forget the poster for a moment and look down at her. "Is that a good thing?"

"It took me a little time to think so," she says, meeting my gaze dead-on, "but yeah, it's a good thing. For all of us. What about you?"

In other words, the subject of her family is closed. And I can relate. I'll tell anyone who'll listen that my parents couldn't be more loving and supportive, but my brothers are an entirely different story. I guess Marisol and I have more in common than I thought. So instead of pushing for more information, I answer her question. "I'm Nuyorican. Born and raised."

"And you wear that label like a badge," she says, stapling one corner of the poster as if it's an exclamation mark on her sentence.

I step back to assess our handiwork, then turn to her. "I wear it like an honor."

She puts up her hands, nearly bludgeoning herself with the staple gun. "Whoa, whoa, whoa. No need to get so defensive, dude."

"Past experiences tell me otherwise," I say, picking up the remaining posters, then slinging my backpack over my shoulder. "Some people can be funny about Latinidad. And I don't mean *ha-ha* funny. I mean, they act as if there's a hierarchy, and Puerto Ricans always seem to be at or near the bottom."

"Well, I'm not one of those people, so drop the sword and shield, Spartacez."

I let out a loud chuckle, surprising myself and, judging by the way her eyes widen, surprising Marisol as well. "You're too much."

Her gaze falls to the ground as she presses her lips into a thin line. After a beat, she says, "So I've been told."

The slight tremor in her voice catches my attention. I take her free hand and gently shake it. "Hey, I didn't mean that in a negative way. If you couldn't tell by now, I don't exactly give off fun vibes. It's rare that someone can get me to laugh out loud."

"Then you need to get out more," she says, easing her hand out of mine and throwing on a carefree expression I now suspect is hiding the most tender parts of her. "In fact, ever think about joining a fraternity? I went on a few dates with the president of ODO last year. We weren't feeling each other, but we're still cool. I could put in a good word."

I groan on the inside. Not this again. Omicron Delta Omega is a relatively new Latinx fraternity here. They reached out to me my first year, asking if I'd be interested in joining their chapter, but I'd rather shovel horse shit all day than join a Greek-letter organization. I already have two brothers I can't stand. What's the point of purposefully saddling myself with more of them?

"No, thanks," I tell her. "Again, not my vibe."

"Yeah, you're right," she says, her head tilted to the side as if she's dissecting my personality and trying to rearrange its contents. "Not your vibe at all."

I'm not touching that comment. I'd rather not know why she thinks so. "Where to next?" I ask, wanting to keep her focused on our assignment so she isn't focused on me.

She looks to her left, then her right, and points toward the center of campus. "Let's hit up Staley Commons. Everyone's always hanging out in front. We'll get a bunch of eyes on the flyer there."

Staley Commons is one of four dining halls on Belmont's campus, and the only place open on the weekend. Its unofficial name is "Commons Meat Market," and as the unofficial name implies, most students go there to see and be seen by their classmates. I usually avoid it at all costs.

"Sure," I say with a sigh. "Let's go."

We stroll along the tree-lined route on Centennial Walk, dodging the occasional student on a bike refusing to stick to the bike path.

On the way, Marisol gets sidetracked by a cute puppy, asking its owner, a middle-aged guy, if she can pet it. When he nods, she drops to her knees in seconds.

"You're such a cutie," she coos to the dog as she strokes its ears. "And look at that wagging tail! Is it a boy?"

"Yeah," the man says, smiling down at her. "Ten weeks old. Name's Ozzie."

"Oh, I love him. Someday I'm going to get a dog just like you, Ozzie." She bops his nose, then jumps up and waves goodbye to them, looking at the puppy longingly as he and his owner resume walking. "My dad says pets are too messy, so we never got one. As soon as I get my own place, I'm going to fill it with a bunch of Ozzies."

"That's going to be expensive," I point out.

"And totally worth the money."

I can easily picture it: an older version of Marisol stretched out on a rug as her adoring puppies climb all over her and she laughs in pure joy. There must be a dopey grin on my face because Marisol stops and asks what I'm thinking about.

"Nothing," I say, my gaze falling to the ground.

Cut it out, Javi. Head in the game.

We continue toward Staley. Beside me, Marisol swings the staple gun in her hand.

"So what do your parents do?" she says.

I want to ask her why it matters, but I bite my tongue. I'm going to give her the benefit of the doubt and assume she's just making conversation. "My dad's a clerk at City Hall in Manhattan. Helps people fill out the paperwork so they can get married. My mom's an elementary teacher."

Marisol blows out her cheeks. "Your mom must be a saint. I mean, I was a devil in grade school."

"You?" I say, tilting my head back. "I can't imagine."

She narrows her eyes at me, a smile dancing on her lips, then shoves me away from her. "I bet I'd like your parents. They raised a good egg."

"You would. They're the best."

"Any siblings?"

"Two older brothers. *Not* the best."

She stumbles to a halt, her eyebrows lifted in anticipation of some juicy family gossip. "Did they gang up on you when you were a kid?"

I relax my jaw. There's no point in getting riled up about them. "Something like that." When I peek at Marisol's face, I notice the wariness in her expression, so I quickly add, "Jesus, they didn't hurt me or anything. Physically, I mean. We just . . . went our separate ways before I started college, mostly because they weren't there for me when I needed them."

"I'm sorry. Unfortunately, there's a lot of that going around."

"Yeah?"

"Yeah." Marisol shakes her head. "What's your relationship with your brothers like now? Do you see them often? Is it weird? Or tense? Or—" She takes a deep breath. "Sorry. Hunger's got me a little loopy."

She's bombarding me with questions before I can formulate my own. That's an impressive superpower. I give her a slow smile, a breather for us both, before answering. "No need to apologize. It's just . . . there's not much to it. We aren't as close as I'd hoped. They're older and only a year and a half apart from each other in age. Kind of always felt like it was them against me."

"That sucks. I'm an only, so I wouldn't know the first thing about sibling dynamics."

"You're lucky," I say, chuckling and absolutely meaning it.

"Didn't always feel like it, though."

I'd like to find out why, but we reach Staley Commons before I can dig into her statement. Another day, maybe. In the meantime, we weave through the crowd of people hanging outside the dining hall. I can't help noticing how the guys track Marisol's movements, their gazes darting to her and away as if they're trying to be cool about checking her out.

We make quick work of our last few posters, then stare at the final one as if we didn't design it ourselves.

A guy appears out of nowhere and throws his arm around Marisol's shoulder. "What's this?"

"Nothing for you to worry about, Spencer," she replies, shrugging out of his hold.

"A date auction?" he shouts. "Holy shit, are you saying I'll be able to win a date with you?"

"I'm sure there'll be someone else you're interested in," she says, grimacing.

"Not likely, babe," he says, reaching out to touch her face.

On instinct, I block his hand and slowly lower his arm. "Chill, man."

He jerks his head back, his eyes bulging in surprise when his gaze lands on me. "Oh, I see how it is." Then he leans in close. "For now. But you won't last, you know. They never do."

"Bye, Spencer," Marisol says, glowering at him.

He smirks at us and saunters back to his posse.

Marisol grabs my T-shirt and pulls me close, her eyes pleading. "If he bids on a date with me, please promise you'll step in and beat him to it." She licks her lips. "It wouldn't be the worst thing in the world, right?"

She's not asking for much, but it feels important to close off the possibility of anything romantic between Marisol and me, even if the attraction I'm sensing is only in my head. After all, she's one of the most popular students on campus. And I'm . . . the opposite of that. She attracts people; I repel them. If I could leave Belmont without anyone ever knowing my name, I wouldn't care one bit. Marisol needs someone on her level; I can't even step on the platform. So believing there could ever be something between us that doesn't end with my heart on the floor would be foolish. I know what it's like to be left behind, and I'd rather not be the reflection in someone's rearview mirror ever again.

"I can't," I say, gently lowering her hands. "I have a girlfriend, remember?"

"Oh, right," she says, twisting her lips to the side as she considers her predicament.

"But don't worry," I add, wanting to ease her stress, "I'll make sure that Spencer kid doesn't win a date with you."

She raises her brows, a question in her eyes. "Oh yeah? How?"

"No clue," I say, shrugging. "But I'll figure something out."

"Well, then, I'm counting on you, friend," she says, poking me in the stomach.

"*Are* we friends?" I ask.

She nods, her direct gaze pinning me to the spot. "If you'd like to be. We can begin by grabbing some lunch together if you want."

I study her for a moment, my lips pressed together. Damn. Spending more time with Marisol is not good for my mental wellbeing. My brain's synapses go into overdrive when I'm around her; it's as if I'm experiencing literal sensory overload. So I hesitate to answer and she notices, her eyes widening in surprise, then narrowing in annoyance.

"Oh, c'mon, Javier," she says, lightly punching my arm, "I don't bite. We're just sharing a meal. We can talk about the auction details if you're worried about what your *girlfriend* would think."

Marisol's point penetrates the chaotic thoughts in my head. She's right. And now I feel ridiculous. I'm acting as though she's some kind of siren hell-bent on tempting me, which isn't fair to her and is actually fucking shitty on my part. By focusing on my attraction to her, I'm undervaluing Marisol's best trait: her personality. She's fun and funny and fearless. Plus, she's that rare individual I can tolerate for longer than a few minutes. I don't need to be *with* Marisol to enjoy the best parts of her. So I place my hands on her shoulders and steer her in the direction of Centennial

Walk. "Yeah, *friend*, let's get you fed. I can hear your belly growling from here."

"Shut up, Javier," she says, leaning into my side as I throw my arm over her shoulder.

"It's Javi."

She looks up at me with a wide smile. "Javi it is, then."

"Sounds good . . . Mari."

CHAPTER 6

Javi

Now

Okay, maybe it was the fake girlfriend that made my relationship with Mari go off course. And yes, I'm aware that lying was a bitch move. But to be (self-servingly) fair, I was young and foolish and couldn't imagine that dating Mari would end in anything other than a total annihilation of my vulnerable heart. Mari claims she knew within seconds and played along. Still, I'm positive Mari and I wouldn't be as close as we are today if we hadn't friend-zoned each other all those years ago. I wanted her in my life; the minor trade-off was a hookup that wouldn't have blossomed into anything of substance anyway. So, no, while I'm not sure precisely when I screwed up, it wasn't fictional Fantasia that got me into this mess.

Which brings me to Mari's very real fiancé. Damn, even the word *fiancé* makes my gut churn.

"So, let me guess what happened at the auction," Alex says as he squeezes a lemon wedge onto his fish. "*You* won the bid for a date with Marisol."

"Actually, no. I had a girlfriend, remember?"

Mari leans forward. "Who was totally made up, by the way."

"Right, but you didn't know that at the time," I say.

"Sure I did. You're a terrible liar." She snorts, her lips quirked up in amusement. "What guy would date a woman named Fantasia and not know about the famous singer with the same name?"

I'm *never* telling her about the Fanta bottle.

"Anyway," I say, stretching out the word, "my roommate at the time, Jeremy, was and still is loaded, so I begged him to win the date in my place. And he did, for five hundred dollars."

"Nice," Alex says, nodding.

Mari huffs out a breath. "But Jeremy didn't even want to go on the date with me. Said it was a gift to LASA."

I shake my head. "Jeremy's a damn liar. It sure wasn't a gift. I had to do his laundry for the rest of the semester to pay him back."

Mari's jaw drops, her fork suspended in midair. "Seriously? Why am I just hearing about this?"

"Because I didn't want you to worry about it. The goal was to get rid of Spencer and that's exactly what I did."

"That's one of the sweetest things anyone's ever done for me," she says, her voice cracking with emotion. "I'm touched."

Alex looks between us, a placid expression on his face.

"It was worth it." I clear my throat, pushing around the lasagna on my plate. It's a rare day when I can't destroy some pasta, so I'm extra annoyed. That doesn't mean I can't be civil, though. "So, Alex, did you grow up on the island?"

"Yeah, in Guaynabo," he says. "I lived there until I was seventeen, then came out here for college."

He probably comes from money, then. *Interesting.* And perhaps it shouldn't be surprising. It makes sense that he and Mari would share similar backgrounds. But is this a love match? I have my doubts.

WHEN JAVI DUMPED MARI

As Alex tries to regale us with colorless stories about his childhood in PR—how that's even possible is beyond me—I stare at Mari, willing her to look in my direction. She refuses to meet my gaze, however, and instead stares off into the distance. I bet she's just as bored as I am. I mean, Alex doesn't immediately strike me as a jerk, but he's no charmer either. He's like stale bread: not inedible but also not ideal most of the time.

Speaking of, the object of my lukewarm contempt is studying me, and because I spaced out I have no idea why.

"Sorry?"

Alex grins amiably. "I asked if we could expect you to bring a plus-one to the wedding."

Why the hell does he care? *Oh, I see.*

"Highly unlikely," I tell him. "I'm not dating anyone." I peer at Mari. "Plus, I'll be too busy fulfilling my man of honor duties. Wouldn't want my date to feel like I'm ignoring her."

Alex's smile slips, and then he studies me as he grinds his jaw. I hope he chisels it down to sawdust. I'm not sure if he's harmless or toxic. That alone would have made me pause had Mari asked for my opinion when they first began dating. Which means I have six weeks to find and expose this guy's faults.

"Well, at the very least, I can introduce you to my sisters," he says. "They'll be dateless too. Either one could work for you."

Either one? As if they're interchangeable? Yeah, no, this guy's a menace. "I'm sure I can manage to be on my own that day," I tell him.

"Suit yourself." Then he rises to his feet and runs a hand up and down his breastbone. "If you'll excuse me, I need to visit the restroom real quick. The wine is going right through me."

My eyes snap shut in disgust. I can't stand when a person mentions their own bodily functions, especially at a dinner table. Keep that shit to yourself, for fuck's sake. I add another tic to Alex's "con" column.

As soon as he steps away, I pounce on Mari, crossing my arms on the table and leaning forward. "What the hell, Mari? Marriage? To that guy?"

Her expression hardens before she takes another swig of the wine she's been guzzling ever since the server took our orders. "Yes, Javi. Marriage. To that guy. Have you seen him?"

I ignore her maddening rhetorical question. What could I possibly say? That he's a ten but his ass is a little too plump? "You've met his parents?"

"His father passed away several years ago, but yes, I've met his mother. She lives in Puerto Rico, so we've chatted on video calls."

"His friends?" I press.

"Also yes."

"What does Patrícia say?" If there's anyone who might be a voice of reason here, it's Mari's mother. She doesn't mince words, and she takes her role as Luiz Campos's counterforce seriously.

"She knows about Alex, but I haven't told her about the engagement. This is all very new, and we keep missing each other."

If Patrícia isn't even aware of what's going on, she won't be much help—yet.

I don't know what else to say. Maybe I need to sleep on the situation and regroup.

Mari's deep sigh fills the silence. "Listen, I know this is a lot for you to take in, and I truly regret not telling you sooner, but Alex is a good guy. We have tons of things in common too. We truly do fit as a couple."

What a ringing endorsement of her lifelong mate and the potential father of her children. *He's sentient, Javi. And he walks up-*

right. He even eats with utensils. I don't buy it, and I don't think Mari buys it either.

"Does your father like him?"

"My father's his mentor."

I sit back and blow out a harsh breath. Jackpot. I *knew* I'd find Luiz's dirty hands all over this farce. But as usual, I need to tread lightly where Mari's father is concerned, so I switch tactics. "Why didn't you put him through our normal vetting process? If you're so sure about him, it would have been an easy thumbs-up."

"Sometimes you just know it's meant to be."

I point at her face, tracing the shape of her in the air. "That right there, that starry-eyed expression. The whole reason we made the pact was to avoid basing our decisions on flimsy shit like that."

She twists her mouth into a grimace and gives me a pitying look. "I was wrong, okay? If you really like someone, it shouldn't matter what anyone else thinks."

"No, it matters a whole hell of a lot," I argue. "If someone's worthy of you, the people who know you best will see it too."

"But that doesn't mean I should relinquish my autonomy over my own love life. Javi, it's time for us to admit that we've been using our dating audit as a crutch. The moment I realized it was holding me back, I was able to let Alex into my life, and now we're committed to each other. Isn't that what you've always wanted for me?"

I could confess my feelings now, but how crass would that be? Her fiancé is only a hundred feet away—what's taking him so long anyway?—and Mari would think I'm only panicking in the face of her unexpected announcement. Besides, I don't want my big moments with Mari mingling with Alex's.

Play the long game, Javi. It'll be worth it in the end.

So I dodge her question. "You should know, this guy isn't getting a pass from me. I'm going to be watching him like a hawk until you say 'I do.'"

"I wouldn't expect anything less," she says, plainly amused.

She has no idea how seriously I'm taking this situation, though. "Mari, I hope you know I only want the best for you. That will never change."

She places her hand on mine. "Then be happy for me. And be the best man of honor in the admittedly short history of men of honor."

I can't picture myself standing next to Mari as she marries someone else, but that's exactly what she's asking of me. My throat is at risk of closing, so I force out the words I know she's expecting to hear. "Sure, I can do that."

Thing is, being the best man of honor *must* mean I'm responsible for ensuring that the bride doesn't make the biggest mistake of her life. After all, isn't that what friends are for?

CHAPTER 7

Mari

Now

"The guy's in love with you," Alex says matter-of-factly.

I've been wondering when Alex was going to share his take on Javi; it's been a couple of hours since dinner, and he hasn't said a peep.

I stop wiping the makeup off my face and meet his gaze in the mirror. "Javi's a good friend, that's all. I assure you, he's not in love with me. There is *nothing* to worry about."

I glance at the tubes and jars in Alex's arsenal, a regimen of serums and creams that keeps his skin baby soft. It used to bother me that Alex is more high-maintenance than most people. But then we traveled together to San Antonio for a weekend getaway, and let me just say, there's no better feeling than realizing you can borrow your man's hyaluronic acid when you've forgotten your own.

"I'm not worried," he says, watching me carefully as he works through his multistep nighttime routine, a pair of striped pajama pants hanging off his hips and his firm chest bare. "Just stating the obvious."

"You're not even a little bit jealous of our relationship, then?" I ask, inwardly wincing at the trace of hopefulness in my voice.

He chuckles as he rubs moisturizer onto his face. "Jealousy springs from insecurity, so no, I'm not even a little bit jealous."

That's partially true, sure, but I think it's more complicated than that. We're all insecure to some degree—insecure in ourselves, insecure in our connections, insecure about our futures—but sometimes we don't express these rational feelings because society tells us being confident is the endgame: "Never let them see you sweat," "Never bend your head," "Believe in yourself and you're halfway there." But the inspirational quote that lives rent-free in my head and resides on a Post-it at my desk is this: "You are allowed to be both a masterpiece and a work in progress, simultaneously." (Thanks, Sophia Bush.)

Alex tends to view issues in black and white; I'm more likely than he is to see the grays in any given situation. I'm also firmly in the camp that believes a little insecurity is normal. It only develops into a problem when that lack of confidence leads to the exertion of control over another person. Nevertheless, I'm grateful for Alex's clear-cut perspective now. How uncomfortable would it be for everyone if the green-eyed monster lurked around every corner as we prepared for this wedding? Especially when there's no basis for it—as I've learned time and again.

I step behind him, pressing my forehead against his back and wrapping my arms around his waist. "Thanks for being so understanding about all this. I bet some other cishet grooms would balk at the idea of their fiancée choosing to have a guy friend in the wedding party."

He turns around and leans against the vanity, then pulls me

into a loose embrace. "I want you to be happy. If having Javier as your man of honor is going to help that happen, I'm certainly not going to stand in the way. You deserve the world, princesa, and I'm going to do everything I can to give it to you."

"Keep talking like that, and I'll drag you to City Hall myself." I tip my head up for a kiss, but we're pulled out of the moment by the sound of the ringtone designated for my mother, a blaring alarm—because if she's calling and *not* leaving a minute-long voice note on WhatsApp asking if I've forgotten her very existence, then something's happening.

I dash to the bedroom and snatch my cell phone off the nightstand. "Alô? Mãe? Tudo bem?"

"Tudo, filha. E você?"

I'm staring at her profile photo, so I request to switch to video, and after a few seconds of fumbling on her end, she appears on the screen with a broad smile on her face and the ends of her relaxed strands peeking out from under a red headscarf. *She's fine.* And just like that, my heart rate slows. One of the drawbacks of having a mother who lives on another continent is that I never know if she's truly okay, and I worry I'll learn from a phone call that she's truly not. We make it work, but I'd be lying if I said it isn't challenging sometimes. "Tudo ótimo! Tento falar com você desde na semana passada."

Alex enters the bedroom, then crouches out of view as he puts on a T-shirt.

I repeat myself for his benefit. "Everything's great. I've been trying to reach you since last week. I have news!"

"Tell me," she says, sitting down at her kitchen table.

"Alex and I are engaged!"

Her eyes bulge, and she covers her mouth with her free hand. "Isso é sério?"

"Yes," I say on a laugh. "He asked last week."

"How did it happen? Did he do something special? Go down on one knee?"

"Nothing like that," I say. "He took me to a jeweler and said I could pick out whichever ring I wanted." I flash said ring at the screen.

"Oh, how . . . nice. It's big."

I motion for Alex to come closer. "And he's right here."

My mother snaps her mouth shut and smiles. "Congratulations! You're a wonderful couple."

"Obrigado, minha sogra," Alex says.

My mother gives him a cheesy grin. "Que lindo! You're learning Portuguese."

"I'm trying," he says.

"That's all we can ask of you," my mother says, nodding.

"I'll let you two talk," he says with a wave, and then he slips out of the room and closes the door behind him.

I give her a knowing look. "Let's hear it." Because I can *guarantee* she's been holding her tongue.

She shrugs, her lips pursed in innocence. "What do you mean? I'm happy for you."

"There's a 'but' in there somewhere, right?"

"Wrong. Only you know *what* and *who* is going to make you happy. If you think Alex is the right person, then I'll support you." She waggles her eyebrows. "Is he good in bed?"

I slap a hand over my eyes and groan. "Nope, we're not going there."

She cackles.

"We're getting married in May," I say, dropping the bomb when she's disarmed.

Her laughter abruptly stops, and she squints at me. "Why so

soon? Don't you need more time to make sure this is what you want? To organize?"

"This *is* what I want," I say firmly. In a less urgent tone, I add, "And my dream venue happens to have a rare opening."

We chat a bit about the particulars: dates, my plans for the run-up to the wedding, her observation that she and my father should minimize their interactions when she comes here for the festivities.

"What does Javi say about all this?" she asks.

The question stuns me into silence. I draw away from the phone, and when I regain the ability to speak, I say, "He's happy for us?"

She tilts her head to the side and peers at the screen. It's like she's standing right in front of me. "Is that a question?" she asks.

"No, it's not a question. I just saw him a couple of hours ago, and he *is* happy for us."

"Okay, but from what you've told me, Javi knows you better than anyone, so I'm curious to hear what he really thinks."

I let out an exaggerated groan, my frustration with Javi's reaction to the news resurfacing. This line of inquiry makes no sense. What does Javi have to do with any of this? And since when did my mother become his advocate? "Who made Javi the arbiter of my love life anyway?"

My mother's forehead creases, and a look of bewilderment overtakes her face. "*You* did, Marisol. *You* did."

Dammit. Why are mothers always so astute?

CHAPTER 8

Javi

Ten Years and Seven Months Before the Wedding

The weather early in our junior year is unseasonably warm, a second summer in the mid-Atlantic blessing us with mild October temperatures even at dusk. People are taking advantage of the reprieve too. Bodies are sprawled all over Belmont Green, and a student practicing Pachelbel's Canon on her violin is providing the perfect soundtrack to help us relax. The violinist isn't playing it straight through, but rather focusing on three of my favorite variations—the ones I practiced for hours when I was teaching myself how to play piano in junior high. If I had a keyboard, I'd be tempted to join her.

Beside me, Mari sighs and straightens the blanket we're sitting on.

"Want to talk about it?" I ask.

Ignoring my question, she removes the lid of the pint of mint chocolate chip ice cream I brought her and digs in. Personally, I think it tastes like Pop Rocks and toothpaste, but to each his own.

"It might make you feel better," I nudge.

"No, it wouldn't," she says, chomping on a spoonful of ice cream. She capitulates within seconds. "I'll just say this: I don't get why I'm the bad person here. All I did was tell him I didn't want anything serious. He acted as if I was asking for a divorce. Not only that, he said I was a tease because I didn't want to have sex with him. The whole thing was wild on every level there is."

"He" is Rob, a guy Mari met a couple of weeks ago. They seemed to be getting along, though I wasn't sold on him, and when Mari backed off, he called her some nasty names. Worse, we're pretty sure he's responsible for defacing the flyers around campus announcing Mari's election to LASA president. The timing's too coincidental, and the language scrawled across the flyers mirrors the names Rob called her when they argued. I'm not a violent person by nature, and a random kid isn't worth an assault charge, but if I could figure out a legal way to make Rob's life miserable, I'd be all over it. We took down the posters this afternoon and—just to be safe—reported our suspicions to campus police.

"You're *not* a bad person," I tell her. "Rob's just used to getting his way and doesn't know how to handle rejection. Fuck him."

A yellow Frisbee lands a few feet away from us, and a guy jogs over to retrieve it. He bends to pick up the Frisbee, then winks at Mari as he straightens to his full height.

Real smooth, cabrón.

Mari glares at him. "My vagina's sealed shut for the rest of the school year. Move along."

He throws his hands in the air, dropping the Frisbee in the process, and backs away.

She sets aside her ice cream—a testament to how annoyed she is—and flops onto her back, throwing an arm over her face. "I need revenge."

I flop onto my back beside her. "What kind?"

"The petty kind."

"Okay, how would you get your revenge?" I ask. "Walk me through it."

She ponders my question a moment and says, "First, I'd glitter-bomb his car."

"Good one."

"Ooh, then I'd sign him up for thousands of marketing emails."

"You'd need access to his account, though. Most of these companies want you to confirm your email address when you subscribe."

She flings her arm out and flicks my forehead. "Must you bring reality into this?"

"Ow . . . and yes. If it doesn't feel possible, this exercise isn't going to be satisfying. Think bigger."

"Okay, how's this? He has a ridiculously comfy couch that he spent an obscene amount of money on. I'd fill the cushions with moldy cheese and anchovies."

"Fuck, that's brutal. He'd never get the stench out."

"Exactly."

"Well done. You could also substitute his social media pics with a photo of a horse and edit his profile name to Bestiality Stan. But you'd need access to his account, so never mind."

She laughs. "That'd be too cruel to animals anyway." After a moment of silence, she turns on her side. "You're right, he's not worth my time."

"No doubt," I say, turning to face her.

"Is this when you tell me *I told you so*?"

I could but I won't. There's no point in rehashing what she already knows: I had a bad feeling about Rob from the get-go. "He hid his true colors. It's as simple as that."

She nods. "I've messed with a lot of frogs."

The words slide over me like tar, weighing me down and darkening my mood. Imagining Mari with other guys just isn't a pleasant thought. Ever. I wish I could protect her from the assholes of the world, but it isn't my place to come between her and any person she chooses to be with. Sometimes I wish it were. "Can I ask you something?"

"Of course."

"This fixation you have with being in a . . . what do you call it?"

"A situationship?"

"Yeah, that. I'm not judging, just trying to understand what that's about. Where's it coming from?"

She blows out her cheeks. "My mom, probably."

"How so? I mean, can you tell me a little more about her?"

"You really want to know?" she asks with a slight shake of her head.

I'm not bothered by the question. Since Mari and I met last year, we've gotten closer, and I consider her a friend. Even so, we haven't shared a lot about our pasts, about the people who matter to us. I'd like to change that. Honestly, I wish I knew everything there is to know about Mari, but telling her that would reveal too much. So instead, I say, "I wouldn't ask if I wasn't interested."

"Huh," she says. "Okay, where to start? Let's see, my mom, Patrícia, met my dad in school. He's first-gen and well off, though he wasn't always. My mom grew up with much more modest means in São Paulo and was here to get a graduate degree in journalism. Anyway, they started dating and fell in love. They both say it was instant fireworks between them, and she couldn't imagine leaving him. So she stayed. And, well, my dad's a bit old-school. It's not that he didn't respect her career; it's just that he didn't prioritize it either. So when they had me—my dad was in law school then—he naturally assumed she'd focus on the home while he did his thing. Which is exactly what happened. Except my mom didn't like the life my dad wanted to live. The entertaining. The long nights at work. His obsession with wanting to maintain his social status and do things she couldn't care less about. They grew apart, I guess."

"That must have been hard for her."

"Yeah, I can't imagine. And it wasn't only about my dad. It was about being in the U.S. too. I mean, people assume being here is always the better option, as if an immigrant couldn't *possibly* want to be anywhere else. But she had a beautiful life in Brazil. A wonderful family that was too far away for her to visit as much as she wanted to. Siblings who needed her help."

"She was homesick."

"Exactly. Plus, I was going off to college soon anyway. And she certainly didn't want to be an empty nester with my dad, so she divorced him and left."

"What was that like for you?"

She lets out a long sigh, her gaze settling on the blanket. "Hard. For a while, I wondered if I could have done anything to make her stay. She assured me it wasn't about me. That she would have taken me to Brazil if I'd wanted to go. But in my mind, that was impossible. My friends were here, my *life* was here."

"Your dad was here too," I point out.

"Not as much of a positive as you'd think," she says flatly. "I overheard him tell her he wouldn't know what to do with a sixteen-year-old daughter." She laughs. "My mother told him to figure it out."

"What's your mom doing now?"

"Working at a daily newspaper in São Paulo and helping her siblings take care of my grandparents."

"Do you see her from time to time?"

"I've visited the last two summers, and I hope to go back next year. My grandparents aren't healthy enough to travel here, so I try to see them whenever I can. I spend the holidays with my dad."

"Are you and your father close?"

She tilts her head from side to side as she considers my question, then says, "He stepped up when my mother left, even though I know he wasn't thrilled about it. So I owe him a lot. But honestly, sometimes I worry I'll get swept up in his hurricane too."

I understand her so much better now. Turns out she has a protective shell as thick as mine. Maybe that's why we click—because we're kindred spirits in a way. A part of me hopes we'll both let our guard down. I get the feeling it'd be worth it. "Let me guess: You're not trying to get swept up in any guy's hurricane while you're in college either."

"Exactly. But don't get me wrong. I'm not hating on love. I'm just not looking for it right now." She stretches, then gives me a once-over. "Your turn."

My heart hammers in my chest. "My turn?"

"Yeah. Give me hope that I'll find a decent person someday. Tell me about your girlfriend."

This is the first time Mari has asked about this person who doesn't exist. I figured she didn't care enough to interrogate me. And since I didn't want to add to my initial lie, I let it be. But I'd like my friendship with Mari to thrive in spite of our significant others, real or fictional, so I put my bogus girlfriend to rest. "We broke up."

Mari bolts upright. "Oh no! Why? What happened?"

She says this in an overly dramatic tone, immediately raising a red flag in my mind.

"It just fizzled," I say, sitting up and avoiding her gaze. "We wanted different things. We were going in different directions."

"You mean you wanted to be here, and she wanted to stay in your closet?"

I cock my head. "Closet? Why the hell would she want to stay in my closet?"

"Isn't that where people keep their blow-up dolls?"

And then it dawns on me: Mari never believed me in the first place.

"She exists, goddammit," I say, my cheeks burning as I try to keep the grin off my face.

"Of course she does," she says, a smile tugging at her lips.

We stare at each other a few beats, and then we both burst out laughing.

"Seriously, Javi. What were you thinking? Fantasia?"

"It's a perfectly beautiful name," I say under my breath. Using my full voice, I add, "Well, if you knew, why didn't you call me out on it?"

"There was no reason to. You didn't want to be available, and I got the message loud and clear."

"It wasn't about you, specifically."

"Oh, it was very much about me, but I'm not mad about it. We're choosing not to be together in that way, and that's perfectly fine."

"We ended up in the right place, though, right?" I say, genuinely believing that to be true.

"Yeah, we did."

She flops onto her back again, and I inch closer, arranging myself so we're perpendicular to each other, my head resting against her side.

"You owe me some honesty, though," she says.

"That's the only lie I've told you."

"I don't doubt it, but that's not what I mean. I need you to share something real with me. Because I've done enough sharing for the both of us."

She has a point. I mean, it couldn't have been easy to talk about her parents just now.

After a beat, I say, "I'm afraid of heights. Like *really* afraid of heights."

"How interesting," she says in an amused tone. "If we're ever in a situation where that information is relevant, I'll bear it in mind. But that's not the kind of sharing I'm talking about, and you know it."

Mari absently runs her fingers through my curls as she stares up at the night sky, an occasional firefly zipping by. Now that the violinist has stored away her instrument, it's soothingly quiet on the quad lawn. With Mari's gentle hands sifting through my hair and the starry view above calming me, it's hard to keep my eyes open. Or maybe I'm avoiding the subject.

"I'm waiting," she singsongs.

"Poking around for dirty secrets?"

She chuckles softly. "Do you have any?"

"Not dirty, exactly."

"That's a shame."

I can't help smiling. Talking to Mari is the best part of my days. Every sentence reveals something about her personality. And the more she shares, the more I want to reciprocate. Even if it dredges up unpleasant memories. I blow out a slow breath, then take a leap. "My junior year of high school, my brothers and I were on the cusp of being signed to a major record deal."

She sits up slightly, dislodging me from my reclined position. I twist my torso to face her, unsurprised by the look of shock on her face.

"*You* were in a boy band?"

"Almost," I say, shrugging. "We hadn't finished any songs, but I was working on a few. I was angsty as hell in high school, and I have the terrible lyrics to prove it. 'Stuck on you like peanut butter' was an actual line I wrote."

"Oh God," she says, cringing.

"Yeah, I know. But in the meantime, we did covers at local festivals and malls. And we were a hit. Our parents were impressed too, so they entered us into a talent search. Not one of those scammy ones, either, but a real one sponsored by Pinnacle Music."

Her brow lifts when I mention the well-known record label, and then she settles back down. Once I return to my preferred position, she asks, "Okay, so then what? Give me all the sordid details."

I bristle, wishing the whole sad episode didn't bother me as much as it does. Mari has no clue that *sordid* is the perfect word to describe what happened, and she certainly didn't mean to hit a nerve. It *was* shameful. I'm tempted to sanitize the details, but she asked me for honesty, and I want to give it to her.

"We had what felt like hundreds of meetings with the label and an outside manager they found for us. It was clear the company was prepared to put some real money behind our group. Then at some point, it started to feel like the original idea of the band—my idea, actually—was being distorted. I wanted to work on stuff that would set us apart. They wanted us to talk about cars and sex. I pushed back, and the label didn't like that, so they dropped me."

"The label dropped you?"

"No, my brothers did."

She gasps. "Javi, no."

"Yeah. They blindsided me too. Didn't break the news to me until a couple days before we were supposed to sign the contract. Said they found someone else who would be a better fit. Asked me if I'd consider taking a more passive role. I was crushed, but I stepped aside. Thing is, I wasn't even mad about the deal. It was the betrayal that really hurt. The group was my idea. My way of strengthening my relationship with my brothers. But they left me behind and never looked back."

"I'm so sorry that happened," she says softly. More urgently, she says, "Tell me there's a happy ending. Tell me they flopped so bad."

I sigh. "Wish I could, but I can't. Their first album was certified gold. Nothing after that came close to the success of the first LP, but they're a bona fide pop group with a huge social media following."

"What did your parents think? How'd your brothers get all this past them?"

"My parents don't know what went down. I just told them I wasn't ready to commit to the group."

"You covered for your brothers," she says, her eyes wide.

"Yeah."

"But why?"

"Because this was a major record deal. A chance for my brothers to do something that would make life easier on my parents. I wasn't going to mess that up for them."

"So this is why you're no longer close with your brothers."

"I don't think we were ever all that close, honestly. I spent my high school years trying to be cool like them, trying to hang around them. But they always brushed me aside. Until the band. But in the end they did what they always did: deserted me."

"Well, then, now it's your turn."

"My turn to do what?"

"To get revenge. In your head, of course. Tell me what you would do."

As usual, she knows just what to say to pull me out of my funk.

"I'd secretly finance a tell-all documentary about their rise and spectacular fall. I just need to wait until they crash and burn, the fuckers. And I'd make sure it was broadcast on multiple networks."

"What's the group's name?"

"The Triborough Boys."

Her fingers pause in my hair. Yeah, she's heard of them. Everyone has.

"I've heard of them," she says matter-of-factly.

"Thanks for not gushing."

"You're welcome," she says, continuing to massage my scalp. "Feel better?"

"Much."

And it's true. I've never shared what really happened with anyone, not even my parents. And although I feel exposed, I'm comforted by Mari's response. It tells me that I can be vulnerable around her and she won't throw it back in my face.

"Hey, Javi," she says.

"Yeah?"

"I'm going to listen to your advice when it comes to guys from now on, no questions asked. It's dangerous out here in these Rob-infested streets, and I could use the help. In return, I'll get rid of all my Triborough Boys downloads. Deal?"

I smile. "Deal."

And you know what? This girl is worth being petty for.

I jump to my feet and hold out my hand. "Let's go to the bookstore."

"What for?" she says, taking it.

I give her a devious smile. "For glitter."

Thursday, October 16, 2014

WhatsApp Voice Message

Marisol, it's your mother. I just want you to know that I put the Sedal Rizos styling cream in the mail to you. Five bottles. It was expensive, filha. Maybe you can find it online now? Tell Javi and the girls I said hello. Oh, and that boy you were dating is a jerk. Esqueça ele! Te amo. Tchau. Tchau. Tchau.

CHAPTER 9

Mari

Ten Years and Seven Months Before the Wedding

My mother's advice is spot-on. Good thing is, Rob's already forgotten, and I'm socializing as usual—well, trying to.

"C'mon, come with us," I plead.

Javi isn't even letting us into his dorm room. Instead, he's standing at the threshold with his arms folded over his chest and his mouth set in a hard line.

"No," he says. "Absolutely not. And if you need me to be clearer, hell to the no."

Sasha snorts and continues to pace the dimly lit hallway. Brittany throws her head back in frustration, though I'm wondering if it's the skintight bandage dress that's making her more irritable than usual. (Honestly, I liked last month's emo look better.)

"Have you been to a single party while you've been here?" I ask Javi, my hands on my hips.

"Nope," he says, popping his lips for emphasis, a habit he

picked up from me. "And I intend to keep it that way. Grain alcohol. Jell-O shots. Puke on my sneakers. Sounds like a damn nightmare. I'll pass."

"Listening to music, dancing, getting to know people," I say, ticking off each point with my fingers.

He stares at me for a moment, then says, "That's supposed to change my mind how? Do you know me or what?"

I *do* know him.

I know that his favorite color is blue.

I know that he *hates* when people speak with their mouths full.

I know that his mother calls him papito, mi cielito, and an untold number of other -itos, and he doesn't mind at all.

I know that he would drop everything if I needed his help (and I'd do the same).

But I also know he wants to be a loner—because it's safer than putting himself out there. So I'm not giving up on him just yet.

"You'll have veto power over anyone I talk to, remember?"

He taps his chin. "Tempting . . . but it's still a no."

"An hour," I beg. "Just give me an hour or two."

"Sorry, Mari, I'm staying in tonight."

As if to underscore how awful drunk college kids can be, the doors of two rooms fly open and a white guy bolts from one to the other, a pair of underwear on his head.

"Yeah, exactly, have fun," Javi says, escaping into his room and pushing the door closed.

Just before the door shuts, a hand shoots out from inside, and soon after, his roommate, Jeremy, emerges and jostles Javi to the side. Giving us a lopsided grin, Jeremy leans against the doorframe. "Well, hellooo, ladies. How can we help you this evening?"

The guy's a trip. His dirty-blond curly hair surrounds his face like a halo, and his skin is always flushed. Sasha secretly (and perfectly) nicknamed him Cupid. Brittany says he favors Justin Timberlake during his *NSYNC days.

"We're trying to get your roommate to quit acting like a thirty-year-old," I tell him.

Jeremy straightens, crosses his arms over his chest, and tucks his hands in his armpits. "Good luck with that. He's got a full night planned applying Preparation H to his hemorrhoids."

Javi smacks the back of Jeremy's head and retreats into the room.

Jeremy shakes it off and asks, "Where you going?"

"ODO's throwing a party at their house on Brickman Street," Brittany says.

"Ten-dollar cover charge," I chime in.

"Ten dollars?" Javi shouts from inside. "Now I'm *definitely* not going!"

"Forget him, Mari," Sasha whines. "He doesn't want to hang with us. Let's just bounce."

Javi's a grump, but he's *my* grump. Sasha doesn't get him, but I do. I've come to think of him as a candy with a hard outer shell and a gooey center. A Mentos personified.

"Okay, fine," I say loud enough for Javi to hear, "but that woman in the public safety workshop said we should attend parties in groups. So we can watch out for each other."

Javi pokes his head out and points a finger at us. "Don't lose sight of your drinks, okay?" He slips away, only to reappear seconds later. "Better yet, don't drink anything at all."

"Sure, sure," I say, pulling on the hem of my black miniskirt.

Javi's gaze follows the action, and then he clenches his jaw before disappearing inside again.

I'll work on him, Jeremy mouths as he closes the door.

"He's fun," Brittany observes as we amble toward the exit. "Reminds me of my dad. Are you sure he isn't one of those people who decide to finish college later in life? Like, do you have actual proof he's our age?"

I roll my eyes. "Just because Javi's not a typical college kid doesn't mean he's ancient."

"Eh, I guess you're right," Brittany says, clutching my hand as she wobbles along in her too-tight heels. "Well, anyway, I'm so glad we're going out tonight."

"You're not slick, you know. You're only hanging on to me because you're about to bust your ass in those ridiculous shoes."

"That too," she says on a laugh.

Before we reach the stairwell, I hear the click of a door locking, and when I look behind me, Javi's walking toward us, his face blank as he throws on a T-shirt. I peek at the sliver of skin visible when he adjusts the waistband of his dark-wash jeans, and my heart skitters. Have I considered what it would be like to give in to the attraction that sometimes simmers between us? Absolutely. But Javi's too special to be relegated to a situationship. And that's all I would ever want from anyone at this stage of my life anyway. He obviously feels the same; I mean, he *invented* a girlfriend to cockblock himself. Remembering all of this, I spin around and link arms with my girls.

"Good choice," I say over my shoulder. "You're going to have a blast, I promise."

Javi grunts in reply.

* * *

Javi is *not* having a blast.

ODO's house isn't huge, but they've removed every piece of

furniture on the main floor, so the space consists of nothing other than the bare rooms and an eerie blue lamp that's serving as the party's only light source. Everyone appears to be holding a red Solo cup in their hand, but as Javi recommended, we're not drinking anything.

"If someone pukes on my sneakers, you're buying a new pair," Javi tells me, leaning in so I can hear him over the booming sound of Don Omar and Lucenzo's "Danza Kuduro" coming from two speakers the size of a small human. I swear they've played it at least three times in the last hour.

"Yeah, yeah," I say over my shoulder, throwing my arms above my head and rocking my hips because that song is still a banger.

A few feet from us, Brittany and Sasha ignore the guys around them as they dance back-to-back. Sasha's crop top is bringing all the boys to the yard, it seems.

A few minutes pass without a snarky comment from Javi, so I glance back at him and catch him sneaking a peek at my ass.

When our eyes meet, his gaze darts to the floor.

"It's a nice butt, isn't it?" I ask, winking at him.

Javi's mouth twitches, and then he rolls his eyes. "You know it is." With a sigh, he makes a big show of looking at his watch. "You've got about thirty minutes left."

This time it's my turn to roll my eyes. "Fine." I stand next to him and scan the crowd, my fingers threaded like an evil villain planning world annihilation. After a moment, I point to a cute Latinx guy across the room. "What about him?"

Javi shakes his head.

"Why not?" I huff, leaning into him.

"He has a girlfriend."

Someone turns up the music even louder, so Javi and I are forced to put our heads together to continue our conversation. Unfortunately, his scent—a clean, earthy smell with just a hint of citrus—tickles my nose and sends my brain to forbidden places.

I draw back and clear my throat. "How can you tell he's taken?"

"Look at his wrist. He's wearing a friendship bracelet."

I snort. "That doesn't mean he has a girlfriend."

"If you're going to question my reasoning," he says, a smile dancing on his lips, "I'll just go ahead and leave now."

"Okay, okay, relax. But we should probably set some ground rules. I mean, you can't just make shit up as you go. You have to have good intentions."

"Of course," he says, nodding. "I only want what's best for you."

I'm skeptical, but I'll trust him—for now. I survey the room again and point at a white guy standing with a group of friends. "What about him?"

"The mullet should be disqualifying all by itself, but he's also a pothead."

"How do you know?"

"He and Jeremy are friends."

I groan. "That's disqualifying too."

He laughs. "It should be. Present company included."

"No, you're exempt, you adorable curmudgeon."

He pulls me into him, kisses my forehead, then releases me. It's a peck, really. Chaste. Friendly. Coming from a place of affection, not lust. Except Javi's lips are butter soft, and he smells amazing. Just like that, my brain rewires itself, decides his kiss is the only one that will do. And I *really* hate that for me. Because I have a sinking feeling that going forward, I'll compare every person to Javi and find them lacking. *No, no, no, brain. We are not going there.*

As if the universe is trying to extend me a break, a slim Black guy appears at my side, his meticulous fade and unwrinkled button-down immediately setting him apart from most of the guys at this party. A Belmont boy who doesn't consider T-shirts formal wear? I never thought I'd see the day.

On the other side of me, Javi clears his throat, so I turn and look up at him.

He tips his head ever so slightly, then walks away to join Sasha and Brittany, who are huddled in a corner guffawing about something. I guess this means he's giving me the green light.

"You're Marisol, right?" the guy says.

His voice is nice—not as deep as Javi's, but nice nonetheless. And he's only a couple of inches taller than me, so I don't have to crane my neck to meet his gaze like I'm always doing with Javi.

"Yeah. You are?"

"Trent," he says, flashing me a wide smile that highlights his straight white teeth.

I lick my lips and extend my hand. "Great to meet you, Trent."

He rubs the back of his neck, then takes a calming breath. "So, uh, would you like to dance?"

His apparent nervousness charms me. I really hope it's not a façade.

I glance at the corner where I last saw my friends and notice that Katy Maldonado has joined them. Ugh, it's bad enough that I still have to deal with her because she's on the LASA board, but now I have to see her here too? Wait a minute. What is she doing? I narrow my eyes. Is she . . . ? Yeah, she's inching closer and closer to Javi, positioning her body to block out my girls and invade his personal space. *Absolutely not.*

"Give me a sec, Trent," I say, and then I yell Javi's name from across the room.

He immediately looks up and finds me in the crowd, a question in his eyes.

I stare at him pointedly, flick my chin toward Katy, and slice a hand across my throat.

He throws his head back and laughs. When he recovers, he gives me a mock salute, letting me know he gets my meaning.

With Javi safely out of Katy's web, I take Trent's hand and pull him onto the dance floor.

This new dynamic between Javi and me is *exactly* what I needed. We're friends, confidants, bodyguards too. And because he matters so much to me, I'm vowing to keep it that way.

CHAPTER 10

Javi

Now

A succession of dings on my phone wakes me from a nightmare in which Mari announces that she's getting married to a bargain-basement Pedro Pascal. Groggy and blurry-eyed, I fumble for my phone on the nightstand. Where the hell are my reading glasses?

Snatching the phone in midair before it clatters to the floor, I hold it inches from my face so I can scan the notifications. Mari's name jumps out at me like a jack-in-the-box. I get yet another fucking scare when I open her email and read the subject line:

From: Marisol Campos <mcampos@camposlawgroup.com>
To: Sasha Campbell <sashacampbell@elitedigital.com>; Brittany Holton <britt@wineanddinecatering.com>; Chloe Rivera <crivera@camposlawgroup.com>; Javi Baez <javier_baezpc@gmail.com>
Date: April 7, 2025, 10:00 am PT
Subject: Alex and Marisol's Wedding

WHEN JAVI DUMPED MARI

Hi friends!

Just wanted to connect everyone in the bridal party and share some details about my and Alex's wedding, which is just six weeks away! Side note: Please excuse the formality of this email; I wanted to put everything in writing so none of you bitches could claim you didn't know what was going on. ☺

Chloe, meet Sasha, Brittany, and Javi. You're my closest friends, and I'm glad I finally have a reason to get you all in one place. Chloe joined my father's firm when I did, and we immediately clicked. She's just as reckless as you are, Sash, so I expect you two will get along great. I hope you'll all have several opportunities to talk as we gear up for the big day (perhaps as you plan my bachelorette party, lol).

Javi has agreed to be my man of honor. Alex's sisters have declined to participate (more on that some other time when there's plenty of wine).

> Wedding-related dates (times are all Pacific)
> Dress rehearsal: Friday, May 16, 4 pm
> Dress rehearsal dinner: Friday, May 16, 7 pm
> Bridal luncheon and wine tasting: Saturday, May 17, 12 pm
> Wedding: Sunday, May 18, 11 am

The wedding venue is Crystal Canyon Farm in the heart of Sonoma wine country. Alex's family will be coming from San Juan and staying in the cottages on the property. We've reserved one- and two-person cottages on your behalf from Thursday evening to Monday morning, and you should be receiving your reservation confirmations later today. If you need different accommodations, simply let me know and we'll arrange them. Additional details can be found at MarisolAndAlexSonomaWedding.com.

I've asked for time off the week of April 21, so if you wanted to plan a bridal party outing featuring a trip to a reputable strip club, my availability is wide open starting that Monday. ☺

Let's get on Zoom to chat face-to-face when you can. The most pressing item is attire. I'm thinking you can choose your own outfit within the wedding color scheme (silver and sky blue). I'll create a Doodle poll to get your availability and send out a video invitation for a date that works for everyone.

I'm thrilled that you're all going to be a part of my big day. I can't thank you enough for joining me as I begin this exciting next chapter of my life.

Big hugs,
Mari

Now I understand the dings.

From: Sasha Campbell <sashacampbell@elitedigital.com>
To: Brittany Holton <britt@wineanddinecatering.com>; Javi Baez <javier_baezpc@gmail.com>
Date: April 7, 2025, 10:02 am PT
Subject: Re: Alex and Marisol's Wedding

That's our girl. Always making lists and checking them twice.

Does anyone know why this wedding is happening in less than two months?

(Leaving Chloe off because I don't know her. *inserts Mariah Carey GIF*)

From: Brittany Holton <britt@wineanddinecatering.com>
To: Sasha Campbell <sashacampbell@elitedigital.com>; Javi Baez <javier_baezpc@gmail.com>
Date: April 7, 2025, 10:03 am PT
Subject: Re: Alex and Marisol's Wedding

She's not pregnant. I asked.

WHEN JAVI DUMPED MARI

From: Chloe Rivera <crivera@camposlawgroup.com>
To: Sasha Campbell <sashacampbell@elitedigital.com>; Brittany Holton <britt@wineanddinecatering.com>; Javi Baez <javier_baezpc@gmail.com>
Date: April 7, 2025, 10:03 am PT
Subject: Re: Alex and Marisol's Wedding

Hey, everyone! Assuming I'm the only one who's local, I'm happy to take the lead on the bachelorette party. My brother's best friend is a stripper. Shouldn't be a problem to ask him for recommendations.

From: Sasha Campbell <sashacampbell@elitedigital.com>
To: Chloe Rivera <crivera@camposlawgroup.com>; Brittany Holton <britt@wineanddinecatering.com>; Javi Baez <javier_baezpc@gmail.com>
Date: April 7, 2025, 10:04 am PT
Subject: Re: Alex and Marisol's Wedding

Thanks for offering to take the lead on the bachelorette party, Chloe. A stripper doesn't seem like Mari's style. Let's put our heads together and come up with a few possibilities. Side note: Is your brother's best friend on Instagram? I might be interested in auditioning him for a private event. ☺

From: Javi Baez <javier_baezpc@gmail.com>
To: Sasha Campbell <sashacampbell@elitedigital.com>; Brittany Holton <britt@wineanddinecatering.com>
Date: April 7, 2025, 10:06 am PT
Subject: Re: Alex and Marisol's Wedding

It's happening in two months because her dream venue has an opening. She's been talking about it since we were in college.

From: Sasha Campbell <sashacampbell@elitedigital.com>
To: Javi Baez <javier_baezpc@gmail.com>
Date: April 7, 2025, 10:06 am PT
Subject: Re: Alex and Marisol's Wedding

Send me your number. I need to speak with you.

My phone rings seconds after I reply to Sasha and close out of Gmail. Shit. I'm not alert enough to deal with her without caffeine in my system.

I sit up in bed and crack my neck. Here goes nothing. "Hello, Sasha."

"Don't 'hello Sasha' me. What did you do?"

"Do? What the hell do you mean?"

Sasha and I haven't talked one-on-one in ages, but I might as well have talked to her yesterday. Some people slip in and out of your life as if they know your door will always remain unlocked for them; Sasha is one of those people.

"Don't play oblivious," she says. "The last time I talked to that girl, she was taking a break from dating, and now she's getting married. And before you try to act clueless, she told me about your pact, so explain to me how everything went sideways."

"Sideways how?"

She takes in a deep breath. "So help me, Javi. This is not the time. Our girl doesn't do anything dating-related without your approval. And now she's getting married in six weeks? Make it make sense."

She's asking the impossible; I don't know what the hell happened either. "Sasha, all I know is that she called me in the fall and said she was taking a break from dating."

"What prompted the break?"

"She needed to regroup."

"From what?"

"She didn't tell me. It's not like I was going to encourage her to date if she didn't want to. She's entitled to take a pause if that's what she needs."

Sasha sighs. "Of course she is. I'm not suggesting otherwise. But none of this is mathing, as the kids say—"

"If you need to tack on 'as the kids say,' then you probably shouldn't be saying it."

"Interrupt me again and see what happens."

I freeze, all of my focus centered on not making another sound.

"All right," Sasha continues. "As I was *saying*, if she supposedly doesn't date a person unless you give them a thumbs-up—"

"It goes both ways," I point out, wanting to be clear that this wasn't some villainous scheme on my part to control her love life. Mari herself came up with the idea, and she's disapproved of a number of women on my behalf.

"Sure, sure, I get that. Regardless, you two have this pact, then she announces she's done with dating for a while because she needs to regroup, and then out of the blue she's engaged."

"That about sums it up."

Well, the part I'm willing to come clean about, that is. If Mari hasn't told Sasha what went down between us, I'm certainly not going to enlighten her.

"So what are you going to do about this?"

I blink several times before answering. "Do? Me?"

"Fa. So. La. Ti. *Yes*, you. The man who loves her."

"As a friend."

"Okay, well, if you're committed to lying to me, then I won't offer to help."

I'm not taking her bait. Yet. Sasha's a blabber. I'm not sure she's a worthy accomplice. Several beats of silence later, I say, "I guess we're just going to have to accept that our friend is getting married."

She sighs. "You've met him? In person, I mean?"

"Who? Alex?"

"No, Timothée Chalamet. *Of course* Alex."

"Yeah, I met him."

"And?" she prompts.

"And I would have disapproved of him had she come to me first."

"Which is why she didn't," Sasha mutters.

"Yeah, I think you're right."

"Oh, and Javi," Sasha says.

"Yeah?"

"You interrupted me twice. I didn't miss that."

"I had a feeling you didn't. My apologies."

Sasha blows out a frustrated breath. "What about his socials? Anything there?"

"Only Instagram and an embarrassingly sterile LinkedIn page. The guy's squeaky clean."

"Ugh, I don't like this."

"Believe me, neither do I."

"Okay, so I'm curious about something. Why'd you two make the pact in the first place?"

"We were kids, Sash."

That doesn't explain why we continued to honor it into adulthood, but that's too long a story to share with Sasha over the phone. And much of it should stay between Mari and me anyway.

"You came up with this at Belmont?" Sasha asks. "It goes back *that* long?"

"The idea of it, yeah."

"Huh, y'all are just full of surprises. I had no clue this was a thing when we were in college."

"It wasn't this big thing. Not really. Certainly not in the way it's supposed to work now. But yeah, the seed was planted back then."

Unfortunately, I suspect the moment we made the pact is when our problems began.

CHAPTER 11

Javi

Nine Years Before the Wedding

What possessed me to take a theater production class in my senior year? And why did I opt to submit an original costume design rather than write a paper for my final?

I. Am. Fucked.

And the person on the other side of this door is the only one who can help me. When I throw it open, Mari stumbles inside.

Her unfocused gaze roams over my (admittedly messy) dorm room. "You took down the Ciara posters."

I place a hand on my heart and dip my head. "It was time."

"Okay, but what are you doing? This is our last night before we cross the threshold of adulthood and become"—she hiccups—"boring. I brought libations. Well, cheap vodka, really, because that's all I can afford without putting it on a credit card and tipping off my dad." She rattles her head around. "Wait. I'm twenty-one now. What's he gonna do?" She gives me a once-over, her lips pursed. "Why aren't you getting ready? Everyone's lining up on Centennial Walk."

The night before graduation, seniors at Belmont take their final turn around campus in a parade in which ninety percent of the participants are wasted. Think keg party meets Mardi Gras. Belmont's administrators insist alcohol consumption has no place in this time-honored rite of passage, but the parade's path is lined on both sides with plastic barrels spaced twenty feet or so apart—not that anyone needs a convenient place to retch or anything.

"I can't go," I tell Mari's backside since its owner is now lying facedown on my bed. "Didn't you get my SOS text?"

She flips over and bolts upright. "I did. Figured you needed help coming up with a halfway decent outfit. What do you mean you can't go? It's tradition."

"No, tradition is actually graduating from college when you spend all four years taking your required classes. And if I don't turn in this assignment by midnight"—I point at my laptop screen—"I won't be doing that either."

She gapes at me, her glassy eyes widening. "You're not"—she lets out a ridiculously loud burp—"done?"

"Anna was supposed to help me finish it," I say, dropping onto the bed beside her and hunching over, "but she bailed. Kept stringing me along for weeks and now she's not answering my texts."

Anna and I met at the school commissary, a tiny convenience store in the basement of our dorm where I was a cashier for my work-study job. She was friendly and flirty, and we hooked up every once in a while. At some point, though, I realized she would always show up when she needed something: snacks, index cards, energy drinks when she was cramming for an exam. I had an employee discount; Anna treated it like her own personal expense account.

Mari's eyes narrow. "I *told* you that girl was a schemer."

"I know," I say, nodding. "And I should have listened to you."

She tilts her head and taps her chin. "So what have we learned from this experience, girls and boys?"

"That I should trust your gut?"

She jabs her pointer finger in the air. "*Exactly.*" With a heavy sigh, she lifts the vodka bottle off the floor and takes a swig. "I'm sorry Anna turned out to be a user."

"I'll survive," I say, shrugging.

"You will," she says with a firm nod. "Okay, so what do you need from me?"

It's as simple as that. There isn't any question in her mind that she'll help me out of this mess. That's Mari in a nutshell. Though she might flip out when she finds out what's involved. "I need a model. For the video."

She scrunches up her face. "Excuse me?"

"Hang on." I jump to my feet and grab the sheet with the grading rubric off my desk. "Here's the description of the assignment: 'Reimagine a costume from a select group of classic Broadway musicals using only items purchased from the Belmont Thrift Shop and/or a discount store. The budget is twenty dollars. You will be graded on (1) the success of your reference costume; (2) the creativity of your reimagining, which must be presented in a video; and (3) the effectiveness of your essay explaining your concept. Your video should be no more than five minutes in length, and your essay should not exceed one thousand words. Receipts itemizing the cost of all elements of the costume must also be provided.'"

When I look up, she's staring at me, her bewildered expression speaking volumes. "Why the hell did you take this class?"

I throw my head back and scrub a hand down my face. "I needed credits for my theater minor."

"And you thought it would be an easy A."

"That too," I say, meeting her knowing gaze. "Anyway, Anna was supposed to model the costume, and since she's gone MIA, I need you to take her place. Except . . ."

She narrows her eyes. "Except what?"

"Except I'm not sure your boozy ass can walk a straight line."

"Bitch, this boozy ass is all you got."

I smile. "I'll take it, then."

"That's what I thought you'd say," she replies, giving me a lopsided grin.

"Are you okay with missing Senior Walk Night, though? You've been talking about it for weeks."

"It's no big deal," she says, waving her hand dismissively. "Sash and Britt are going to be pissed, but making sure you get your degree is way more important."

Maybe it's the fact that we're graduating tomorrow, and we're heading our separate ways soon—Mari to California, where she'll start USC Law in the fall, and me back to New York, where I'll be doing who the hell knows what—but I'm feeling sentimental. I can't imagine what the last three years at Belmont would have been like without her. Unfortunately, the real world is snapping at our heels, and I can no longer outrun it. If I could, I'd freeze this moment.

Mari rises from the bed and snatches the grading sheet from me. "What musical did you choose?"

I swallow before I answer. "*Cats.*"

"Oh hell no," she says. "For the love of all that's holy, Javi, why didn't you choose *West Side Story*? Or *Grease*?"

"I was trying to challenge myself," I grumble.

She snorts. "Well, congrats, you succeeded."

"Okay, but don't give me too much shit. It's also the first musical

I ever saw live on Broadway. My mom took me when I was a kid. For my sixth or seventh birthday or something." I shrug. "I don't know, it's special to me."

Her eyes soften in understanding. "Aw, that's really sweet."

"Now don't get me wrong, I had no damn clue what was going on half the time. But I was fascinated by the music, the costumes, the fancy theater. And almost everyone was *so* skinny. I remember that for some reason."

"Okay, fine, I'll give you a pass on this one. If it's special to you, then it's special, period. Is the costume finished?"

"Mostly. I just need to add a few things here and there."

"Let's see it, then."

I pull the costume, still on a hanger, from the back of my tiny closet and present it to her.

She studies it, her head tilting from side to side, and then her gaze darts back and forth between me and the costume. "First, let me preface this question by telling you it's coming from a place of love and deep respect. Second, what the fuck is that?"

I grimace and hold it away from me so I can examine it through her eyes. The full bodysuit's white to accentuate the details. And I chose the spandex fabric because it'll shimmer under stage lights. For the patches of fur, I dyed cotton balls orange and black, which I thought was genius. Maybe I went overboard with the embellishments, but that's what a reimagining is all about. It probably isn't going to win any design contests. Still, I can easily picture a version of this in the musical. "Is it *that* bad?"

She bares her teeth as she considers it, her expression broadcasting her skepticism. "It's a bedazzled Muppet at a burlesque show. *Mad Max* meets *Where the Wild Things Are*."

I bark out a laugh and hold the costume in front of me. Well, shit. Now that she's described my creation that way, I can't unsee any of it.

Mari circles me, inspecting the piece from all angles. She steps closer and peers at the sleeves. "Is that . . . ? Are those the little toe separator thingies you use when you're getting a pedicure?"

"I think so," I say, squinting. "I picked them up at the dollar store. I wasn't sure why toes needed to be separated, but they fit the brief. The idea is that this cat has developed a protective shell to ensure no one strokes it."

"Like, through evolution?"

"Maybe," I say, wrinkling my nose. "But she also lays certain parts of her figure bare because that's the one thing she's comfortable sharing."

Her gaze darts to mine and she holds it for a long moment. "Or maybe it's not that deep and she just likes to have a good time. All those pesky alley cats trying to police what she does with her own body need to mind their own business. Or maybe, just maybe, this cat should be a Puerto Rican boy from New York who's always hiding himself from the world."

She raises an eyebrow, and my mouth falls open. What? Why am *I* in this? Is she pissed because she thinks I was talking about her? "Shit, Mari. This isn't personification or anything. It's a *character* I came up with."

She blinks a few times. "Yeah, yeah, I get that. I'm just helping you flesh out the *character*." She smiles. "And actually, it's genius. Do you have a number in mind?"

"I do," I say, nodding. "It's called 'Cantankerous, Coquettish Calico Cat.'"

"I love it," she says, clapping loudly. "Your professor's the only person who's going to see this video, right?"

"Yeah."

Mari blows out a breath. "Okay, then let's get this over with." She puts out one hand, and with the other, makes a circling motion with her index finger.

"What?" I ask.

She rolls her eyes. "Turn around so I can put it on."

"Here?" I ask, my voice rising.

"Yes, here. Where else would you have me change? I'm not going all the way to the bathroom and getting caught out there in this outfit. It's the night before graduation. There are wall-to-wall people in the dorms."

"Oh, okay, yeah, sorry, here." I hold the costume out to her, then spin on my heel as soon as she takes it from me, my heartbeat a steady drum in my chest. I flex my fingers at my sides, trying but failing not to notice every whisper of fabric as it comes off her body. Fuck, fuck, fuck. This is Mari. *Do. Not. Proceed.*

Mari grumbles as she puts on the outfit, making it slightly easier for me to scrub the reckless images from my brain.

"You all right over there?" I call out.

"Yeah," she says, huffing. "Almost done. It's . . . really . . . tight." She sucks in a breath and grunts. "Okay, you can turn around now."

When I do, I don't know whether to laugh or cry. On the one hand, she *does* look like a bedazzled Muppet. On the other hand, the parts of her body that I can see—her thighs, the curve of one hip, the slope of her shoulders—cause a pang to take up a permanent place in my chest. It's all a suggestion. A hint of what's underneath. But Jesus, her body is *unreal*. Lush and toned and just . . . perfect.

Mari's gently biting her lip, waiting for my reaction. That little habit seems unnecessarily cruel somehow.

"It'll work," I croak.

"It better," she says, a hand cocked on her hip. "So what else?"

"The headpiece," I say, snapping my fingers. It's safer to keep my mind on the assignment. "And the leg warmers."

"Oh God," Mari mutters.

I dig through the closet, tossing clothes behind me as I search for the box I put the headpiece in. "I'm really, really grateful, Mari. Seriously, you're saving my ass."

"It's a nice ass, and it deserves to be saved."

I know if I look at her, she'll be standing there with a teasing grin on her face. So I don't turn around—because I can't handle Mari flirting with me right now. Any other day, sure, but not tonight. Not when we're in this small dorm room and I'm already thinking about parts of her I usually excel at ignoring. So I pretend I didn't hear her comment and focus on finding the headpiece. "Here it is!"

"Yay," she says with fake enthusiasm.

"It's just a wig," I explain, walking toward her. "The ears and whiskers are attached, so there's no need to mess with makeup."

"What's this netting?" she asks as I place the wig on top of her head.

"It goes over your face. To match the theme that she's keeping herself hidden."

We're so close I can feel her body heat. There's no way she can't feel mine. As it is, I'm itching to wipe the sheen of sweat above my lip.

Mari looks up at me and searches my face, then she angles her chin, a question in her dark brown eyes.

My brain sends signals through my body, nudging my hand to touch her, begging me to inhale her scent, but I take a huge step back instead. "I was thinking about what you said earlier . . ."

"Yeah?" she says softly.

I clear my throat. "About how I should listen to your advice when it comes to women. I think . . . I think you're onto something. And maybe you should keep listening to mine. It's worked for you so far, and the one time I didn't listen to you, things went to shit."

She studies me for a few torturously quiet beats, then takes a deep breath, letting it out slowly. "You know what? Those are all excellent points. Staying focused is going to be even more important when I'm in law school. I can't afford to go off track now. So here's what I propose: Neither of us will date someone the other doesn't approve of. And if you find yourself getting all starry-eyed for someone, I can wade through the bullshit and make sure the person's worth your time." She pauses, then says, "I *really* need you to do the same for me."

I don't immediately answer her. Needing something else to do with my hands, I grab the vodka off the floor and take a careful sip. "Let's do it," I say, staring at her over the rim of the bottle.

"This requires trust," she says in a solemn tone.

"It does."

"And we can't second-guess each other."

"Exactly. We'd be giving each other free rein to stop a potential relationship in its tracks."

"Okay, then," she says, nodding. "Let's shake on it."

So we do, and thus a pact is born, though whether we'll ever use it is an entirely different story.

We make quick work of the video, and then I scramble over to the desk to read my essay one last time. Mari hands me the liquor and encourages me to take a swig for good luck. I know my limits, so I take a tiny sip instead, then return to the assignment from hell as Mari takes off the costume.

My mother's ringtone pierces the quiet, and I automatically hit speaker on my cell phone and continue to scan the screen.

"Everything okay?" I say absently.

"Papito," my mother shouts on her end of the line. "I found a TJ Maxx!"

Of course she did. TJ Maxx is my mother's second home; she can find one in the middle of a torrential rainstorm *without* the benefit of GPS. I'm not surprised she came all the way to Belmont for graduation and found one here too.

"That's great, Ma. Have fun."

"Do you need fresh underwear for tomorrow? There's a sale!"

I grab the phone and take her off speaker, blowing out my cheeks before responding. "No, Ma, I'm good."

"Okay, see you in the morning!" she says.

When I look up, Mari's grinning at me. "I can't wait to meet them in person."

"The feeling's mutual, believe me. I made you sound better than you actually are, so she's already in love with you."

Mari, now back in her regular clothes, twists her lips. "Whatever, dude. I'm fabulous, and you know it."

Damn right I know it, which is a pain; suppressing my feelings for Mari would be a lot easier if I didn't.

As I edit the essay, Mari floats around the room, inspecting my shit. "Do you still have my M&Ms?" She reaches into the top drawer where she keeps her candy stash and pulls out a box of condoms instead. "Unopened, Javi? Seriously?"

"It's a fresh box."

"Why extra small, though?"

"What?" I fly across the room, bringing the vodka with me, and grab the box from her hands. "That's not what I bought!"

She falls over in laughter. "So typical. Figures that would be the only thing to get your ass out of that chair."

I hand the bottle back to her and shuffle back to said chair. "No more liquor for me. I can't hang."

"Lightweight," Mari says, wandering over to a set of papers on my minifridge. She lifts the stack. "What's this?"

"Um, just something I'm playing around with in my spare time."

"Is it a script?" She peers at the pages more closely. "Wait, there's stage directions for choreography too. Are you writing a *musical*, Javi?"

"It's nothing, really," I say, shrugging. "Remember how I worked with the theater camp last summer?"

"Of course. But I thought you just worked on lighting and building the sets and stuff."

"I did," I say, nodding. "But I also watched and listened. And, well, I'm a songwriter at heart, so I couldn't help thinking about telling a story onstage. Anyway, it was just an idea. Not like it's ever going to see the light of day."

"Why not?"

"Because it's just for fun."

"And what are you planning to do that's *not* just for fun? After you finally turn in this assignment and get your diploma."

Her tone pokes me in the chest. Probably because I'm trying to turn in this final hours before it's due, and the whole situation feels like an omen of what's to come of my life. "I don't know, Mari. Not all of us have our entire existence plotted out by a dad who also happens to have a job waiting for them after law school."

I squeeze my eyes shut. Fuck. That was uncalled for.

"Ouch," she says, pressing a hand to her chest and stumbling back as if she's taken a direct hit, which she has—an unfair one at that.

I'm out of my seat before she can even blink, my hands threaded together as I prepare to plead for her forgiveness. "Can we forget what I said? I didn't mean anything by it."

She pins me to the spot with a hard stare, her nose flaring. "Of course you meant something by it. Words have meaning. That's kind of their point."

"Okay, well, I meant something by it," I say, pulling her into my arms, "but it was a shitty thing to say, and I apologize. Profusely."

Mari doesn't shrink away, but she doesn't return my embrace either; although her head is resting against my chest, her arms are hanging limply at her sides, as if she wants no part of this hug.

I hold her enough for the both of us. "You're my favorite person in the world, Mari, and it kills me that I said something that made you hurt for even a second. I'm nervous about the future, and I snapped at you out of frustration. That's not an excuse, it's an explanation."

"Fine," she says, gently pushing me away. "It's forgotten."

The tense set of her shoulders tells me otherwise. But here's the thing about Mari: She doesn't usually hold grudges for long. She brushes the hurt away as if it never happened in the first place. I get what she's doing, but I *hate* that I'm the one making her do it now. Times like these I wish I were perfect so I wouldn't have snapped at her at all. But I'm not—far from it, in fact—so I'll be sitting with this guilt for a long time.

Mari crosses the room and sits on my bed, her hands smoothing the ripples of my comforter. "You're worried about going back home. Nervous about being around your brothers again."

She's not asking a question; she's simply stating truths I'd rather not face. But talking this through with her feels like the appropriate penance for what I said, so I sit beside her. "I should be grateful. I'll be living rent-free in a home they bought for my parents. They even offered me a job helping promote the group."

She shakes her head. "They're offering you scraps. Because they know they took something from you, and now they feel like shit about it."

"Well, it's not like I have a ton of other options."

She turns to me and grabs my hand. "That band was *your* baby, and they stole it from you. Don't let them off that easily."

"Sure, so I'll work at some med office filing patient charts, since that's the only job I could get," I grumble. "That'll show 'em."

"Hey," she says, grabbing my chin. "Don't knock honest work, especially when it doesn't cost you your self-respect."

"You're right," I say, meeting her gaze head-on. "I'll tell them no."

"Damn right you will," she says with a firm nod. "And maybe while you're filing patient charts you can work on that musical over there."

"Maybe," I say, shrugging.

Mari stands and wanders over to my desk, where she grabs a stack of yellow Post-it notes. After making a big show of rolling her shoulders, she bends over and starts scribbling.

"What are you doing?" I ask.

"I'm writing your first review," she says, nibbling on her lower lip. "Wait. Someone who writes a musical—what's their job title?"

"A librettist," I say, grinning as I watch her ponder how to word this so-called review.

"Perfect." She writes some more, then strides across the room and stops in front of me, handing me the Post-it with a cheesy smile on her face. "Read it."

"Okay, okay," I say, raising the note to eye level. "'Javier Báez's untitled musical is an absolute masterpiece. Báez is the librettist of our generation.'" There's an arrow pointing to the other side. On it, she wrote, *Marisol Campos, the only critic who matters.*

I look up to find Mari watching me. She leans in and drops a gentle kiss on my forehead. "You're going to do great things. In your own time. Please believe me."

In this moment, I do believe her. Because Mari's rarely wrong, so if she has faith in me, there's an excellent reason why, even if I'm not sure what it is just yet.

"Thanks for saying that. It means a lot. And since we're talking about the future, I need you to promise you won't forget about me when you're some big-deal lawyer in California, all right?"

"I'd never," she scoffs playfully. "That's a promise."

I hold out my arms for a hug, and she eases into my embrace.

"Te quiero, Mari. Para siempre."

"Para sempre," she says softly.

Our languages aren't identical, but they're close enough that the differences don't truly matter. Just like Mari and me.

Thursday, September 15, 2016, at 1:34 p.m.

MARI: hey, how's the job?

JAVI: all right

boss is an asshole

MARI: that sucks

JAVI: how's school

MARI: good, I feel all lawyerly and shit ☺

JAVI: ha

MARI: when are you going to come visit me?

JAVI: just say the word

MARI: let's plan on something during my first long break in December

JAVI: sounds good

CHAPTER 12

Mari

Eight Years and Five Months Before the Wedding

People are gawking, and my arms might fall off soon, but Javi's reaction will be *so* worth it. Where the hell is he anyway? Was he the very last person to get off the plane?

An elderly woman with the scent of hair spray preceding her sidles up to me and whispers, "I hope he says yes."

"Me too," I tell her with a wink.

Is Javi going to kill me for holding up a sign that says I'M HAVING YOUR BABY! WILL YOU MARRY ME? Absolutely. Do I care? Absolutely not. Someone needs to get him out of his funk, and I'm the only someone he'll tolerate on his best days, let alone his worst.

Seconds later, I'm bouncing on my toes, my gaze zeroed in on the exit double doors, when Javi finally strolls through them, a navy duffel bag slung across one shoulder. I watch him search for me in the crowd, and as I hoped, his jaw drops when he spots me and reads the sign in my hands. At this point, everyone in the immediate vicinity is staring, probably wondering how all of this is going to go down.

I give him a goofy smile. "Gotcha!"

Oh shit. Javi doesn't look amused. Did I miscalculate the depth of his slump?

"You've got a lot of nerve asking me to marry you," he bellows. "Is the kid even mine? I mean, it's bad enough that you cheated on me with my brother, but now you're trying to get me to raise his kid too?"

A quick glance around confirms that people are shifting in their seats, trying to get a better view of the (fake) drama.

I wrap my arms around him, unable to contain my laughter. "Okay, fair enough. You got me."

Apparently he's committed to the role, though, because he throws me off him, drops his duffel, and then paces in front of me massaging his temples. Serves me right for thinking I could embarrass him in a public place. Javi hates attention, but he also hates that I think he's predictable, and my stunt only works if he reacts the way I expect him to.

"This is just like you," he shouts, his nostrils flaring. "Treating me like garbage and expecting me to come crawling back to you. Where'd you even go last night?" To a young Indian man sitting on a nearby bench, he says, "I went to visit my little sister in New York."

(Javi doesn't have a sister, the rat.)

"She's sick," he continues. "I had to go alone because this one"—he aims a thumb in my direction—"couldn't be bothered to answer her phone. I bet she was with my brother."

"That's terrible," the guy says, his eyes narrowed on me.

I scan the crowd and notice several people trying to secretly record this undeniably juicy slice of life. Which is when it registers that my prank is getting entirely out of hand. The *last* thing I need is to go viral for being an asshole with questionable morals.

"He's acting," I tell our audience as I pull Javi along. "Came all the way to L.A. to be discovered. What do you think? Should he quit his job making dildo casts and move to Hollywood?"

"Why not do both?" someone shouts, a hint of amusement in their voice.

"Not a bad idea," I reply.

We're forgotten within seconds. It's L.A., after all. Which gives me a moment to study Javi as we face each other. He may not be in good spirits, but he looks great. Broader shoulders. Sharper cheekbones. A bit more facial hair. It's entirely possible that he hasn't changed at all, but my eyes are amplifying everything about him because I've missed him so much.

"Always so extra," Javi says playfully. "Give me that damn hug you promised."

We come together in a tight embrace, my head resting against his chest. He smells amazing, though I wish I hadn't noticed. I also wish hugging Javi felt like hugging a brother. It never has.

"This is what I needed," he says, his voice managing to be both soft and gruff at the same time.

"Did you check a bag?" I ask.

"Do I look like an amateur? Of course not."

"Oh, thank God." I step back and pull on his jacket, tugging him toward the exit. "First, we need to get you out of those clothes. You're not in New York anymore, Toto."

Javi smiles as he surveys the frenetic activity around him. I follow his gaze, noticing the moment he and a woman exchange a flirty glance as they pass each other. Javi's a handsome guy, so I shouldn't be surprised someone finds him attractive. Still, it's strange—and unsettling for some reason.

"Dímelo, what do you have planned for us while I'm here?" he asks, snatching me out of my thoughts.

"Well, if it's okay with you, I thought we could have dinner with my dad. He's paying, so that's a big bonus."

Javi blows out his cheeks. "I don't know, Mari. Your dad doesn't seem to be my biggest fan."

"My dad isn't anyone's biggest fan. He's like that with everyone, even me."

"That's . . . concerning."

"It's really not. Just smile and eat the most expensive steak on the menu."

"Sure, that'll stick it to him," he mutters.

I roll my eyes. "Anyway, tomorrow I thought we could grab breakfast at my favorite diner and then head out to the Santa Monica Pier. Also, don't kill me, but a law school friend is throwing a party, and I told her we'd swing by. The one wrinkle is that I have a study group early Sunday morning, so I can't take you to the airport, but I'll arrange a Lyft. Hope that's okay."

"It's all good, Mari," he says, his eyes shining with affection. "I'm here to hang out with you. Whatever we do is fine with me. Except for the dad part."

We jostle each other as we stroll through the airport, generally making a nuisance of ourselves and not caring one bit. I inwardly sigh in relief. You never know with Javi. If he doesn't want to deal with people, he simply won't, but he's being a good sport about it, so I'm going to be extra careful not to deplete his sociability reserves this weekend.

Walking arm in arm, we head outside. "I sprang for parking in the terminal. Because you're special."

Javi laughs. "I'm honored."

"You should be."

He takes my words at face value, missing—or intentionally ignoring—my deeper meaning.

When we get to my car, Javi gapes at me. "A Beetle?"

I laugh. "Daddy dearest wanted to get me a BMW for graduation. I just wanted something to get me from point A to point B. This was the compromise."

"I can't believe you said all that with a straight face." He gestures at the passenger side. "Where am I supposed to go in this tiny-ass car?"

"Don't worry, you'll fit."

He narrows his eyes, and I give him a wink. Oh, this weekend is going to be fun.

On the ride to my apartment, Javi and I fall back into our usual pattern. That is to say, I pepper him with questions, squeezing out the answers by circling back as many times as necessary to the topics he wants to avoid. Something's off, though. I mean, Javi's never been an open book, but *this* book is glued shut and double-wrapped in cellophane. "How's work?"

He grimaces and stares out the window. "Next subject, please."

"Okay, but your boss sounds like an ass," I say. "Just because someone's stressed doesn't mean they get to take it out on everyone."

He shifts in his seat. "Let's not talk about my job, okay? I want to have a good time with you this weekend. Talking about work is just going to put me in a foul mood."

"All right. Well, how's the musical coming along, then?"

He shrugs. "It's going, I guess. I work on it here and there. But I'm hoping to get more done now that . . ." He squeezes his eyes shut.

"Now that what?" I ask.

Javi opens his eyes. "Now that I have a better handle on the themes I'm trying to convey."

"I'm happy to hear it's coming together. Can't wait to watch it in a theater one day."

He smiles, but I get the feeling it isn't genuine. What is going on with him?

"Speaking of theater," he says, perking up a bit, "a patient told me I have a face for acting. Asked if I ever thought about doing commercials."

"Was this person hitting on you?" I ask on a laugh.

"I don't think so," he says, his brow furrowed. "I mean, she gave me a card and everything. She's a casting agent. Seemed legit."

"Well, she's right, but would you want to do that? I picture you as a behind-the-scenes kind of guy."

"True, but if it pays the bills, I'd get over my stage fright real fast."

"Then you should go for it. In fact, this could be your foot in the door to making connections with people who might have pull on Broadway. Entertainment circles are really small. At least that's what my dad always says."

"Thanks for the vote of confidence, but Broadway's aiming too high."

"When it comes to you, there's no such thing. If Broadway's what you want, then Broadway's what you'll get."

He chuckles. "Damn, Mari, you really are great for my ego."

I'm not stroking his ego, though; I truly mean every word. I wish Javi could see himself the way I do. He's thoughtful and creative and one of the smartest men I know. There isn't anything he couldn't do if he put his mind to it. But sometimes that mind is riddled with self-doubt and throws him off track.

My little pep talk seems to have made a difference, because the conversation flows more smoothly after that. I ask about his parents and his brothers. As usual, his parents are great, and his brothers are grating on his nerves. Javi complains that because Manny and Leandro paid for the house he lives in, they think they should also have a say about what he does in it.

"You could move out," I suggest.

"That's easier said than paid for."

"Point taken. Well, look, you can continue to work the nine-to-five with . . . what's the name you call your boss?"

"Comemierda."

"Ha, yes, such an elegant way to call someone a shit-eater. If you keep working with the comemierda, then you'll give yourself time to work on the musical. And by living at home, you can save money until you're ready to leave. There's no rush on any of this. We just graduated. You have time to figure things out."

"You didn't waste any time figuring it out," he says.

"My choices were mapped out for me, remember? If I had told my father I wanted to do anything other than go to law school, he would have had a coronary. Consider yourself lucky that you get to make your own decisions."

"Consider yourself lucky that you'll be gainfully employed in three years."

"Touché. Between us, though, there's a small part of me that wants to rebel against my dad. Maybe because it feels like I'm giving in to him." I sigh. "In the end, it doesn't matter, because I actually enjoy studying law, and if I went a different route just to assert my independence, I'd be shooting myself in the foot."

"Yeah," he agrees, readjusting his seat belt so he can face me. "Plus, this is your calling. A more argumentative person never existed."

"That's absolutely not true."

"See?" he says, raising a brow.

"Okay, whatever," I say with a grin.

"Anyway, this weekend is all about catching up, so tell me what's new with you."

"Me? Hmm, let's see . . . Oh, my torts prof is looking for an assistant and said I should interview."

"That's fantastic . . . Uh, what's torts?"

"Basically, civil wrongs. As opposed to criminal ones."

"Woman, that explanation did absolutely *nothing* for me."

Javi's joking again, which is a good sign. Although I can't help noticing that his mood is light when we're talking about me and that it plummets when he talks about himself. I want to ask him what's truly going on, but this weekend feels fragile, a test of our relationship, a test of what it could become, and I don't want him to shut down. *Baby steps, Mari. Baby steps.* "Okay, in real-world terms, crimes can be punished by the justice system. Like a prosecutor brings a case on behalf of the people. A tort is just the bad stuff you might get compensated for that isn't necessarily criminal. A slip-and-fall accident. A faulty product. Stuff like that. An example: A personal injury lawyer brings a case against McDonald's because their client purchased a scalding cup of coffee, accidentally spilled it on themselves, and got third-degree burns. That's a lawsuit we studied in class."

"*Okay*, professor. *Now* it makes more sense to me. Are the courses interesting?"

"Most of the time, yes. Other times I sit in class and Google how to get a job on a cruise ship. Anyway, Henrickson has an endowed professorship at the law school and she's really well respected, so it's a big deal that she's interested in working with me."

"Well, then, I'm proud of you, but I'm also not surprised. I assume you're going to interview with this professor?"

"Absolutely," I say, nodding vigorously. "I'd be a fool not to."

"Then you'll get the job, no question."

I smile so wide he must be able to see it in my profile. "You're good for my ego too, Javi."

* * *

Javi drops his duffel bag in the entryway and kicks off his sneakers.

It feels good to see him in my apartment. In the place where I feel most like myself. Where everything is here because *I* chose it—from the books on the shelves to the pots of aloe vera I purchased because my thumb is whatever the opposite of green is and these suckers are almost indestructible. In a way, this trip confirms that Javi and I are choosing each other too. That we're not letting ourselves drift apart simply because we live on opposite sides of the country.

"So this is where one of our country's brightest legal minds gets shit done, huh?" he says.

"No, this is where I experience an existential crisis every ten days or so. Also where I binge *Suits* even though the show is wildly unrealistic."

"You have time to watch TV?" he asks, scanning the space as he circles the living room. "I pictured you studying twenty-four-seven and getting grilled by your professors."

I bring the gallon-size container of Purell over, and without a beat of interruption in our conversation, he puts his palms face up so I can pump sanitizer onto his hands. "Turns out the image of a stodgy professor embarrassing you in front of your peers isn't all that realistic either. If you keep up with the readings, you're usually fine."

"Damn," he says, rubbing the Purell in, "I would have applied to law school had I known that."

"You should have. You're certainly judgy enough."

He gives me a playfully frosty look, then bends at the waist to read the spines of the books on my shelves. *"The Costs of Accidents: A Legal and Economic Analysis. Studies in Contract Law. Fundamentals of Modern Property Law."*

"Riveting stuff, right?" Crossing to the kitchen, I open the fridge and peek inside. "Do you want something to drink? I bought the Newman's Own lemonade you like."

He doesn't immediately answer, and when I hear a faint snore, I laugh—because he's still bent at the waist in front of my bookshelf.

"Javi!" I shout.

"Huh? What?" he says, pretending to wake up. "Oh, sorry. I fell asleep reading these titles." He raises his arms overhead and stretches to emphasize his ridiculous point, and his taut stomach comes into view. My heart thumps. *Yes, asshole, I know you're there; no need to announce yourself. Now calm the hell down.*

Needing a distraction, I pour Javi a glass of lemonade and thrust it into his hand. "Here, smartass."

He takes a long sip, and I do *not* watch his Adam's apple bob. No, I absolutely do not. And anyway, this seems like an excellent time to unload the dishwasher.

From the safety of my self-imposed distance, I ask, "Are you hungry? Need to take a shower?"

"Shower. Definitely." He leans on the pony wall separating the living room and kitchen and lets out a long yawn. Then, with a smile tugging at his lips, he says, "That one was real. The flight wiped me out. Would it be okay if I took a nap after the shower? I just need an hour to recharge."

"Of course," I say, wiping my hands on a tea towel. "I'll show you where everything is in a sec." I pause and meet his gaze.

"So, um, you can either sleep in my bed or out here on the couch. Fair warning, though: My bed's a queen. I'm fine with either. You choose."

I turn away, busying myself with unloading the dishwasher in the hopes that we can skip any awkwardness if I'm as nonchalant as possible about our sleeping arrangements. The silence roars in my head while I wait for his answer, and I can't help noticing that he's taking entirely *too* long to respond.

A millennium later, he says, "I'm good on the couch." After a beat, he adds, "Did you ever notice I never sat on the same sofa as you for movie night? It's because you have the coldest feet in the world."

"I do not," I scoff.

"You do," he says, pretending to shiver. "Glacial."

"Whatever," I say, shrugging. "More room for me."

He grabs his duffel bag and follows me down the hall. I stack a set of fluffy towels on his outstretched arms and open the bathroom door. "Let the water run a bit before getting in. The heater's a little moody like you."

"Cute," he says, hanging the towels on the shower frame.

I swipe a box of tampons off the vanity and shove it in the drawer underneath. Next, I wipe a smudge off the mirror. He watches me fuss and doesn't say a word.

"Okay, then," I say, my gaze tunneling to the floor. "I'll let you get settled." Before I can escape, he shoots out a hand and stops me. I stare up at him, my eyes widening.

"It's a great place," he says softly, his deep brown eyes drawing me in. "Thank you for having me. I'm really happy to see you."

Ordinarily, I'd hug him in a moment like this, but I hesitate, and I'm not exactly sure why. I've never *not* been attracted to Javi. That is a fact. But sex between friends muddies the waters. Sex between friends who now live on opposite sides of the country and need to acclimate to a new normal would turn the waters to sludge. But none of this matters, because Javi and I have moved well past a fling. And oh my God, why is my brain preoccupied with sex? I am *definitely* overthinking this. It's just a hug.

I rise on my toes and wrap my arms around him, my entwined hands resting on the back of his neck. "I'm really happy to see you too."

Javi pulls me even closer, erasing the space between us, and his minty breath whispers across my cheek. Images of what could possibly come next flash in my head, and heat curls down my spine. I release him like he's on fire.

Avoiding Javi's gaze, I shuffle backward out of the bathroom and slam the door shut. "Have a great shower! Dinner with my dad's at seven," I call out. Then I rest my head against the door and inhale a gulp of air.

Okay, maybe I'm actually *underthinking* this.

CHAPTER 13

Javi

Eight Years and Five Months Before the Wedding

Mari's dad doesn't like me.

When Mari introduced us at graduation, she described me as one of her best friends. Luiz Campos replied, "It's very good to meet one of Mari's *classmates*." Emphasis his.

Okay, maybe I read too much into that brief interaction, but tonight it couldn't be clearer that he wishes I had nothing to do with his daughter.

Exhibit 1 is the restaurant we're in: Chi Spacca. There's a bone-in porterhouse on the menu priced at almost three hundred dollars. As if he's telegraphing that I'd never be able to give Mari the life she's accustomed to. Pork loin for one hundred ten dollars? My mother's world-class pernil is turning over in its aluminum-foil grave. I could make this evening easier on everyone and clarify that I have no romantic interest in Mari, except the idea of occupying real estate in this supposedly important man's brain is so fucking satisfying.

We're sitting in a semicircular booth in a "prime location," according to Luiz. Not that I care. Mari has wisely taken the spot between her father and me—seriously, we need the buffer—but there's no way to avoid the man's flinty stare.

When the server arrives at our table and recommends that we begin with the affettati misti, Luiz asks my thoughts on the starter before our server can even recite his spiel. Mari's dad must not realize that a kid from the South Bronx will look up the restaurant's menu in advance of a meal and familiarize himself with what's on offer to avoid this very situation.

"I was hoping we'd order that," I tell him with a smirk. "Apparently, Chef Colby's pâté is not to be missed." I look over at Mari. "What about you?"

"I'm definitely up for that," she says, her bright eyes letting me know she's game for joining my mischief.

The server clicks his heels and trots away. Meanwhile, Luiz simmers. And there's Exhibit 2.

He's a good-looking man, I'll give him that. His salt-and-pepper curly hair is immaculately styled. The suit he's wearing is most certainly bespoke. And although I have no idea what kind of watch he owns, I'd bet a whole year of my salary (such as it was) that it's not a Casio. None of it makes a bit of difference in my mind, but the air of superiority that surrounds him like an aura guarantees we won't be friends anytime soon—if ever. I'm actually kind of shocked that the precious human sitting next to me has this man's genes.

Mari claims her dad is slow to warm to people he doesn't know; I think he's already made up his mind that I'm someone he doesn't *need* to know. I mean, what else is she going to say? He's the only family she has in the States, so he skates by simply because he's present.

"So, Javi, what are you up to in New York?" Luiz asks, studying the wine menu.

He can pretend to make small talk all he wants, but I know damn well he's waiting for an opportunity to cut me down; if I told him the truth—that as of last week, I'm unemployed—I'd be handing him the scissors on a silver platter. So I lie: "Well, for now I'm working at a medical office. In the records department. I'm also looking into doing some commercial acting. I have a few auditions lined up in the new year."

"You do?" Mari says, grabbing my hand and shaking it. "You didn't tell me that part. How amazing!"

I nod. It's killing me to keep the truth from Mari, but I don't want to ruin this trip. She's worried about me as it is; I can't imagine how she'd react if she knew I had no job to return to.

Luiz's gaze settles on Mari's and my intertwined hands.

"You could have done that without a degree," Luiz says.

"Pai, não seja mal educado!" Mari exclaims.

"Eh, Ele . . . apaixonado por você. Não importa . . . diga."

I catch a word here and there—"he" and "in love with you" stand out in particular—so I get the gist of his comment.

Mari sucks her teeth. "Sorry, Javi. I told my dad not to be rude. He apparently left his manners at home."

"It's all good," I tell her. "He isn't saying anything I haven't already heard from my brothers." To Luiz, I say, "But you're wrong, you know. I'm using my degree to write a musical."

"Maluco," Luiz mutters.

"Fica quieto," Mari says to him through gritted teeth.

Yeah, so far, this dinner has been a blast. I commit the word "maluco" to memory; I'm looking that shit up later.

"Speaking of your brothers," Luiz says. "They're making a

name for themselves, no? Be sure you let them know if they ever need representation, I'd be happy to consider the group."

As if he would be doing them a favor. This man's something else. I may not be my brothers' biggest fan, but even I know they're at the pinnacle of their career, and anyone who rides on their coattails could stand to do *extremely* well.

"I don't talk to them about band stuff," I tell Luiz. "I'm not really involved."

"No, I suppose not," he says with a smirk.

Mari heaves a deep sigh.

Luiz feigns embarrassment and throws up his hands. "Okay, okay, I'll be nice." He winks at her. "For you."

Not because everyone should strive to be nice, or decent even. No, he'll be "nice" because his daughter is disappointed in him. It's not Mari's fault her father's a jerk. Maybe it's the universe's way of ensuring balance: one asshole for every good person. Keeps things interesting.

A middle-aged white guy appears at Luiz's side and clasps his shoulder. "Good to see you, Luiz."

Luiz quickly rises and pats the man on his back. "Dennis, how are you? So glad you stopped by." To Mari and me, he says, "Dennis is the manager. If I need to wine and dine a potential client at the last minute, Dennis here saves the day. A top-notch individual in a town where there aren't many left."

Dennis preens as he gets his kudos, and when the server arrives with our appetizer, Dennis excuses himself and slips off to greet the patrons at a table nearby.

"He's a decent man," Luiz says when Dennis is out of earshot. "Started as a busser here and worked his way up the ranks. There's hope for you yet, Javi."

"Stop it," Mari hisses. "You're being ridiculous."

She's absolutely right, and he absolutely deserves what's coming to him. With a pointed glance at Mari, I jump up and slam my hands on the table, attracting the attention of the diners around us. "I love this woman," I shout, glaring at Luiz, "and I don't care if you don't think I'm good enough for her! We're getting married—whether you like it or not!"

I peek at Dennis, who's now frowning at us. Luiz must see Dennis's reaction too, because he straightens his tie and laughs nervously.

"Sit down," he tells me through clenched teeth. "You're embarrassing yourself."

"Wrong," I say under my breath. "I'm embarrassing *you*."

"Now's a good time to apologize, Pai," Mari tells him, her mouth curved in amusement.

"I'll do no such thing. Your friend needs thicker skin."

She scowls at her father, then jumps to her feet as well. "I love this man, and no one's going to stop me from being with him. Besides"—she places a hand on her stomach—"I'm having his baby!"

A few guests gasp, someone says, "Oh shit," and Dennis rushes over.

"Is there a problem here?" he asks. "Perhaps you'd like to take this conversation somewhere else?"

Luiz pulls out a kerchief and wipes his brow. "Dennis, my friend, there's no problem. They're just joking." To us, he says, "Sit. Both of you."

"Apologize," Mari urges him.

"Okay, okay, I'm sorry, all right?" Luiz says, plastering on a smile. "Now sit down so we can finish this meal." He waves his hands around and addresses our audience. "Nothing to see here, folks. Just a small misunderstanding."

Dennis looks between us, his jaw tight. "Please refrain from engaging in any further disruptions."

"Of course," Luiz says. "We'll be on our best behavior, I promise."

Mari and I plop down and grin at each other.

After Dennis leaves, Luiz stares at me, his eyes shooting sparks. "You're a real wiseass, kid. Maybe I underestimated you."

Throwing up my hands in mock surrender, I repeat the words he told his daughter earlier: "Okay, okay, I'll be nice." I wink at Mari. "For you."

She snorts, her eyes shining brightly, and warmth fills my chest. I'll be honest, I get a thrill thinking about how she backed me up in pranking her father, that small act of defiance a not-so-subtle indication that she's siding with me tonight.

Man, this woman's special.

She truly deserves the world.

I wish I could be the kind of guy who could give it to her.

CHAPTER 14

Mari

Eight Years and Five Months Before the Wedding

Saturday morning, Javi and I eat at Derby's Diner, where we demolish the best blueberry pancakes on earth—because *of course* I'm qualified to confer that title. To my delight, Javi and my favorite waitress, Gloria, a Filipina server who says she doesn't look old enough to be anyone's grandmother (it's true), immediately click. Their rapport likely was fated; in a former life, Gloria was a cabaret performer in Chicago, and she isn't shy about showing off her vocal chops as she delivers the patrons' meals and charms the hefty tips off them. She wraps up a slice of apple pie for Javi, telling him with a wink and a smile that it's on the house.

"Do you enjoy what you do?" he asks her.

"I *love* it," she says, slipping a pencil in her bouffant-styled ash-gray hair, her hands on her trim hips. "Can't you tell?

"I can," Javi says on a laugh. "But I'm also wondering if you miss being onstage."

She waves a hand behind her. "Oh, honey, that was *ages* ago. A different *lifetime* ago. I was a natural. A true talent—if I do say so myself. But our priorities change. Our wants and desires blossom into something else. These days, I want to spend all of my time with my grandbabies. Working here means I'm off at two, and I don't think about this place until I return the next morning. It's all about perspective."

Javi nods. "Absolutely."

Gloria reaches over and pinches Javi's cheeks in that way only older women of a certain generation can get away with. "You're such a cutie." She meets my gaze, her eyes flashing with mischief. "Don't lose this one, sweetie!" Before I can clarify that Javi and I aren't together, she saunters off singing a line about rocking someone's world.

Javi and I grin at each other.

"She's a firecracker," he says.

"Now you see why I love her," I reply.

While we wait for the check, Javi jots down notes in his phone, his fingers typing at warp speed.

"What's got you so excited?" I ask.

"Gloria's given me an idea about the musical. A possible backstory for one of the characters. And I can see the number in my head, so I'm trying to write down my thoughts before I forget it all."

I love seeing this side of him. This passion. It's an unguarded moment. More often than not he appears ambivalent about writing this musical, but right now, I can plainly see that it's more important to him than he lets on.

"So this trip isn't a total bust, then?" I ask.

He looks up from his phone and squishes his eyebrows together. "A bust? Mari, I'm spending time with you. How could that ever be anything less than perfect?"

"Well, now you're just trying to get me to drop my panties."

He blinks a few times, then stares at me, his eyes huge as saucers. "That's not what . . ."

I throw my head back and cackle, drawing the attention of a few customers.

He flattens his lips into a thin line. "Cute."

"You say that a lot about me," I say, giving him a pointed look.

"I do. It's an acronym."

"It is?" I ask, leaning over the table because he's blowing my mind. "What's the acronym?"

"Can. U. Take. Embarrassment." He chuckles, though I don't get what's funny. "Think about it: I say it every time you do something awkward."

I stare at him, my brain whirring as I repeat the acronym in my head. "Seriously?"

"No," he says with a grin. "I made that shit up on the spot."

I throw a napkin at him. "Rude."

"Admit it," he says, brushing off his shoulders and waggling his eyebrows. "I almost had you."

"Yeah, you did," I say, holding back a smile. "Even though it didn't make a bit of sense, I knew there was an insult in there, so I was about to make you sleep on the floor tonight."

"The day's still young," he says.

Now that I think about it, he's right. The pier should be fine, but we still have a party to go to after that. And as Javi and I both know, parties are his kryptonite.

* * *

"Tell me who's throwing this get-together again," Javi asks as we climb the flight of steps leading to the entrance of an impressive apartment complex a short drive from campus. It's gated. And I know from our host that there's an infinity pool on the roof. Javi will *love* that.

"Her name's Rielle, and she's a first-year law student like me. I met her during orientation. She's good people."

"Cool," Javi says, though I know he's reserving judgment on whether Rielle is, in fact, good people.

"So mostly law students will be here?" he asks.

"Yeah, that's my guess. But don't worry, we're a chill bunch. And we don't have to stay long. I just promised to swing by. She's excited to meet you."

Javi stumbles to a stop and pins me in place with a wide-eyed stare. "Me? Why would she be excited to meet me?"

"I told her about you, silly," I say, rolling my eyes. "Mentioned that you were visiting."

With his lips pressed together, he pulls on the sleeves of his burgundy knit shirt, straightening the cuffs before he resumes walking. As we enter the vestibule, he puffs out a breath and rolls his shoulders. "Okay, let's do this."

"Gracious, you're acting like I'm sending you to the gallows."

"Close enough," he says, his eyes shining with humor.

I nudge Javi to my side and link arms with him. "Just be yourself. Everyone's going to love you."

"That's never my goal," he quips.

Which is unquestionably true, and one of the things I like most about Javi. In a world where most of the men his age are cosplaying through life, Javi's content to be himself. As if he's daring anyone to fault him for who he is so he can fault *them* for being superficial. It's a test many people fail, my father among them. I'm sure his reserved demeanor is a defense mechanism too. After all, the defenses you build are born from experience, and no one should tell you they aren't warranted. Javi and I don't move through the world in exactly the same way, but there are enough similarities between us that I understand and can empathize with the land mines he's trying to avoid.

When we exit the elevator, our jaws drop. I'm no stranger to opulence, but this rooftop space is on another level. Actually, it's on two levels, both of which feature sleek black-and-white decor and panoramic glass windows that don't disturb the amazing 360-degree views. There's plenty of velvet banquette seating, and heated lamps cleverly disguised as decorative columns frame the perimeter. The infinity pool puts a bow on the whole vibe.

"Jesus," Javi says, looking dazed. "The rent prices here must be astronomical."

"I know."

"Let's get drinks, stat."

"Definitely." There's a chill in the air, and I could use something to warm me up anyway.

We're weaving through the surprisingly big crowd when I hear my name being called. I turn and see Rielle gliding toward us, the picture of effortless chic in a white V-neck that's doing amazing things for her cleavage, a pair of boyfriend jeans, and a pink cashmere sweater wrapped around her waist. As she strides in our direction, Rielle's chocolate-brown hair bounces and cascades over her shoulders as if she's auditioning for a shampoo commercial.

"I'm so glad you came!" she says, immediately tugging me into a light embrace. When we separate, her gaze lands on Javi.

"You must be the friend from New York," she says, holding out her hand.

Javi shakes it. "Yeah, I'm Javi. Good to meet you . . ."

"Rielle," she supplies with a flirty smile. To both of us, she says, "The open bar is by the DJ. Feel free to order whatever you'd like."

She looks around. "There should be servers passing around hors d'oeuvres somewhere. Let me check the kitchen. Marisol, want to come with?"

"Uh, sure," I say, thoroughly confused yet knowing based on her conspicuous attempt at optical telepathy that she wants to speak with me in private. "I'll just be a minute," I tell Javi. "Want to grab us drinks?"

"No problem," he says. "What'll you have?"

"Any white is fine. Except moscato."

Javi grins. "You got it."

Rielle pulls me away, then links our arms together and leans in. "He's hot as fuck."

"He's smart as fuck too," I say a bit grumpily.

"I'm sure he is," she says with a saucy smile, "but I'm not interested in that."

"Well, you shouldn't be interested in anything having to do with Javi considering you have a fiancé."

"Boyfriend," she corrects.

"My point remains."

And now I'm rethinking my earlier assessment that Rielle is "good people." What even is this?

We reach the kitchen, where she briefly speaks with someone on the catering staff, then turns back to me. "You two are just friends, right?"

"Correct."

"So you wouldn't mind if I chat with him?"

"He's a grown man, Rielle. And you're an adult too. I don't really have a say in this."

She playfully clips me on the shoulder. "Oh, c'mon, you know what I'm really asking here. Girl code. Would you be pissed?"

"The better question is, would your *boyfriend* be pissed?"

"We're open, so no, he wouldn't."

My stomach drops. This guy, whom I've never met, was my ace in the hole, the one factor I was relying on to convince both Rielle and Javi that they shouldn't talk, hook up, whatever. Now it appears there's nothing stopping them from getting together, and I'm horrified to discover that I desperately wish there were an obstacle I could throw in both of their faces.

"Well, then, have at him," I say flatly.

"Thanks, I will," she says with a sassy toss of her hair.

I watch her saunter out of the kitchen and glide in the direction of the bar, where Javi's still waiting in line.

But I don't want Rielle to "have at" Javi, as I so glibly suggested. Not if I'm truly being honest with myself. And because I'm overthinking everything this weekend, I'm trying to process why that would be the case. Am I just being territorial, which itself isn't cool, or am I grappling with feelings I buried so deep I can't even recognize them when they surface?

Is there a word that takes overthinking to another level? Uber-overthinking? If so, that's what I'm doing. In the end, though, I can't forget that Javi and I are committed to being and *remaining* friends. Whatever happens tonight, I need to keep that goal front and center in my unruly mind.

CHAPTER 15

Javi

Eight Years and Five Months Before the Wedding

This party isn't as unpleasant as I assumed it would be. So far, the only con is that the two white guys ahead of me in line won't shut up.

"How's Civ Pro treating you?" one of them asks the other.

"Durbin's a prick. He's spending all of his time talking about substantive due process. I couldn't give a fuck. When are we going to actually open up the federal rules of civil procedure?"

"Yeah, I hear ya. He's known for focusing on a bunch of bullshit we'll never use in real life."

"It's tiring. I wish I could . . ."

Noticing that something (or someone) has caught his friend's attention, the second guy, the shorter of the two, follows the first guy's gaze. "Ah, you spotted Marisol."

Well, now my eyes are laser-focused, and my ears are in stealth mode.

"Damn, every time I see her I get tongue-tied," the tall guy says. "I don't know what it is about her, but that woman is messing with my head."

"She's the whole package, that's why. Smart, gorgeous, has a dad who could give you a summer internship." They both chuckle; I take mental notes to be shared with Mari later.

"Man, I tried to talk to her once," the short guy continues, "and she shot me down in seconds, so if she's giving you the time of day, take it. Just know that whoever bags her is going to have to be on point. A woman like that is not entertaining scrubs."

"Yeah, yeah," the tall guy says, licking his lips. "I think I can meet that bar. But I'm also not averse to a onetime hookup—"

"Excuse me," I say.

The short guy spins around. "Yeah?"

I point at the bartender, who's patiently waiting for these two knuckleheads to move up. "It's your turn."

"Oh, sure. Thanks."

Seconds later, an arm slips through mine.

"Took you long enough," I say.

"Oh, you were waiting for me?" asks a velvety voice that doesn't belong to Mari.

I turn and see that the person whose arm is linked with mine is Rielle. "Sorry, I thought you were Marisol."

"I hope you're not disappointed," she says, smiling coyly.

"No, no, just surprised."

She leans in close and says, "I'm hosting so I need to make the rounds, but I'd like to get to know you better before the night is over."

"Sure, sure," I say, my throat garbled. "I'll be around."

"I'll look for you later," she says with a wink.

"Sounds good," I say with no enthusiasm. Because one, I'm not playing in Mari's playground; that would be inconsiderate as hell.

And two, Rielle does nothing for me. No spark, no thump in the chest, no tingle down my spine.

I finally order a club soda for myself and a glass of chardonnay for Mari. And this time, when an arm links through mine, I know it's her.

She relieves me of the wine, takes a sip, and makes a face of disgust. "Thanks, but I'm definitely passing on that." After setting the glass on a high-top table nearby, she asks, "Doing okay so far?"

"I'm fine. Was working intel on the bar line."

Her eyes widen. "Oh, do tell."

I point at the guys who were ahead of me, both of whom are now lurking in a corner. "The tall one over there has a crush on you."

She looks over at them and wrinkles her nose. "Ugh, Nelson's the tall one. Brad's his lackey. They're both insufferable. Pass." She studies me for a moment, then mutters something to herself before saying, "And just a heads-up: Rielle wants to get to know you better."

"She suggested as much a minute ago."

"Any interest?" Mari asks carefully.

"None whatsoever."

"Well, Rielle's staring at you as we speak, so you might want to figure out how you're going to handle it."

My gaze travels past Mari to those two guys in the corner, one of whom seems poised to walk over here. "Well, don't look now, but I think the guy who has a crush on you is about to make his move."

"Oh no," Mari says, fake terror in her eyes. "Help me."

I scan the room, noticing that the billiards table is free. "Let's play pool. It'll give you an excuse not to talk to him and keep Rielle at bay. Two birds, one stone."

"But I don't know how," she whines, her mouth curved in an adorable frown.

"Don't worry, I'll teach you."

I drag Mari across the room and grab two sticks off a stand-alone cue stick wall. Mari listens intently as I go over the basics.

"How do I shoot?" she asks.

"Okay, let me show you the open bridge." I gesture ahead of me. "Get in front and I'll guide you."

Mari takes her cue stick, which is significantly shorter than mine, and leans over the table. I do not look at her ass in the snug jeans she's wearing, though I'm tempted to.

"Now what?" she says over her shoulder.

"Okay, set your hand on the table and spread your fingers apart. Then place the cue stick in the V between your thumb and index finger."

"Sounds . . . dirty."

"Behave."

"Okay, okay. Like this?" she asks, trying to get the placement correct.

"Not quite," I say. "Here."

I lean over, the front of my thighs resting against her backside, and spread her fingers apart, positioning the cue stick behind the ball.

It's a big mistake. I know it. She knows it. The whole fucking world knows it.

Because being this close to Mari does something to me—to us—that I don't think we can ever undo. She feels . . . perfect. Curvy, strong, warm. And the vanilla scent she always wears surrounds us like a cage, trapping me in a lust-induced daze and throwing me even more off balance. I picture myself lifting her top and trailing kisses along her spine. I imagine her body laid out on the table, my face between her legs. I—

"Now what?" she says softly.

What the hell, brain? Focus. We're playing pool.

I clear my throat and back away. Then, with my hands fisted at my sides, I inhale a huge breath and exhale. "Guide the stick back and forth along the V, then glide it forward quickly."

"Wow, that sounds *really* dirty," she says on a laugh.

I ignore the joke. I have to. Because I'm barely holding myself together as it is. "Shoot, Mari."

And she does. Very well. The seven ball smacks into the corner pocket and drops with a satisfying thud.

Mari jumps up and down. "Yes, yes, yes!"

"She's a natural," the tall guy from before—Nelson?—says as he sidles up to us.

I give him a curt nod. "That she is."

"Enough talking, sir," Mari says to me. "Now that I've figured out the mechanics of this game, there will be no stalling."

Nelson hovers, edging closer to the table as Mari and I continue to practice. We pretend to ignore him, though we're both aware of his presence. Mari keeps brushing against my side, her body never more than a few inches away from mine. I know *why* she's sticking close to me, but it's wreaking havoc on my psyche too. Nelson needs to go.

After one particularly brilliant shot on Mari's part, he tries to high-five her, but she sidesteps him. This guy can't take a hint to save his life.

When she passes me on my left, she whispers, "He's just going to hang around waiting for an opening."

"Don't give him one," I whisper back.

"How do I manage that?"

I take the pool stick from her and rest it against the couch behind us. "Do you trust me?"

She draws back and studies my face, her brow pinched in confusion. "Of course I do."

"Then follow my lead."

Before I can fully think through my plan, I'm lifting Mari onto the edge of the pool table and stepping into the space between her thighs.

Mari looks up at me, her bottomless brown eyes round as saucers. "What are you doing?" she asks in a shaky voice.

"Making it clear that you're unavailable."

Her eyes flash with heat, and then she's lifting her chin, her mouth open in anticipation. My heart pounds as we close the distance between us; it gallops furiously when our lips finally meet. I let Mari control the pace. Let her decide how we're going to play this. We're tentative at first, our lips grazing then retreating. But then the kiss switches gears, an unmistakable urgency to it, our tongues mingling possessively as if they're meant to be knotted together. Somewhere along the way, she grips my waist while my hands slide to her ass and pull her closer. I'm not sure if it's encouragement or pure pleasure, but she lets out a needy moan, and the sound sets my skin on fire. As if I need a reminder that my solution to our problem has gone off the rails, my dick presses painfully against the fly of my zipper.

And there's the spark I didn't feel for Rielle. There's the thump in my chest. There's the tingle down my spine.

For Mari. My best friend.

And now I have to pretend that kiss was just a means to an end. Fuck.

* * *

Mari's over at the bar talking to a classmate. They're standing close to each other as they chat, and the moment she throws her head back in laughter, the guy inches closer. I don't blame him. I don't blame her either. But damn, that kiss fried my brain; apparently it did nothing to hers.

I nurse a soda and watch a couple play pool.

Minutes later, Mari pops up at my side. "Sorry about that. I was trying to get away, but Jason's a talker."

"Don't worry about it," I say. "Ready to go?"

She stares at me a beat too long, her sultry, black-rimmed eyes roving over my face.

"What?" I ask.

"Nothing," she says, linking her arm with mine. "And sure, let's get out of here."

In the car, Mari queues up a playlist titled "Anthem." The first track is "Girl on Fire" by Alicia Keys.

This boy's on fire too—but for a very different reason.

"Your theme song?" I ask, trying to redirect my thoughts.

Her lips curve into a confident smile. "Exactly."

"It's perfect for you."

"I'm glad you think so," she says in an amused tone.

It's also a timely reminder that Mari's going places. She's bound to do great things. Her smarts will open doors for her; her charm will ensure she gets a seat at the table. And she deserves it all.

Mari drums her fingers against the steering wheel and sways to the song's rhythm. "So, I was thinking we could watch a movie tonight. Your choice. I'll even try *Citizen Kane* again if you want."

"You hate that movie."

"I don't *hate* it," she says, glancing over at me. "I just wasn't enamored enough to watch it until the end."

Sadly, I can't even remember the plot. I'm stuck on that fucking kiss. Did it even happen? Was it all a dream? Mari's certainly acting as if I made that shit up in my head.

I say nothing, which I guess signals to her that she needs to convince me to spend more time with her.

"We can get into some comfortable clothes," she says breezily. "And make popcorn. I promise not to snore when you try to convince me of Orson Welles's genius."

That sounds like the worst idea in the world. I'm not sitting next to Mari all night. She'd probably want to rest her head on my lap like she always did during movie nights at school. No, thank you.

I stretch in my seat and make a big production of yawning. "Honestly, Mari, I don't think I'll be able to keep my eyes open. I'm drained. I think I'll just head to bed."

"Oh . . . okay. No problem." She side-eyes me, then focuses on the view through the windshield. "Hey, are we good? I mean, about what happened back at the party. You're not weirded out or anything, right?"

"Not at all, and yeah, we're good."

If we want to keep it that way, I'm going to follow her cue and erase it from my mind. Or try to, at least.

Good luck with that, Javi.

Monday, December 19, 2016, at 3:30 p.m.

MARI: thanks again for visiting me this weekend

sorry I had to run out so early

and sorry if some of it was a little too much for you

JAVI: it wasn't

always good to see you

MARI: I meant about the thing, at the party

JAVI: let's forget about it, okay

we did what we needed to do

we're good

MARI: okay

MARI: but be real, my dad annoyed you

JAVI: definitely

your dad's not you, though

please remember that

MARI: true

anyway, I need to study

have a great week!

JAVI: you too!

Sunday, January 1, 2017, at 12:01 p.m.

MARI: waited long enough for you to wake up

happy new year!

wishing you an amazing 2017!

JAVI: lol, I'm out of a job

MARI: shit, I'm so sorry

JAVI: not your fault

just need to regroup

MARI: want to talk about it

JAVI: nope

MARI: pick up on FaceTime

JAVI: I need some space

please

I'll reach out when I'm ready

MARI: okay

just remember I'm here for you

JAVI: thanks

you're an amazing person

don't worry about me I'll be fine

Tuesday, January 10, 2017, at 4:17 p.m.

MARI: been calling you

are you ever going to pick up?

Saturday, January 28, 2017, at 3:12 p.m.

MARI: hey, was thinking of visiting you for my birthday give me a ring when you can

Friday, February 17, 2017, at 1:12 a.m.

MARI: are you okay

what's going on?

Saturday, February 25, 2017, at 8:34 p.m.

MARI: just saw your post on IG

good to know you're okay

Monday, March 20, 2017, at 9:19 p.m.

MARI: thought you'd at least call for my birthday ☹

Wednesday, March 22, 2017, at 2:24 a.m.

MARI: I know you're getting my messages, I can see the read receipts

this is me giving you space

reach out when you're ready

PART TWO
The Weed

Wednesday, April 8, 2025

WhatsApp Voice Message

Marisol, alô é sua mãe. Você se lembra de mim? Listen, I was thinking. Do you need me to come sooner? I know you said you have everything under control, but I can be there a week before the wedding if you need me. Let me know if I should change my ticket, okay? Beijos! Tchau, tchau, tchau.

CHAPTER 16

Mari

Now

My mother's typical do-you-remember-me message makes me chuckle. *The drama.* I set a reminder to call her tonight so I can reiterate that she doesn't need to get here early. I *do* have everything under control.

As I'm putting my phone away, my father appears at my office door.

"Marisol, I have great news!" He sweeps inside holding a few sheets of paper, a big smile on his face. With an uncharacteristic flourish, he sets the papers on my desk.

"What's this?" I ask, bending at the waist to switch into my pumps. Since I'm due to meet with a potential client in ten minutes, this isn't the ideal time to pore over legalese.

"It's a new contract with Crystal Canyon Farm." He waggles his eyebrows and does a little shimmy.

I sit up and purse my lips, tilting my head to study him better. Have aliens finally infiltrated the earth and planted body doubles that aren't as skilled at mimicking humans as they ought to be? Because this person certainly *looks* like my father, but he isn't *acting* like him. For one thing, Luiz Campos doesn't waggle his eyebrows. And as for the shimmy, I was not aware he could even move his upper body like that.

Wait, did he say Crystal Canyon Farm? Oh God, the wedding venue. What has he done? I lunge for the pages, inspecting them more closely. "What's going on? What's changed?"

He slips his hands into the pockets of his slacks and puffs out his chest. My father isn't an overly expressive person—or an affectionate one. There isn't much other than money (or the prospect of making it) that could get him *this* animated. A shiver runs through me.

"Se calma, Marisol. Everything's fine. Great, in fact. I was thinking that you're my only daughter, and I need to do my part, so I paid for a few upgrades. Essentially, they're making us their priority for the entire weekend, and they're including a tour of the vineyards after the wine tasting."

"Pai, you didn't have to do that," I say, absolutely meaning it. "We're perfectly capable of staying within budget."

He shakes his head. "No, no, that's my point. You shouldn't have to. I don't want to spare any expense when it comes to this wedding. And I don't want your mother to say I didn't do enough. Plus, you and Alex deserve to get married in style. After all, you're only going to do this once, right?"

"That's the plan," I say evenly.

What my father doesn't understand is this: I chose Crystal Canyon Farm because the setting is naturally exquisite. It doesn't need any embellishments or add-ons or whatever he has in mind. Alex and I just want an intimate wedding where we can celebrate with the people we love. But as usual, my father's focused on making a statement—to our guests and to my mother, especially, not that she'd care. If I don't monitor him closely, he'll hire Cirque du Soleil to perform at our reception. Considering he's already aiming to make this wedding a circus, that would be entirely fitting. Even so, I need to be careful about how I curb my father's enthusiasm; given how rarely it makes an appearance, I don't want to quash it altogether.

"When it comes to our big day, Alex and I think less is more," I tell him carefully. "You have your style, and we have ours. I appreciate that you want to contribute, but please run these things by me before you make any changes."

I internally high-five myself. That felt *great* to say out loud.

"Okay, okay," he says, throwing up his hands. "I didn't realize that a father giving his daughter the wedding of her dreams would be a problem."

The wedding of *his* dreams, maybe.

I rise from my chair, round my desk, and kiss his cheek. "I have someone waiting for me in conference room A. Can we talk more about this later?"

"Fine," he says, frowning.

He picks up the contract from my desk and follows me out of my office.

We walk alongside each other in the direction of the smaller of the firm's two conference rooms. A few of the administrative assistants in their cubicles lower their heads as we pass. That's the Luiz Campos effect: Everyone wants to hide when the surly boss is near. Sometimes I get a little thrill knowing he doesn't trigger that reaction in me, then I remember that he's *my father*, and I get a little sad that not being intimidated by him is somehow a win. Sasha's dad smothers her with love and affection; my father's more likely to smother me with criticism.

You're not aggressive enough, Marisol.

That hair's a little much for a business setting, no?

We're not running a charity, you know.

Sure, I no longer shrink in my father's presence, but I don't flourish in it either.

We reach the conference suite, a sleek space with a single floor-to-ceiling window panel that spans the length of the room and a glass enclosure that makes its occupants visible from the outside. There are no late-night shenanigans to be had here on my father's watch (those happen in the copy room).

He looks past me and studies the person patiently waiting for me, a steaming cup of coffee resting on a coaster in front of her. "Who's that?"

"Lisa Randle, an indie filmmaker. She's interested in getting our advice on privacy issues that might come up for the documentary she's working on."

"That doesn't sound lucrative."

I snort. "For us or for her?"

"Either," he says, faking a smile as he waves to Lisa.

I'm not a particularly creative person, but I love facilitating creativity. I respect artists' contributions to society and want to help them get their work out to their audiences. My father likes creatives too—but mostly because they make him money. I can't deny that my father has built a formidable business from nothing. I just wish he were motivated by more than maintaining his own social status. He used to say he worked so hard because he wanted to make his immigrant parents proud. Wanted their sacrifices to mean something. But they're gone now, and he's surpassed their wildest dreams, so he can no longer use them as an excuse for the person he's become.

I point a thumb behind me. "I need to get in there."

"Hope it's worth it," he says before walking in the direction of his corner office.

What he's really saying is that he *expects* it to be.

As I'm poised to enter the conference room, he calls out to me.

"What's up?" I ask, my hand on the doorknob. I'm mindful of Lisa Randle's time; my father is not.

He looks down at the Crystal Canyon Farm contract. "There's a list here of the room reservations I'm paying for. Who's this Javier Báez person?"

I frown at him. "That's Javi, my friend from college. You had dinner with him once, remember? He's going to be the man of honor."

"You still talk to him?" he asks, his brow lifted in surprise. "I thought you two lost touch."

"We ran into each other in New York a couple of years ago. We're more than good now."

We're good friends too—as we should be.

CHAPTER 17

Mari

Two Years and Two Months Before the Wedding

Verbally eviscerating gaslighters is the *best* part of my job. Today, I'm planning to do just that, so I'm practically skipping toward this on-location shoot in New York's Central Park.

Chanelle Heyward is both a client and a friend. She doesn't suffer fools gladly, and she isn't easily distressed. Chanelle *is* at her breaking point, however, which is why I'm taking this midday detour to settle her nerves and knock a few heads.

A Black security guard stops me at the traffic barricade. "May I help you?"

"Hi, my name's Mari Campos. I'm here to see Chanelle Heyward, one of the stars of the film. I'm her lawyer."

"You have any ID on you?" he asks, eyeing me curiously.

"Sure." I fish out my wallet from my purse and hand him my driver's license. "I have membership cards for the New York and California bars if you need to see those too."

He inspects the license, then hands it back to me. "No need.

Ms. Chanelle told me to expect you. She's in trailer B. Just follow the bike path and it'll be on your right."

"Thanks," I say, giving him the universal head nod.

It takes me only a couple of minutes to find Chanelle's trailer, a double-wide she shares with two of her co-stars. The set is twenty yards away. I quickly locate the source of Chanelle's issues: a collapsible water tank off to the side and numerous sprinklers spaced three feet apart in the shape of a circle.

As expected, dozens of people are milling about. A makeup artist drifts from actor to actor, checking out each face and occasionally pulling out a tool from his apron to tweak a look. Meanwhile, a middle-aged white woman (probably the set director) flaps her hands as she barks orders to her listless staff.

Before I even knock, Chanelle's trailer door swings open.

"Oh, thank goodness you're here," she says in a rush.

I hustle inside and shrug off my coat and gloves. The spacious trailer is bright and warm, and I'm pleased to see that it's also clean and nicely appointed. Anything less would make me even more annoyed than I already am.

As usual, Chanelle looks great. Natural makeup highlights her flawless brown skin, and the swooping front layers of her chin-length bob frame her face perfectly. It boggles my mind that anyone would want to ruin her appearance.

"Tell me the latest," I say, finding a spot on the love seat against the far wall.

"I did exactly as you suggested," she says, pacing in front of me. "Told them I wouldn't do the scene unless they assured me a stylist would be on set to fix the havoc the rain would wreak on my hair. Declan huffed. Said he didn't have time for this shit. Said time is money. Said I'm wasting his time. Then he stormed off. Time, time, time, that's all he cares about." She wrings her hands.

"It was so awkward. I didn't want to make a fuss. Didn't want to be *that* girl. But this is my career, my brand. Why should I look like a Chia Pet simply because they can't hire people who are well-versed in doing textured hair?"

I stifle a chuckle. "First, under no circumstances would you ever look like a Chia Pet. Pennywise from that *It* movie, maybe."

"Bitch," Chanelle says, throwing a napkin at me. She's smiling, though, which is precisely what I was aiming for.

"Second, there is no such thing as being 'that girl' when it comes to equity. They need to create an inclusive environment, and if that requires them to hire beyond their typical pool of hairstylists, then so be it."

"You'll talk to Declan, then?" Chanelle asks.

"Of course. Is he on set?"

"Yeah, they're doing some background shots. Holding off on everything else until I'm, as he put it, 'no longer hysterical.'"

"Oh no he didn't," I say, narrowing my eyes.

"Oh yes he did."

"Wait here. I'll walk over now."

Chanelle bites her lip as she watches me slip on my coat and gloves. "Good luck."

"Won't need it," I say, brushing off my shoulders.

Outside, I scan the set and immediately spot Declan speaking to someone on the production team. Although his reputation in the business isn't great, he's an accomplished director with a golden touch. Difficult yet talented men like him thrive in Hollywood; it's everyone else's job to steer clear of the shrapnel when they inevitably go ballistic.

Declan continues to speak to the person as he watches me approach. His eyes flicker with annoyance, but he masks his irritation quickly. He knows it wouldn't be wise to have a highly regarded entertainment lawyer at a well-respected firm on his ass. I'm here to underscore that fact.

When his staffer departs, I offer my hand. "Declan, it's good to see you again."

He wiggles his fingers. "They're dirty. Wouldn't want to muss up that fancy outfit."

I suspect Declan's hands are clean and declining to shake my hand is a power play in his unimaginative brain. I'm not even a tiny bit bothered.

"Yes, well, thanks for the courtesy. Listen, I don't want to take up too much of your time. I understand from Chanelle that you're planning to shoot in the rain and then immediately follow it with a restaurant scene. As you know, she's understandably concerned about getting her hair wet."

He rolls his eyes. "Ms. Campos, Chanelle can do whatever the hell she wants to fix it. I'm not a stylist."

"No one's asking you to be a stylist, Declan. We *are* asking you to abide by the equity and inclusion provisions of the SAG-AFTRA agreement."

He straightens. "I have no idea what you're talking about."

"You should. But I'll send over a copy anyway. It's in Chanelle's contract too, which incorporates the SAG-AFTRA agreement as an addendum. In short, if you're unable to provide someone to do her hair, she can find someone herself and get reimbursed. People in the industry are wondering how the provision is going to play out in the real world. Might be a news item that could gain traction. How would you like to proceed?"

He stares at me for a long moment, then blows out a frustrated breath. "I'll take a look at the agreement tonight and get back to you," he says through gritted teeth.

"And you'll skip the restaurant scene for now?"

"Fine," he says, flaring his nostrils. "We'll do it after we sort the hair thing out. But it's going to fuck up the schedule. And now I'll have a bunch of extras with nothing to do."

"I'm sorry about that, but I commend you for wanting to do what's required by the agreement."

"Is there anything else?" he asks sharply, his arms crossed over his chest.

"That's it from me."

"Thank goodness," he says, not even trying to say the words under his breath.

I type a quick text to Chanelle letting her know the restaurant shoot will be delayed until further notice, then deeply inhale the frigid air, the scent of my freshly eviscerated nemesis invigorating me. I slowly scan the area, and before long my gaze is drawn to the actors standing around waiting for their cues. One of them immediately snags my attention. Because I know the guy.

A tsunami of moments floods my brain: challenging him in class, sitting with him on Belmont Green, helping him the night before graduation, *kissing* him on a pool table. God, that was so long ago, yet the memories feel close enough to touch.

In a stupor, I walk in his direction, my heart barreling through my chest, and when I reach him, I eke out the only word my brain can manage.

"Javi?"

CHAPTER 18

Javi

Two Years and Two Months Before the Wedding

I hear a familiar voice and my brain is overrun with memories. Of all the poor decisions I've made in my life—and there have been *many*—ghosting Mari is the one I regret the most. I think about that choice every day.

No, my mind *must* be tricking me. Cruelly playing out a scenario in which Mari and I are still friends and I didn't just abandon her. Well, *abandon* might be too strong a word. Mari didn't need me. I needed her. And yet I cut her out of my life as if she didn't matter. How fucking wrong I was.

But wait. This person's saying my name.

"Javi? Javier Báez?" they repeat.

I look up, and there she is. Marisol Campos. The friend who got away.

My hands tingle, and a wave of heat washes over me. As if joy is coursing through my body and can no longer be contained in such a small space. Then reality sets in. What I did. What she didn't deserve. She remembers too, apparently, because the lightness in her eyes quickly fades, replaced by a dazed expression.

People are bustling around us, but I only have eyes for her. My gaze is greedy, bouncing around as I take in what time has changed. She's leaner, especially in the face, her cheeks more sculpted than I remember. Her hair's just as curly but now sits on her shoulders. And maybe it's a little lighter? Her clothing is refined. Elegant. A sumptuous coat that flares out at her hips, a long skirt that ends below her knees, and a pair of brown leather boots that add inches to her stature. She looks . . . expensive. I don't know how else to put it. And she's waiting for me to acknowledge her.

"Marisol Campos," I manage to say.

"Javier Báez."

"I can't believe it's you."

"Same."

The word floats in the air, then plummets to the ground. I'm the villain here. She knows it. I know it. It's an uncomfortable status for me. I'd rather be invisible and unproblematic. In this situation, I'm anything but.

She squints at me. "It's been . . . what? Six years?"

"Six years and three months." Her eyes widen, so I shrug and add, "Give or take." I clear my throat. "What brings you to Central Park?"

So. Fucking. Awkward.

"One of my clients is in the film. Chanelle Heyward."

My eyes bulge. That's big-time. Chanelle is one of the film's leads.

"What about you?" she asks.

"I'm an extra."

She nods. There's nothing to say, really. But I can tell she has questions. Or perhaps I just want to give her answers. Well, as much as I can.

"It's amazing to see you again. Do you have time to catch up later?" I ask, my words tumbling out in a rush. "Maybe we could grab a drink somewhere?"

She tilts her head, assessing me. Probably seconds from chewing my ass out. "I'm here on business," she finally says, "and my schedule's really tight. I don't have any time to catch up, unfortunately. I need to do a walk-through of a client's premises tonight. But maybe next time I'm in town?"

"Sure, sure, I understand. Of course you have things to do."

She chews on her lower lip a moment, then says, "You could come with me? To do the walk-through, I mean. It's in Chelsea, though, so I'm not sure if that's too much of a hassle."

A chance to reconnect with Mari? I'd agree to climb Mount Everest for an opportunity like this. "No, no. That's not a hassle at all. Whatever, whenever. Just tell me where I need to be."

She nods, her expression painfully bland. It's only right, but it still hurts.

"I'll text you the address," she says. "You have the same number?"

"I do."

She looks up from her phone. "I do too."

It's an accusation. Every bit of it justified. After all, the rift between us is of my own making. What will she see when she texts? Will she see the last messages she sent me? My stomach twists at the thought.

Seconds later, my phone buzzes. I quickly glance at Mari's message, noting that it's nothing more than a downtown address. As if that's all she's willing to commit to writing under the circumstances. I fully understand. I did this to myself. But I also want to undo it—even though I don't deserve to.

"I'll be there, Mari. I . . ." I was going to say "I promise," but what a fucking joke that would be.

"I'm looking forward to it," I tell her, genuinely meaning it.

"Great," she says, her small smile flipping the switch on her lifeless expression and giving me hope that I'll get the do-over I so desperately want. "I'll see you then."

She walks away without a backward glance, and I watch her until she disappears into Chanelle Heyward's trailer.

I don't know what my future holds, but now I'm wondering if Mari was always meant to be in it. If this is my second chance, I'm going to do my level best not to mess up.

* * *

Could this be the place? It's eerie as hell. And why are some of the windows boarded up?

I glance at the address Mari sent me, then stare at the building number above the brownstone's door. The 2 is barely hanging on. Yup, this is the right location, but what is it?

I jump when I feel a tap at my shoulder.

"Hey, you," Mari says, smiling brightly.

She's still wearing the same expensive-ass-looking coat, but she's changed into jeans and sneakers. Reminds me of the old Mari. Before she became a big-time lawyer. Yeah, I looked her up—for the first time in a while—and my girl's been kicking ass and taking names. This year, she made *Forbes* magazine's 30 Under 30 list in Law & Policy. A year before that, her local bar association nominated her for a rising star award. I couldn't find an Instagram account (the old one had been deactivated), so I know nothing about her personal life, not that IG is a reliable source in any case. One thing's for sure: Mari's on the path to greatness, while I'm still asking for directions.

I point at the building. "We're headed in here?"

"Yeah," she says with a decisive nod. "I'm doing a walk-through of the premises to advise my clients about any liability issues. They want to hard launch as soon as possible. Since they plan to serve liquor, it's especially important that they minimize their exposure to legal complaints. I told them about you, and they gave me permission to have you tag along. I was thinking you and I could talk at the bar afterward."

"Sounds good to me," I say, trying to peer through a curtainless window. "So, this place. It's like a modern-day speakeasy?"

She grins. "Of sorts. The liquor's legal, of course."

"I meant the vibe."

"Oh, I know what you meant, but I don't want to say too much. It's better if you experience it yourself." She gestures at the short flight of stairs leading to the basement level. "Shall we?"

I follow her to the entrance, and suddenly the door's opening—seemingly on its own. It's pitch-black in there, but mist, or maybe smoke, is emanating from inside.

I'm fully prepared to run and drag Mari with me, but she crosses the threshold and immediately looks around, her phone in hand as if she's readying to take notes.

I guess we're doing this—whatever "this" is.

Making the sign of the cross, I step up to the door and follow her inside.

CHAPTER 19

Mari

Two Years and Two Months Before the Wedding

I'm a petty person when I need to be. This walk-through is proof of that. Particularly because I asked my clients to do their worst. I mean, it's only fair. Javi *did* ghost me all those years ago, so why not ghost him now? In a manner of speaking, that is.

Maybe I shouldn't be entertaining him at all, but I've always had a soft spot for Javi, and the passage of time has dulled the pain of his rejection. It's not as if I'm planning to rekindle our friendship. No, it's too late for bygones. Still, we're adults now, and I've always wondered why Javi decided to drop out of my life. Let's call it curiosity.

Behind me, Javi's quiet as he takes in the intentionally ominous scene. I must say, the creak of the floorboards is a nice touch.

"What is this place?" he whispers.

"This is all part of the experience. To evoke the feeling that you're doing something illicit."

There's a protective film on the floor that crackles with every step. Several strides in, I slip on a wet spot. It's a hazard that needs to be removed from the final iteration of this nighttime attraction, but for tonight, I'm amused.

Since I, too, have a role to play, I let out an exaggerated yelp. "Oh God, is that blood?"

Javi fishes out his phone and angles the light to illuminate the ground. "It's definitely red. Is this a damn crime scene, Mari? How well do you know these clients?"

"They gave me the go-ahead to do the walk-through minutes before we entered. I doubt there's been a murder since then. I'm being ridiculous. It's probably just paint."

"We have two seconds to figure this out," Javi says in a low voice. "Otherwise, we're leaving."

A figure suddenly appears by the stairs, and before I can decipher who or what it's meant to be, it scurries away.

"Goddamn," Javi exclaims. "What the fuck was that?"

"What? What?" I whisper, faking a tremor so he thinks I'm just as alarmed as he is. "I didn't see anything."

"You didn't see that person?" he asks, his voice tight. "They scrambled away like a subway rat. Actually, subway rats will just stare you down while they drag a slice of pizza across the train tracks. This was something else."

I look back at him. "Maybe you're seeing things?"

Even in the dark, I can't miss his brown eyes narrowing.

"That's my point," he says. "I *am* seeing things."

Before I can respond, a figure taps Javi on the shoulder. Javi leaps in the air like an Olympic gymnast, spins around, and yells, "Holy shit!" In milliseconds, he lands on his feet, hauls me behind him, and throws up his hands as if he's readying for a full-on brawl.

We're staring at what looks like a zombie. Gray scaly skin punctured by bullets, a mouth filled with dirty yellow teeth (though the canines are missing), and leeches embedded in this monster's bare chest. If I weren't in on the prank, I'd be sprinting to the door.

"En el nombre del Padre, y del Hijo, y del Espíritu Santo. Amén," Javi chants. "¡Vayase, Demonio!"

Feigning terror, I plaster the front of my body against the back of Javi's. "Are you praying?"

"I don't know what the fuck I'm doing," he whispers. "I'm hoping this is a fever dream and I'm going to wake up any minute now. Would you look at me the same if I pissed my pants? It's a definite possibility."

The snort escapes me before I can suppress it, and I'm unable to hold it together after that. Resting my hands on my knees, I let out a deep belly laugh as my eyes well. I wanted to go the distance, but there's no way I can.

Javi whips around. "Are you *laughing*?"

I slowly straighten to my full height and wink at Javi. "Gotcha!"

The zombie chuckles, and I immediately recognize the voice as that of Tripp Holdings, one of the owners of this spooky venture.

"Tripp, is that you?" I ask.

"It sure is," Tripp says, his wide grin making him appear vastly less intimidating than he did moments ago. He lumbers away, and after a few seconds, the basement lights flicker on and off, then finally remain on—barely. Tripp takes one look at Javi and says, "I'll give you two a moment."

Javi's staring at me, his face scrunched up in a way that suggests he's partly annoyed and mostly confused. "What's going on?"

"Just a little joke," I say with a smile.

His face clears. "Ah. Payback, I suppose."

I wondered about this—whether he'd give me the opening to skewer him as he deserves. I was totally prepared to be cordial and leave the past in its place, but now that he's acknowledged what happened between us, the saltiness I vowed to suppress seeps out of my pores. I meet his stare with my own glare. "So you agree payback is fitting."

He sighs, then twists back and forth as he scans the space around us. There isn't much to see. The room's huge, but there's no furniture to speak of, and the only décor is the tarlike black paint covering the walls.

"Can we sit somewhere and talk?" he asks.

"Ah, *now* you're ready to talk? Six years later?"

He grimaces. "You have every right to be mad at me. You owe me nothing, Mari. But just remember I was young."

"And dumb," I add.

"That too," he says, his lips curving into a cautious smile.

"Well, then. Let's get your dumb ass a drink."

I gesture for him to follow me down a narrow hall that leads to the heart of my client's concept: a bar and lounge area with a vibe that's both ominous and sensual. There's so much to absorb. High-top tables draped in rich burgundy velvet and enclosed in wrought-iron cages. Midnight-black chandeliers with crow-shaped candelabras dripping in crystals. Two-seater settees framed by gold-polished spikes facing the bar.

Javi's jaw drops as he takes in his surroundings. "What is this place?"

I climb onto one of the settees and scoot over so he can join me. "It's called Friday Night Frights. Think haunted mansion meets vampire den meets speakeasy."

"Right. Because making someone shit their pants before you ply them with alcohol makes a lot of sense."

I hold in a chuckle. "I'm not here to judge my client's ideas. I'm here to ensure those ideas don't lead to a lawsuit."

"Fair enough," Javi says, easing onto the spot beside me.

The bartender, who's also Tripp's longtime partner, sidles over; his hair is entwined with lifelike snakes, and he's wearing a cape made of heavy brocade. "Hey, baby girl. May I interest you in a cocktail?"

"Hey, Samir. I could use three, but I'll settle for one." Gesturing to Javi, I add, "This is Javier. We knew each other in college."

Javi's gaze meets mine before he takes Samir's outstretched hand. He has absolutely no right to be affronted by my perfectly accurate description of our connection. "Nice to meet you."

"Likewise." Samir spins and plucks a menu off the liquor shelf. "Here you go. Let me know your pleasure."

I quickly scan the cocktail descriptions and pass the menu to Javi. "I'll try the Mummy Martini."

"Just a club soda for me, thanks," Javi says, handing Samir the menu. "The Count Vodkula sounds impressive, though. Belvedere's a good choice. I'd go with that too."

Samir tilts his head, his eyes widening in surprise. "You bartend?"

"On the weekends," Javi says.

"Well, all right, then. A Mummy Martini and a club soda coming right up," Samir says. As he backs away, he laughs ominously.

We watch his performance with raised brows.

"Too much?" he asks, noticing our underwhelming response to his theatrical cackle.

"Needs work," I say, charitably.

Samir chuckles. "Noted."

Once Samir's out of earshot, I turn to Javi. "So that answers one of my questions. You're acting during the week and bartending on weekends."

"Which is ironic since I have the world's worst poker face and

I can't hold my liquor for shit." He lifts a finger in the air as though he's just remembered something. "Oh, and I'm working on my grand opus."

"The musical?"

"Yeah," he says, lowering his chin. "Still."

"That just means it'll be fully cooked when you're done. What's it about?"

"The working title is *The Mailroom*. It's about the people who work in the mailroom of this nameless corporation. The contents of an interoffice memo spill out and everyone learns that there's a plan to promote from within, that someone in the mailroom is going to move up in the ranks and fast. So each of the main characters thinks about the life they have now and the life they want. The life they always dreamed of."

"How'd you come up with the idea?"

"My dad inspired it, actually," he says, straightening his shoulders. "One of his first jobs out of high school was working in a mailroom in Midtown. For Aramark. You know, the food company?"

I nod, not wanting to interrupt. Not when Javier's eyes are brightening as he speaks, his passion for this project evident in his lively demeanor.

"Anyway," he continues, "my dad told me he learned a big life lesson there. See, a coworker kept coming in late, and everybody used to tease her about it. An older woman, Jamaican. And he said one day everyone was leaving and she was pleading for someone to give her a ride home. She needed to get there in a rush. And my dad decided to do her this favor. And when he dropped her off, she invited him in for coffee before he got back on the road. So my dad says he walks in and discovers that this woman needed to get home to relieve the caretaker watching her disabled teenage son."

"Oh, that's why she was always late," I say.

"Exactly. And after that, he never let anyone tease her about not being on time. I'm sure he told me this in the context of teaching me empathy. He always says we never know what people are going through, and we should be mindful of that." He looks up and frowns, as if he can't believe he got caught up in his own words. It's wonderful to be reminded of the boy I once knew. The one who became so animated only around me. "So yeah, it's really about these people who have challenging lives outside the mailroom and what getting a promotion would mean for them."

"With a running commentary on the proletariat and bourgeoisie, of course."

"You know me well," he says, nodding enthusiastically.

"What about costumes? Any bedazzled Muppets?"

We grin at each other, remembering his senior design project.

"Nothing like that," he says after a beat. "Just normal workwear."

"So, this musical. There's a catch, right? I just know there is."

Javi nods, his lips curving into a devious smile. "The mailroom supervisor planted the fake memo as a way to improve productivity. Because *he's* gunning for a promotion. But if you tell anyone that twist, I'll never speak to . . ."

He fidgets with the napkin in his hand.

I enjoy seeing him squirm. It's satisfying in a way I didn't expect. "That threat's lost its force, considering you stopped speaking to me for no apparent reason."

"Mari—"

"Here we are," Samir says jovially, unaware he's interrupting. He places our drinks in front of us, then disappears in a cloud of literal smoke (courtesy of the bag of dry ice he's dragging behind him).

I take a sip of the martini, savoring the espresso flavor that hits my tongue. "Listen, Javi, let's forget about it, okay? Everything happens for a reason and all that." It's a flippant response that doesn't quite fit the relationship we once had, but that's entirely my point. We *don't* have the relationship we once had, and the fault for that sits squarely on Javi's shoulders.

Javi, meanwhile, stares at his glass, worrying his bottom lip. He's struggling with his thoughts. I can tell because there's a little divot between his eyebrows that always appears when he's grappling with the very heady musings in that overcomplicated brain of his.

We're adults now. Who the hell cares why he dumped me all those years ago? Right now, Javi's just a handsome man I ran into on a business trip. Admittedly, we have *history*, but none of it matters.

He's just a guy.

A guy I wouldn't mind getting to know (again) while I'm in New York.

So I absolve him of his sins and give him a reprieve, knocking his knee with mine. "Seriously, Javi, there's no need to explain. Let's enjoy the night and see where it takes us, okay?"

"Yeah?" he asks, his eyes glinting with hope, and relief, and maybe a little interest.

"Yeah."

CHAPTER 20

Javi

Two Years and Two Months Before the Wedding

I should explain to Mari why I ghosted her all those years ago. Tell her I was worried that our relationship would interfere with her goals. That I would hold her back. But also, that I couldn't have been more into her if I tried. That I was shook by the kiss we shared at that party. That I'd lost my job the week before that fateful trip to L.A., and I didn't have the balls to tell her. That I'd already started pulling away in my mind because I couldn't let her see me knocked down, so how good a friend could I really be?

I could explain how her dad's attitude made everything worse. How he made it abundantly clear I was going nowhere, whereas Mari was absolutely destined for greatness, and I would do nothing but impede her progress. I could even tell her how I toyed with the idea of instigating a fight with her so I could make a clean break but scrapped the plan because I didn't want to suggest that she was at fault in any way. I could reveal that on the plane back to New York, I'd decided that my own brain and her dad could go fuck themselves. That she could be my world if I were brave enough to tell her so. But then a week later, I did what she told me *not* to do and accepted my brothers' magnanimous offer to be their personal assistant—gofer, lackey, whatever you want to call it. Because I needed to eat. Because I had a college degree that looked great on paper and was absolutely worthless in the real world. Because I lived in a house they bought with the money they made off the band *I* started, and I needed savings to get the hell out. I could tell her that I fetched their coffee, their dry cleaning, the gifts for their girlfriends. That I quit the day Manny called me in the middle of the night and asked me to run out to the drugstore for a box of condoms. I didn't want her to see any of that. Didn't want her to know that version of me. So I didn't answer her texts. Because she didn't need me like I needed her. And wouldn't it be better for the both of us if we accepted that our friendship had gone as far as it was meant to?

Sure, I could tell her all this now, but everything happened so long ago, and what would be the point of dredging up the past anyway? Zero percent of that explanation would paint me in a flattering light. Worse, if I bring up how her father made me feel, it might cause tension between us—because even though I don't care for the guy, he's Mari's sole parent in the States, and she's protective of him. So I accept the reprieve she's granted me and console myself with the facts: She's doing well. No—more than that, she's *thriving*. And she doesn't seem to be holding a grudge. I can't know with certainty that disappearing made a positive difference in her future, but I'm going to pretend it did.

I stare at the condensation on the outside of my glass and draw in a fortifying breath. When I look up, Mari's watching me with a knowing smile.

"You're overthinking, aren't you?" she asks.

I drop my chin sheepishly. "Probably." Wanting to redirect the conversation, I broach my least favorite topic. "So, how's Luiz?"

"My father's fine," Mari says. "Wants to loosen the reins at work but doesn't know how to stop micromanaging everything."

"You two are good?"

She shrugs. "As good as we'll ever be, I think. We're like oil and water."

More like snake oil and water.

"Always have been," she continues. "The one thing we have in common is our love for the firm."

"It's doing well?"

"It's doing great. We're booked and busy and showing no signs of slowing down. We're even thinking about expanding to New York. I'm testing the waters with a few clients, mostly friends who appreciate the free help. My hope is that when my father retires, I can steer the firm's culture in a different direction. Focus on smaller clients making truly impactful content. That's the long-term goal, at least."

"I'm glad everything worked out, then."

She tilts her head, her brow knitted.

"I mean, I'm glad the business is doing well," I add. "So what's the plan? Will you run the firm one day?"

"We've never sat down and talked about it, but yeah, that's my plan. Or what I'd like to happen, I should say. I still need a few more years under my belt before it's even a possibility, though."

"If you want it to happen, then it will."

"Thanks for the vote of confidence."

I shouldn't ask about her love life—it's none of my business—but I can't help myself. "I don't see a ring."

"I'm not a ring person," she replies with a wink.

Silence simmers between us until she says, "If there's a question you're frothing at the mouth to know the answer to, just be direct about it."

I roll my eyes. "Are you single?"

"Yes."

"Dating anyone?"

"I date," she says. "But there's no one I'm dating regularly. Or exclusively. It's rough out in these streets. I'm incapable of heeding red flags even when they're flying at full mast right in front of my face. Plus, I get bored very easily."

"I'm not seeing anyone either."

"I don't recall asking, but thanks for sharing."

"Still a smartass, I see."

"Don't stop," she whispers, fluttering her eyelashes as she twirls the cocktail straw in her glass. "You're feeding my praise kink."

I moisten my lips and let out a slow breath. "You have one?"

She leans in, places her hand on my thigh, and gives it a light squeeze. "Absolutely."

My heart races, and a surge of adrenaline runs through me. Adult Mari has ten times the confidence of her younger self, and she's equally compelling. She's probably broken a lot of hearts in the time we've been apart.

I stare at her, taking all of it—this new Mari—in.

Likely misinterpreting my silence as a negative reaction to her flirty behavior, she straightens in her seat and clears her throat. "How are your parents? Where are you living? Have your brothers flopped yet? Tell me everything."

I laugh. "Okay, okay, let's see. My parents are good. They're in a bowling league, if you can believe it. And they travel now. Mostly to visit family in PR, but it's a start. They've been making noise about wanting to open a food truck, but they can't agree on what they'd sell. I did move out, although I have three roommates because the cost of living here is ridiculous."

"I bet," Mari says, nodding. "I once stayed in a hotel room so tiny I could wash my hands in the sink while lying in bed."

There doesn't seem to be any judgment on her part, which shouldn't surprise me but does, so maybe my expectation that she'd be unimpressed with my current situation is just me projecting.

"And your brothers? Manny and Leandro, right?"

"Yeah, that's right. They're still singing. Not as much as they used to, but they get invited to festivals and stuff like that. Manny's still a playboy. Leandro's married now and has a kid. Ana Luz. She's the sweetest thing on earth."

"Aww, you're an uncle," she says, rubbing my arm playfully. "I love that for you."

I shift closer, enjoying her teasing touch and wanting more.

She clocks the movement and smiles slyly. "How are things between the three of you?"

"My brothers and me?" I shrug. "We're fine. They've tried to explain themselves over the years, but I'm not interested in hearing what they have to say about the band. I'm over it."

"Are you?" she asks, lifting a brow to convey her doubt.

"I am."

"If you say so."

"What about your friends from Belmont?" I ask, wanting to change the topic. "Sasha and Brittany. You still in contact with them?"

"Absolutely, yeah. We don't see each other in person as much as we'd like to, but FaceTime is a godsend. Sasha's in Chicago working as a marketing expert extraordinaire. Brittany's a sous chef for a catering company in Virginia. She has a tyrant of a boss she's secretly in love with."

"Damn, sounds complicated."

"It's completely on brand for Brittany, though. They'll probably be married within the year."

"That's wild. Man, Sasha and Brittany. Haven't seen them since graduation."

"And what about your old roommate? The guy who was always high. What was his name again?"

"Jeremy. Yeah, we still talk. He's some big finance guy out in L.A."

"The pothead now has a big pot of money," she quips.

I chuckle. This feels so fucking easy, I'm mad at myself for ever losing touch with her. Mari's one of a kind. I can't think of many people I have this instant rapport with. Our relationship in college wasn't just born of circumstance. No, it was her. Us. A connection that's never been replicated.

Thirty minutes later, Mari's told me all about her life in L.A. and it's all so, I don't know, *mature*. The condo she bought in Culver City. The international book and supper club she joined just a few months ago. The teenage girl who's shadowing Mari at work because she's interested in the law (and who Mari is desperately trying to dissuade from being a lawyer). The roundtable conversations about equity and inclusion in Hollywood that the firm hosts, a monthly industry-wide event she convinced her father to sponsor. She sounds content. Settled. Pleased with her life choices. Honestly, when I grow up, I want to be like Mari.

The guy who scared the shit out of me when we came in—Tim? No, Tripp—sidles over and taps Mari on the shoulder. "I hate to interrupt, but I'm wondering if you have any feedback."

Mari grins sheepishly. "Oh, right. Sorry, Tripp. The evening got away from me. Let's chat in your office."

She rises from the bench. To me, she says, "This shouldn't take long, but I don't want to presume that you don't have things to do. If you need to—"

"I'll wait. I'm enjoying this," I say, pointing between us. "And I was thinking I could walk you to your hotel."

She smiles and gives me a once-over, a faint blush tinting her cheeks. "I'd like that."

When she returns, she hands Samir her credit card, and I scramble to catch up, fishing mine out of my pocket.

We stare at each other as we wait for Samir to return. The silence is killing me, so I break it. "What are you thinking?"

Mari slides into my personal space and ghosts her lips against my ear. Softly, so softly I almost convince myself I imagined it, she says, "I'm thinking the universe brought us together again for a reason. Let's not disappoint her."

I remember this feeling. Because I experienced it the last time we were together. A need so fierce it almost brings me to my knees. God, the things I would do to this woman if the slate were clean. But it isn't. By tacit agreement, Mari and I have never explored the possibility of a romantic relationship. The costs always outweighed the potential benefits. Because we valued our friendship over everything else. Because boyfriends and girlfriends came and went, but we were always solid. Until I fucked it all up and disappeared on her. Which is how I *know* she's telling herself I'm nothing more than someone to keep her bed warm for a night. Precisely the person I never wanted to be.

As hard as it is to resist her, I do it anyway and step back. "I guess you can't hold your liquor as well as you used to."

She huffs. "I'm not even a little bit drunk, but if that's what you need to tell yourself, then sure, let's go with that."

Samir returns with our credit cards and receipts. After we sign off, Mari gestures to the exit. "Shall we?"

"We shall," I say, looping my arm through hers.

Mari's staying at a place only a couple of blocks away, one of those boutique hotels that looks like a regular-ass residential building. There isn't any security, and the lobby bar is teeming with people who are obviously inebriated.

"Let me walk you to your room," I say.

She slips me a curious glance, her teeth pressed into her bottom lip. After a beat, she asks, "Is that a pickup line?"

I stop and face her, irresistibly drawn to the sparkle in her eyes, the hint of mischief in her smile. "Is that what you want it to be?"

She playfully purses her lips, a tiny shrug her only response. Flirting with Mari feels like uncharted territory. A dynamic we never fully experienced in college because we weren't prepared to cross the platonic boundary of our friendship. I'm not sure I'm prepared to cross it now, either, but I'm *so* damn tempted to.

Mari threads our hands together and leads me to the bank of elevators. On the way up, we stand side by side, hands still entwined, my fingers grazing hers.

"How long are you here?" I ask.

"Leaving tomorrow afternoon."

"Will you be back any time soon?"

"Not that I know of. I mean, I travel out here every few months, but I don't have any concrete plans. Why?"

"I just thought it would be nice to see you again."

"Hmm" is all she says in return.

When we reach her floor, we get off, and I trail behind her. She reaches her room and points at the door. "This is me."

I nod. "Okay, you have my number. I hope you use it."

Mari holds my gaze for a long moment. "Will you answer?"

"I will."

She takes in a deep breath, lets it out slowly, then pulls me in for a hug. Against my ear, she whispers, "Why don't you stay a little while longer? With me."

There's no way I can say no to what she seems to be offering, and yet that's exactly what I do. "It's been really good seeing you again," I say, stepping back and squeezing her hand, "and I understand the impulse, but we're older now, maybe even wiser. And perhaps this is the universe telling us we need each other. And shit, I'm just going to say it: I miss my friend. So let's not go there, okay?"

She stares up at me, her eyes glistening. "I kind of hate that you still know the perfect thing to say at any given moment."

"It's a gift I use only sparingly."

"Going to be honest, though. I was looking forward to finally seeing your dick."

She crosses her eyes and sticks out her tongue, and I can't help barking out a laugh.

I lean in and press a gentle kiss on her forehead. "Take care of yourself. And call me. If you want."

"I'll think about it," she says, her mouth twisted in a playful grin.

I've said all I can say to convince her to give me a second chance. Now it's up to Mari. As I walk to the elevator, there's a heaviness in my chest that's at odds with how happy I am to have been in Mari's presence again. I turn around and catch a glimpse of her as she slips inside her hotel room and shuts the door.

It would be a cruel outcome if our story ends here, but if it does, I only have myself to blame.

CHAPTER 21

Javi

Now

Apparently the man of honor has duties beyond trying to convince the bride to dump the groom. Who knew?

"Thanks for coming with me," Mari says, linking her arm with mine as we enter Diamond House, the Highland Park event space that's hosting the wedding we're crashing today. Okay, to be fair, Mari was told we could stop by, so we're not exactly crashing anything, but it feels weird as hell to be rolling up to a stranger's marriage celebration to help plan your own.

I pat Mari's hand. "No need to thank me. Just want to be sure I'm doing my part."

"You dressed up," she says, eyeing my light gray suit. "I'd say you're doing all right. And seriously, I know you're going all in on the musical, so I'm grateful that you ditched your work for a little while." She rests her head against my shoulder. "You're the best."

Would she still think so if she knew I spent the last few days scouring the internet for information about Alex that would make her call off the wedding? Hmm, I should probably keep that fact to myself. Especially since I didn't find anything.

We walk through the brightly decorated lounge, a long, narrow room with four discrete conversation areas anchored by oversize sofas and plush armchairs. There is no specific color scheme; color *is* the scheme. A few people are chatting off to the side—one person's taking a call—but the activity's otherwise sparse in here. The most arresting feature is the four-panel sliding glass door that leads to the courtyard, which is where the true festivities seem to be happening.

"So which one of you had the idea to hire a live portrait artist for the wedding?" I ask.

"Alex suggested it," she says, running a hand over the back of a mint-green velvet couch as we pass it. "But he knows I'm a bit of a micromanager—"

"A bit?"

She jostles my shoulder with her own. "Watch it. As I was *saying*, since Alex knows I'm a micromanager and he knows Diamond House's owner, he arranged for us to get a preview of what it would be like. I'm not really worried about the portrait itself. But I *am* curious to know how the artist interacts with the guests. Whether having a person watching every detail changes the vibe. I want our guests to enjoy themselves, so if it's a mood killer, I'll just tell Alex I'm not comfortable with the idea. He'll understand."

"And Alex is too busy to do this with you?"

"He had a conflict." I remain quiet, so she adds, "Please don't read anything else into it. We're busy people."

"Fine, fine," I say. It *isn't* fine, though. We're all busy—some of us more so than others—but being "busy people" sounds like a ready-made catchall Mari can pull off the shelf whenever she needs to account for her partner's absence. As if she's expecting it'll come in handy as an easy explanation that won't cause people to think less of him. "Still, I'm allowed to probe, remember?"

"I remember."

"So, does he have a good excuse for not being here?"

"He does," she says firmly.

"I won't complain, then. Besides, his loss is my gain."

She squeezes my arm. "Exactly."

We walk outside to the courtyard, a large area that's sealed off from rest of the world by enormous tree hedges that resemble the walls of a maze. I look down at the patterned concrete floor—a seemingly never-ending spiral of black-and-white diamonds—and almost sway on my feet. Wow, whoever designed this place was definitely trying to make a statement—or create a headache-inducing optical illusion. I blink a few times and lift my face to the sun, enjoying the warmth on my face. It's a perfect L.A. day, and since I've pretty much been holed up in Jeremy's condo, I haven't experienced many of those firsthand. I'm smiling as I study the guests, a diverse mix of people whose attire is as eclectic as the venue's décor.

"Do you know anything about the couple getting married?" I ask.

"Alex said one of the guys is a studio set designer. I'm not sure what the other guy does."

The crowd and the venue make sense to me now. A creative person would appreciate this setting; it celebrates color, honors nature, and features conversation-worthy elements at every turn.

"There's Sienna, the artist," Mari says, pointing to a young Asian woman standing at the far end of the courtyard, a thin paintbrush in her gloved hand. She's wearing brown ankle boots and a long black dress cinched at the waist by a wide brown leather belt.

Her canvas is propped on a wooden A-frame easel, and guests are peeking over her shoulder.

"I never would have guessed," I joke.

Mari rolls her eyes and pulls me along as she makes her way over. We wait at the edge of the crowd and watch Sienna work. She's friendly with everyone and comfortable speaking with both adults and the little kids bouncing on their toes to get a closer look.

I study the canvas, trying to imagine what the finished painting will look like. The celebrants, an interracial couple, are almost complete, the image of them dancing while their guests are gathered around them matching what's actually happening in front of us.

Mari and I inch closer, waiting for the opportunity to introduce ourselves. When several kids lose interest and scamper away, we settle into the spot they abandoned.

Mari clears her throat. "Sienna, I'm Marisol Campos, we spoke last week about the possibility of you doing a live painting at my wedding in Sonoma."

Sienna turns to Mari with a bright smile. "Yes, yes, hello, hello! So great to meet you." She places the paintbrush in the drawer attached to the easel and stares up at me.

"Hi, I'm Javier."

"Nice to meet you, Javier," she says, using her ungloved hand to shake mine.

She picks up the paintbrush again and gazes out at the couple still dancing in the center of the courtyard. "They agreed to two dances so I can get this right. I'll refine the rest in my studio. Happy to answer any questions you have."

"I'm just so fascinated by this," Mari says, her words rushing out as if they're tripping on themselves. "But since you're only capturing a moment, how do you ensure you have enough time to"—she gestures at the painting—"do what you do."

Sienna crooks her finger and points to a spot in front of the easel. There, a small digital camera sits on a tripod. It's so unobtrusive I didn't notice it until now. "This is my assistant, Mr. Nikon. What I'm doing here is for the atmosphere. But if there are adjustments to be made, or heaven forbid, I make a mistake, the moment is stored in my camera and I can refer to it when I'm back in the studio."

"I see," Mari says. "And I read on your website that the couple chooses the moment they want memorialized."

"Yes," Sienna confirms.

"But what about the guests?" Mari asks. "How do you incorporate them?"

"That's your choice too," Sienna says. "I can highlight specific guests and ignore everyone else, or I can paint everything as I see it. The pricing varies, obviously, but everything's really dependent on your preferences. I can be as inconspicuous or as present as you need me to be. And I'm not easily distracted, so someone talking my ear off isn't going to affect the finished product."

"What if the couple just wants a portrait of them?" I ask, curious about the process. "With no one else around, I mean. That's the kind of special moment I can easily imagine putting up in my home."

"Many of the couples I work with opt for a portrait of just themselves, so you and Marisol wouldn't be doing anything out of the ordinary if you went that route."

Mari straightens. "Oh, Javier isn't my fiancé."

Sienna's gaze flickers between Mari's face and our linked arms. After a moment of silence, Mari eases out of my hold. "My fiancé, Alex, couldn't be here. Javier is my man of honor."

"Oh, that's so sweet!" Sienna gushes.

"How'd you even get into this?" Mari asks, plainly wanting to skip right over the awkwardness. "It's *so* specialized. *Wonderful* but specialized. I didn't even know there was such a thing as live wedding painting until Alex, *my fiancé*, mentioned it. Isn't that interesting?"

Sienna's eyes widen, and then she turns back to the canvas.

Yeah, not awkward at all, Mari.

Sienna studies the portrait, thinking for a few beats before responding. "Honestly, I'm an artist, but I'm also a romantic at heart. As cliché as this may sound, I love romance, weddings, expressions of love. Making a living capturing these magical moments is a privilege."

A middle-aged woman (who's practically breathing down my neck) takes a sip of wine and says, "It's such a beautiful depiction of them. Reminds me that those two were meant to be."

"Best friends turned lovers," a younger woman beside her observes wistfully.

"A hard-fought happily-ever-after," a third person agrees.

Sienna takes in a sharp breath and draws the paintbrush away from the canvas as if she's been burned. For a long moment, she just stands there, her gaze clouding.

Mari frowns and reaches out to touch Sienna's shoulder. "Sienna? Everything okay?"

In answer, Sienna throws her head back and wails.

"Oh my God, oh my God," Mari chants. "What's wrong? What can I do? Are you hurt?"

"Only my heart," Sienna sobs. "I"—she sniffs—"ruined"—she whimpers—"everything. With David."

The "with David" part comes out as a blubbery mess that makes Mari and me wince.

Mari throws an arm around Sienna and looks at me. *I'm going to take her to the bathroom*, she mouths.

Good idea, I mouth in return, my face tight as I absorb this baffling turn of events.

With a decisive nod, Mari says, "We'll be right back," and leads Sienna to the lounge area inside. Seconds before they disappear from view, Sienna tucks herself against Mari as if she's being consoled by a close friend rather than a stranger and potential client—though I'm guessing the latter's no longer true.

What the hell? Is this one of those fever dreams again?

I'm frozen in place, unsure what to do. Stay here and guard the portrait? The digital camera? Yeah, that seems like the responsible thing to do. I peek at the crowd to gauge how many people witnessed the spectacle, and that's when I notice one of the celebrants—the white one—marching toward me.

By the time he reaches me, he's pasted on a smile and shaken out his hands. "Listen to me carefully," he says, his voice low and strained. "Do not do anything that would suggest something's wrong. Nod if you understand."

I nod.

"Who are you?" he asks.

"I'm Javier. You don't know me. I'm here with my friend Marisol. She's considering using the artist for her own wedding."

"Nice to meet you, Javier. I'm Ian."

"Good to meet you. Congrats on your wedding, by the way."

"Thanks. What happened to Sienna?"

"She got overwhelmed all of a sudden, I think. Upset about something."

"Oh dear, that's Sienna for you," he says, shaking his head. "Listen, my very new and very anxious husband did not want Sienna to do this live portrait thing because she's . . . not exactly reliable, and if he has any inkling that something's gone awry, I will never hear the end of it. So can you pretend that all is well until Sienna returns? Consider it your wedding present to us. And if anyone asks, you're her assistant."

"Uh, sure, I can do that," I say, stunned into agreeing to whatever he asks.

"Great. And be sure to grab a beer at the bar. On us, of course."

"Yep, that's very nice of you," I say on autopilot. "Take care."

Ian strides away, returning to his groom, who's dancing with an older Black woman. Given how the pair are gazing at each other, I assume she's his mother, but who the hell knows? What a strange day.

I pick up the paintbrush and wave it around, hovering near the painting but being careful not to touch it.

"It's magnificent," a man behind me says. "Bethany, come here, honey," he bellows to someone else. "Check this out!"

I give the guy a tense smile and notice out of the corner of my eye that his attempt to get his companion's attention has drawn several more people over. Shit. If I touch this canvas, I risk ruining the couple's wedding portrait. What the hell am I supposed to do? And where the hell are Sienna and Mari?

"So what happens now?" the guy asks, unknowingly mimicking one of the thoughts in my scrambled head.

Excellent question, sir. I have no fucking clue. To him, I say, "Well, I, um, I'm not the lead artist. I'm her assistant."

"Which means what? Are you working on the background, then?"

"Exactly that," I say.

"Oh, show us how it's done!" the guy's companion exclaims. "We're so invested." She indicates a section of the portrait. "Look, Bill, I think that's us!"

Thanks to an art history course in high school, I vaguely remember a style of painting that was just dots. Pointism? No, pointillism! How much damage can I really do if I just add a speck? I can't imagine it would make that much of a difference.

Slowly and very carefully, I use the paintbrush to add a single dot to the canvas. "There you have it, friends. That's the process."

I twist around to see everyone's reactions. A dozen people are staring back at me, most of their faces scrunched in confusion. My good friend Bill is wrinkling his nose. My gaze floats over the guests and lands on Mari, who's standing at the edge of the dance floor, a hand over her mouth and her shoulders shaking in barely concealed amusement. Before I can figure out how to drag her into my nightmare, Sienna appears at my side and gently removes the paintbrush from my hand.

"Thank you," she says. "I've got it from here. And sorry about"—she waves the brush—"whatever that was."

"No problem," I say, knowing Mari will give me the backstory later. "Feeling better?"

"Yeah," she says.

"Good. I'll let you get back to it."

I escape and find Mari at the bar, where she's ordering a glass of white wine and a virgin mojito. She hands the mojito to me. "That was quite the performance. You earned this."

"Well, now that I'm part of the wedding staff, I feel entitled to some hors d'oeuvres too. Shall we?"

"We shall," she says, waggling her eyebrows.

After ransacking the hors d'oeuvres display, we find an open cocktail table and dig in.

"Mmm, I love arancini balls!" Mari exclaims.

"That's great, but maybe you shouldn't shout that in public."

She throws a hand over her mouth and laughs, then turns to her chicken lollipop. "This is nice," she says between bites. "This reception, I mean. It's modest yet elegant and not fussy at all."

"Is that what you're going for?"

Her smile slips. "Not sure that's an option anymore. My father wants to make a statement. Wants it to be memorable. And even though it's turning into more than I envisioned, I don't want to totally disregard his wishes. My father gets to do this only once. What's the harm in letting him have this?"

"It's your wedding, though," I urge. "Yours and Alex's, rather."

"Of course it is. And that hasn't changed. It's just that I've had to compromise here and there. That isn't necessarily a bad thing."

I tilt my head and peer at her. "Mari, you do know you don't owe your father anything, right? He did nothing more for you than what fathers are *supposed* to do. There's no debt you need to repay."

"Sure, there's no debt, but that doesn't mean I can't acknowledge that he did something many men wouldn't have done. Seriously, what father would want to be saddled with a moody teenage daughter when her mother dashes off to another country?"

In other words, she does feel indebted to him even though she claims she doesn't. I bet Luiz not only knows this but also uses it to his advantage. "Unless what you've been telling me all these years isn't true, your mother didn't dash off anywhere, and she would have taken you with her if you had wanted to go." I squeeze her hand. "Besides, you're a goddamned treasure. Your father's *lucky* to have you in his life."

Her eyes well up. "There you go being good for my ego again."

"Eat some more balls," I say, bumping her shoulder with mine. "It'll make you feel better."

She snorts, and then she throws her head back in laughter, wiping her eyes with a tissue.

An elderly couple shuffles over, the gentleman of the pair holding a plate of his own food. "This looks like the fun table!"

"May we join you?" the woman asks.

"Of course," I say, shifting closer to Mari to make room for them.

"I'm Tom," the man says. "And this is my wife, Barbara."

"Pleased to meet you," Mari says. "I'm Marisol, and this is my friend Javier."

Tom turns to face the people dancing in the center of the courtyard. "It's a lovely wedding, isn't it?"

"It is," I say, nodding. "Mari was just saying it's modest yet elegant."

"That's how ours was," Barbara says, tearing off a piece of chicken from the leg and popping it into her mouth. Damn, she's really going to town on that thing.

Tom chuckles. "But it was different back then. We didn't do all of the stuff people do nowadays: releasing butterflies, wedding painters, photo booths. Goodness, whatever happened to just saying 'I do' to the person you want to spend the rest of your life with?"

"Simpler times," I say.

"How long have you been married?" Mari asks them.

They stare at each other, their eyes glowing with affection. "Forty-one years," they say in unison.

Mari leans in conspiratorially. "So what's the secret to a long and loving marriage?"

Barbara covers Tom's hand with hers. "We were best friends first."

Go, Barbara, go. If I didn't know any better, I would think Barbara's a plant, paid by yours truly to remind Mari that Alex isn't the guy for her.

Mari swallows, her eyes downcast, then says, "That's lovely.

We wish you all the continued happiness you deserve." But her head's already on a swivel, searching for the exit and signaling in no uncertain terms that she's ready to leave.

I knock twice on the table and wave goodbye to Tom and Barbara. "It was wonderful to meet you."

"Take care, you two," Barbara calls after us.

As we make our way through the lounge, I tap Mari's arm. "Sienna's a no, I take it?"

Mari snickers, her eyes flashing with amusement. "Sienna's a I-think-the-fuck-not. Thanks for coming with me, though. I still had fun."

"It was nothing," I say. "But what was her deal anyway? Why'd she melt down like that?"

"She had sex with her friend David last night, and now she's worried they've ruined their friendship."

"Oh shit," I say, stopping short in the middle of the lounge.

Mari turns back to me, her eyebrows raised. "Exactly. Now where have we heard that before?"

CHAPTER 22

Mari

Two Years and Two Months Before the Wedding

I can't believe I threw myself at Javi within hours of seeing him again.

I can't believe he passed on the chance to have sex with me. Me!

Why didn't I let him finish the haunted speakeasy experience? I should have shown him no mercy.

Sighing, I throw a hand over my face. Oh God, could this night get any more embarrassing?

It's only been a few minutes since Javi left, and I've spent every one of them second-guessing myself. Did I come on too strong? Not strong enough?

A knock on the door of my hotel suite startles me out of this unproductive headspace. I heave myself off the soothingly plush couch and shuffle over. When I open the door, Javi's staring back at me.

"You sure about this?" he asks, his gaze steady and heated.

I'm not familiar with this version of Javi. The one whose jaw is clenched, whose burning eyes take me in greedily, the one who looks poised to devour me on the spot. I'm transfixed by the pure need that seems to be pouring off him in waves. Am I sure about this? For now, absolutely. Tomorrow? Who the hell knows? Still, I grip the lapel of his bomber jacket, tug him inside, and say, "Yes, I'm sure."

He's on me in seconds, grabbing my waist and bringing my body flush against his. He dips his head and narrows in on the sensitive skin of my collarbones, sliding his mouth over them, then running his nose along my neck and under my chin. His lips are cold, which tells me he walked outside before returning. How many steps did he take before he decided to turn around? What made him change his mind? Do I even care?

We fumble with his jacket, clumsily easing him out of it and letting it drop to the floor.

Am I really doing this?

Are *we* really doing this?

He watches me watch him, his gaze following mine as he slowly bends and presses his mouth against the fabric covering one of my breasts.

Ah, so we're diving right in. There's a vague warning in my brain that he's setting the tone, communicating that this isn't the start of our love story by bypassing the most intimate of moments, the first kiss. Then again, I suppose we already had one of those six years ago. Besides, this is what I wanted: the ability to lose myself in him for a night—no more, no less. *Don't overthink this, Mari.*

Javi places an open-mouthed kiss on my nipple over my T-shirt, then gathers the fabric with his teeth and drags it across my beaded tip. I briefly close my eyes but open them quickly, not wanting to miss even an instant of the surreal sight before me.

My clothing is a barrier, a dam to be broken. But also the cliff's edge. Everything underneath is precarious. Thrilling. *Risky*. I'm desperate to push us both over the precipice, so I grasp the hem of my T-shirt and lift it to my shoulders. I'm bare from the waist up and thrillingly exposed, my chest rising and falling as if the air's been knocked out of me. In a way, it has. This is more than my senses can handle; my brain can hardly keep up.

Javi steps back and looks his fill, then lets out a low hum of appreciation. "Jesus, I want to press my lips against every fucking inch of your skin. Just lay you out on a bed and love on you for days."

I easily picture him making good on that promise, and I'm so aroused, my skin feels too tight, too confining. Wordlessly, Javi finishes what I started and lifts my top over my head, then makes quick work of his own sweater, discarding both behind him. Now we're facing each other, bare-chested and panting. He snakes one hand around the back of my neck, pulling me close. His other hand palms one of my breasts, then rubs the nipple.

Javi's lips finally connect with mine, and we groan into each other. His lips are soft, his breath is sweet, his mouth is *masterful*. His hands slide down to my ass and squeeze; my hands slide up his chest and worship. I don't want to stop kissing or touching him, but I'm impatient for more, so I undo my pants, let them drop to the floor, and step out. I'm standing in the middle of the room, wearing a sheer black thong, as Javi's gaze roams over me, his pupils blown wide.

"Fuck," he says, softly. "Let me—"

"Yes, whatever you're thinking, yes," I eke out.

He spins me into his arms, my back to his chest, then whispers, "Lead the way."

I take his hand and walk to the bedroom. It's brightly lit and small, the bed predictably its dominant feature. The coverlet is pristine, and there are small signs of my mad dash to change into something more comfortable before I met Javi at the bar—a towel haphazardly draped over an armchair, my skirt laid out on the mattress.

Javi picks up my skirt and lays it neatly on the armchair, then turns to face me at the foot of the bed, crowding me with his body, until my only option is to fall back. He toes off his shoes and crawls onto the bed, resting next to me on his side. I take his hand and place it on my stomach, then draw it down my body until it's nestled at the juncture of my thighs.

Javi finds his way beneath my panties and teases the tight curls there. He edges torturously closer with each pass, and then he ghosts a finger against my clit. The effect is instantaneous. Electric. I flinch and let out a deep moan.

"You like that?" he breathes against my neck, repeating the move.

"I love it."

"How about this?" he asks, slipping a finger inside me. "Do you want me here? Filling you?"

"Oh God, yes," I cry out. "But first I need to touch you too."

I turn into him, careful not to disrupt his skillful exploration, then flick open the top button of his jeans and slowly drag the zipper down. My gaze never leaves his face as I trail a digit across his stomach, burrow inside his pants, and dip into his boxers. I wrap my hand around him, relishing the warmth, the thickness, how deliciously rigid he is for me. For *me*.

"Mari," he hisses, thrusting into my hand, "that's it. Keep doing that. Just. Like. That."

Our gazes meet, and then his eyes roll as he takes in a shuddering breath.

"God, Javi, that look on your face has me . . ."

Astonishingly, he grows even harder in my palm.

"You're making my fantasies come true," he says in an awestruck voice.

And although he's plainly enjoying my touch, he doesn't forget about me for one moment, alternating between closing his eyes in bliss and opening them to watch me as he rubs my clit in agonizingly slow circles.

I bite my lip, arching into him when he picks up the pace.

"Yes, Javi, oh God, that feels so good."

I'm close, so incredibly close, but I know from experience that my first orgasm is always the strongest, and I want Javi inside me when that happens, so I rest my hand on his. "Wait."

"What's wrong?" he says, his brow furrowed in concern.

"Nothing's wrong," I say, pushing him onto his back and straddling him so that my ass is resting on his thighs. "I just want to come on your cock."

"Jesus, Mari," he says, taking in an unsteady breath, "no better sentence has ever been spoken."

I love that he's affected by my words, that picturing us together unbalances him. "Let's get you out of these jeans."

He lifts his butt off the mattress, and I yelp, clumsily hanging on as he tugs his pants and boxers down and kicks them to the floor. Once he settles, I position myself above him and reach for his dick.

"Hold up," he groans. "We need a condom."

"Oh shit, I can't believe I forgot."

I mean, I *really* can't believe I forgot. I *never* forget. I scramble off the bed and dive for my purse. I'm back within seconds, a strip of condoms in hand—because if this turns out to be as good as I'm anticipating, then we're definitely going more than one round.

Javi tears off a packet and rolls the condom on himself. I'm shaking with need by the time he's done. I lean forward, my breasts within inches of his mouth, and guide him inside me. He palms my breasts, then traces slow circles on my areolas, ghosting in spirals that end at my nipples. He pinches them when I sink onto him, and I'm flooded with sensation, as if a current is flowing through me and leaving a trail of heat in its wake.

"Fuck," we both cry out.

It's a tight fit, but I'm not tentative at all, the twinge of pain from the fullness only heightening my arousal.

"Come down here, so I can kiss you," Javi says.

I lean over and touch my lips to his, my hair creating a cocoon around our faces. Javi's tongue teases mine as I rock into him slowly. He threads his fingers through my hair and massages my scalp. I'm warm all over, the skin between my thighs is slick and tender, and my nipples are so tight it's nearly painful. This feeling is . . . intoxicating.

"I won't be able to last very long," he warns, tightening his hold in my hair. "It's been a while."

"What do you need?"

"I need you to grind on my dick . . ." he whispers.

"Runner-up for the best sentence ever spoken."

"*While* I play with this gorgeously soaked pussy."

"Ding, ding, ding, we have a winner," I groan out.

I rest my upper body on his chest and snuggle into the crook of his neck, inhaling his scent, a mix of his natural pheromones and a hint of citrus that tells me he's using the same cologne he wore in college. Something about that tugs at my heart, reminds me of the guy I once knew so well I would have sworn we'd be in each other's lives forever.

Don't let him fool you, Mari. Don't make this more than it is. Clearing my head of sentimental notions, I lift my ass and impale myself on Javi, contracting around him on each stroke. Making good on his promise, he fondles me, ghosting his fingers over my lips and clit, then toying in my wetness.

"Jesus," I pant out. "You are *really* good with your hands."

My thighs are burning, but it's the kind of ache that only intensifies every sensation. I'm sweating, working him furiously, and trying to maintain a rhythm while he overwhelms me with his touch, until he grasps my waist and takes over, lifting then dragging me down as he plunges upward.

"Oh my God, Javi, yes," I say, sitting up, "don't stop."

"Touch yourself, baby," he says, and my fingers fly across my clit. I rub, and I rub, while he fucks me from below, the corded muscles of his forearms straining from the effort.

Javi doesn't even have to ask if I'm close. He's so attuned, his gaze locked on my face, there's *no way* he won't know the moment the first tremor pulses through me. It doesn't take long either. My heart pounds, my ears throb, and a burst of heat surges up my sternum as the orgasm rolls through and over me. The force of it stuns me into silence. Fittingly, my mouth forms the shape of an O, but no sound comes out. Then all I can do is lock my thighs around Javi's hips as he bucks under the assault of his own climax and shouts my name.

Pure. Bliss.

I collapse against him and try to catch my breath. "Holy shit, I'm going to need carbs and electrolytes before we move to round two."

He chuckles. "Mighty forward of you to assume we're doing this again."

I rise up, placing my elbows on the mattress and caging him in so that his face is centimeters from mine. "Or we could end it here?"

Javi lifts his head and captures my mouth. Against my lips he says, "Definitely not. A million times wouldn't be enough."

"A million times sounds impossible."

"A goal worth striving for," he says, wearing a lazy grin and watching me through heavy-lidded eyes.

I return his expression with a satisfied smile of my own, but inside I'm smacking a hand across my forehead. What the hell was I thinking? Treating Javi like any other man has never been my strong suit. But now? He's given me a glimpse of what we could be. And once again shown me that there's just something about him that speaks to my soul.

Or is *this* why it's described as mind-altering sex?

Because my brain is *definitely* scrambled, and that can only mean danger for my tender heart.

CHAPTER 23

Javi

Two Years and Two Months Before the Wedding

I'm staring at the ceiling as Mari sleeps soundly, her head resting against my chest. My arms are aching and my neck is stiff. I stick out my tongue. Yeah, that's sore too. I slip out from under Mari, throw on my boxers and jeans, and walk on Jell-O legs to grab a water from the minifridge. If she tries for round four I'm going to cry. The woman is as relentless in bed as she is outside it.

Leaning against the counter in the living area, I survey the room, eventually drifting over to the desk. Mari's planner sits open, a steel-tipped mechanical pencil resting on it. The month's entries are riddled with so many items there's hardly any empty space left. Her days seem to be nothing but meetings, appointments, and reminders. She's even jotted a time next Tuesday evening to call her mother. A flash of light on her laptop snags my attention, and then I see a notification alerting her that she has thirty-four unread texts and emails. Damn.

I sit on the couch and guzzle the much-needed water. Nothing about last night was a mistake. When I close my eyes, I picture Mari riding me, her eyes heavy with lust. Just the memory of it makes me want to risk another round. But this morning feels fraught. As if we inflicted irreparable damage on a relationship that hadn't even had the chance to re-form. I don't want to be just another guy to her, but I'm also not at a point in my life when I can be *the guy* for her. Not that she'd even want me to. Fuck. I hate being human. I should have kept walking last night. Should have gone home and jerked off and called it a day. But Mari asked me to stay, and despite all the red flags warning me not to, I selfishly took the slice of heaven she was offering.

My hand brushes against her coat, which is carefully draped over a sofa arm. Is this cashmere? Where the hell does cashmere come from anyway? I tug on the lapel and glance at the label. Dolce & Gabbana. Even I know that shit is expensive. Sighing, I lean back and close my eyes. That coat is a form-fitting reminder that I am not, and never will be, on Mari's level.

"What are you doing out here?"

My eyes pop open, and my chest tightens at the sight of her. She's standing in the archway that leads to the bedroom, a sheet wrapped around her body, her voluminous curls tousled to one side. She looks . . . beautiful. Irresistible. And utterly out of reach. Which is a strange thing to think considering what happened last night, but it's true. In the light of day, I can't ignore that Mari remains unattainable. Sex didn't bring us closer together; it only underscored that in terms of everything else we've grown farther apart.

I point to the water bottle in my other hand. "I was thirsty."

She takes one step toward me, then hesitates. "Are you coming back to bed?"

"I need to head out soon," I say, bracing my neck. "I'm due on set at nine a.m. I have a speaking role."

Her eyes widen. "That's great."

"Don't get too excited. I literally say, 'I have a reservation for two under Ramirez.'"

"Hey, the Latine rep counts for something," she says, tucking the sheet beneath her before she sits next to me. "How any movie set in New York can get away with having no people of color is beyond me."

"It's magical realism." I shrug. "Or magical *surrealism*."

She huffs. "Magical erasure too."

After a few beats of silence, she asks, "So, want to talk about it?"

"Talk about what?"

"The student debt crisis and its effect on our nation's economy," she deadpans.

I nod gravely. "I mean, the threat to the housing market is real."

She bumps me with her shoulder. "C'mon, Javi, this is me you're talking to. And we're grown-ups. Or we're supposed to be."

"Fine, let's talk," I say, taking her hand in mine. "Can we grab coffee somewhere nearby? I'm wiped out."

She gives me a suggestive smile. "Put it on ya last night, didn't I?"

She sure did. Our chemistry isn't the problem—but everything else is.

* * *

Mari takes me to a crowded coffee shop around the block from the hotel. We order regular coffees and take them to a corner that's partially obscured by the jackets hanging on a vintage coatrack. Across from me, Mari quietly fixes her cup of coffee, the sugar in the glass shaker she's holding flowing like sand in an hourglass.

"Do you want some coffee with that sugar?" I ask.

"It's seven a.m., Javi," she says in a don't-fuck-with-me tone.

I throw up my hands then sip my coffee, seizing on the moment to study her in the morning light. She's dressed more casually than when I first saw her, a pair of worn jeans sitting low on her hips. The all-white Adidas she's sporting feel like a flex, as if she's reminding me that she's always had an impressive sneaker game. Her lips shimmer under the shop's overheads, but she's otherwise makeup free, most of her curls tucked under a knit beanie with a pompom on top. If I were asked to describe an outfit tailor-made to disarm me, what Mari's wearing now would be my answer. There's history here, a stroll down memory lane to a time when Mari and I couldn't imagine being anything other than the very best of friends. Plus, she looks adorable. And judging by the attention she got when we walked in, I'm not the only one who thinks so.

She blows out a breath and leans back in her chair, a coffee stirrer in her hand. "The floor is yours, my friend."

"Okay, well, I'll start with this: Last night was amazing. Everything I hoped it would be and more."

She sips her coffee, then blows on it, and I focus really hard on not staring at her lips. "But . . ."

I lean back and stare at her. "That's your line."

She laughs. "What? Why me?"

"Because it will *always* be you."

"You're gaslighting me right now. Admit it."

I shrug. "Then it wouldn't be gaslighting." A few beats of silence later, I add, "This is when you tell me last night was a one-time thing."

"Or a three-time thing," she says.

I raise an eyebrow. "Or a one-time three-round thing."

"I'm not sure going down on me counts as a whole round. So two and a half."

"The last word is yours. Have it."

We smile at each other until she straightens and lets out a long breath. She sets her cup down, leans forward, and rests her elbows on the table. "Or we could try to see if this thing between you and me has wings."

Her words ignite a tiny flame of hope in my mind, but I snuff it out quickly. It would be *so* easy to disregard logic and simply get swept away by what she's suggesting, but I lost Mari once, and I can't risk that happening again. Our reunion is still new, still fresh. One wrong move, and she'll be gone forever. "Mari, let's be serious. You'd chew me up and spit me out within weeks."

"And how do you know that?"

"Because you're you and I'm me."

She scrunches up her face. "What's that supposed to mean?"

"We're just different, Mari. You have a certain lifestyle you're accustomed to. I can't give you that."

"I don't recall *asking* you to," she says, drawing back in frustration. She blows out a breath and scans the shop.

I give her a moment, then I say, "Of course not, but I'd want to. Or be able to, at least."

Her gaze snaps to mine. "So what I want means nothing?"

"You know that isn't true . . . It's just . . . You're zigging, and I'm zagging. In life, I mean."

She groans, then squares her shoulders. "Javi, let me be clear: I don't need you to be anyone other than exactly who you are. Right now. In this moment. That's enough for me."

"Well, it's not enough for me." I straighten, my eyes searching hers. "And anyway, what are we even talking about? You have a whole life in L.A., and I'm here in New York—"

"Doing what, exactly?" she asks, her mouth pursed in annoyance.

My heads snaps back and I glare at her. "So much for being enough."

It's not until she sees my reaction that she realizes there was only one way that question could have landed. "I didn't—"

"You want to know what I'm doing, Mari? I'm making a living. That's what us mortals tend to do. And don't look at me like that!"

"Like what?" she whisper-shouts, exasperation threaded in her voice.

"Like you pity me!"

"I *don't* pity you, Javi."

She says the words so softly, I wonder for a second if I imagined them.

"I have dreams too, Mari. And I'm working on them, all right?"

"I know you are," she says, her voice urgent and strong. "I don't doubt that for a second."

Mari was the first person to learn I wanted to write a musical. She believed in me back then. She believes in me now. And I know she's likely as frustrated as I am that the musical is still unwritten. This moment crystallizes what we've always been for each other: Friends. Confidants. Supporters. Everything else just muddies the waters until all that's left is a murky mess.

Mari sighs. "So this really was a one-time thing."

I sit up and peer at her. "Isn't that what you wanted? Be honest, wasn't your plan to fuck me and move on?"

She drops her gaze and stares at the floor. "Yes, that was exactly my plan."

"But you miscalculated. Because you didn't count on still caring about me."

"Yes, dammit, yes," she says, hanging her head.

I miscalculated too. I thought I'd finally get her out of my system. Rid myself of the infatuation not even six years apart could diminish. But all I've done is grafted her onto my body and made her an essential part of me. I *want* to be the person who can work *with* her to build the life she's accustomed to. I *want* to be the person she'd proudly introduce to her old law school friends. I *want* to be the person she deserves. But I'm not that person right now. Maybe I never will be. "Just so you know, I never stopped caring about you."

"Same." She takes my hand and threads her fingers through mine. "So where do we go from here?"

"Let's do what we do best."

"And what's that?" she asks, her eyes boring into me.

"Be friends."

Because we can make this friendship real. We can shore it up, give it the type of foundation that'll weather whatever life throws at us. A romantic relationship would crash and burn, and there's no way I'd survive the wreckage. Being friends is the only answer that makes sense. We both know it. So what if it hurts a whole hell of a lot?

CHAPTER 24

Mari

Two Years and Two Months Before the Wedding

Maybe Javi's right. Maybe we're only meant to be friends. But how are we supposed to unwind the past twelve hours and pretend that we didn't touch every inch of each other's bodies? And why am I even contemplating giving this man a moment more of my time?

Because I like him, that's why. Because I remember the guy who brought me ice cream when I broke up with a boyfriend. Because the adult version of Javi isn't perfect, but he's sweet and gentle and ridiculously sexy, all of which is extremely compelling. And also because my relationship with Javi feels like a blot on an otherwise impeccable résumé. As if I worked toward a goal and didn't accomplish it. That can't stand.

I massage my temples, the piping hot coffee I was eagerly anticipating cooled to a tepid and inferior version of its former self.

A handsome white guy with dark hair and even darker eyes approaches our table.

"May I?" he asks me, pointing to the sugar pourer.

"Of course," I say, absently.

"Happy to bring it back. Wouldn't want you to go without."

I look up at him. He's standing at an angle that makes it impossible for Javi to see his face, and after he gives me a wink, I realize that he purposely positioned himself this way to flirt with me. I'm grumpy, but I also want to mess with Javi. When the guy's gone, I say, "He was cute."

"And an asshole," Javi observes flatly. "He flirted with you even though I could be your boyfriend."

"You aren't."

"That's not the point." Javi turns around and glares at the guy, who's sitting a few tables over. "And he has three sugar pourers at his table, so apparently he's not leaving this place without *someone's* number. Maybe even three."

How is Javi that observant? I would have assumed a server had left them there by accident. I purse my lips and blow out a slow breath.

"*And*," Javi says, holding his index finger in the air, "he has a tan line where his wedding ring should be."

Oh damn, that does it. I drop my head and slump my shoulders.

No. I'm not the one who should be dejected; these guys can go straight to hell. With a huff, I straighten, and then I shout loud enough for the attempted philanderer to hear: "Did you two coordinate this performance to show how terrible men can be?"

The guy slides down in his seat and turns away from us.

Javi's eyebrows shoot up to his hairline. "What did *I* do?"

"Have you not been sitting here the past twenty minutes? Or is being a ghost your entire personality."

"I deserved that," he says gravely.

"You sure did."

WHEN JAVI DUMPED MARI

God, I'm a disaster. *Where's your pride, Mari? Where the hell are your bad-bitch vibes?* Okay, enough already. I am friend-zoning this man now and forever. And thanks to him, I know just how to do it.

I roll my shoulders, take a cleansing breath, and place my clasped hands on the table. "Be friends, you say?"

"Yeah," Javi says. "Just like we used to be."

"Before you bounced out of my life."

"If you need me to do penance, I will. It's only fair."

"I'm not contemplating anything drastic—"

"But you're contemplating *something*."

"Well, of course. I'm *always* contemplating something."

Javi side-eyes me. "Out with it, then."

"I want us to make good on our pact."

His brows snap together. "What pact?"

"The pact we made in college. The one about gatekeeping each other's dates. We said we would vet them, remember?"

"Yeah, I remember. We were kids, and you were drunk off your ass."

"And yet I remember it like it was yesterday. C'mon, Javi, it's still a good idea. I'm shit at dating, and I need someone to sift through all the crap and find me a gem of a boyfriend. You're . . ."

"Also shit at dating, sure," he finishes. "But I fail to see how you can help me."

"Okay, stay with me a minute. What happened with the last person you dated?"

Javi sighs. "Um, it turns out she wanted to get to my brothers through me. As soon as I invited her to meet the family, she was all over Manny. It was embarrassing as hell."

"Ugh, I'm sorry about that."

"It wasn't a big deal," he says, shrugging. "We weren't serious or anything."

"Well, here's where I would come in. I can ask the hard questions, the ones the person you're dating would never answer honestly if you asked them."

"How so?"

"Well, I would chitchat with her. I could be like, 'Javi's great, but have you met his brothers? They're really hot. And successful. I mean, Javi's cute and all that, but his brothers sing, and have money, and—'"

"All right, all right, there's no need to get so immersed in the role." Javi leans forward and rests an elbow on the table. "Let's say I'm *cautiously* entertaining the idea of making good on the pact. How do you see us doing this?"

"It'd be a thumbs-up, thumbs-down proposition. Either you approve or disapprove. If you disapprove, then I'd respect your judgment and move along. Honestly, I'm often blinded by thick lips and an even thicker dick."

Javi grimaces.

See, Mari? This is good. This is what platonic friends do.

"But once the person receives a thumbs-up," I continue, "I remove you from the equation, and it's all up to me—and him."

"And we'd do this for how long?"

"For however long the arrangement is serving us."

He straightens, then nods. "I'm not sure we need to be so literal about this pact. I mean, what if you come up with bullshit reasons why I shouldn't date someone?"

I square my shoulders and cross my arms over my chest. This is my moment, dammit. I've literally been training for years. "Because, my friend, every contract imposes a duty of good faith, and our pact would be no different. I would have an obligation to use my best efforts to help you avoid a mistake, and you would have that same duty."

"But what if I don't want to date?"

"Then you don't have to. It's only when you *do* date that the pact is in play."

"I feel like I'm missing something. Something big. Like this might bite me in the ass at some point."

"Why would it?"

"I don't know," he says. "You ever do anything like this with Sasha and Brittany?"

"Oh God, no. They're as hopeless as I am. See, the beauty of this is that it addresses the crux of the problem: our tendency to lose our objectivity when we start dating someone new. Remember how you always thought Rob had nefarious intentions?"

"I don't think I used the word 'nefarious.' Sounds like SAT vocab."

"My *point* is, I was so smitten it didn't even occur to me to look for flags. But an impartial observer sees things you're bound to miss."

"Like a woman who wants to date one of my brothers."

"Or a guy who's dating several women at once and claiming he's exclusive with each one."

He cocks his head, frowning. "That happened to you?"

"It did," I say, remembering the jerk who wasted far too much of my time in law school.

"If I could possibly help you avoid an experience like that, it'd be worth it. How would this work, though? Practically speaking. I mean, I'm here and you're . . . there."

"Well, I can be here often enough to do reconnaissance on your behalf when you need it. And then there's always FaceTime and video meetings and all that. I communicate with most of the people in my life through a screen anyway." I throw up my hands. "We're smart people. I'm sure we can figure it out."

"Are we really smart, though? Especially if we're going to these extremes to get our love lives on track?"

Well, Javi doesn't need to know this, but getting my love life on track isn't the only reason I want to honor the pact. I also want to keep him firmly ensconced in the friend zone, and the pact will ensure that happens. "As usual, you're overthinking this. It'll be good for us, I promise." I offer my hand. "So, what do you say? Are you intrigued enough to at least *try* making good on it?"

He stares at me for a few beats, then says, "Yes, I'm sufficiently intrigued to accept your proposal on a trial basis."

We shake on our agreement, and the moment feels promising. Friends don't let friends date trash. And although watching Javi with other women will be tough, that's exactly the kind of wake-up call I need.

CHAPTER 25

Mari

Now

Chloe examines my figure in the first selection, then meets my gaze in the mirror. "You look like you're going to the Met Gala, and the theme is Vulvas: Portal to Pleasure."

"I look like a twat?" I ask on a laugh.

She nods, her expression grim. "One that's been battered by a dark romance hero who wants you to take it like a good girl. It crinkles at the slightest movement, has numerous textured folds, and *comes*—ha!—in blush pink, for God's sake. Pop a bottle of champagne while you're wearing that thing and you'll look like you're squirting."

The lore around the firm is that Chloe once told a judge to go fist himself and was sanctioned for it. Being independently wealthy has its perks, apparently. It isn't old money she's living off either. To hear her tell it, she joined an investment management club at Spelman and tested her knowledge by making some impressively lucrative stock purchases for herself and her family. Point is, she doesn't *need* her job, and because she's scarily brilliant, it's actually *our firm* that needs *her*.

I chance a glance at the shop's bridal consultant, Benji, whose bubbly personality deflates like a popped balloon whenever Chloe opens her mouth.

He studies me with a practiced tilt of his head, his lips compressed into a thin smile. "What do *you* think?"

"Sorry, Benji, I'm going to pass on this one. I know you wanted me to try something out of the box, but this isn't what I had in mind. I'm going for classic, stylish, maybe a touch of edge."

"In other words," Chloe adds, flipping through a bridal magazine, "she doesn't want to look like a twat."

"No, she just wants to be friends with one," Benji mutters under his breath as he carefully pulls down the gown's hidden zipper.

My eyes pop open, and I dart a glance at Benji's face in the mirror. We exchange a mischievous smirk, and then he announces that he'll be back with more options before he scurries down the hall.

"I heard that," Chloe says when he's gone. "That's the kind of clapback I wish I'd come up with on my own. Benji and I could definitely be friends."

I step out of the gown and hand it to the lady lurking in the corner—who's likely worrying that I'm going to mar its silk. "You're both too bitchy to be friends. It's a rule."

Chloe gives me one of her patented smiles. This one's titled "Unbothered." She sighs. "Okay, given that you harassed me into serving as a bridesmaid at your outdated and hasty homage to the patriarchy, I suppose I should offer to give you a hand. So, this is me asking if you need help."

"Thanks for that *incredibly* sincere offer," I say, slipping out of my heels, "but I've got everything under control."

"Thank goodness," Chloe says, "because I don't know what I would have done if you'd actually asked for my assistance."

"Retch, probably," I say.

She blows out a breath as if she's preparing to do the unthinkable. "But seriously, if there's something I'm supposed to be doing, tell me, okay? I have no idea what's involved in planning a wedding—nor do I want any of that taking residence in my brain—but I can follow step-by-step instructions really well."

"I'll keep that in mind, but I truly am in good shape on most things."

"Excellent," she says, dropping onto the settee strategically situated in front of the riser. Chloe's sprawled in a way that's taking up all the seating, but since no one else is here to join us, it doesn't matter.

Benji returns with another staff member in tow. "Okay, here's something I think is right up your alley. A sleek bodice, some volume on the bottom, and loads of drama from the back."

Chloe chuckles. "The last woman I dated was loads of drama from the back too."

Benji rolls his eyes. "Anyway, the beauty of this number is that you can step into it, so no need to worry that you'll smudge your makeup or mess up your hair when you put it on."

He helps me into the dress, a surprisingly uncomplicated feat, and admires the finished look. With all of the flair one would expect of a person trying to make a hefty commission, Benji covers his mouth and circles me, his eyes bright with wonder. "I think this is the one."

"I think this is the one," Chloe agrees, her eyes turning suspiciously glossy the longer she stares at me.

I look at my reflection. Boasting a modern square neckline,

expertly placed pleats, and a slit that will allow me to dance at the reception, the dress is truly stunning. Best of all, it has pockets! Because who doesn't love easy access to snacks on their wedding day? "Okay, we have a serious contender."

"Você está linda, filha," a voice says behind me.

I whirl around, and my breath hitches. "Pai, o que o senhor está fazendo aqui?"

He dips his chin and jams his hands in the pockets of his slacks. If I didn't know him better, I would assume he wants to flee, but nothing flusters my dad, so there must be some other explanation for his uncommonly tentative behavior. "Você está experimentando seu vestido de noiva. Um pai não deveria estar aqui?"

It's sweet that he thinks he needs to be here as I try on wedding dresses. Bittersweet too. Because I wish my mother were here, but she isn't. I sniff away the tears that are threatening to fall. What is going on with me?

My father approaches with his hands outstretched, but Benji stops him with a swing of his elbows and a jut of his hips. "Sorry, no can do-oh. This dress is expensivo."

"Did you just . . . ?" Chloe asks, from her perch on the couch. "Not even my Dominican, Spanglish-loving ass would fix my lips to say such a thing."

"Benji," I say, taking in a so-help-me breath, "my father speaks English."

"Oh, right, apologies," he says, a flush creeping up his cheeks. "Even so, the dress . . ."

My father glares at Benji, who quickly grasps that he's in dangerous territory, puts up a shaky hand, and takes a giant leap backward.

"This is what I've always wanted for you, Marisol," my dad says, gazing at me with affection.

WHEN JAVI DUMPED MARI

He cups my cheeks and, for the love of God, *squeezes* them, causing me to freeze. In all of my thirty years, my father has *never* touched my face; it's disconcerting on a number of levels to be experiencing this phenomenon at my big age.

Benji whimpers as he chews on a cuticle.

"Hang on," I say to my father. "Let me put Benji out of his misery and get this off. I'll be right back." I take several steps, then turn around, my head swiveling like a bobble doll. "Where's my phone?"

"Here," Chloe says, handing it to me. She's biting her lip and doesn't look half as composed as usual.

"Just . . . give me a moment." I trot off like a runaway bride and lock myself in a dressing room in the rear of the shop. After a few deep breaths, I swipe to the favorites screen on my phone and tap on Javi's name.

He picks up immediately, thank goodness.

"Hey, Mari, what's up? Everything okay?"

There's clattering and a stream of chatter, some of it boisterous, in the background.

"Are you in a *bar*, Javi?"

"Yeah, I am," he says, sounding amused. "Technically, I'm interviewing for a bartending position. Near Jeremy's. Figured I could use the extra cash and the inspiration. People talk all kinds of shit when they're throwing back drinks."

"Oh shoot, never mind, then," I say, willing my breath to even out, "you're busy—"

"No, wait! Let me go somewhere quiet. Stay on the phone."

I close my eyes and count in my head while he keeps me on hold. Less than a minute later, I hear a door shut.

"Okay, I'm all yours," Javi says. "What's up?"

"I just . . . Hang on, I need to sit down."

A knock at the dressing room door startles me, and I let out an embarrassing yelp.

"Marisol?" Benji calls out. "Would you be so kind as to give me the gown?"

"Uh, yeah, give me a minute, Benji. I'm taking it off now."

I drop the phone on the bench and put Javi on speaker as I step out of the dress.

"Mari, everything okay?" Javi asks. "Are you safe?"

The question almost brings me to tears. No, I don't feel safe at all, but Javi's asking about my physical safety, an entirely different concern.

"Javi, I'm fine. I'm trying on dresses. For the wedding." There's no response. "Javi?"

He clears his throat. "I'm here."

"Give me a sec." I open the door and hand the dress to a twitchy-eyed Benji, and then I sit on the bench, wearing only a bra and panties. Blowing out a long breath, I rest my head against the wall. "Okay, I'm back, and my father's here."

"Your dad's where exactly?" he says, sounding troubled.

"In the boutique, not in my dressing room. He just . . . showed up."

"And that's a bad thing?" he asks softly.

"No. Why would it be? He's trying, I guess. But now I'm thinking about my mother and the fact that she *isn't* here. She's coming to the wedding, of course. Which isn't the same thing at all, and I'm just sad about it. Did I tell you she didn't see me off to prom either?"

"You did."

"Right. It's just . . . she's managed to share in the big moments—graduating from college and law school and now my wedding—and I'm really grateful for that because she doesn't like it here, but *I'm* here too, and I just wish she were around for the small moments:

the birthdays, the dinners, whatever. Even though I'm an adult, I'll always need my mom, you know? Meanwhile, my dad's out there, trying to be supportive, trying to be present. And I feel like shit for thinking that's not enough. That *he* isn't enough. Ugh, this wedding is bringing up feelings I thought I'd dealt with."

There's a pause, and then Javi says, "My therapist tells me the goal isn't to deal with an issue but to process it. To make sense of it within your life's history, not just to interrogate it and put it in a box never to be heard from again."

"You're seeing a therapist?"

"I am."

"Since when?"

"A few months. The point is, what you're feeling right now is entirely normal. And the next time you see your therapist, you can talk about it, process it."

"Not put it away in a box."

"Exactly."

"Maybe I should pay *you* to be my therapist."

He chuckles. "That'd be like the foolish leading the—"

"Are you calling me *foolish*?"

"Of course not. I'm offended you didn't take issue with me calling myself foolish."

"Why would I? Being self-aware is an essential part of growth."

"Anyway," he says, stretching out the word, "we're talking about you, not me, and I have a suggestion."

"Let's hear it."

"Maybe you and your mother need to have a heart-to-heart. Finally get whatever's bothering you out in the open instead of skirting around it and pretending everything's okay."

"Now you *really* sound like my therapist," I grumble.

"I'll take that as a compliment."

"You would," I say, smiling.

"What does Alex say?"

"About what?"

"About the situation with your mother. About her attending the wedding."

I frown. "I haven't told him much about it. I mean, he knows my parents are divorced, obviously, but I haven't gotten into any specifics."

"Well, your therapist knows about it. And I know about it. Maybe the man you're going to marry should know about it too."

"Yeah," I say, sniffling. "Maybe. I just . . . didn't want to think about all of this today or anytime soon."

"Where's your father now?"

"He's up front. With Chloe." I squeeze my eyes shut. "Oh God, she's probably showing him how to open an OnlyFans account."

"I'm pretty sure your father already *has* an OnlyFans account."

"Ew, stop." I giggle, then erupt into full-blown laughter. "Thanks, Javi. I needed that."

I hear someone speaking to Javi in the background, and then when he gets back on the line, he says, "Hey, listen, I need to return to the bar so I can finish this trial run. I'm probably not making the best first impression—"

"Oh, sure, I understand. Sorry to interrupt. Thanks for helping me through this meltdown."

"Always." He pauses, then says, "So you're not going to put these feelings away in a box after we get off the phone, right? And you're going to give yourself the grace to be sad about your mother without thinking you're being disloyal to your father?"

"Yes, Daddy," I say, rolling my eyes.

"Don't say shit like that without warning me. I just busted a nut."

I snort. "Good luck on the interview."

"Thanks, I'll need it."

"Bye, Javi."

"Bye, Mari. Te quiero. Para siempre."

"Para sempre."

As if I need Javi to call me out on putting my feelings away in a box. He's the reason I've been doing it for much longer than even he knows.

Saturday, May 18, 2024

WhatsApp Voice Message

Hi Marisol, it's your mother. I just remembered something about the recipe: Tell Javi that he should try to get both types of starch (azedo and doce) for the cheese bread. Look for polvilho on the package, okay? And tell him to send pictures! Te amo. Tchau. Tchau. Tchau.

CHAPTER 26

Mari

One Year Before the Wedding

How can you tell someone's a good friend? When your own parent communicates with them through you. I take a screenshot of my mother's cooking tip and forward it to Javi. The read receipt appears immediately, so I tap the call button.

"Hey, I'm in Manhattan," I tell him when he picks up.

"What for?" he asks.

"Tripp's having an issue with the liquor license for Friday Night Frights. I'm appearing at an emergency hearing this afternoon. Was thinking we could have lunch tomorrow."

"Oh damn, Mari, I can't. I'm going to a birthday party."

"Boo, that sucks. Who's the birthday party for?"

"Um, well, I'm seeing someone new."

"Oh, *really*? And it didn't occur to you to share the news? Because of the pact, of course."

"It's fairly recent, so I thought I would wait a little bit before I asked you to do your thing."

"Mr. Báez, you are *not* complying with the spirit of our agreement. I'm supposed to evaluate any potential girlfriends as soon as possible."

"I know, I know, it's just . . . I've been busy. And I wasn't even sure if this was going to go anywhere."

"Fine. I'll give you a pass this time. So, does this unvetted person in your life have a name?"

"Sofia."

"Is it Sofia's birthday?"

"No, it's her . . ."

"I'm having trouble hearing you. Say that again."

"I said it's her son's birthday."

"She has a *kid*?"

"Yeah, she has a kid. It's not a felony."

"I didn't say it was," I grumble. "It's just . . . you've never suggested that you want kids or would want to date someone who has them."

"Well, it's early days, so . . ."

"And I trust you've already perused Sofia's social media accounts?"

He sighs. "Of course."

"And?"

"And she likes to party. And bowl. That's all I can tell so far. No immediate red flags."

"Okay, this works out, then."

"How?"

"Well, since I'm in town, I can go with you to the party."

He chuckles. "How the hell am I supposed to spin that?"

"Easy. Tell her a close friend from college is here for only a day, and you invited her to stop by."

"That's kind of rude."

"It's a kid's birthday party. It's not that deep. How old is he?"

"Four."

"Latine?"

"Yeah. Puerto Rican."

"Oh, for God's sake, Javi. There's gonna be like three hundred people at this party."

"You're right," he says on a laugh. "Okay, fine, fine, fine. The party's in Harding Park, in the Bronx. Twelve p.m. Want me to pick you up around eleven?"

"No, I'll meet you there. If we arrive together, she might be suspicious of me. A drop-by feels more appropriate."

"You're quite the schemer."

"It's in my DNA. Send me the address."

I hang up and riffle through my suitcase. What the hell does a person wear to a four-year-old's birthday party? Actually, my outfit won't even matter. I'm on a mission, and it has nothing to do with impressing someone.

* * *

"Three-thirteen's right up there," my rideshare driver says, pointing at a beige-and-brown bungalow on a quiet, tree-lined street. The white iron fence is decorated with streamers and birthday balloons, and as I suspected, there are more than a dozen people hanging out around the perimeter of the house. Small Puerto Rican flags border both sides of the short driveway. Because of course.

"That's the East River?" I ask, taking in the breathtaking view of the city from this hidden gem of a neighborhood.

"Sure is."

"Thanks."

"No problem, dear. Have fun."

I climb out of the car and wave goodbye. After texting Javi a quick *hi, I'm here*, I walk to the water's edge just a few feet away. Javi's thumbs-up follows within seconds. A minute later, he strolls over, casually dressed in blue jeans that hug his thick thighs and a forest-green T-shirt that gives everyone a partial view of his muscular arms. He's also sporting my personal kryptonite: a five o'clock shadow that complements his strong jawline. On the one hand, seeing him with someone else is a necessary part of my Get-Over-Javi plan. On the other, seeing him at all, *especially* when he looks like this, makes it nearly impossible to remember the point of the plan.

"Hey, there," he says, folding me in his arms.

I snuggle into him a little longer than is warranted. "Hey, you."

"Let's get you something to drink. They're serving—"

A young woman with long curly hair rushes up to us and grabs Javi's arm. "Papi, we have an emergency."

Papi. So it's like that, huh? This must be Sofia.

Javi eases out of our embrace and turns to her. "What's going on?" He glances at me, then taps his forehead. "This is my friend, Mari, by the way. The one I told you about."

"Hi, Mari, so nice to meet you," she says with what appears to be a genuine smile. "And so sorry to interrupt, but I have a bunch of restless four-year-olds and the entertainment just canceled on me."

"Oh no, what a nightmare," I say. "Is there anything I can do to help?"

"I'm hoping Javi can."

"What do you need?" Javi asks.

"So I hired a guy from work to play Elmo, but the rat bastard claims he's sick. I should have known he would bail, so this is totally on me. Anyway, I have the costume and the music. And really, I'd get my brother to step in, but he's too short, and you just happen to have the perfect build and height for the suit."

"You want me to play Elmo," Javi says slowly, his head tipped to the side. "From *Sesame Street*."

Sofia grimaces sheepishly. "Just an hour." When Javi flinches, she adds, "Or a half hour. I'll take *anything*. For Danny! I figured since you're an actor, this would be easy for you."

"Calling me an actor's a stretch. And anyway, why can't Danny's father do it? Isn't he here?"

"Angel? No, he wouldn't even know how to act. He only wants to drink beer and make trouble."

I chuckle on the inside. Javi doesn't need a relationship gatekeeper; Sofia's going to tank the possibility of dating him all on her own. Still, I know him well. He's a softie at heart, and there's no way he won't do this, not when Sofia's little boy is somewhere in the backyard waiting for his favorite furry monster to make an appearance.

"But I don't know anything about *Sesame Street*," Javi says, scratching the back of his head.

"I do! I can coach you through it!" I say.

Javi's eyes grow wide as saucers, as if he's telepathically telling me to go straight to hell without passing Go.

Sofia throws her exquisitely manicured hands across her chest in relief. "Oh my God, you two would be lifesavers."

Javi sighs. "Fine, fine. I'll do it. Little man deserves to get his birthday wish."

Twenty minutes later, I'm outside Sofia's bedroom, waiting for Javi to change into the costume while Sofia and the other parents wrangle the kids for a quick lunch before the special guest arrives. Sofia's grandmother, who I've since learned owns this home, keeps shuffling past me in her housedress and slippers. She appears to give zero fucks that there's a party going on outside and is uber concerned with the strange lady—me—standing in her hallway.

From inside the room, I hear a clatter, then a thump, so I knock on the door. "Everything okay in there?"

"No," Javi yells back.

"Are you dressed?"

"Yeah."

"May I come in?"

"If you must."

I slip inside the room and come to a halt. "It's . . . brown."

"Uh-huh."

It's . . . more than that. The costume's matted. As if this muddy monster took a dive in the river out front, shook himself dry, and kept it moving. Also, there are no monster feet; Javi's lace-ups are peeking out from the frayed hem. In short, this is the Wish.com version of Elmo.

"Say something," he pleads.

"I can't," I say, holding back a laugh. "I'm officially dead."

He points at me with an accusing finger. "You got me into this mess!"

"Me?" I say, daintily placing my hands on my chest. "All I did was offer to help."

"That was enough," he says grumpily. With an exaggerated sigh, he slaps his furry hands against his sides. "This is never going to work. They're going to know they're being bamboozled, and they will be merciless."

"They're four-year-olds; they won't care. Just give them what they expect. Elmo is kind. Elmo listens. Elmo speaks about himself in the third person."

"Elmo sounds like my abuela."

"No, Elmo sounds like someone who's just inhaled helium. Maybe you should practice that."

Javi clears his throat. "Hello, boys and girls. I'm hot as fuck in here already."

"Javi, you can't cuss out there."

"No, I'm telling *you* I'm boiling *inside here*. I'm never going to make it more than ten minutes. Let's just get this over with."

I take his hand and help him navigate the short set of steps to the home's fenced-in backyard, where two dozen toddlers are running around bopping each other with neon pool noodles even though there is no pool to speak of. It's easy to spot the birthday boy, who's wearing a red cape and a crown.

"Do you want me to introduce you?" I ask.

Javi groans. "I want you to shoot me with a tranquilizer gun."

I try but fail to keep a straight face. It's a pleasant day in May, but I imagine it's much hotter in the costume. I'm not surprised he's extra grumpy. Still. "Oh, hush. The kids are counting on you. Remember, it's Danny's big day."

After signaling the DJ with a pinch of my fingers, he turns down the merengue playing through the speakers at each corner of the yard.

"Hey, everyone," I say, trying to project my voice over the cacophony. "We have a special treat for you today!"

The kids turn in my direction, several sets of eyes bulging when they spy Javi behind me. A sweet little girl immediately starts crying; another runs away and hides in the folds of her mother's skirt.

Danny, the guest of honor, stomps his foot. "That's not Elmo!"

A chorus of "that's not Elmo" reaches a fever pitch, and Javi slips behind me as though I'm his shield.

"No, no," I say, wishing I hadn't volunteered to help my friend. "This is . . . Elmo's cousin . . . Guillermo! He came all the way from Puerto Rico to celebrate with you."

Javi puts out a furry arm and waves hello. There's a chorus of chuckles from the adults, and then the DJ plays a kids' song I'm not familiar with.

I dodge to the left, leaving Javi at center stage.

"Hello, boys and girls!" he says in a high-pitched voice. "Guillermo is *so* happy to be here!"

"Guillermo's boring!" one of the older kids yells.

A guy nursing a beer by the DJ booth cups his free hand and shouts, "If Guillermo's from Puerto Rico, he should dance salsa for us."

Sofia swats the guy on the arm. "Stop it, Angel. Don't be messy."

The DJ, who's plainly a co-conspirator, places a new record on the turntable, and the sounds of salsa fill the air.

Everyone looks at Guillermo expectantly.

For my ears only, Javi grumbles, "I'm never dating again," and then he shakes his hips from side to side. Even I know what he's doing looks more like merengue than salsa.

"Guillermo needs a partner," the unaptly named Angel suggests.

"Guillermo's friend can be his partner," Javi says, taking my hand and spinning me into his arms.

"You're getting me back, aren't you?" I ask, unable to keep the goofy grin off my face.

"Damn straight," he says, moving with more grace than any six-foot monster should possess.

I can see people in the periphery recording our performance, and it doesn't bother me one bit. Javi and I are going to tell our children about this one day. Well, not *our* children. No, the children we *each* have. Separately. *Ugh, turn your brain off, Mari.*

I refocus on my steps. And although Javi's a decent dance partner, the kids are getting restless again, an occasional squeal piercing the air when someone gets whacked by a pool noodle. I nudge his shoulder with mine. "Psst, you should interact with the kiddies."

He scans the backyard and gives me a thumbs-up, then grabs one of the pool noodles and joins the others in their bopping game. Minutes into the spirited noodle duel, the kids band together and go after Javi, who makes a big show of dropping to the ground when the children rush him all at once.

"Guillermo gives up!" he says, laughing. "You win!"

I can't help smiling as I watch all the antics. Obviously I can't see Javi's face, but the joy in his voice must mean he's grinning. So much for being bamboozled; these kids are having the time of their lives.

Suddenly someone's standing next to me. When I look up, Sofia's watching Javi and the children.

"He came through for us," she says to me.

"That's Javi," I reply.

"He's going to be a great father someday."

"Maybe," I say, shrugging.

She turns her head in my direction and looks at me as if she can read my thoughts. Now I'm wondering what she thinks she knows. Did she catch me in an unguarded moment? Was I looking at Javi with yearning? No, that can't be.

"He's an amazing guy," I tell Sofia. "Not perfect by a long shot—"

"Nobody is," she says.

"But he has a good heart," I continue.

She points at Javi, who's still tussling with Danny. "And he's comfortable with kids."

"Have you met his brothers?"

Sofia groans. "I have, but we didn't talk much. Between us, I wasn't all that impressed. They're so into themselves, it's ridiculous."

I was hoping she'd reveal something about her character that would raise a red flag, but other than her inability to purchase a convincing Elmo costume, nothing jumps out at me. And that's a disappointment. Perhaps I'm not as good a friend as I think I am.

"So you'd like to explore this?" I ask her.

"I would," she says with a firm nod. Her eyes search my face. "Do I have your blessing?"

Huh, did Javi tell her about our pact? Why would he? That would undermine the whole (stated) point of it.

"I mean, he obviously cares what you think," she quickly adds. "I get the sense that he wouldn't pursue anyone unless they had your approval."

Well, I'm not entirely sure that's true. But maybe my opinion still counts for something. And maybe Sofia wants to know if I'm a potentially disruptive force. Whatever the case, it's clear to me that seeing Javi in a relationship isn't the answer. To move on, I need to focus on me. Preferably (but not necessarily) with someone else.

So I turn to Sofia and tell her what she wants to hear. "You don't need my blessing. But I think you'd be good for him."

She lets out a small breath. "Thank you."

Javi waddles over, his furry arm loosely hanging over Danny's shoulder. "Guillermo needs water and a break."

"Of course," Sofia says. She leans into Javi. "And thanks for doing this. You can take off that silly costume now."

He nods with his big ol' monster head.

Sofia steers Danny in the direction of a picnic table with a cupcake tower in the center while I guide Javi back inside. He immediately takes off the head piece. The hair at his crown is mussed up, and he's sweating so much he looks as if he's just emerged from a shower. And yet he's perfect.

I swallow. Hard. "That was great, and now I need to take off."

"What? Already?" he asks, his eyebrows snapping together. "You don't want to stay for a cupcake?"

"No," I say, rubbing my belly. "I ate something earlier that isn't agreeing with me."

"Do you need something?" he asks, looking around. "Tums?"

"No, I'm fine. Nothing a long nap and plenty of water can't handle."

"Okay," he says. "I wish we'd had more time to catch up."

"Me too, but I'm sure I'll be visiting again soon."

I stride through the living room, practically sprinting for the front door.

"Mari," he calls out just as I'm poised to escape.

I turn around, one hand on the doorknob.

"So, what do you think of Sofia?" he whispers. "Do you approve?"

"We didn't get to talk much, but I like what I saw. She obviously cares about her son, and she had some nice things to say about you."

"Yeah?" he asks, grinning.

"Yeah. So if you're interested, I say go for it."

His gaze falls to the ground for a beat, and then he raises his head, takes a deep breath, and nods. "Okay."

But it doesn't *feel* okay to me. And getting to the point where it does is vital.

CHAPTER 27

Javi

Ten Months Before the Wedding

Mari picks up on the second ring, a wide smile on her face even though she's sitting in her office at seven a.m.

"Wow, this is super early for you," she says. "Must be important."

"It is."

Her playful expression morphs into a frown. "What's up?"

"I did some digging, and you're going to have to pass on that date with Brian Wilcox."

She sighs. "Oh God, what's wrong with him? I checked Instagram and didn't see anything concerning."

"I checked Facebook."

"Shit." There's a pause, and then she says, "Wait. *You* have a Facebook account?"

"Blame my mother. She made us all get an account because she wants us to mark ourselves safe during a national emergency."

She snorts. "I love her."

"And she loves you. *Anyway*, as far as I can tell, Mr. Wilcox turned into a ghost on January 6, 2021. No posts on Instagram. No posts on Facebook. No posts on TikTok."

"Javi," she says, her brows drawn together. "So based on those facts alone, you want me to assume he was at the Capitol. Way the hell on the other side of the country."

"It's a possibility."

"I bet Sofia doesn't have a digital footprint on January 6."

"Sofia and I are no longer dating, so that's beside the point."

"What? When did that happen? Why?"

"A few weeks ago. She's trying to work things out with her ex. For her kid."

"I'm sorry, Javi."

"It's okay. Wasn't meant to be."

She peers at me as she chews on the corner of her bottom lip. "Did you care for her?"

"I liked her. She's a good person and loves her son to death. We should leave it at that."

She nods. "Okay, well, let's think about this a bit. *I* don't even have a digital footprint on January 6."

"*You* are not Brian Wilcox, so that's also beside the point."

"And *you* are a mess," she says, tearing up in laughter. "I'm hanging up now."

"Wait! There's something else!"

"What?"

"He went to a Kid Rock concert."

"Well, Kid Rock had his moment back in the day. I'm not going to fault Brian for what he did when he was younger."

"It was three months ago."

"Shit."

"Exactly."

"I never would have guessed."

"Luckily for you, I'm here to steer you in the right direction."

"Ugh, bye."

She hangs up on me, and I don't even care. I'm taking my role as her relationship gatekeeper seriously. After all, that's exactly what she asked for. If any person is going to date Mari, they'll need to get through me first.

CHAPTER 28

Now

I asked for an ordinary bachelorette party, and they organized *this* instead. A two-night rendezvous at Starfish Oasis, an all-inclusive adults-only resort in Belize. One short nonstop flight away from each of us, Belize could easily dub itself paradise on earth, and I wouldn't disagree. I'm mentally kicking myself for not traveling here sooner.

The five of us—Sasha, Brittany, Chloe, Javi, and me—just dropped off our bags in our rooms (Javi, Chloe, and I are sharing a two-bedroom suite, while Sasha and Brittany are rooming together in a double), and now we're touring the grounds to get a taste of what's on offer.

Unlimited top-shelf liquor, butt cracks, and hedonism seem to be the specials of the day. To the left, a group of guests have fashioned their own twerking competition as the resort staff look on with amusement. To the right, an older gentleman with snow-white

Fabioesque hair and an equally eye-catching Speedo is doing planks poolside.

Javi whistles when he spots the guy. "Damn, I want that kind of endurance when I'm his age."

"Maybe you should be asking for his level of endurance at your current age," I quip.

He smirks, then opens his mouth to respond but quickly closes it.

Yeah, wise move, Javi. Because although we're in the best company, we're also in *mixed* company. Meaning, none of the women know that Javi and I hooked up in the past. *Numerous times* if we're counting discrete sexual acts. Now that I think about it, we shouldn't be alluding to hookups at all. Sasha will sniff out our dirty business quicker than she'd snatch a wig off someone who's rude to her, and that's real fucking fast. I'd prefer to not spend our time here answering questions or having our every interaction examined under a microscope.

"I'd settle for that man's glorious hair," Chloe says. "If there's one thing I'd like to take into my golden years, it's getting my hair pulled during sex." Wearing a seductive smile, she glances at Javi. "Is that something you're into?"

"You're going to have to be more precise than that," Sasha says to Chloe. "Which hairs are you asking about, exactly? I mean, depending on the time of year, I can lay the sleekest edges with my pubic hair."

I screw up my face. "For the love of all that's holy, Sasha."

Brittany sighs. "It's going to be a looong weekend."

I pull Sasha along as she cackles her ass off. "You need a sitter."

"And a muzzle," Brittany adds.

We amble down the path to the private beach, a thick and lush canopy of palmettos providing much-needed shade, and I stumble to a stop when the breathtaking view of the sunlit sea appears. I look at my friends; they're all in awe too.

"We're not worthy," Brittany says.

Sasha tsks. "Speak for yourself." Sweeping her hands in an arc, she adds, "I deserve all this and more. Now, let's get changed for dinner. I want to be the first in line at the buffet."

"Because you think they'll run out?" Chloe asks.

"No, because I don't want anyone breathing on my food," Sasha says.

I nod. "Precisely."

"You know the people who make it also breathe on it, right?" Javi asks.

Sasha glares at him. "Go away, Satan."

"Okay, children," I say. "As the guest of honor, I'm requesting that we minimize the squabbling and maximize the debauchery."

"The bride has spoken," Chloe announces. "She's marrying her Prince Charming in less than a month. What she says, goes."

I glance at Javi, whose face is fixed in a wooden expression.

"You okay, J?"

"What? Oh. Yeah, I'm fine. Just a little tired."

"Well, get untired, my friend," Sasha says, linking her arm with his. "Because tonight, we're divulging all of our deepest, darkest secrets, and no one will be spared."

Javi's gaze darts to mine.

Well, aren't we off to a promising start?

* * *

Sasha has secured a prime spot that's close enough to the bar for us to easily replenish our drinks yet far enough away from the DJ that we can hear one another. The latter isn't necessarily ideal, because I have a feeling I'll want to use hearing troubles as an excuse at some point tonight. Still, the air is sticky and sweet, and I'm pleasantly languid, as if molasses is running through my body and forcing me to slow down.

"Okay," Sasha says, a cocktail in hand, "here's how this game works."

Sasha, whose springy curls are piled high on her head, is wearing a burnt-orange maxi dress that skims her lush figure, and her dark skin is glowing in the firelight. I'm in awe of her personal style.

"Each of us draws a card," she continues. "And each card poses a question. You can either answer the question or pass it on to a person of your choice. But, and there's a big *but*, the person you pass to gets to ask you a true-or-false question of their own and you *must* answer it."

"I can't just drink a shot or something?" Chloe asks.

Sasha lifts her nose in the air. "Nope."

"Point of clarification," Brittany says, raising her index finger.

Sasha peers at her. "Yes, my love. What is it?"

"Is this an actual game, or did you make these cards yourself?"

"I made them myself," Sasha says.

"God help us," Javi mutters.

"Hey," Sasha says, flicking a napkin at him. "Be appreciative of my efforts. I got these custom made." She leans over and presses her face into my neck. "Because nothing's too good for Mari."

"And you're already tipsy," I observe.

"Indeed," she replies. "Why aren't you?"

I take a sip of my espresso martini, the perfect after-dinner drink. "I'm pacing myself."

She squints and points toward the beach. "If you stand *just* over there, you'd be a literal stick in the mud."

"Sand isn't dirt," Brittany notes.

"Oh my fucking God, let's get back to the game," Sasha bellows, digging into her purse.

She pulls out some sort of vial and pops three pills into her mouth.

"What are those?" I ask, frowning.

"Magnesium." She gestures at her head. "For migraines."

"Ah," I say.

"I'll volunteer to go first," Chloe says as she gathers her long dark hair in a messy topknot.

"All right, all right," Sasha says, shimmying her shoulders. "Now we're talking." She picks up the stack of cards and places it in front of Chloe, who draws from the middle.

"Read it out loud," Sasha prompts.

Chloe reads the card in her head, then smiles. "This is easy. The question is, 'Have you ever participated in a threesome?' And the answer is yes, and also a foursome and a fivesome. Men and women."

"I suspect much of this game will be a cakewalk for Chloe," Brittany says.

Chloe smirks. "What can I say? I went through a period of deep introspection and exploration in my early twenties."

"Sounds like you went through a period of deep *penetration* in your early twenties," Sasha says.

Chloe grins. "That too."

We all laugh, and then Sasha declares, "Your turn, Brittany!"

Brittany jumps up, her caramel-brown shoulder-length bob swinging with the movement. She gingerly plucks a card from Sasha's hand, then reads it aloud. "What's the hottest sex you've ever had?" She bites her lip, then peers at Javi. "I'm passing this question to Javi."

He groans. "Fine. True or false: You've never had sex in public."

"True," Brittany says, puffing her chest. "One hundred percent true."

Chloe traces the rim of her cocktail glass with her finger. "Okay, Javi, now spill. And *don't* lie."

I brace myself for whatever he's going to say. I don't want to interrogate my brain, but I can't deny that hearing about Javi's sexual exploits makes me uncomfortable. It probably shouldn't, but it does. I make a mental note to discuss it with my therapist.

He swallows. "The hottest sex I ever had happened against a hotel door."

My heart gallops in my chest. Is he . . . ?

"Get it, Javi," Sasha whoops. "Tell us more."

"And don't leave out a *single* detail," Chloe adds.

"It was just . . . frantic and all-encompassing. You know the kind of sex where walking even a few feet to a bed is impossible. The kind where you're not completely unclothed because you can't wait to sink into someone. Like you need it almost as much as you need your next breath." He looks up and notices everyone's rapt expressions. "Shit, I've said too much."

"No, no," Chloe argues. "You haven't said enough."

He shrugs and takes a sip of water. "Well, that's all you're going to get."

It's a superhuman feat to keep my expression bland, to pretend I'm unaffected by Javi's description of the hottest sex he's ever had—sex that I'm almost certain happened *between us*. A swath of heat engulfs my body, making me squirm. I don't like this game; it's putting me in an entirely unproductive headspace. I'm getting married next month, and I should *not* be thinking about sex with someone else. I clear my throat. "I'm going to say something, and I hope you don't take this the wrong way."

"Uh-oh," Sasha says. "Sounds like I'm about to take it the wrong way."

I turn to her. "If you knew me, *really* knew me, you'd know that I wouldn't want to spend this time together talking about the bullshit we did when we were younger."

Sasha's eyes go wide. "I thought we were having some harmless fun?"

She looks as confused as I feel.

"I'm sorry, you're right. It's just . . ." I stand up. "I don't want to do this. It's not you, guys. It's me. I'm going to take a walk." I take a step and put up a hand when Javi rises to join me. "Alone."

No one says a word, and honestly, I feel like shit for ruining the mood, but I can't help how I feel. That was uncomfortable for me, and I could just murder Javi for messing with my head.

I make my way to the beach and slip out of my sandals when I get there. Several couples pass me, strolling hand in hand and reveling in their love. I want what they have, but while the literal goal is within my grasp, I'm not sure the depth of emotion I'm striving for will develop soon enough.

No, Mari, stop it right now. Alex is a great guy. He's done nothing to make you doubt him. You need to keep your head straight and focus on securing the future you've always wanted.

I sink my toes in the sand, then plop on my butt, bringing my knees up and resting my elbows on them.

"Hey, you," Sasha says as she lowers herself onto her knees. "You couldn't throw a fit away from all this mess?"

"I'm sorry, Sash," I say, resting my head against her shoulder. "That was uncalled for. Maybe the jet lag's getting to me."

"It's all right. But I don't think it's jet lag. It was the game."

"Yeah."

"Care to tell me what happened back there?"

"No," I mutter.

"Care to respond in the affirmative if I guess correctly?"

"No," I mutter again. "But I will."

"Okay," she says, sifting the fingers of her left hand in the sand. "So, something Javi said set you off. And I'm thinking that the person he had the hottest sex of his life with . . . is you."

I groan.

"I knew it!" she says, her enthusiastic response dislodging my head off her shoulder. "You two-bit hussy."

I snort. "Okay, Cowboy Carter."

She shifts her entire body so she's facing me. "I'm not surprised, you know. You two have been circling each other for years. More than a decade if you count college. So what's the big deal?"

"It's *not* a big deal."

"Lie to me one more time, and I'll bury you right here."

"Okay, fine. I don't want it to be a big deal, but it is."

"Mari, you're getting married in literal weeks. To someone who's *not* the big deal in this scenario."

There's no judgment in her tone, but there *is* concern. If our roles were reversed, I'd be concerned too. But Sasha doesn't know Javi like I know Javi. Or understand how much I want what he can't give me. What even my parents couldn't give me. And Alex is the right person for me. There's no doubt in my mind that we'd have an amazing life together. Plus, my father likes him, which is a feat in and of itself.

"Sasha, it's all going to be fine. I'm suffering from wedding jitters, that's all. Alex and I are a perfect match. Alex and I make sense."

"Has Alex ever fucked you against a hotel door?"

I yelp. Hearing those words out loud is so . . . shocking. "No, but I think he'd be up for it if I asked him to."

"That's not the kind of sex you ask for. It's the kind that happens. Because you can't keep your hands off each other."

"Hmm" is all I say. "Anyway, what's going on with you?"

She draws back. "What do you mean?"

"The pills, Sash. When did you start getting migraines?"

She licks her lips. "I don't get migraines, but don't share any of this with them: I have AFib. It's a heart condition. At my age, it's likely caused by stress. Totally manageable, hence the pills. I just . . . when you tell people something's wrong with your heart, it's a thing. I don't want it to be a thing."

"Kind of like how I don't want my and Javi's past to be a big deal."

"Exactly."

"But it's a thing, Sash."

"It is."

"Thanks for telling me, even though I had to pry it out of you."

"I could say the same to you."

"So, this thing, what shouldn't you be doing?"

She swallows, then stares out at the sea. "Drinking too much. But good luck stopping me from doing that."

"I don't need luck. It's the bride's prerogative."

"Shit, Mari, don't do this to me. If I don't drink, I won't be any fun, and then you'll replace me with Chloe."

"Chloe's a friend, but she's not you. She could *never* be you."

"She thinks she's hot shit just because she paid for this extravagant weekend jaunt. It's giving *The Other Black Girl* vibes."

"Didn't read it. But Chloe doesn't think about money. She doesn't have to. It's both her best trait and her worst. I assure you she isn't using it to one-up anyone. Besides, she can't. Not where you're concerned."

"Promise?"

"Promise."

"Okay, because she's a basic bitch, and I was starting to question your taste."

"Sash, Chloe's not a bitch."

"A ritch, then."

"What's a ritch?"

"A rich bitch," she says, a *duh* expression on her face.

"That's not any better."

"I can't improve on the truth."

"What about women supporting women? Whatever happened to that?"

She draws back and rests a hand over her heart. "In this day and age? Oh, I'm all for it, but my support needs to be earned. It isn't automatic anymore. And another thing: You know Chloe put Brittany and me in the double room because she wants to have a threesome with you and Javi."

I snicker. Sash is in usual form; nothing's rare when it comes to her. "I'm not even going to dignify your speculation with a response."

"Because deep down, you suspect it's true. Anyway, we're getting off track. Now, at the risk of losing my first-in-class status as your best woman friend, I need to ask: What's going on with you and Javi?"

"Nothing's going on, Sash. He just threw me for a loop when he essentially confessed that he'd had the hottest sex of his life with me."

"And that threw you for a loop, why?"

"Because I wasn't expecting it."

"Well, then, let me ask you this. If he had described a hookup with someone else, would that have been worse?"

Oh God, that would have been ten times worse. And isn't that the crux of the issue?

Sasha stares at me, then takes my hand, covering it with hers and patting it gently. "Like Britt said, it's going to be a looong weekend." She jumps to her feet. "C'mon, let's go to the bar and get a drink for you and a mocktail for me. Then you're going to explain how Javi had the hottest sex of his life with you and we still ended up here."

I take her hand and struggle to my feet. "Sash, *I* don't even understand how we got here."

"That's a problem, sweetie."

She's right. Good thing I'm in the *perfect* place to bury my head in the sand.

"By the way," Sasha says, linking her arm with mine, "when was this dirty little escapade between you two?"

I drop my head. "Seven or eight months ago."

When I look up, Sasha's staring at me, her eyes bulging in shock. "Oh."

Precisely. What else is there to say?

CHAPTER 29

Javi

Eight Months Before the Wedding

"¿Qué es la que hay?" my old college roommate, Jeremy Slaughter III, asks, rising from his chair.

We're meeting for lunch at Spago, a restaurant that seems more L.A. than L.A. itself, and Jeremy's apparent newfound facility with the Spanish language—*Puerto Rican Spanish*, no less—is blowing my mind. "No me digas," I say in reply as we meet in the middle for a handshake and hug. "¿Puedes hablar español? ¿Desde cuándo?"

He throws up his hands. "Whoa, whoa, whoa. I just looked that shit up on Google. That's all I got, dude."

"You haven't changed one bit," I say on a laugh. "Still doing the least even though you were born with the most."

"It's a gift," he says.

"From your daddy and *his* daddy."

He gives me a shit-eating grin. An insult is a compliment in Jeremy's world.

"Anyway, I didn't ask you to lunch so you could break my balls," he says, flagging a server down.

"I know, I know," I say, looking around. "So when are the others getting here?"

"What others?" he asks, his brow knitted in confusion.

"You . . . you said you wanted me to meet with potential investors. Wasn't that the point of this trip?" I squeeze my eyes shut, then open them, my jaw clenched. "Jer, tell me you didn't bring me all the way to L.A. for nothing."

"Of course not," he scoffs. "Chill, man."

Before I can grill him, our server approaches, introduces herself, and asks if we want tap or bottled water. Jeremy asks for sparkling.

"Tap's fine for me," I tell her.

Once she's gone, I lean forward. "So, what gives, Jer? You gave me names. Tanner. Rubenstein. Jones. I did research."

Jeremy grimaces. "It's the nature of what we do, man. People tell you they're interested, and then poof, they've moved on to something else."

"So they didn't even want to meet with me?"

"They bailed," he says, lifting his shoulder in a half-assed shrug. "I'm sorry about that."

"You couldn't tell me all this before I got on the plane? I dipped into my savings to come."

"It didn't matter."

"Why the hell not?"

"I needed to get you here."

"Why?"

"Because I want to back your musical, you dumbass!"

I let out a stunned breath. "Why would you want to do that?"

Jeremy leans forward, rests his elbows on the table, and steeples his fingers. "That should be obvious: You're brilliant, man. I knew it in college, and I know it now. The idea is gold too. But you need to finish it. I can't get more investors if there's nothing to show them." He clears his throat, as though even he's surprised he said that much. "So, where are you in the process?"

"It's not done. I still need to figure out the skeleton and the compositions."

"That's what you said last year. And the year before that."

"Because it's a *passion* project, and I need to pay my bills in the meantime."

"I thought you'd say that. Which is why I needed to see you face-to-face. To tell you that I want to give you the breathing room to finish the musical. Stay at my place here. I'm hardly around anyway. You can write, think, take long walks on the beach, whatever the fuck you need to finish. All I ask is that you keep me updated on your progress."

"I can't just uproot my life," I say, even though I'm already contemplating that very thing.

Jeremy laughs. "Mari predicted you'd say something along those lines."

I frown at him. "Mari? You two talk? About me?"

"We saw each other a few weeks ago. I hired her father's firm to look over an agreement for me."

"And this proposal came up?"

"I mentioned in passing that I wanted to get you here. To finish the damn musical." He takes a sip of his water, then continues: "She seemed to think it was a great idea but didn't think you'd go for it."

"Because she knows me so well . . ."

"Hey," he says, tapping the table. "We weren't conspiring. You're a mutual, that's all. And we both care about you."

It all sounds entirely harmless, but my clothes suddenly feel like they're cutting off my circulation. I can't help but wonder whether they see me as a charity case. Whether they discussed lighting a fire under my ass and came up with this plan.

The server returns to take our orders, interrupting my train of thought. That's probably for the best.

When she's gone, I say, "I'm actually going to see her later tonight."

"Mari?"

"Yeah. She's dating some new guy. Going to meet up with them at a restaurant in Culver City, and then, because I'm such a good friend, I'm going over to her place to put together a bookshelf."

"You know you can buy fully assembled bookcases these days, right?"

"Just doing what was asked of me," I say.

Jeremy sighs. "Back to this date. That doesn't bother you? Seeing Mari with other men?"

I draw back and tilt my head. "Why would it?"

"Oh, c'mon, Javi, this is me. That woman had you whipped from the moment you met her."

"We're friends."

"I don't doubt that."

"It's safer that way."

"For whom?"

"For both of us."

"Okay. Whatever. I'm not here to analyze your friendship with Mari. Just remember that I'd better get an invitation to your wedding."

"Yeah, that's not happening," I say, shaking my head.

"Are you dating anyone?" he asks.

I shrug. "Not really."

He gives me that damn shit-eating grin again. "I rest my case, then."

"There is no case, so drop it."

"Fine, fine," he says, throwing up his hands in mock surrender. "Listen . . . just . . . Promise me you'll think about my proposal?"

I blow out a breath and smile at him. Even though I'm wired to give him a hard time, Jeremy's a good guy. "Yeah, I'll think about it."

Honestly, I'm not sure I'll think of much else while I'm here. Correction: I'll be thinking about Mari as well. Because I'm wired to do that too.

* * *

ME: what's this guy's name again?

MARI: Sam

ME: got it. be there in 10.

MARI: Great. See you soon.

* * *

Twenty minutes into this dinner, it's abundantly clear to me that Sam is the assholiest of assholes. Un pendejo to rival all pendejos. Worse, with the runny nose he keeps wiping, he is either allergic to all organic matter or has a cocaine problem. In the short time we've been here, he's snapped his fingers at the waitstaff, answered his phone at the table, and placed his hand on Mari's thigh.

What are we even doing? Why is Mari entertaining someone

like him? Doesn't she see that she deserves a person a thousand times better than this one?

He's attractive enough, I suppose, but when he isn't being rude, he's so damn bland. I'm hard-pressed to understand what Mari sees in him. It's . . . infuriating.

I stare at my friend, willing her to look at me, but she's taken a sudden and single-minded interest in the menu.

Now *Mari*, on the other hand, is exquisite. She's wearing a fitted, low-cut top that shows off her gorgeous collarbones, and her tousled hair makes her appear carefree. She keeps nibbling on her glossy bottom lip, which is maddening for some reason.

"So, Javi," Sam says, flipping back his wavy blond locks as if he's posing for a photo, "Mari tells me you're a jack of all trades."

Mari finally lifts her gaze from the menu and meets mine, her lips flattened into a thin line.

"Did she?" I say, still peering at her.

"Well, yeah. She said you act, you bartend, you write." He turns to Mari. "What was it again? A play or something?"

"All accurate. She could have just sent you my résumé."

Mari slams the menu closed. Now her nostrils are flaring.

Good. Why the hell is this guy in my business? And why the hell is she talking with Jeremy about me?

"Where's our server anyway?" she asks, swiveling her head to scan the cavernous dining area.

I lean forward and place my clasped hands on the table. "Probably hiding in the kitchen considering Sam here snapped his fingers at her."

"Are you okay?" she asks me.

"I'm fine," I say, leaning back in my chair.

Sam looks between Mari and me, then swallows thickly. Even he can tell this evening isn't going well.

He straightens in his seat when our server arrives, his eyes locked on her as if she's a lifeline he sorely needs. "Ah, here she is!"

Our server—Amanda, according to her name tag—wisely regards Sam with suspicion. "Does anyone have questions about the menu?"

Not surprisingly, Sam has numerous questions, and as he runs through them, I cock my head at Mari, my eyebrows drawn together. This dinner is a waste of everyone's time. I'd rather be alone with my friend. I'd rather catch up with her. Ask her how things are going with the firm, her mom, the aloe vera plant she's trying to nurse back to health.

Okay, maybe I'm also pissed that the potential investors I'd expected to meet with bailed on *The Mailroom* before I could tell them all about it. So now I'm annoyed that I don't have good news to share. And yeah, I'm a little hurt that Mari never mentioned that she and Jeremy talked about me. There's just a cyclone of thoughts whirling in my head, and I'm not likely to be good company until it dissipates.

Sam orders a crabcake entrée. Mari orders salmon.

"And you, sir?" Amanda asks me.

"Can I just skip to dessert? Move this along, perhaps?"

Amanda snorts, and I smile at her in return.

Mari clears her throat. "He'll have the skirt steak—medium—garlic mash, and the asparagus tips."

"That sounds perfect, actually," I say, handing my menu to Amanda. "Just what I would have ordered."

"I know," Mari says flatly. "That's why I ordered it."

Okay, so now we're both annoyed. This is a shit day, and I'm over it.

Amanda scurries away, leaving our disastrous trio to brood on our own. If someone dropped us on a deserted island and tasked us with working together to survive, we'd perish, no question. I look over at Mari, who's uncharacteristically quiet and wearing a scowl. Damn, I'm the person responsible for her mood. Not Sam, me. Maybe *I'm* the asshole. But I can salvage this. For Mari's sake.

"So, Sam, what keeps you busy?"

It's how I usually phrase questions aimed at getting to know someone. Ever since my mother told me that asking someone what they "do for a living" is rude.

"I'm a finance guy," he says, settling into his chair as if he's preparing to recite a dissertation on the topic.

I humor him. "What does that mean exactly?"

"So, I'm a venture capitalist. That's how Mari and I met. She was a speaker on a panel about the legal implications of investing in startups." A corner of his mouth lifts as he meets Mari's gaze. "I also do some investing of my own. Side projects. Mostly in the entertainment industry. Not a musical or anything like that, but I can't say it's out of the question."

My gaze snaps to Mari. Is that what this evening is really about? She's engaging in matchmaking for my career? It would explain why she's giving this guy even a minute of her time. Oh hell no. I am absolutely ending this now.

"Well, it won't be mine," I tell him. "Someone else has expressed interest."

Mari's eyes grow wide, and her shoulders rise. "Who?"

"Jeremy."

"That's fantastic news," she says, beaming at me.

"Not sure I'll accept. It's something to think about, though."

Mari squints. "But—"

"Here we are, friends," Amanda says, placing my meal in front of me. Another server handles Mari's and Sam's plates.

I give Mari a pointed look. "We'll talk about it later." Meaning, she and I will talk about it when we're alone. Sam can go somewhere and invest in a personality for all I care. "Let's dig in."

She forces a smile, then nods.

The conversation won't be pretty, but it's obviously necessary—and long overdue.

CHAPTER 30

Mari

Eight Months Before the Wedding

After dropping Sam off at his place and declining his invitation to come in for a "nightcap," I make a quick stop at my condo to squeeze out of my Spanx and change into clothes comfortable enough to kick Javi's ass in. I slip on a pair of flip-flops—bypassing the Havaianas for the Kenners since I'm aiming for agility—and grab my car keys off the entryway table.

In the elevator, I cross my arms over my chest and repeatedly tap my foot. I am empty-your-entire-bladder pissed at Javi. The *gall* of that man. He was rude to Sam, was snippy with me, and added absolutely nothing to the admittedly stilted and inane dinner conversation.

Okay, fine, Sam isn't the most alluring person I've ever dated, but that's precisely the point of the pact. Javi is supposed to act as the gatekeeper. Suss the guy out and give me his thoughts *after* the meal. Instead, Javi was ornery from the moment he sat down, and

WHEN JAVI DUMPED MARI

I cannot for the life of me understand what bug crawled up his butt and died there.

Once at the hotel, I stomp over to the check-in desk and ask the clerk to let Javi know I'm here. After the clerk directs me to room 303, I bang on the door.

"Hang on, damn," I hear Javi shout from inside the room.

He swings the door open, his bare chest staring back at me, a towel hung around his shoulders. In seconds, I take in the jaw-dropping sight before me: his pecs, his chiseled arms, the abs, the happy trail that disappears beneath his navy joggers.

I walk past him and whirl around. "I am so mad at you right now."

"Why?" he says on a chuckle. "I haven't done anything."

"You were an ass tonight."

"No," he says, shaking his head as he closes the door. "Your date was an ass. You know that, right?"

"That's the point of all this, Javi. He seemed like a decent guy, so when he asked me out, I said yes. And this is where you're supposed to come in. Instead, you seemed entirely put out by the whole thing. As if you didn't want to be bothered."

"Because I *didn't* want to be bothered," he says, flinging the towel onto a nearby armchair. "That guy doesn't deserve to breathe the same air as you." He presses his palms together in a pleading gesture. "You gotta help me out here, Mari. *You* are the first line of defense. There's a floor, and that guy was *well* below it."

"You could tell all that in the three minutes you spared to even speak with him?"

"I could tell the moment he snapped his fingers to get our server's attention."

"Oh yes," I huff, pacing in front of the door. "We mustn't forget about Amanda."

He draws back, his brows knitted. "What's that supposed to mean?"

"You were fawning over her. It was embarrassing."

"I said maybe ten words to her the whole night."

"You said a lot more with your eyes. The poor woman didn't deserve to be ogled like that."

"I don't even remember what our server looked like," he says, scrubbing the back of his head. "I assure you, I wasn't ogling anyone. But it's *interesting* that you were paying such close attention." Then he laughs. Actually laughs.

I'm so angry, I'm practically vibrating, and my skin feels three sizes too small for my body. I don't like this. I'm not myself tonight. And I'm *so close* to saying something we'll both regret. "You know what? It was a mistake coming here. I'm leaving. And forget about helping me with the bookshelf. I think we both need to cool off and pick this up when we've calmed down."

Javi throws up his hands in an exaggerated shrug. "I'm already calm. You're the one who's blowing things out of proportion. The truth is, I'm the one who should be upset, but I'm trying to salvage what I can of this trip."

I draw back. "Oh, really? And why should *you* be upset?"

"Because apparently you've been talking about me with everyone."

"Everyone who?" I ask, frowning.

"Jeremy."

"He visited my firm," I say, unable to keep the exasperation out of my voice. "We both know you. *Of course* you'd come up."

"Well, it didn't sound like a 'hey, how's Javi doing' conversation. You apparently talked about the nudge I needed to finish the musical."

I slap my hands against my sides. "And what's wrong with that?"

"I'm not a fucking project, Mari," he says, bending to meet my gaze head-on. "You don't have to fix me. *Improve* me. It's as if finishing this musical is more important to you than it is to me. Why would that be?"

"Because it matters to you, Javi. That's all. I want you to be happy, and I get the sense that you aren't."

He chews on his bottom lip, studying me in silence while I try not to squirm. After a few tense beats, he blows out his cheeks. "Fine. Then what about Sam?"

"He asked about the person he was meeting for dinner. We weren't talking about you for any other reason."

"So it never occurred to you that Sam might be interested in funding the musical?"

"Not at all. There's nothing to fund."

A muscle in his jaw twitches.

I regret the words as soon as I say them, but part of me wonders if Javi needs a bit of tough love. Or am I just trying to make myself feel better? "Sorry, I didn't mean it—"

He stops me with a hand. "No, you were right. We should pick this up another time."

"Fine," I say, striding to the door. I turn back. Javi's standing there, shoulders slumped as he stares at the floor. "Javi, I don't think you realize how much I care for you. No matter what you say, no matter what you do, there's this core part of me that wants *everything* for you because I think you deserve it. Problem is, I can't want everything for you if you don't want it for yourself."

"Wait," he says, placing his palm against the door to stop me from opening it.

I spin around and stare up at him. "What?"

"Let's not do this," he says, caressing my jaw. "This isn't us."

After a few beats of tense silence, I clip him on his shoulder. "God, I could just kill you sometimes."

He presses a kiss against my forehead. "Pero te quiero." He kisses a cheek, then the other. "Para siempre." He approaches—for a peck on the nose, I suspect—but I meet his mouth instead. Javi takes in a sharp breath against my lips. Slowly, as if he's giving me a chance to consider where this is headed, his hands slide to my backside as he deepens the kiss. But I don't want to think, I just want to *feel*. My hands roam everywhere: his shoulders, his back, his waist, his ass. I squeeze him there. He hisses and drops to his knees, his head resting against my belly as he pulls down my leggings. I step out and kick off my chinelos.

Javi presses his lips against my mound, then looks up at me. His intense gaze doesn't leave mine as his fingers slip under my panties. He dips inside, moans in satisfaction, and pulls out, showing me my arousal. "So. Fucking. Ready." He brings his hand to his mouth and closes it around a single digit, then licks it clean, his eyes closed. I'm blissed out on desire, impatient and needy, strung so tight that I'm panting.

Javi's lips skim my stomach as he tugs off my underwear, his big hands stroking me reverently.

"Come here," I whisper, pulling him up from his crouched position. "I need to touch you." He attacks my mouth as if it's his last meal; I attack his sweatpants as though they're keeping me from mine. With his joggers at his thighs, I grip him, reveling in the way his cock swells in my hand.

"Fuck, Mari, that's it," he says, his head thrown back.

I lift my leg, hook it around him, and use it to draw him closer, bringing our feverishly hot bodies flush against each other.

Javi looks over his shoulder. "There's a perfectly good bed only a few steps away."

"Too far," I reply, rubbing him against my clit.

"Mari," he says, groaning. "I want this. I do. But we need a condom."

"I'm on the pill," I say, as I drag my mouth along his neck, "and I haven't been with anyone for a while. And I was tested last month."

"Was tested a while ago, and I haven't been with anyone—"

I don't even wait for him to finish his sentence before I'm guiding him inside me.

"Oh fuck yes," he says, surging upward as he lifts me off the floor.

The sensation of being stretched, being filled, is overwhelming; it dulls some senses and sharpens others. My vision goes hazy, blood thrums in my eardrums, and Javi's unique scent permeates the air around us. Javi's relentless, his body driving into mine over and over, with such force and at such a pace I can hardly catch my breath. My hands roam over his shoulders, and then I hang on for dear life.

"This is going to be embarrassingly quick," he breathes against my neck a few minutes later.

"Oh God," I say, my eyes squeezed shut, "I'm going to come soon too."

He surges into me one last time, and we both fall apart, our bodies trembling.

"Mari, Mari, Mari," he chants.

I'm unable to form words; my mouth hangs open as the pleasure courses through me, makes me shiver, wrings me dry.

As soon as the orgasm recedes, though, the doubts and the questions wrap around me like thorny vines and pull me back down to earth. Javi and I always come together like this. Like an aside. Like a detour. As if we can simply erase any potential damage to our friendship by returning us to our factory settings whenever we'd like. But I should expect more, shouldn't I? Not just someone who's only with me whenever the mood arises. No, I need someone who wants my heart with such ferocity that he can't imagine an existence without me.

He kisses my neck as he works to even his breathing.

I reprimand my undisciplined brain while I disentangle myself from his embrace.

"I need to use the bathroom," I murmur.

"Of course," he says, pulling his joggers up and tucking himself in. He points. "Right there."

"Thanks," I say, not looking at him as I bend to pick up my leggings.

Because I don't want to see the concern in his eyes. Or succumb to whatever fantastical notions he has in his head. Enough is enough.

CHAPTER 31

Javi

Eight Months Before the Wedding

Mari's been in the bathroom awhile, and I can't help wondering if she's in there just staring at her reflection in the mirror and shaking her head.

That's what I would do.

When she reappears, fully dressed, refreshed, and as beautiful as ever, she puffs out a short breath. "There's something about this"—Mari waves a hand between our bodies—"about us, together, that isn't right."

An ache settles in the pit of my stomach. "What do you mean?"

She dips her chin. "I don't know that *I* even know what I mean, but it's as if we don't know what we are to each other. It's all murky and messy. As if we're doing this all wrong. I mean, look at us, Javi. I had a date earlier, and we just had sex against a door. What the fuck?"

She isn't wrong, but I don't know what to say or do about it. It's hard to move toward something if you don't know how to get there. I'm . . . stuck.

"We said we'd always prioritize our friendship," she says. "What we're doing isn't that. So what happened just now makes no sense. It's chemistry. Pheromones. Maybe a little frustration. But it isn't growing." She hesitates.

"Say it," I urge her.

"I don't think we're growing as people either. Isn't that what this is all about? What *life* is about?"

I cross my arms over my chest. Widen my stance. "So I'm holding you back?"

"Or I'm holding *you* back," she says, her eyes glistening.

"I'm not following," I say with an edge to my voice I'm unable to suppress.

She peers at me for a long moment. It's an uncomfortable silence. One in which she's plainly weighing her words. Eventually, she asks, "Why didn't you accept Jeremy's offer?"

"What?"

I'm not being deliberately obtuse; I'm genuinely confused. Seconds ago, we were talking about our convoluted friendship. Which . . . fair. And now she's talking about Jeremy?

"Don't 'what' me, Javi. You know exactly what I'm talking about. He's offering to back the musical. Why wouldn't you immediately say yes?"

"Because Jeremy's just throwing money my way. He doesn't give a shit about the musical."

"Yeah, but he cares about *you*, he's investing in *you*, so who the hell cares if he gives a shit about the musical? Accept the help and make your dreams come true."

"It's not that simple. Money comes with strings."

"Yeah, that kind of money usually does. Is he asking you to sign something? Because I could take a look at—"

"No, there's no contract."

"What's he asking for in return, then?"

"To be kept in the loop. Regular updates—so far."

She throws a hand on her chest and gasps. "The nerve of the guy!"

"Okay, okay, you've made your point. Now close your mouth so you don't use up any more of that sarcasm."

"My supply is endless."

"That's for damn sure."

She stares at me for a long moment, and then her eyes widen, as if she's had some kind of epiphany. "You're scared."

"Don't be ridiculous."

"You're worried you'll fail."

"Everyone worries they'll fail."

"Yes, most of us do. But we also don't let those worries get in the way of our goals."

"That's not what I'm doing."

"Then why are you always"—she makes air quotes—"working on the musical? As if it's a literal job title. I'll tell you why. Because as long as you're *working* on the musical, you don't have to be the guy who wrote a musical that flopped."

I scoff. "I'm just a guy who acts and bartends."

"And who's writing a musical that will one day be onstage," she says, her voice rising. "And I wouldn't be a friend if I didn't call you out on this limbo you seem to be in. If I didn't push."

"But what if I'll always be just a guy who acts and bartends?"

She lifts my chin and stares up at me. "You'll never be *just* anything, Javi. Not to me anyway."

"You're biased."

"I am. I'm not afraid to admit it." She leans into me. "Do *you* want to be the guy who acts and bartends?"

"No, I want to be the guy who wrote a musical that made it to off-Broadway."

"Broadway."

"Let's not push it."

"Whatever. So what's stopping you?"

"Me?"

"Exactly. So tell yourself to get out of the fucking way."

I thought I understood all of the facets of my love for Mari, but this moment has sparked the kind of love I feel down to my very soul. This woman owns me. And it's not that I don't want to be with her. Or to try. It's exactly the opposite. But I'm not in a place where doing so would be wise. I'm a mess. I'm a work in progress. Mari's anything but. And I know how power imbalances work. My brothers have taught me that lesson over and over again. How the person with the upper hand either uses it to their advantage or feels taken advantage of. I doubt Mari would fall in the first camp, but she'd definitely fall in the second. I suspect that's exactly why she's so invested in my future. Because Javi the bit actor and bartender is okay as a friend, but Javi the creator of a Broadway musical—and it's *always* Broadway, never off-Broadway—would be a better match for her. Plus, there's a snag that could unravel our whole relationship: her dad. Talk about a power imbalance. He's convinced Mari that he did her a favor by *letting* her remain in America with him while her mother returned to Brazil. Every move she makes is aimed at ensuring he doesn't regret the purported sacrifice. But we can't have that conversation. Because she needs her dad's approval. So I have to work around him. Or do what Mari does: seek his acceptance, which he'll never give me.

"Anyway," she says softly. "This can't happen again."

"Okay, fine, whatever you want. I get it."

"We're friends, Javi," she says with more urgency. "Let's keep it that way."

I want to ask Mari to wait for me. To give me a chance to get myself together. To give me the space to make the changes necessary to be worthy of her. But that wouldn't be fair to anyone, so I remain quiet. In my head, though, I'm planning my next steps. I'm going to finish that damn musical. I'm going to get my own place. I'm going to tell my brothers to go fuck themselves. Okay, so maybe I won't do that. But I'll consider a therapist. Someone who can help me work through the baggage I carry around like an anchor. And *then* Mari and I will finally be equals. And *then* I'll fall at Mari's feet. And *then* her father will be forced to accept me.

In the meantime, I'll be the best damn friend she's ever had.

I hope that's enough.

CHAPTER 32

Javi

Now

It wasn't enough. Which is why I'm spending the weekend celebrating Mari's upcoming marriage to someone else. And although waking up in a Belizean paradise is surreal, my first thought isn't about the crystal-clear waters I can see from my room's balcony. No, my first thought is Mari. Last night's game upset her, and I can't help thinking that my careless answer is the main reason her mood plummeted. I tried to speak with her about it, but she came into the suite she's sharing with Chloe and me and went straight to sleep.

I sit up in bed, stretch, and pad to the bathroom. After a quick piss, I flick the light off and bump into Mari. Literally.

"Oh!" she says, quickly tugging her robe closed. "Sorry, I'm just going to . . ." She points at the bathroom door, a weak smile plastered on her sleep-lined face, then slides past me and shuts herself inside.

Should I wait? Give her space? Why am I so indecisive when it comes to her?

I loiter in the living area, rearranging the few personal items we scattered yesterday. After folding Mari's sweater, I bring it up to my nose and inhale the traces of her scent, which is how Mari finds me when she emerges from the bathroom.

She meets my gaze, then glances at her sweater in my hands. "You're such a weirdo."

I laugh nervously and lay the sweater on the couch's arm. "Was just checking to see if it smelled like smoke or food or . . ."

"Sure," she says, smiling.

We're okay. That smile tells me so. But is *she* okay?

"Making coffee?" she asks, peeking around me.

I swivel to face the counter. "Not yet, but I can do it now."

"Please," she says, shivering. "I can't think straight without it."

As I'm rinsing the pot in the sink, I say, "You disappeared on us last night."

She settles onto one of the counter stools. "I went for a walk on the beach, and then Sasha joined me. And well, you know how Sash can be, so we ended up playing Spades with some of the bar staff. Benito makes a mean rum punch, by the way."

"I'll keep that in mind."

"What did you guys do?"

"Brittany escaped to the room. Chloe and I sat by the pool for a bit, then came back here."

"Hmm" is all she says in response.

I fiddle with the coffeepot and get the drip going, and then I turn to her. "Look, I just wanted to clear the air. About what I said last night during the game. I was just speaking the truth, but I didn't think about how uncomfortable that would be for you, and I should have. I'm sorry."

She waves off my apology. "It's all good. Really. I was just thrown off. And I'm stressed. I'm getting married in less than a month."

My heart does a double thump in my chest. "Second thoughts?"

"Not at all. I'm just a perfectionist, as you know. My mind can't stop thinking about the thousand and one things I need to do before the big day. I mean, we haven't even put together a list of songs for the DJ, although Alex claims he'll take care of it."

I hand her a cup of coffee with cream and three sugars—just like she used to like it.

"Thanks," she says, before taking a sip. She licks her lips, then hums her appreciation, and I do my best to pretend that none of that affects me in any way.

Clearing my throat, I say, "Well, putting together a list is easy. How many songs do you need?"

"DJ says twenty-five to thirty. She just wants a sense of the vibe we're going for."

"Might be better to start with the songs you absolutely do *not* want to be played and go from there."

"Ooh, that's a good point," she says, grinning.

"Hang on." I jog back to the bedroom and grab my phone. "I'll type the songs in my notes app."

"We don't have to do this," she says on a laugh.

"Why not? I'm your man of honor. Shouldn't I help with something?"

She rolls her eyes, a smile tugging at her lips. "All right, fine."

We move to the couch, taking our coffees with us, and face each other.

"Okay, number one song you don't want played at your wedding. Go."

Nursing her mug, Mari answers without hesitation. "'Macarena.'"

"What? I've been practicing the dance ever since you told me you were getting married."

"Absolutely not," she says, her nose in the air.

"Okay, okay," I say as I start the list on my phone. "What else?"

"'Baby Got Back,'" she says, setting her coffee down.

"But think of all the Beckys!"

"There is not a single Becky on my guest list," she says, trying but failing to keep a straight face.

"Think of Chloe, then. She's definitely a 'Baby Got Back' kind of girl. Shit, she probably knows all the lyrics."

She snorts. "Absolutely not. 'Despacito' can go also."

I drop my phone onto the seat cushion and slap a hand against my forehead. "Now you've gone too far."

"Actually, that one can stay. Luis Fonsi could sing the phone book and sound good."

"What about 'WAP'?"

"Good Lord, no. My father would expire on the spot."

"Hmm, let's keep it, then."

Mari barks out a laugh and shoves me, but I grab her hand and hold it to my chest. She immediately draws in a long breath. Her gaze slowly meets mine, and her mouth opens a tiny fraction. Enough for me to know she's as affected by our closeness as I am.

"Oh God, I'm hungry," she blurts. Her eyes widen, and then she jumps up. "For food. We should get dressed!"

"Sure," I say, trying to remember what we were doing seconds ago. "But wait, the list." I chuckle. "I'm going to send it to Alex. See if he can take a joke."

"He can take a joke," she says, pouting as if she's offended on his behalf.

"We'll see about that," I say. "I'm going to add a few more too."

"Whatever," she says, striding away. "See you at breakfast."

When she's gone, I shoot Alex a quick text: *Mari told me about the list for the DJ. This should do the trick.* He responds within seconds: *Thanks. I'll take a look when I'm not driving. Having fun?*

I don't know how to answer that. Am I having fun spending time with her? Always. Am I having fun celebrating Mari's impending marriage to him? No. Every second that brings me closer to that fateful day is a second I regret. But I hit the thumbs-up option anyway and call it a day.

CHAPTER 33

Mari

Now

After breakfast, the group heads out to the beach and secures one of the first-come, first-serve cabanas that sit on a low dock directly above the sparkling waters of the Caribbean. I let my legs hang off the planks, dipping my toes and enjoying the shade. A school of herring zigzagging through the water snags my attention, but it's gone so quickly I wonder if it was a mirage.

"This is the life," Sasha says from her spot on the bed beneath our canopy. She's wearing a polka-dot bikini that's doing very good things for her figure and a wide-brimmed hat that harks back to the pinup models of the 1950s.

Brittany sits beside Sasha, wearing a practical navy suit with a square neckline, her nose inches away from her e-reader. She lifts her sunglasses and watches Chloe and Javi swim around. Chloe's attempting to dunk Javi, but he's evading her efforts, ducking underneath the water whenever she gets close enough to tackle him.

"Those two seem to be getting along," Brittany observes.

"Indeed," Sasha says.

I shrug and pretend I haven't noticed. "Chloe gets along with everyone."

"Not me," Sasha singsongs.

Chloe screams in delight when Javi grabs her ankles, and then she kicks at him and swims away.

"Hey, Campos," Javi says as he treads water. "Coming in?"

"Not yet," I yell back, refusing to meet his gaze.

Instead of joining them, I lift my face to the sun and close my eyes. Doing so has the desirable effect of shutting out the image of Javi submerged in the sea, water droplets clinging to his sharp jaw and his broad, sun-bronzed shoulders.

Gah. Now would be a perfect time to mentally run through the list of tasks I need to complete before the wedding. But I can't do that with all this fucking *noise*.

Oh God, I'm being a brat. On a vacation in my honor, no less. How petty am I to begrudge my friends having a little fun?

"Are you drafting a brief in your head?" Javi asks.

I stick my tongue out at him. "No."

"What are you doing, then?"

"Running through my to-do lists."

"Not the point of this trip, Mari. Come in here so I can show you how to have fun."

"Damn," Sasha purrs. "You don't have to make it sound so dirty."

"Mind out the gutter, Sasha." Javi twirls around, hiding his face, and then he floats on his back and closes his eyes.

I crane my neck to look at Sasha and wrinkle my nose at her when she finally spares a glance in my direction. She's zero percent intimidated and simply raises a brow at me. Brittany looks between us, her eyes narrowing as if she's trying to piece a puzzle together.

That's not even the annoying part. No, the annoying part is Javi's suggestion that I don't know how to have fun. I most certainly do—in theory. In actuality, I never give myself *time* to have fun anymore. Every hour of every day is accounted for, including the ones I set aside for sleep. Alex and I aren't even going on a honeymoon; we agreed it would be nearly impossible to sync our schedules and we're both too busy at work to take any more time off. We're alike in this sense—both driven, both goal-oriented, both practical. Alex doesn't complain when I stay at the office until midnight; instead, he uses it as an opportunity to do the same, and then we return to either my place or his afterward.

There's another way, a voice inside me implores. But I ignore it. A structured life isn't an inferior life; it's composed, tranquil, comforting. Being impulsive can be freeing, but it has its drawbacks too. Still, I haven't taken a vacation in forever, and this little sojourn is refilling a well I hadn't noticed was empty.

I swing my legs onto the dock and jump to my feet. Before I can talk myself out of it, I back up and take a running leap into the waves below. I plunge into the water and hover submerged for a moment before coming up to the surface. It's exhilarating. My curls will pay for my spontaneity, but I don't care. There's something about being suspended in the ocean that humbles you; it reminds you that life here is more vivid and wondrous than anything you've got going on in your supposedly significant existence. While I'm holed up in my office accumulating billable hours, this incredibly complex ecosystem is growing, rebuilding, *evolving*.

When I open my eyes, Chloe's pulling herself out of the water, and Javi's a foot away, a lazy smile lifting his lips at the corners. "There she is," he says with a wink.

I huff. "Going to belittle my workaholic tendencies?"

His brows snap together. "Damn, Mari, that wasn't what I was doing. This is your bachelorette celebration. The run-up to your wedding. Whatever." He licks his lips, and I look away. "I just thought the point was to relax and have a little fun."

When did that become Javi's line? It used to be mine.

"I know, I know," I say, throwing my head back. "I'm sorry. I'm projecting."

"I did notice your nipples are more prominent than usual in that swimsuit," Sasha yells from her spot in the cabana.

Despite the distance between us, I try to splash her while everyone else laughs.

"You're such a menace," I tell her.

She grimaces at the few water droplets that land on her towel and stares at me pointedly. "If you two lower your voices over there, I won't be able to hear your conversation."

Taking the hint, Javi and I drift farther from the dock.

"She has no filter," Javi says.

I groan. "Tell me about it."

"So, listen, I've been meaning to tell you something. Good news, actually."

"What is it?" I ask, my heart pounding in anticipation. I'm already happy for him, and I don't even know what "it" is.

"I officially moved out of my old apartment. Got my own place in New York. My new lease starts when I get return."

"That's amazing. You're making moves. Ditching the roommates and finishing the musical."

"I landed that part-time bartending job too," he says, his eyes twinkling. "Can't totally live off Jeremy while I'm here."

"Sounds like you're zigging, not zagging."

He gives me a lopsided smile. "Yeah."

"Hey, listen, about Jeremy's place: Can I drop by to see it one day? I'm so curious about the condos in Brentwood."

"Of course. And believe me, it's spectacular."

"I bet. Maybe we could hang out when you're not working on your masterpiece."

"Sure, although I assume you'll be too busy being a newlywed, and since I'm trying to make the most of the time I have, I'll be holed up at Jeremy's whenever I'm not bartending."

"Being a workaholic like me."

"No one can be a workaholic like you."

I splash him in the face—mostly because he's such a gorgeous jerk.

He sputters on a laugh, then reaches out to grab me, but I quickly swim away, his hands grazing my heels. I turn back and grin at him. This feels right. Feels like us. We're good friends, and that's perfectly fine. And absolutely enough.

* * *

Oh shit. Javi's never going to let me hear the end of it.

Back at the suite, I continue to scan the contents of Alex's email to our DJ, searching for the punch line. Sadly, there is none. Is he being serious right now?

Attached to the email is a list of songs, the very songs Javi and I put on the do-not-play list. But it gets worse, because I can only assume that Javi added several more, including the ultimate breakup song, "Flowers" by Miley Cyrus, and "Te Boté," the lyrics of which are the very definition of petty.

Since the rest of the group is napping before dinner, no one's here to witness my mini meltdown. I'm muttering to myself as I call Alex.

He picks up on the second ring. "Hey, princesa. I was wondering when I'd hear from you."

"Hi, Alex. Everything okay on your end?"

"Yeah, yeah, working as usual. What about you?"

"Well, I just read your email to the DJ, and I'm confused."

There's a rustling of papers, and then I hear the clickety-clack of his keyboard.

"All right," he says, "I have it in front of me. What's unclear about it?"

I scoff. "Did you even look at the list?"

"Of course I did. I added a few too."

"And nothing about the list struck you as odd?"

"Not really, no," he says. "Should it have?"

This is the moment Javi appears at the threshold of the room I'm sharing with Chloe. Of course.

I wave him off and scoot to the other side of the bed, facing away from him. "Javi sent you a list of songs I absolutely do *not* want played at our wedding reception."

"And that's what I sent to the DJ."

"Exactly."

Alex is quiet for a long moment. Finally, he says, "Well, that's unfortunate."

I hold back a laugh. "He sent it as a joke. To see if you'd be a good sport about it."

"I failed, huh?"

I blow out a breath. "It's fine. I'm stressed. You're stressed. There's a lot of stuff going on. But please fix it. Maybe explain that was the do-not-play list, and the list of preferred songs is still to come."

"Sure, sure," he says amiably. "I'll take care of it as soon as we get off the phone."

And this is why we get along so well. He's so . . . agreeable. Hardly anything gets him bent out of shape. He's calm. Collected.

Though Javi would definitely say he's uncool. But whatever. Javi doesn't know Alex like I do.

"Okay, great," I say, rising from the bed. When I turn around, Javi's standing at the door silently dancing the Macarena. I snort, then spin around. "Alex, we're heading to dinner, so I'm going to jump off."

"No problem. I'll pick you up at the airport tomorrow afternoon."

"Sounds good. Take care."

"You too, sweetheart."

I toss the phone on the bed and fall back onto the mattress.

Javi knocks on the doorjamb.

"What?" I growl.

"I hope, for everyone's sake, the kids get your sense of humor."

I grab a pillow, ready to toss it at him, but he's gone before I can lob it.

* * *

"Last call for any contenders," the resort emcee says, holding his mic by the cord and taking a whirl around the tables of guests. "Winner gets an amazing prize!"

"Go on," Chloe urges Sasha.

"No, *you* go on," Sasha replies with a flick of her hand.

The emcee weaves through the crowd and plants himself in front of us. He's tall, dark, and shiny, the latter a result of his gold lamé jacket. "Anyone?"

"What's the prize?" Brittany asks even though there's zero percent chance she'll get up there.

"A prestige bottle of Veuve Clicquot 2015!"

We ooh and aah as he likely expects us to, but no one volunteers to shake their ass on a stage in front of strangers, most of whom are either already on Drunk Island or one cocktail away from getting there. How surprising.

"What about the bride?" the emcee prods.

I stare at him blankly. How the hell does he know I'm getting married?

"The sash with the word 'bride' on it probably gave it away," Chloe says, guessing the source of my confusion.

"Oh, no, thanks." I glance beside me, where Javi's quietly sipping a water and scanning the crowd, and I can't resist getting him back for all the teasing he's subjected me to since Alex's DJ fiasco earlier today. As I wrap an arm around Javi's shoulder, I say, "But my friend here will do the honors."

Javi jerks in his seat and scrubs a hand across the back of his head. "No. No. And *hell* no."

I pout, batting my eyes coquettishly. "Oh, c'mon, Javi, *please*? You're my man of honor. Don't you want me to be happy?"

He stares at me, his lips compressed into a grimace that suggests he's not buying my bullshit, then says, "And it's still a no."

"Boo," the emcee says into the mic. "Her man of honor won't come up here and win a premium bottle of champagne for her." He raises his free hand at the crowd, waving it as he continues to boo. The crowd delivers, joining in the public shaming. Oh no, this is getting out of hand! I thought he'd experience a moment of panic, and the emcee would move on; this is far worse than that.

I stand and wave my arms in the air. "It's okay, everyone. Just a joke between friends." Unfortunately, there's no reasoning with drunk people, so now they're chanting, "Get up! Get up!"

Javi sets his glass down and eyes every person at our table. "If you take photos of this— You. Will. Pay."

Brittany, Sasha, and Chloe squeal with delight and clap their hands as Javi rises and strides to the stage. He's dressed casually, his olive board shorts hanging low on his hips and the front of his fitted white V-neck jersey stretched across his broad chest. There's a hum in the audience once people see *who* they were egging on.

I sit back to enjoy the show, pleasantly buzzed after two post-dinner cocktails. This is what it's all about, isn't it? Making memories. Javi will probably exact retribution, but that's a worry for another time.

Eight contestants for the still-undisclosed game huddle in a circle while the emcee talks to them, likely explaining what they've signed up for. I giggle when I notice that the older gentleman who walks around in his Speedo all day is among the competitors. He's upgraded his outfit by donning a loose button-up shirt that completely covers the bikini so he looks like he has nothing on below. This is going to be a scream.

A server appears at Chloe's side and asks if we'd like any refills from the bar.

"I'll take one of those rum punches," Sasha says.

"Should you?" I ask under my breath.

"Yes, Mom," she says, with a roll of her eyes. "One little drink isn't going to kill me."

Brittany looks between us. "Okay, what the hell's going on?" She peers at Sasha. "Don't think I haven't noticed that you're not drinking during this trip." Her eyes widen, and she leans over. "Are you pregnant?" she whisper-shouts.

"Shut your mouth, girl," Sasha says. "I would need to be having sex for that to happen, and that's definitely not happening."

"Then what's going on?" Brittany asks, her brow knitted in concern as she catalogs Sasha's face.

Sasha sighs. "I have a thing. It's *really* not a big deal. My heart skips beats when I'm stressed."

"Why didn't you just tell me?" Brittany asks.

"Because you tend to hover and nag even when you don't have a reason to. I didn't want to give you a reason."

Brittany folds her arms over her chest. "I tend to hover and nag because I *care*, you ingrate. And anyway, it's not *not* a big deal. It can lead to strokes and blood clots."

"How do you know?" Sasha says, her head tilted.

"Because my dad has AFib too. And yes, it can be managed, but you can't pretend it isn't a thing." She huffs. "I'm so mad at you for keeping this from me. Why does she know"—Brittany juts her chin in my direction—"and I don't?"

"Why does Mari know you're sleeping with your boss and I don't?" Sasha asks in return.

Brittany whips her head in my direction. "Holy shit, Mari, you *told* her?"

"She didn't say anything. I just smoked you out, Little Miss Sunshine."

Chloe's head swivels from person to person as she throws back the honey-roasted cashews our server dropped off when we first arrived.

"Okay, okay," I say, putting my hands out in an effort to calm the tension. "This is getting a little heavy for a bachelorette celebration."

"That's life for you," Chloe observes.

I flare my nostrils. "Yes, Chloe, thanks for that illuminating contribution to the conversation."

"Yes, yes, yes," she says, shimmying her shoulders, unaffected by the attitude in my voice, "*there's* the fire I knew was in you the whole time! Get it, girl!"

What the hell? When did I become this person who needs to get her spirit coaxed out of her? I take in a deep breath. As usual, Chloe's derailing my thoughts. "Now, ladies, we're friends, okay, and sometimes friends don't share everything they should, or they share in their own time."

Chloe points a cocktail straw in my face. "So is *this* when you tell us that you and Javier fucked against a hotel door?"

I gasp. Sasha cackles. Brittany lets out a whoosh of breath.

"How does everyone know this?" I cry.

"Oh please," Brittany says. "That little tantrum you threw last night was a dead giveaway."

I rest my forehead on the table and groan.

"Chin up, sweetie," Chloe says. "It's showtime, and I have a feeling you're going to want to see this."

I reluctantly sit up and turn my attention to the stage, where Javi and seven other people are standing in a row.

The emcee swings his hips from side to side, then says, "All right, all right, my friends. Here's how this competition is going to go. For those of you who don't know, Tanya Carter is our country's Beyoncé. No, Rihanna. Anyway, we're going to play one of her most popular reggae songs, 'Bad,' and we're going to have a dance-off. The winner will be determined by the audience's applause. I'll eliminate two people until we get down to the last two for the final contest. Sound good?"

The audience whoops and cheers in response, and then the emcee waves a finger in the air and chants "Bop, bop, bop!"

On the far side of the stage, Javi scrubs a hand down his face. Our eyes meet, and I stick my tongue out at him. He laughs, and I'm giddy just thinking about what's about to go down. Also, I'm *absolutely* taking pics.

The music is infectious—it truly is impossible to sit still—so we're all getting an upper-body workout, grinding to the beat in our seats. Javi moves from side to side, seemingly content to get eliminated quickly. Speedo Guy tries to secure the win in seconds, whipping his shirt off and swiveling his hips like he's in a music video. The crowd goes bananas, and Speedo Guy revels in the praise. I'm ready to call Speedo Guy the champion, but Javi gets this peculiar glint in his eye, points to me, and mouths, *This is for you.* Then he peels off his shirt and chucks it into the audience.

Sasha throws her arm over my shoulder and jostles us. "Ahhhh, this is epic!"

And it is. But it's also confusing. Javi doesn't enjoy the spotlight, so to see him lose his inhibitions this way is breaking my brain.

Chloe takes in a deep breath and flutters her eyes closed. "Look at that man's abs."

That's precisely what I'm trying *not* to do. Unfortunately, it's nearly impossible to focus on anything else, especially when he's doing body waves that emphasize their definition, each contraction giving me a different ridge to concentrate on.

"Is someone recording this?" Brittany asks, wheezing and wiping her eyes with a tissue. "For posterity."

"And blackmail," Sasha adds, winking at me.

"Shouldn't the emcee decide who's out by now?" I grumble.

Thankfully, the emcee runs behind the contestants, eliciting the audience's vote by hovering a hand over each person. Two white women who are so sloshed they can barely stand up straight extend their middle fingers at the crowd when they're eliminated, while Javi and Speedo Guy easily move on to the next round, possibly on the strength of our table's applause alone. Before long, four more contestants are out, predictably resulting in the two early favorites making the finals.

Javi and Speedo Guy, who the emcee tells us is Gianni, an Italian-born and Argentinian-bred American retiree with seven children, move to opposite sides of the stage to plan their final efforts to win over the crowd. Javi and the emcee put their heads together, then signal a few of the resort staff over. What is he up to?

My gaze snags on Gianni as he does push-ups on the stage in preparation for the battle. How is any of this happening? Will Javi ever live down his defeat by a seventy-year-old man unironically wearing a bikini twenty-four hours a day?

I prepare my phone to record the final contest, and when Gianni begins to hump the stage, I lose it. My hands shake as I try to capture every moment of this lopsided battle, but then Javi raises his hands in the air, and the servers he was speaking with earlier step onto the stage and throw pitchers of water at him. Javi grinds, licking his lips and flicking water at the women closest to the stage. But he's not done, because he drops to the ground, slaps at the water puddled on the stage, and then draws a finger across his lips, recreating the iconic moment when Tom Holland performed Rihanna's "Umbrella" on *Lip Sync Battle*.

The crowd goes wild.

And that, my friends, is how you win a dance contest.

I didn't think Javi had it in him, but he's been full of surprises this weekend, hasn't he?

"I am deceased," Sasha shouts, collapsing in her chair and throwing a hand over her heart.

"And I have video evidence that it happened," I say, lifting my phone in the air triumphantly.

"What a way to end this amazing trip," Chloe says on a chuckle.

And it has been exactly that: amazing. Even with so much going on, I can always count on my friends to get me out of my head.

We wait for Javi to collect his prize, and then he returns to the table, still bare-chested and panting.

"That was something," I tell him, slow-clapping.

Handing me the champagne, he pins me with his eyes, then winks. "Anything for you, Mari."

Something about his phrasing dampens my spirits and kicks my brain into overthinking mode. It may be true that he'd do anything for me *now*, but that wasn't always the case. After all, he vanished from my life *for years*, and only a chance encounter brought us back together. A small part of me will never forget that fact.

I suppose my long memory is a good thing. In the end, it's what led me to Alex.

CHAPTER 34

Mari

Seven Months and Three Weeks Before the Wedding

I'm drafting an email to my father proposing that we explore the possibility of expanding to New York when I hear a knock at my office door. I look up to see Alex Cordero, the firm's resident thirst trap, standing at the threshold.

"Well, if it isn't the rainmaker," I say with a smile.

He inches forward, heat staining his cheeks. "It was nothing."

"Don't tell my father that. He's been floating through the hallways since Atlas Music signed the retainer. Congratulations, by the way. You're bringing in the kind of clients that are going to grow our business."

"Well, all these new lawyers we're hiring need work on their plates. With Atlas on our roster, the associates shouldn't have any trouble meeting their billable-hour targets."

"That's certainly true."

He stares at me in silence. It's about to get awkward, so I ask, "What's up? Is there something you need?"

"Actually, there is. I was—"

My father glides into the office, unconcerned that he's interrupting a conversation, and slaps Alex on the back. "There he is: the man who's going to retire me before I turn sixty-five."

Alex has the good grace to look embarrassed by my father's praise. "I don't think I'll be doing that single-handedly, sir."

"No, no, of course not. But people need leaders, and you're certainly on your way to being one of them. This deal with Atlas Music has put everyone on notice: Keep up with Alex Cordero or get left behind."

"Yes, that certainly sounds like something our millennial employees would say to themselves," I joke.

Alex grins at me, and my mouth twitches. It's a moment of camaraderie that tells me he's not completely under my dad's thumb. Thank goodness.

"Well, I don't pretend to know what you people think anymore," my father says, "but I understand the language of success, and you, Alex, are helping us thrive."

"Speaking of thriving," I say, "I was just drafting an email to you about the New York office. The paralegals are putting together a list of real estate agents we can contact about leasing opportunities."

My father thrusts his hands in his pants pockets and ducks his head. "Let's hold off on that research, Marisol. Atlas Music wants us to revamp its licensing agreements, and we're going to need plenty of manpower to get it all done within their time frame. We'll need your help. And the help of the paralegals too. Let's focus on the business we have before we start considering business we're not sure we'll ever get."

"But—"

"We can talk about it another time, Marisol. I need to get on a call."

"Sure," I say glumly.

My father fist-bumps Alex on the way out.

Well, shit. I move the email I was typing to my drafts folder.

"For what it's worth, I think opening a New York office is a great idea."

"Your opinion's worth a lot, apparently," I grumble.

"He's just riding the high of the Atlas deal. It won't last forever, so don't give up on New York."

I nod. "Never planned to. That's kind of my thing: not giving up."

He gives me a lopsided grin. "That's kind of what I like about you." He spins on his heel and walks to the door.

"Oh, Alex, wait!"

He turns back. "Yeah?"

"Didn't you come in here to ask me something? What's up?"

"Right! I'm operating on my C game," he says, shaking his head. "I, uh, I stopped by to see if you'd be interested in grabbing coffee or getting dinner sometime soon. Whenever you want."

I immediately think about Javi. About what the terrible, no-good date with Sam and subsequent hookup with Javi revealed. About being stuck. About always wondering what I mean to him. And although the way my father thinks the sun rises and sets in Alex's eyes is a yellow flag, I'm intrigued by the fact that he hasn't let his success or my father's man crush get to him. I said I wanted to move forward, so this is me doing just that.

I smile at Alex and resist the urge to twirl one of my curls. "Dinner would be nice."

CHAPTER 35

Mari

Now

"Welcome to Jeremy's not-so-humble abode," Javi says, standing back and ushering me inside.

I step over the threshold and gape at the ridiculously large space. "Oh wow... I hate him."

Javi grins, his expression easygoing and his outfit—a black T-shirt and blue jeans—matching that vibe perfectly. "I felt the same way when I first saw it. He even has empty cabinets in the kitchen."

"The bastard," I say, my fingers splayed across my chest. "Two bedrooms?"

"Yeah, and two bathrooms."

"Is he around?"

"Nah, he's in Europe with his parents."

"What an asshole," I say, only half joking. Because seriously, this truly is too much square footage for one person. Reminds me of my dad's house.

Javi laughs. "He's a good guy, though, and he's doing me a real solid by letting me stay here. It's exactly what I needed."

I don't miss the way he scans me from head to toe. When he notices that I'm staring at him and likely witnessed his blatant perusal, he drops his gaze to the floor. "Can I, uh, get you something to drink?"

"No, thanks," I say, dropping my purse on one of two sofa tables that span the length of a ginormous U-shaped sectional. I circle the room, digesting Javi's new workspace. Four freestanding chalkboards are lined up against the wall opposite the sectional, and the dining table is littered with legal pads, crumpled paper, red markers, and pencils. A keyboard on its own stand is positioned in front of a highbacked lounge chair. "So this is where the magic happens."

"Or the chaos."

"How's it going?"

"Sometimes it's going; other times I want to throw it all in the trash."

I stand in front of one of the chalkboards. "What's happening here?"

"I'm working through the structure of each of the acts." He points at the chalkboard next to it. "Here's where I keep notes on characters, try to flesh them out." He taps the third with his index finger. "This is where I keep track of lyrics I want to build into whatever songs I write."

"Will you do the music too?"

"No, not yet," he says. "I'll need to collaborate with a composer for that."

"When will that happen?"

"It's not a given that it *will* happen," he says, stretching, then scrubbing a hand down his face. "If there's enough interest in what I've written, I might be able to convince someone to work with me on the music. One of my friends who was in the musical theater department at Belmont, perhaps, if I can call in some favors. Maybe just two or three songs. Enough to workshop it to potential backers and secure enough money to do the rest."

I blow out a short breath. "That's quite an undertaking."

"It is."

"And you're doing it."

"I am," he says softly, his gaze piercing mine. "Thanks to you."

"Me?" I ask, genuinely shocked. "How so?"

"You encouraged me. Convinced me to set my pride aside and accept Jeremy's help. Made me realize I wasn't focused on finishing, because I was too scared. A wise person once said I was getting in my own way."

I remember the moment as well as he does. "That was when you decided to finish the musical?"

"Yeah."

"Then I'm honored to have played a small role in your decision to finally finish your magnum opus."

"You didn't play a small role. You were *the* reason I decided to finish."

I shiver at the intensity of his expression. What is he saying? That he finished the musical for me?

I'm in desperate need of a pithy response to cut the tension, but my brain has turned to mush; thankfully, it senses my panic and kick-starts my memory. "Oh, I almost forgot!" I sprint to my purse as if whatever's in it will save my life. I dig inside and pull out the envelope. Returning to Javi, I hand it to him. "Here," I say, as he opens the flap. "It's a belated invitation. To a party my dad's throwing in honor of my wedding." His head whips up, and his face goes blank. I've never understood the idea that someone can look right through you, but I get it now, and it's not a great experience.

"My and Alex's wedding, I mean," I say, unable to keep myself from making it even more awkward than it already is. I roll my eyes. "Still getting used to thinking of us as a pair."

"Hmm" is all he says as he glances at the linen cardstock.

"Will you come?" I ask hopefully. "It's next Saturday. Most of the people attending will be colleagues who weren't invited to the wedding because we're trying to keep it intimate, and since you're in the city for a bit, I figured you might want to get out of Jeremy's house."

"Of course I'll be there," he says, his mouth curving into a wide smile. "How else am I going to do my due diligence where Alex is concerned?"

"Oh God," I say, throwing my head back. "You're not still on that, are you?"

He shoves his hands in the back pockets of his jeans. "Listen, until the wedding happens, I'm going to put that man through his paces."

"Knock yourself out, Javi, but you're wasting your time."

"If I'm spending my time ensuring your happiness, it could never be wasted."

"You know, sometimes you talk like a hero in a romance novel."

He furrows his brow. "I don't know what that means. Is that a bad thing?"

"No, no," I say. "It's just . . . a thing I've noticed."

"What else do romance heroes say?" he asks, his expression equal parts intrigued and baffled.

"'My heart stopped the first moment I saw you.'"

"Guys talk like that?" he asks, wrinkling his nose.

"Well, they also say things like 'You're so wet . . . and tight.'"

As soon as the unfiltered words escape me, I remember that Javi isn't Sasha or Chloe or Brittany, and we shouldn't be talking about wetness or tightness at all.

"That makes sense," Javi says, tipping his head from side to side. "Telling someone they're dry and loose would probably kill the mood."

I snort and turn away. "On that note, I'm going to leave you to your work. I don't want your ideas to *dry* up."

He gives me an adorable pout. "But I thought we could have lunch. I can call something in. I'm on a first-name basis with the dim sum place down the block."

"Maybe some other time," I say, glancing at my watch. "I need to get to the office."

He scrunches his face. "On a Saturday?"

"Well, yeah. I'm going to be taking several days off for the wedding, so I need to make up for it somehow."

I'm already walking to the door when he says, "It doesn't count as time off if you need to replace it."

I wave away his comment. "Bye, Javi, I'll see you next Saturday. Promise me you'll be on your best behavior." When he says nothing in response, I turn back, my hand on the doorknob. "Promise."

He shakes his head. "Sorry, Mari, I won't make a promise I can't keep."

"Ooh. Gauntlet. Thrown."

It's cute that Javi is operating as if our pact is still in place, but there's no way he's going to change my mind about marrying Alex. No way at all.

CHAPTER 36

Javi

Now

Luiz Campos's home is trolling me.

Lifestyles of the Rich and Odious. It's not the home Mari grew up in; it's the home Luiz purchased after Mari's mother left him and he felt the need to, as Mari put it, "level up." I always knew Mari's dad was wealthy, but seeing that affluence firsthand is more daunting than I ever would have guessed.

The Lyft driver leaves me outside the gates, where I punch in the code Mari gave me and sigh at the prospect of spending an evening with people who will inevitably ask me how I know the guests of honor. How would they respond if I told them I'm in love with Mari and would give my left nut to drop-kick Alex off the face of the earth? Eh, I should probably keep that to myself.

As I climb the steps to the massive double doors, I squint against the brightness of the spotlights trained on the house; there are enough of them to light up the Eiffel Tower. It's not only the excess I'm appalled by; it's that Luiz Campos gets to live like this.

You know who should be the beneficiary of all this opulence? Ms. Camacho, my sixth-grade teacher at Our Lady of Mount Carmel, the nicest, most hardworking person I ever met. I mean, she taught horny middle school boys about the perils of seeking the pleasures of the flesh. Now *that* was a tireless and futile endeavor deserving of a reward.

A woman in a catering uniform answers the door and steps back to let me in, her bland expression likely signaling what kind of evening this promises to be. "The festivities are in the grand room."

"Thank you. Should I be scared?"

Her eyes widen, then narrow before she gives me an impish smile. "Very."

Luiz, or whoever decorated this place, sure likes tiered chandeliers. The furniture's obviously bespoke, or at least it's the kind that doesn't come in a box with instructions for its assembly. In fact, half the shit in here looks like it belongs in a museum.

I smooth my hands over the front of my thighs before venturing down the hall toward the sounds of classical music and polite chatter; along the way, I dodge a few servers rushing past me with empty hors d'oeuvres trays.

The party space is stately, with high-gloss tile floors and ceiling-height windows in an area that's as wide and tall as an aircraft hangar. Okay, that last part's an exaggeration, but the effect on my psyche is the same. A magnificent black baby grand piano rests on a dedicated platform in the far left corner of the room.

It doesn't take me long to find Mari in the crowd. She looks stunning in a sleek white dress that ends just above her knees. Her curly hair is subdued into an intricate hairstyle that emphasizes the almond shape of her dark brown eyes. She's standing next to Chloe, their heads close together as they talk, both of their gazes bouncing around the room. I smile to myself—because I know bochinche when I see it, and in a gathering like this one, I bet there's plenty to gossip about.

When Mari spots me, her eyes gleam with affection, and then she's gliding across the room in my direction, her friend in tow. "You made it!"

"I told you I would," I say, meeting her halfway for a quick hug.

When I step back, Chloe pats my stomach. "Just making sure the abs are still there."

I chuckle. "Never change, my new friend."

"I don't intend to," she says with a wink.

We stare at each other, perhaps a beat too long, because Mari clears her throat and says, "Well, I'll leave you to chat. You'll both be in the wedding"—she crosses her eyes—"obviously, so it's great that you two are getting along. Yeah, okay, I'm going to make the rounds."

Mari rushes off, leaving Chloe and me staring after her.

"She thinks we had a moment back there," Chloe observes.

"That's not what that was, right?"

"Right. We're both still wondering why any of this is happening," she says, gesturing at the room.

"Exactly."

"But we're going to support our girl."

"Of course," I say, nodding gravely.

She leans in. "While providing numerous opportunities for her to consider her choices, just to ensure she's certain."

She's a co-conspirator, then. I wasn't sure about Chloe before, but now I'm a fan. "Precisely what I was thinking, though not in such eloquent terms."

Chloe laughs. "I'm so glad we're on the same page." Her gaze snags on someone by the open bar. "Excuse me, I have a junior associate to intimidate."

"I bet you can achieve that simply by existing."

She turns around and hugs me. "I'm rooting for you."

I'm in a daze as Chloe walks away, thrown off by her statement. I don't want anyone to root for me; I want everyone to root for Mari. Even if we can't figure our shit out, I want her to be happy. That's the primary goal. If that means she ends up with Alex, then I'll have to accept her choice. In the meantime, though, I need to engage in some reconnaissance.

I look up and scan the area around me, my gaze eventually landing on Mari, who's watching me with a frown. I lift an eyebrow in question, to ask her what's up. She motions me toward one of the room's two entryways.

She meets me there. "You doing okay?"

"I'm fine. Why?"

"Figured this might be a lot for you."

"It *is* a lot . . . but I can handle it."

"Come with me," she says, holding out her hand.

I don't ask her where we're going, and I don't really care. I'm with Mari. That's enough. She leads me down a long hallway, then up a winding staircase that ends at a massive landing. A few steps later, she pushes open a door and we're in a bedroom. Judging by the Usher and Rihanna posters on the walls, it's a teenager's bedroom. A light blue comforter and a dozen stuffed Minions of various sizes cover the bed.

"It's a time capsule," I say, slowly spinning to take it all in.

"He hasn't changed a thing in here since I left for college."

I walk over to the nightstand on the far end of the room and pick up a framed photo. In it, a woman is blocking her eyes against the sun's rays as she stares at the sea. "Is this Patrícia?"

"It is," she says, nodding. "I love this photo so much. It's how

I think of her, even now. Sometimes I have to remind myself that my mother no longer looks like this, that she's aged."

"It's hard to think of our parents growing old, but with age comes wisdom; that's what my father says, at least."

Mari stares at the portrait, her gaze vacant.

I lay a hand on her arm. "Well, now it's my turn to ask: Are *you* okay?"

She laughs. "I'm doing great."

"Any wedding jitters? I can parachute you out of here at a moment's notice. Just say the word."

"That won't be necessary, but thanks for the offer," she says, giving me a half smile.

"Then what do you need, Mari?" My voice sounds strained and just a bit urgent to my own ears. She *must* hear it too. "You can ask me for anything, Mari. *Anything.*"

"I need you to be my friend," she whispers.

I pull her into my arms and hug her close. "I am, Mari. I am."

And I could be so much more if she asked me to. But I'm beginning to think that'll never happen. Could it be that I've been kidding myself this whole time? Do I still have a shot? Or have I lost her already?

* * *

Now that the party's in full swing, I easily blend into the crowd and drift over to the baby grand—I can't help myself. It's a beauty, and nothing like the Yamaha electric keyboard I begged my parents to buy me so I could teach myself how to play. Unlike the well-loved keyboard I used in my teens, this piano is décor, ornamental rather than functional. An instrument capable of creating soul-stirring melodies relegated to the role of demonstrating status. I lay my fingers on the black keys, the sharps and flats that alter a note's natural pitch. I hit middle C and glance around; no one notices, so I mess around bit, seeing if the piano is in tune, and it most certainly is.

When I look up, servers are whipping through the room handing out glasses of champagne, and then Luiz taps his own glass with a cocktail fork.

Chloe joins me by the piano, two glasses of champagne in her hands. "Want one?"

"I'll pass, but I don't mind holding it," I say, taking a flute.

"Not ready to drink to their union?" Chloe asks.

"Something like that."

"Good evening, everyone," Luiz says, his deep baritone commanding everyone's attention. "Thank you all for coming out tonight to help me celebrate the fast-approaching marriage of two of my favorite people: my daughter, Marisol Campos, and her fiancé, Alejandro Cordero, who goes by Alex for short. Now, what you probably *do* know is that theirs is a whirlwind romance, and no, Marisol is not pregnant."

Someone in the audience gasps, and Mari grimaces, but the majority of the guests laugh, because that's what Luiz expects them to do, and he's their boss. "But what you probably *don't* know is that Alex is an accomplished musician, and in honor of his wife-to-be, he's prepared a special performance."

So *that* explains why Alex is nowhere to be seen.

Excited chatter runs through the crowd, followed by tittering among the onlookers when Alex makes his way to a chair at the head of the room.

Oh, come the fuck on, he's a guitarist *too*?

"Hello, everyone. I know this may seem a little self-indulgent, but I'd like to share my gift for music with my future wife, and what better way to do that than to serenade her during this celebration of our forthcoming nuptials?"

Well, I can think of a thousand better ways off the top of my head, all of them involving sharing his *gift* with Mari in private. This guy's something else.

"This is a piece I learned in college, which was only a year ago." Everyone laughs, and Alex winks. "It's called 'Mi Luna,' which means 'My Moon.'"

I'm inexplicably annoyed with the whole production, but then he starts playing, and it's as if Carlos Santana is in the room. Alex is *good*. Great, even. How the hell does one person get the luck of the draw on smarts, looks, love, *and* artistic talent?

After a few minutes, Chloe nudges me with her shoulder. "It's all too polished, too perfect, isn't it?"

"I was thinking it's unfair, but I like your take on it much better."

Chloe leans over and whispers in my ear, "Do you play?"

I nod, my gaze bouncing between Alex and Mari as he wows the crowd with his guitar skills, the final chords of his song rising to an admittedly sensual crescendo before he plays the last delicate notes. He's showered with enthusiastic applause, and Mari wraps her arms around him in a tight embrace.

"Well?" Chloe asks.

"Well, what?"

She sucks her teeth. "No, I meant, do you play *well*?"

"I'm self-taught, but yeah, I'm a decent piano player."

"Excellent," she says.

"Why?"

In answer, Chloe leans back and sweeps her fingers across the piano keys. Every single person in the room turns in our direction, their gazes landing on us like one of the spotlights on Luiz's ridiculous home.

"Ooh, someone's challenging Alex to a music duel," Chloe says in an excited tone.

I survey the people in the room, looking for this challenger.

"Psst, it's you," Chloe says before allowing herself to be swallowed by the rush of people moving forward to witness the impromptu competition.

I raise my hands in surrender. "Oh no, that was a mistake. Carry on, everyone, and well done to the groom."

Alex's eyes narrow on me as he approaches. "Not so fast, Javier. Why don't you show me what you've got. Mari tells me you're a musician too."

"Oh, I couldn't," I say, inching away from the piano.

"Unless you're not up to the challenge."

I turn right the fuck back around and plop onto the piano bench, cracking my knuckles as I stare Alex down.

He smirks; I simmer.

The melody that immediately comes to me is the one I've been toying with for months, for a song that will serve as the musical's refrain. It's called "What If," and although it isn't finished, it's nearly perfect because I've tweaked and expanded on it for hundreds of hours. My fingers glide over the keys as I play the intro and first verse, an homage to the show tunes of early Broadway, and then I transition to a melody punctuated by African and Caribbean rhythms that matches the vibe of the character I envision singing the song's chorus and bridge. I'm so immersed in the piece that I'm surprised when I see Chloe and a few others nodding their heads and tapping their feet. When I'm done, I press a hand to my heart and thank everyone for their generous applause. Warmth radiates through my body as I absorb the positive reception. It's exhilarating, a peek at what I can accomplish if I just set my mind to making *The Mailroom* the best it can be.

I find Mari in the crowd, standing in a corner, and she looks just as proud as I feel: She's clapping furiously, and her eyes are glistening.

Alex pats me on the back, a little too hard for it to be called a good-natured show of camaraderie. Perhaps this is the start of *his* villain origin story.

"Great job, friend," he says.

"Thanks. I didn't mean to upstage you or anything."

He raises a single brow. "You didn't."

"Of course I didn't. I'm just saying I wasn't *trying* to."

"Good to know," he says before walking away.

Chloe tiptoes toward me, her eyes wide with mischief. "That was perfection!"

"No thanks to you," I grumble. "Now he hates me."

"He hates everyone who makes him look bad." She shrugs. "It was bound to happen. I just moved things along."

"Great. Now I have a target on my back, and I'm not even sure it isn't deserved."

I search for Alex in the crowd and quickly find him talking to Mari's father, whose eyes are shooting daggers at me.

Oh shit, make that *two* targets.

PART THREE

The Bloom

Thursday, May 15, 2025, at 9:30 a.m.

MARI: Hey everyone

Can't wait to see you this weekend!

Just so you have it on your phone, here's the schedule

<u>Friday, May 16</u>
Dress rehearsal @4pm
Rehearsal dinner @7pm

<u>Saturday May 17</u>
Luncheon and wine tasting @12pm

<u>Sunday, May 18</u>
Ceremony @11am
Reception @12pm

JAVI: I'll see you this evening!

SASHA: who dis 😂

BRITT: can't wait! ♡

CHLOE: will there be a bar at the reception?

CHAPTER 37

Javi

Now

Wow, Crystal Canyon Farm is *unreal*. Now I understand why Mari chose this wedding venue. The landscaping is lush, an abundance of flowers and vegetation blooming as far as the eye can see, and the main building, a barn that's been converted into a multiuse space, is decorated with high-end furnishings and museum-quality art. Best of all, the views of the valley below are postcard perfect. Smells good as hell in here too.

I step out onto the circular driveway and set my suitcase beside me as I wait for Mari, who insisted that I "stay put" so she can greet me. Before long, delicate hands cover my eyes, and I take a moment to bask in her touch. If only this were a different kind of reunion, one that had nothing to do with her upcoming marriage. Haters gonna hate, and dreamers gonna dream.

"Luiz? Is that you?" I ask.

She laughs. "Damn, my hands are *that* rough?"

"Of course not," I say on a chuckle.

"It's good to see you, friend," she says, settling in my arms as soon as I wrap them around her. We hold each other tight, communicating so much while saying nothing at all. She draws back, tucks a wayward curl behind her ear, and squints up at me. "How was the flight?"

"Too quick. I couldn't even take a nap. As soon as I closed my eyes we were here."

"Well, you can rest now. The cottages are fully stocked with drinks and snacks, and room service is available twenty-four-seven. Everything's being charged to our account."

"Nice. I guess I'll be ordering a steak, then."

"Order whatever you like. You're a guest of the bride and groom."

I peer at her, trying to gauge her mood, looking beyond the sunglasses hiding her eyes and searching for what's underneath the surface. She's glowing, her serene expression revealing nothing, but she can't stand still, and there's a current of restless energy buzzing around her, as if she's hanging on to a live wire behind her back. "How's the bride holding up?"

"Not as frazzled as I thought I would be," she says, rolling her shoulders. "I might have gone a little overboard checking my lists more than twice, but there's something to be said for being anal."

I waggle my eyebrows. "There's something to be said for doing anal too."

She snorts, her eyes sparkling with mischief. "Javier Báez, behave."

I straighten and don a serious expression. "Done."

"There's the man of honor!" Alex shouts, approaching us with another guy—a relative, probably—in tow. There's a twinkle in his eye. Pep in his huge-ass step. Which immediately puts me on high alert. Why are they in athletic gear, and why is he so sweaty?

He throws his arm over my shoulder. "My good man, how are you?"

"Fine," I say. "How . . . are you?" I'm aiming for friendliness, but even I can hear the wariness in my voice.

"Good, good," he says. "How was your flight?"

"Good, good," I reply.

If he's going to give me bullshit answers, I'll do the same.

He studies me for a long moment, then says, "Listen, I wanted to personally invite you to participate in my bachelor celebration."

Oh, okay, sounds benign enough. "Let me guess," I say, rolling my eyes. "A strip club."

He tsks. "Mari would have my head on a platter. Wouldn't you, my love?"

Mari laughs. "In the final days before marrying me? I'd give you a pass."

He winks at her. "Be that as it may, we have other, more grown-up plans."

"Which are?" I say, trying to keep my voice neutral.

"Skydiving," he replies, mimicking a bomb going off.

My stomach drops.

Mari's brow furrows in concern. "Actually, I don't think that's a good idea. Javi's afraid of—"

"It's fine, it's fine," I blurt. I'm not letting this guy get under my skin. And I'm certainly not telling him about my fear of heights. Weakness is this guy's fuel, so while a fear of heights isn't one, he would definitely treat it as such, and I refuse to give him sustenance. *Starve, asshole. Starve.* "I'm definitely up for it."

Alex raises his perfectly defined brows. "You are?"

I nod. "I am. Who else is going?"

"It'll be me"—he taps the guy next to him on the arm—"my cousin Joel, here, and my uncle Ramón."

I cross my arms and widen my stance, feigning nonchalance. "Sure, sure, why the hell not?"

"Why the hell not, indeed." He gives me a toothy smile, then glances at his cousin, who's staring at me like a hyena eyeing its prey. Assholes are so much more irritating when they travel in pairs.

"Well, all right," Alex says, rubbing his hands. "Will this be your first time skydiving?"

"Yeah."

"You'll need to go in tandem, then."

Thank God. That means I'll be in someone's expert hands. "Works for me."

"Excellent. The transportation to the jump site is already set. Just wear comfortable clothes and meet us out front at seven a.m. tomorrow."

"I'll be there."

He places a finger under Mari's chin. "We're going to check out the gym and the courts. Want to join us?"

She scrunches her face, her eyebrows shooting up. "Do you see these day-two curls? I would never."

Alex shakes his head, an indulgent smile on his face. "My bad, princesa. I'll see you later, then."

"You will," she says, smiling at him.

He kisses Mari on a cheek, a move that *shouldn't* affect me but does. This man is going to be Mari's husband. Maybe even the father of her children. My stomach twists; it's probably going to be in knots this whole weekend.

Alex taps his cousin on the arm again, and then they walk off, bouncing a basketball between them.

Mari and I watch them disappear over a footbridge.

"You don't have to go skydiving with them," she says. "No one will think less of you if you pass."

"Nah, it's fine. The scared-of-heights thing was so long ago, when I was a kid. This should be good for me. Besides, I need to spend more time with Alex. You can learn a lot about a guy when he's around other men."

She looks askance at me. "Javi, please don't get yourself hurt trying to find something wrong with Alex. It isn't worth it."

"Marisol Campos, it *is* worth it, and I won't get hurt. I'm just going to be strapped to some instructor's back and land on the ground twenty seconds later. How bad could it be?"

Mari pulls down her sunglasses and gives me a flat stare. "I'm not answering that."

* * *

Mari sees us off the next morning.

"Bring him back in one piece," she tells Alex as our group climbs into the passenger van that will take us to the drop zone.

"Princesa, we're not going off to war. It's skydiving. Only ten fatalities a year. It's safer than driving."

"Still, watch out for Javi," she admonishes. "He's not experienced like you are."

"Of course," Alex says, nodding.

I brace the doorframe to hoist myself into the van, but Mari clutches onto my long-sleeve T-shirt and yanks me back. Without a word, she wraps her arms around me tightly.

"Mari, I'll be fine," I say into her hair.

"Don't try to be cute up there," she says against my chest. "Just go up and come down."

I lightly tap her chin and give her a confident wink. "That's the plan."

Alex looks between us, his mouth flattened into a thin line. "Any day now. We have a schedule to keep."

Mari kisses Alex on the cheek—seemingly (and satisfyingly) as an afterthought—then chews on her thumb as she waves goodbye to us from the property's driveway.

I pass Joel and his father, Ramón, both of whom greet me by way of a head nod. As soon as I'm seated, I take deep breaths, trying to empty my brain of any worst-case scenarios. There's a reason so many people do this, right? But maybe *I'm* not supposed to be doing this. I mean, I'm firmly in the camp of folks who think if you get chewed up by a shark, you were somewhere you weren't supposed to be. By extension, if my ass gets chewed up by an airplane propeller, I can't really fault anyone but myself. Oh, and Alex. I can definitely fault him. Because who the hell chooses skydiving as their bachelor party outing?

Which reminds me that I don't know enough about the guy and should use this as an opportunity to get some dirt on him.

I study his face as I consider what approach to take. He's movie-star attractive and wears his confidence like a second skin. But as Chloe observed, it's all suspiciously perfect. I need to find the cracks in his shiny exterior.

"So, Alex, are you nervous about getting married in two days?"

A couple of rows ahead of us, Joel turns his head to the side, as if he's trying to listen in over the soft rock music playing through the van's speakers.

A smile tugs at Alex's lips before he responds. "Nervous? No. How could I be? I'm marrying Marisol. She's literally perfect."

I throw up a hand. "I love Mari too, but I think we can both agree she isn't perfect. I mean, no one is, right?"

"Where's the flaw?" Alex challenges.

I turn to face him, propping one leg over the other. "The way she leaves toast crumbs in the margarine tub."

He laughs. "I don't eat that crap, so I don't mind."

"Well, what about the way she stands at the refrigerator door and blocks everyone else when she's grazing?"

"That's a flaw?" he asks, his eyebrows drawn together. "I think it's adorable."

"Okay, but I bet you sleep through all those classic black-and-white movies she forces you to watch: *Casablanca*, *Seven Samurai*, *Sunset Boulevard*."

"No, no," he says. "I loved them all."

"Oh yeah?" I'm getting more frustrated with each word out of his mouth. "Which was your favorite?"

He ponders my question a moment, then says. "Um, *Citizen Kane*, maybe?"

"*Interesting*." And truly enlightening. "You two are a match made in heaven, then."

"We really are," he says, straightening his shoulders.

I close my eyes to signal that, as far as I'm concerned, this conversation is over, but Alex whispers my name, forcing me to engage once again.

"Psst, Javi."

I open an eye to find Alex angling his backpack so only I can see its contents. "Want a shot of tequila?"

"No, thanks. I read last night that you shouldn't eat or drink anything that can make you nauseated. Besides, my tolerance for anything but beer is nonexistent."

He draws back. "Aren't you a bartender?"

I laugh. "Part time, yeah. It's one of life's great ironies."

"*Interesting*," he says, tapping his lips with his index finger.

He shoves the backpack under his seat and fishes out his phone.

I tilt my head and study him with suspicion. "Aren't *you* going to take a shot?"

"Oh no," he says, his gaze fixed on his phone screen. "I need to keep my head on straight for the jump."

"So why'd you offer *me* a shot, then?"

He gives me a once-over, then grins. "Because you're a first-timer. To loosen you up."

"Huh, I see."

I'm not buying it. But whatever. I'll be in someone else's hands, not his.

* * *

"Javier, you'll be riding in tandem with Alex," the lead instructor, Mason, says during the safety briefing.

I swallow. Hard. "Excuse me?" I ask, trying to blink away my confusion.

We're in a small building outside the air hangar where First in Flight Skydiving runs through the protocol for each jump. I now realize why Alex has been so buddy-buddy with the staff: He knows them.

"That's right," Alex says, throwing his arm over my shoulder. "I was an instructor here during law school. I still do jumps on an as-needed basis too."

"What about them?" I ask, jutting my chin in the direction of Joel and Ramón.

"They're both experienced," Mason says. "You're the only newbie."

I turn to Alex, letting out a deep, heavy sigh. "So you're trained for this?"

"Yep," he says, grinning at me. "Licensed, certified, and up-to-date. Plus, I have over seven hundred jumps under my belt. Trust me, you're in good hands."

Well, that's unfortunate. "Ever had an accident?"

"Not one . . . though there's a first time for everything."

My eyes bulge, and he lightly punches me in the stomach. "I'm just messing with you, man. You'll be fine."

Alex's cousin chooses that moment to stick his phone in my face. Shit, they're recording this too? I give him a thumbs-up, although I'm anything but okay. The waiver alone, all *four* pages of it, isn't helping to calm my nerves either; it may as well have said *you will die, and it's no one's fault but your own.*

"Hey, Mason," Alex says. "We should let Javier practice on the creeper board. Give him a sense of positioning."

Mason angles his head, his lips pursed, then says, "We could just show—"

"No, no," Alex says, staring at him pointedly. "We should get him on the ground."

What the hell does that mean?

"Ah, all right," Mason says, jutting his jaw out. "I'll go get them."

I'm pacing when Mason returns with a jumpsuit and two contraptions that remind me of those rolling boards mechanics use to get under the body of a car.

"Here's your jumpsuit," he tells me. "You can go behind that dressing curtain and put it on over your clothes. Then, when you're ready, we'll get you on the creeper board and show you how it's done."

I shuffle away, wondering what decisions got me to this point. Why did I let bravado talk me into this situation? I puff out short breaths in the dressing area as I tug on the jumpsuit. A quick inspection in the mirror gasses my head up, though. Now that I see the entire outfit, though, I'm actually impressed. I look legit. I just need theme music, a badass turbojet, and a cool call sign like *Papi Chulo*.

I reenter the training area and put my arms out at my sides. "Ready."

Alex nods, his foot on one of the boards Mason brought in earlier. "Here you go," he says, kicking the contraption my way. It slides over the distance between us, and I stop it with a tap of my heel.

I look down at the board, then lift my gaze to him. "What am I supposed to with it?"

"You lie down on it, Javier. It'll mimic your horizontal position in the air. Helps you practice how to hold your arms and legs in a starfish stance during the jump."

My gaze swings between Alex and Mason. "Is this necessary?"

Mason remains silent, while Alex sighs.

"Don't you want the jump to be a success?" Alex asks.

"Of course I do."

"Then get on your belly and practice."

So I do. Reluctantly. The position is odd, and for a fleeting moment I wonder what I look like from everyone else's perspective, but then I start moving around on the board, my legs bent at the knees, and my arms out to the sides, and I can picture how this will be useful for the actual jump.

"You're getting all this," Alex asks his cousin.

"Sure am," he replies.

Alex rests his foot on my back and shifts me from side to side. "Keep your head tucked to protect you from that initial blast of air."

"Got it."

Mason kicks the other creeper board in Alex's direction. "You're an instructor. Show him."

There's a gruffness to Mason's tone, almost as if he's annoyed, although Alex doesn't seem fazed by it. In fact, Alex doesn't hesitate to take Mason's suggestion, dropping on his haunches and extending his body as if he's surfing. "Now, it might get choppy out there," he says to me, "so I'll help you get used to that."

I'm unsure what Alex means, but then he grabs the edge of my board and spins me in a circle. My hands fly out, trying to keep my balance, but I'm completely disoriented.

"Okay, I think I'll be able to handle it," I squeak out, trying not to get dizzy.

Except he doesn't stop and instead spins me even faster, his laughter echoing off the walls of the training room.

"Uncle!" I cry out. "Uncle!"

"What's up?" Ramón asks.

"No, not you, uncle. I meant—"

Fuck this.

I press my hands against the ground and propel myself over to Alex like a sea turtle on crack, and then I grab his arm and push him with all the strength I can muster, sending him crashing into a folding chair.

"That's enough, children," Mason says on a chuckle. "Let's get everyone on the plane."

I roll off the creeper board and jump to my feet. Which is a mistake. Because I stumble around, trying to regain my equilibrium, and run into the mobile privacy screen, toppling it over.

After I recover, Mason stands in front of me, inspecting my face. "You didn't drink before you got here, did you?"

"Just water, I promise."

Joel and Ramón laugh their asses off. Alex rubs his elbow. And

I glare at the man who'll be responsible for bringing me back to earth from fifteen thousand feet in the air.

This is a disaster.

* * *

"This is going to be fire!" Joel shouts, jumping in place. On a plane. Why would someone need to lift themself in the air when they're already at ten thousand feet and climbing?

Damn, I think I'm getting lightheaded.

I tap Alex on the shoulder. "When do I actually get attached to you?" I yell over the sound of the plane's engine.

He whirls around from his spot near the plane's door. "You don't. Just hold on to me as tight as you can."

I stare at Alex in a daze. That can't be right, but my central nervous system is shutting down, and I'm not able to tell what's real anymore.

Ramón laughs good-naturedly. "Stop messing with him, mijo. He's a good guy."

Alex smiles sheepishly. "Fine, I'll strap you in now. We'll be jumping soon."

My stomach drops, but there's nothing I'm willing to do about it. I'm going to see this through even if it kills me—literally.

The door of the plane lowers, and I hang onto a bar to get a closer look. The first thing I notice is a kaleidoscope of blues blanketing the sky. The air appears hazy, the clouds close enough to touch. The peaks and valleys seem richer in texture from this vantage. Up here, the deep green of a tree line stretches forever and parts of the terrain resemble a jigsaw. The wind's also smacking the shit out of my face.

Alex walks behind me and attaches my harness to his at four

different points. There's very little space between us, and if I'd known yesterday that skydiving would require Alex and me to be literally attached at the hip, I would have pretended to be felled by a bout of dysentery to get out of it.

"How does that feel?" he asks against my ear.

"So good," I say in a seductive whisper, trying to get my mind off what's about to happen.

He smacks the side of my head, then pulls it back to rest against his shoulder so I don't block his view. We watch Joel and Ramón jump out of the plane as if they're walking out the front door of their homes; they make it look *that* easy. And then it's our turn.

I squeeze my eyes shut, say a quick prayer, and blow out a deep breath.

"Let's do this," Alex shouts, and then we're marching forward in unison, looking like discount stormtroopers, I'm sure.

Holy shit, holy shit, holy shit.

I grab the plane's doorframe in a last-ditch effort to delay the inevitable.

"Let go," Alex yells, peeling my fingers off the plane.

Before I can even brace myself, he's pushing us forward, and we're jumping out of the plane together. Fifteen thousand feet from the ground.

I'm weightless. A speck floating in the air high above the great big world below. It's surreal—and unsettling. It reminds me of the time my brothers got me drunk while my parents were away for the weekend. I was only sixteen, and the cheap liquor they snuck into my cup overloaded my senses. I hated that feeling, and I've been queasy about alcohol ever since. Pushing that memory away, I try to focus on the here and now. Before long, I regain my equilibrium and can't help taking in the wonder of it all. I'm suspended in the earth's atmosphere. How cool is that?

And then there's pressure, as if I'm being pushed upward and might never land.

They told us we'd be free-falling at one hundred twenty miles per hour, but other than the flapping of my cheeks as the wind hits them, I can hardly tell.

This is unlike anything I've ever done before, and I wish Mari were here to experience it with me. She'd love it. Maybe one day we could do this together.

Alex spins us around a few times, then says, "I'm going to release the parachute now. You'll feel a bit of a jerk when I do."

The soundlessness in the sky contrasts starkly with the roar of the plane's engine moments ago, so Alex's voice permeates the quiet, yanking me back to reality just as harshly as the jolt from the parachute's release. That's when I remember: Mari and I won't be going skydiving now or in the future. She's getting married in two days—to the guy strapped to my back; as exhilarating as it is out here, my heart still sinks.

I'm so wrapped up in my thoughts, I almost miss that we're steadily making our descent. The wind is smacking my face, my stomach's churning, and the ground is coming at me fast. Seconds later, I land on my ass and bounce three times before Alex topples over me, halting my forward momentum.

After he helps me up, he slaps my back. "You did good. And the video's going to be hilarious. Marisol's really going to get a kick out of it."

This is all one big game to him. What a jerk.

Panting, I give Alex a thumbs-up. Then I chuckle to myself while I make plans in my head. I'm going to wipe the smirk off this man's face if it's the last thing I do.

CHAPTER 38

Mari

Now

Teddy, our wedding officiant and a member of the family that owns Crystal Canyon Farm, claps his hands, his ruddy face and thick beard reminding me of one of my favorite professors at Belmont. When people say that someone has kind eyes, they're thinking of someone like Teddy; there's a genuine warmth in his gaze, as if nothing and no one could ever dim his optimistic view of the world. It's calming. And I'm immensely grateful that he'll be the person officiating the ceremony. "Okay, everyone, let's gather together so I can walk you through what to expect on Sunday."

I look over the group of people assembled to take part in the ceremony: My girls are here, of course; Alex is flanked by his parents, cousin, and uncle; and my father's at the edge of the circle—on the phone. My mother won't be here until tomorrow, but I plan to acknowledge her presence at the wedding in my own way.

It's a gorgeous day on a piece of land that truly captures the essence of nature's beauty: rolling hills, picturesque vineyards, gardens overflowing with wildflowers. Everything's coming together exactly as I envisioned it.

I glance around, then tap Sasha on her arm. "Hey, have you seen Javi?"

"Nope," Sasha says, shrugging.

Alex's ears perk up, and he drifts over to us. "He might still be recovering from our skydiving adventure this morning."

I frown at him. "You said it went great, though."

"It did," he says, nodding. "But let's just say he had a time of it."

"Did he get nauseated or something?"

"Not that I know of, but jumping out of an airplane spikes your adrenaline like nothing else can."

I sigh. So much for everything coming together as I envisioned it. "Hey, Teddy, can you give us a minute? We're missing one more person."

"Certainly," he says.

I fish out my phone. "I'm going to check on Javi." As I'm scrolling to my favorites, a yip in the distance catches my attention. I scan the garden and gasp when I spot Javi strolling toward us, a small dog wearing a blue-and-silver bow cradled in his arms.

"What the hell is that?" Alex asks, squinting at Javi as he approaches.

"I think that's called a puppy," Brittany says, her lips twitching in amusement.

Javi reaches us, a broad smile softening the sharp angles of his face. "Sorry I'm late. This little guy needed to pee multiple times while we were on the road."

I lean over and cup the puppy's sweet face, drawn to his clear gray eyes. "Who's this?"

"This is Chocolicious," Javi says, "a Labrador retriever and pit bull terrier mix. And my wedding gift to you." He slides a devious look Alex's way. "To the both of you, of course."

My mouth drops open. On the one hand, I'm in love. On the other hand, this is neither the time nor the appropriate gesture. I straighten to my full height, my brow furrowed, partly in confusion and partly in consternation.

"Excuse me, everyone," I say, pulling Javi away from the group. When we're out of nosy ears' reach, I stare him down. "What is this?"

"Hear me out," he says, snuggling Chocolicious like a baby. It's fucking annoying. And precious. And every bit of this is messing with my head.

"I'm listening," I say.

"Well, I know you said Alex isn't a fan of pets—"

"So you did this to mess with him."

"I always want to mess with him. That's just how it is, okay? But really, this is for you."

I blow out a frustrated breath. Is he being serious right now? "How can this be for me, Javi? You *know* my *future husband* doesn't want a pet."

"Yes, but *you* want a pet, and you once told me that you imagined having your dog play a part in your wedding. Remember?"

I pinch the bridge of my nose. "Yes, I remember. And that's really sweet of you, Javi. Shortsightedly sweet. Still, I can't keep him." The little guy chooses that moment to nudge my arm with his nose. Dammit.

"I knew you would say that," he says, shifting Chocolicious in his arms. "So I have a proposal."

"I shouldn't be listening, yet I am."

"Here's what I'm thinking: He's yours, but I'll keep him. And whenever you visit New York, you can come and see him. And whenever I come here, I'll bring him along. We'll have joint custody."

My heart can't take this; it really can't.

"This way," Javi continues, "you get your wish"—he raises an index finger in the air—"which, I might add, will be the cutest thing your wedding guests will ever see—"

"I was hoping *I* would be the cutest thing my wedding guests would see."

"No," he says, playfully sticking his nose in the air. "You will be stunning. Glorious. Incandescent, as some of those romance heroes like to say. 'Cute' will not cut it."

I laugh. "You're such a clown." I wipe the smile off my face when Teddy walks up.

"Just checking that everything's okay," he says good-naturedly.

"Sorry, Teddy," I say, narrowing my eyes at Javi. "Just a little hiccup . . . and a last-minute alteration to the run of the ceremony."

Teddy tilts his head. "Oh?"

"Yeah," I say, taking Chocolicious from Javi and nestling him in the crook of my arm. "This little guy's going to be walking down the aisle too."

Javi beams at me, his whole face lit with happiness. I really need to squash this soft spot I have for him; it's the source of many bad decisions.

I hold out my hand. "Hang on . . . Chocolicious is walking down the aisle with you."

Javi nods, his chest puffed out like he's Superman. "Deal."

"And you need to make arrangements for his care while he's here."

"I already did. Jeremy's picking him up before tonight's dinner and bringing him back Sunday morning."

I'm touched by Javi's gift. I really am. Especially now that I know he put so much thought into it.

"Fine," I say to Javi, and then I snuggle into my new puppy and bop him on his adorably tiny nose. "Let's go meet everyone."

I take three steps toward the garden before I stutter to a stop. Oh God, I didn't even consult Alex about adding a dog to the lineup.

My therapist is going to have a field day with that one.

CHAPTER 39

Javi

Now

I don't know much, but I know Alex is a dick.

He's regaling everyone with a fictitious account of my skydiving exploits, and I've never seen him so animated.

"So, we're just about to jump," he tells us, his eyes eerily bright and his wine sloshing in its glass, "and Javi grabs onto the plane's doorframe as if his life depends on it."

Okay, sure, that part's true. He's still a dick, though.

Most of his relatives are eating up the entertainment, laughing boisterously no matter what he says. It's clear to me, and probably to anyone else with a smidgen of insight into family dynamics, that he's their golden child and his two sisters are the castoffs. Danila and Mirna do nothing but whisper to each other, their disdain for everyone around them affixed to their faces like permanent makeup. Worse, Mirna has the longest fingernails I've ever seen on a person not seeking to hold a Guinness World Record. It's decided: I'm putting them in the script somehow.

Mari clears her throat and takes a deep breath. "Señora Cordero, are you enjoying your first visit to California?"

Alex's mother covers her mouth with a linen napkin as she finishes chewing. When she's done, she says, "Yes, it's very nice."

We wait for her to say more, but she looks back down at her plate and eats another forkful of feijoada. I mean, I get it. These black beans are delicious; every time I discover a hunk of meat hidden in the sauce I mentally high-five myself.

Alex takes his mother's silence as an opportunity to continue speaking. "Marisol, get this." He throws his arm over the back of her chair. "Your friend here tried to point out your flaws, but I told him you were perfect."

Shit, that's true too. He's probably still pissed about Chocolicious, but this isn't going to end well—for him.

"Oh, really," Mari says, giving me a smirk to go along with her scorching side-eye. "And what flaws are those?"

"Hmm, let's see," Alex says, tapping his chin with his index finger. "One was that you always leave toast crumbs in the margarine tub. Another is how you stand in front of the refrigerator grazing until you've had an entire meal. And apparently he can't stand all those black-and-white classics you love so much. I told him *Citizen Kane* happens to be my favorite."

Mari presses her lips together and heaves a deep sigh. We exchange a glance, and then she says: "*Citizen Kane* is a directorial masterpiece, but I couldn't sit through it. And *I* don't leave crumbs in the margarine tub; Javi does. *He's* the one who stands in front of the refrigerator like he's a bouncer stopping people from getting into a club. I used to complain about it all the time." She turns to Alex. "I *hate* black-and-white movies, and the only reason I know this is because when we were at Belmont, Javi used to drag me to the theater in town to watch them." She jumps to her feet. "I need to use the restroom. Excuse me."

The rest of the group sits in stunned silence.

Chloe, who was probably a diplomat in another life, leans forward and settles her gaze on Mari's father. "Luiz, what's the most ridiculous legal matter you've ever worked on? I'm sure you have a great story."

Luiz, always ready to seize any moment as his own, blessedly appears to recognize the need to defuse the situation. "Ah, there have been quite a few, Chloe. You know, I once had a client who refused to work on any movie set that used artificial turf. Something to do with . . ."

To my right, Sasha pretends to snore.

To my left, Alex leans over Mari's empty chair and whispers, "You played me."

"You played yourself," I whisper back. "You didn't have to bring up any of that stuff. Instead, you tried to make me look bad and only ended up proving how little you know about her."

A muscle in his jaw tics. "So that's how it's gonna be, huh?"

Sasha sets her elbows on the table and glares at us both. "Be quiet, you two. She's coming back."

We both straighten in our seats, and Mari sits down, her face damp, as though she splashed it with water. I didn't intend to share any of my and Alex's earlier conversation with Mari; it was simply a part of my own due diligence. But now that it's out, Mari's hurt by its implications, and for that, I regret the silly mind game I played.

"Everything okay?" I ask.

She gives me a weak smile, her eyes vacant. "Everything's fine."

Across the table, Chloe blows out her cheeks. I understand

where she's coming from; listening to Luiz *is* exhausting. Her gaze bounces around until it settles on me. "Javi, tell us about this musical you have in the works."

I wipe my mouth and drop the napkin onto my lap. *This* I can handle. And the more I work on it, the more confident I am talking about it. "The tentative title is *The Mailroom*. It's about a group of mailroom workers who discover that their company is looking to promote from the inside and wants to choose a candidate from the mailroom. The discovery leads the employees to think about their dreams, what's caused them to be stagnant, what they hope for their futures—"

"So it's autobiographical," Alex says, faking a smile. Mari scowls at him, and he throws up his hands. "Aww, c'mon, I'm just kidding."

I relax my face, flattening my expression to signal that I'm completely unbothered, and then I continue: "It's about the inevitability of failure, the power of reinventing ourselves, the importance of knowing our self-worth, and the consequences of the choices we make. So, yeah, I suppose it is somewhat autobiographical. And aspirational."

"Can't wait to see it," Chloe says.

"Me too," Brittany and Sasha say in unison.

I stare at Mari, willing her to look at me, but she's fixed her sights on a spot beyond her father's shoulder. Chloe's less subtle about it; she waves both hands at her friend and barks out, "Hey, you okay over there?"

Mari's head snaps back. "What? Sure. Of course. Just . . . a little distracted." Using her hands, she mimics an explosion around her head. "There's a lot going on in my brain."

Alex places his hand over hers and whispers into her ear.

I wish he'd disappear, which is laughable. Not only does he have every right to be here, but he's also half the reason why we're gathered in the first place. He's the fiancé. The future husband. This is just as much his rehearsal dinner as it is Mari's. If there's anyone whose presence is questionable, it's me. Fuck, I wish I were a drinker.

Mari slowly rises to her feet and picks up her champagne flute. Alex follows suit.

She takes a deep breath and curves her mouth into a wide smile. She's positively beaming. How she isn't suffering an injury from all that whiplash is a mystery. "Alex and I want to thank you for being here and for your continued support as we embark on this next phase of our lives together. We're excited to see what the future holds for us, and we're so delighted to be starting the journey with all of you." She raises her glass. "To weddings and new beginnings."

A round of hear-hears and cheers ensues as everyone clinks glasses. Alex's sisters are noticeably subdued, but that might be because Mirna can barely wrap her long-ass fingernails around the champagne flute, and Danila looks to her sister for any behavioral cues.

Mari's gaze roams over the faces around the table and eventually lands on me. There's a question in my eyes, one I know she's not going to answer.

She toasted to weddings and new beginnings. What about toasting to love?

CHAPTER 40

Mari

Now

Chloe, who's standing beside me, takes one look at the person who's running the wine tasting and gasps. "Fuck. Me."

I pinch her elbow. She yelps, then dramatically rubs the spot as if it's actually sore. "Coño, Mari, that hurt."

"Behave," I tell her. "He's a professional and deserves your respect."

She eyes him dreamily. "I'll gladly kneel at his feet and call him 'sir.' How's that for respect?"

"You're growing on me," Sasha says to Chloe, nodding in approval.

Brittany and I, the levelheaded individuals in this chaotic foursome, stare at each other and shake our heads.

"My name is Sebastian Price." With his pale green eyes and salt-and-pepper hair, he's a dead ringer for journalist Jorge Ramos. Honestly, I can see why Chloe's smitten. "My family owns Crystal

Canyon Farm," he continues, "and I've been a vintner and sommelier here for just under ten years."

Chloe leans over. "I'll happily call him my silver daddy too."

"Enough," I whisper.

Sebastian paces the terrace as he shares the vineyard's story, making sure to exchange eye contact with each person in the wedding party. Every person who's here, that is. Alex's mother chose to abstain, and the men are apparently still sorting out last-minute alterations to their wedding attire with the tailor Alex hired. I glance at my watch. Shouldn't they be here by now?

No sooner than the thought occurs to me, Alex makes his way up the winding path overlooking the valley below. The members of his entourage, including my father, trot behind him single file. I scan the group, searching for Javi, and sigh in relief when I spot him bringing up the rear.

"Hey there," I say to Alex when he reaches me. "How'd it go?"

"Great," he says, kissing me on the cheek. "A minor snafu with Javier's suit—a stain or something, I don't know—but the laundry valet's taking care of it, and it'll be ready in time for the ceremony tomorrow."

I pat him on the chest. "Thanks for handling all that."

"Of course," he says, tucking me under his arm. He turns his attention to Sebastian, who's running through what to expect during today's tasting.

"We'll start here on the terrace," Sebastian says, "where you'll get to enjoy several of our white wines. Two pieces of good news: The first is, although we're technically calling this a tasting, your fine host, Mr. Campos, has arranged for an upgrade that will offer more wine than we usually provide."

Everyone whoops and cheers.

"The second," Sebastian continues, "is that there was a request for nonalcoholic options, and you'll be pleased to know that we have several: two whites, one red blend, and an alcohol-free IPA."

Javi raises his hand.

"Yes, sir?"

"How does that work?" Javi asks. "Are they actually wines?"

Sebastian, who's standing with his legs apart, crosses his arms over his chest.

Chloe moans, then whispers, "Jesus, that stance should be illegal in the continental United States."

Brittany snorts.

"I'm glad you asked," Sebastian tells Javi. "We call them alcohol-extracted wines. Essentially, we develop the grape using our traditional winemaking methods, and then we use spinning cone technology to remove the alcohol. You'll get as authentic a wine tasting experience as possible—the depth of the aromas, the fullness of the flavors, and the lushness of the fruits—without the alcohol."

"That's dope," Javi says. "I'll definitely stick to that for the duration of the tour."

Sasha nods. "Me too."

Sebastian spreads his arms wide and motions for everyone to follow him to the tasting table. "Gather around, friends. Once everyone's seated, we'll bring out the flights."

The group splits in two, the women drifting to one side of the table, and the men gravitating to the other. Oddly, Alex doesn't sit across from me, but I'm happy to see that he's engaging Javi in conversation at the far end of the table.

Javi catches me staring at them and waves.

"Behave," I shout, playfully pointing my finger at him.

Just then, a dozen servers descend upon us, each holding two trays of wine flights, so I miss his response.

"Who's getting the alcohol-free options?" one of the servers asks.

I hover my hand over Sasha's head. "This one right here." Next, I gesture to the far end of the table. "And that guy over there sitting by the groom."

The server places Sasha's flight in front of her, then strides in Javi's direction.

Sebastian walks us through the selections, though Danila and Mirna are tossing back their glasses like they're marathon runners snatching Dixie cups from volunteers along the route.

"Oh, this is good," Sasha says. "You wouldn't even know there's no alcohol." She raises one of her glasses in front of my face. "Try it."

I take a sip and straighten my shoulders. "Wow, you're right, that would have absolutely fooled me."

Javi waves from his corner of the table. "Hey, Sasha, it tastes like the real thing, doesn't it?"

"It does!" she exclaims.

I prefer reds, so I take dainty sips of the white, fully expecting to get to the good stuff later. For now, though, I'm delighted that everyone seems to be having a great time. And because there's nothing on the schedule until tomorrow's ceremony, we can all enjoy ourselves without worrying about going overboard.

I've planned this weekend perfectly, if I do say so myself.

CHAPTER 41

Javi

Now

Where has nonalcoholic wine been all my life?

"It's good, yeah?" Alex asks.

I pound a closed fist against my chest and burp. "Damn good." I look over at him, catching a sly twist of his lips that disappears as soon as he notices I'm watching him. "How's yours?"

He raises a shoulder, appearing unruffled. "It's fine. The chardonnay is okay, but I'm not partial to whites, myself."

"You should talk to someone about that," I say with a straight face.

He stares at me, his expression flat and unamused. "Because I'm a white Latino." He rolls his eyes. "Good one, Javi."

Well, he's no fun.

Alex scans the area around him, then signals a server. The woman rushes over, a black tray in her hands, and they share a whispered exchange before she nods and jogs away.

It's beautiful out here. All sunny and shit. I make a hole with my thumb and index finger and stare at the sun through it. It's bright, so bright.

I survey the people at the table, grinning at the good vibes on display. Everyone looks so happy. Even Alex's sisters, Cruella and Ursula, seem to be enjoying themselves. Mari looks beautiful too. All sun-kissed shoulders and big, fluffy hair. Fuck, it's hot. I unbutton the top two buttons of my half-sleeve. I wonder what Chocolicious is doing right now? That little shit is needy as hell, but I'm keeping him forever. God, that moment when I first picked him up at the shelter and he snuggled against my neck and fell asleep? So damn cute. Are there bees out here? Wow, that's a pretty butterfly.

"Javi!"

I shake my head and look around. "Yeah?"

"Here's another flight," Alex says, placing a tray in front of me. "Figured since we'll be visiting the vineyards next, you might want to get your fill of the nonalcoholic stuff now."

We bump fists. "Thanks for looking out, man."

A line appears between his eyebrows. "Looking out where?"

I blink a few times. Is he . . . ? "Never mind." I down the first glass.

The guy running the tasting—what the hell was his name? It reminded me of the Little Mermaid: Flounder? Scuttle? Sebastian!—whistles to get everyone's attention. "Okay, friends, gather whatever belongings you have and follow me out front. We're going on a joyride!"

"Yippee!" I say, throwing back the last of the three glasses as I rise from my chair.

Mari materializes out of thin air.

I jump back and wobble on my feet. "Shit, you scared me!"

"Are you okay?" she asks, inspecting my face.

"I'm fine." I motion her over. "I'm just high on life."

Her face clears. "Oh, goodness, you are *such* a mess." She links her arm with mine and pulls me along. "C'mon, it's time to get on the bus."

"Okay!"

Damn, I need to concentrate really hard right now because the cobblestones on this path seem to be moving.

Mari tells me to "wait here," and when I look up, I rock on my heels. "It's a party bus!"

We climb on and I grab onto the pole, opting to stand while everyone else sits. Unfortunately, the music sucks. Still, I move my hips to whatever song is playing because I'm so keyed up.

In front of me, Alex's cousin, Joel, taps his father on the arm a few times and points at me. "¡Mira, está perreando el poste!"

"I am not grinding on the pole!" I shout.

Everyone stops talking and stares at me.

I gulp, then make the shape of a gun with my fingers and point it in the air. "Just a joke between friends. Pew, pew, pew."

Mari pulls me down into the seat next to her. "I told you to behave."

"I'm really hot," I say, fanning myself.

Mari turns to Alex, who's sitting on the other side of her. Their heads are together, and she's scowling at him while he's shrugging his shoulders. Hmm, what's going on there?

Oh, we're here already?

I climb off the bus and rest my hands on my waist, stretching my hip flexors. It's gorgeous out here. Like a Monet painting.

Our tour guide motions for us to form a circle.

I raise my hand. "Scuttle—"

He chuckles. "It's Sebastian."

"Shit, right," I say, smacking my forehead. "Sebastian, are these vineyards sustaichable?"

"Do you mean sustainable?"

I drop my head and point a finger to the sky. "Exactly that."

"I'm glad you asked," he says, "and the answer is yes. We use organic and sustainable farming methods to grow and cultivate our wines." He points to a section of the vineyard and motions for everyone to follow. "Over here, you'll see . . ."

I dip between the rows and rows of grapevines, wanting to explore the vineyard on my own. It's so peaceful here. And hot. Really fucking hot. I take off my short-sleeve (good thing I wore a rib tank underneath), trip over a small mound of dirt, and wrap my shirt around my neck like a scarf. Ah, much better. Are these grapes ripe? Is that when they're plucked? Harvested? Whatever the hell it's called? My head spins. Shit. I think I'm drunk. But I didn't have any alcohol, so how the hell is that even possible?

"What are you doing in there?" someone cries. "And why aren't you wearing your shirt?"

I look up, taking a few seconds to clear my brain and focus on the person's face. "There she is. The most beautiful girl in the world."

"You're drunk," Mari says, frowning. "How is that possible?"

"I was asking myself the same thing. Great minds . . ."

"They must have given you the wrong wine," she says, shaking her head.

I shrug. "Don't know." I walk up to her and throw my arms around her shoulders. "But I do know that I love you."

"I love you too, Javi," she says absently. Then she bites her lip as if she's trying to figure something out.

"No, Mari. I *love* you, love you."

She takes in a sharp breath and looks away. "What a mess." After a few seconds of silence, she wraps one of her arms around my waist. "Let's get you back on the bus."

"Okay," I say, yawning. "I could use a nap."

"And I could use a reset button," she mutters.

I want to ask her what she means, but I'm too tired to form the words.

Alex encounters us on the way, and I use all of my remaining strength to jump behind Mari. "You did this to me," I say, using Mari as a shield.

He grimaces. "I did no such thing. It was a snafu."

Mari gives him a sidelong glance. "There's been a lot of those this weekend."

"Princesa, he's trying to cause trouble," Alex pleads, his expression uncharacteristically flustered.

"Let's just get him to the cottage," she says solemnly.

I want to plead my case too, but my brain isn't cooperating. Not that it would do any good. After all, I told her I loved her, and she didn't even care.

CHAPTER 42

Mari

Now

Standing behind me, Alex meets my gaze in the mirror. "Want to walk over to the restaurant early? We could grab a drink before they arrive."

We're having dinner with Alex's mother and sisters tonight, and he's uncommonly nervous about it. I'm tickled by this facet of his personality; turns out my seemingly unflappable fiancé is capable of getting his feathers ruffled.

I swipe some gloss across my lips and smile. "A drink to fortify us?"

His mouth twitches. "To loosen us up. And be warned: She's going to ask you about babies."

"Why would she? Other than having been one decades ago, I have no expertise on the topic."

He points a finger at me, his bright eyes twinkling. "That," he says on a chuckle. "Don't do that. Just humor her. For me."

I turn around and cup his chin. "It's going to be fine. I'll be on my *best* behavior. Promise." Stepping back, I add, "But I still have a few things to do, so go ahead without me and grab a drink for yourself. I'll finish up here, then check on Javi."

A muscle in his jaw tics, and he lets out a slow breath. "I'm sure he's fine."

"You're probably right," I say, slipping on my shoes. "I still want to see him with my own eyes."

Besides, Javi and I need to talk. *Really* talk. And since Alex has nothing to worry about, there's no reason to mention that part.

Alex opens and shuts his mouth. After a beat, he plucks at the cuff of his shirt and says, "Sure. Please don't be late, though. My mom's pretty easygoing, but she hates to be kept waiting."

"I'll be there *on time* and ready to charm," I say, resting a hand against his chest.

He draws me to him and presses a kiss against my forehead, then stares at me for a long moment, his eyes unblinking. After a deep breath, he walks to the door. On his way out of the cottage, he says, "See you soon, princesa."

The endearment is meant as a reminder, and it works. I recall that he's vowed to cherish me. That he wants to build a life with me. That he's prepared to promise me forever. What else could I possibly ask for?

Someone knocks at the door, and I flinch. Goodness, I really need to ease up on these heavy thoughts. I swing the door open. "Did you forget—"

I look up and stop short, processing *who* I'm looking at. My mother's staring back at me. She's *here*. We haven't been together for two years, not in person, not like this—not when she's close enough to touch. I fight back tears, my knees nearly buckling as she wraps me in her arms.

"Oh, Marisol, it's so good to see you," she says softly.

The feel of her skin. Her sweet scent. The warmth that engulfs me. It's all too much. An embarrassingly loud sob escapes me. When I finally gather the strength to speak, my voice is shaky: "I thought you were getting in late tonight. Alex and I planned to pick you up from the airport." I look behind her. "Where's your stuff?"

She pats my hand, a smile tugging at her lips. "Everything's fine, filha. May I come in?"

I slap a palm against my forehead and pull her inside. "Sorry, sorry, I just wasn't expecting you so soon."

"The people in Atlanta were wonderful," she says, removing her blazer. She doesn't do casual when she travels; if anything, she dresses up. "I told one of the workers at the gate that I was coming here for your wedding, and he put me on an earlier flight." She waggles her eyebrows and whispers, "A first-class seat too."

"Ooh, fancy," I reply with a smile. I study her face, try to figure out what's changed. The blunt bob that ends at her chin is new. "You cut your hair!"

She leans forward, partially covers her mouth, and whispers, "It's a wig."

"Well, it looks great. And I'm so glad you made it." Twisting around, I ask, "Do you need anything? Water? Bathroom? Something to eat?"

She gently places her hand on my arm and grins at me. "I don't need anything, filha. I'm here for you. Is there anything *you* need from *me*?"

"Being here is enough," I reply.

Her eyes glisten. "Sometimes it doesn't feel like enough, but thank you for saying so."

I take in a sharp breath and exhale. Perhaps my mother needs to confront her feelings about our separation as much as I do. Maybe we could unpack them together. But not now. Not less than twenty-four hours before my wedding. "We have so much to talk about, so much to catch up on, but I'm supposed to have dinner with Alex's family."

She straightens and plasters on a smile. "Don't change your plans. The trip was exhausting. I could use the rest." She grimaces, her eyes crinkling at the corners. "I'll need my strength to deal with your father tomorrow. But don't worry, we'll have plenty of time to see each other. I'll be here for a week."

"Good," I say, nodding. "We'll spend so much time together you'll be sick of me."

"Wonderful," she says, her face brightening. Then she frowns. "But shouldn't you be spending time with your new husband?"

I laugh. "I think I can manage both. No honeymoon, remember?"

"Oh yes, I remember," she says, lifting her eyebrows.

"Mãe," I warn.

She pretends to zip her lips.

I look at the digital clock behind her. "Oh God, I'm going to be late if I don't get out of here now. I need to see Javi before dinner."

My mother's face positively sparkles at the mention of his name. "I can't wait to hug him for real. That boy is so fun!"

"He can't wait to see you too."

Minutes later, on my way to Javi's room, a thought strikes me upside the head: My mother never expressed any excitement about seeing Alex in person for the first time. How odd.

Javi immediately answers the door, looking hungover and definitely worse for the wear in a tank and a pair of jeans slung low on his hips. He doesn't say a word as he motions me inside.

"How are you feeling?" I ask, wrapping my arms around my middle.

He scrubs a hand down his face. "Like shit, but I'll survive." He looks around him, then gestures at the couch. "Wanna sit down?"

"Sure."

I settle in and pat the cushion. He sits next to me, stretching out his legs, then smoothing his hands on his thighs.

"What happened earlier?" I ask. "How'd you get so drunk?"

He blows out a breath and shakes his head. "I have no clue. You heard what I told Sebastian. I made it clear that I wanted no alcohol, and that obviously isn't what happened." He grimaces. "Was I a wreck? I don't remember half the shit I said or did. Damn, I need to apologize to everyone."

"You were fine. A little outlandish at times, but the group was tipsy as a whole, so you didn't stick out or anything."

"Thank God," he says.

"You said some things, though. To me."

He draws back, his eyes roving my face. "Something bad?"

"No, you said you love me."

"That's nothing new," he says, bumping my shoulder, a smile dancing on his lips. "I do love you."

I could leave it at that and walk away. It would be so easy to pretend I didn't understand what he meant. But if Javi and I are going to remain in each other's lives, we need to get this out in the open now. "No, you said you *love* me, love me."

"Damn," he says, squeezing his eyes shut. "Drunk Javi is stupid as fuck."

I hold my breath.

"I mean, it's true," he continues, running a hand over the back of his head, "but I wouldn't have said it that way if I had been sober. That was probably Alex's plan. To get me drunk so I could make a fool of myself."

I exhale on a sigh. What does Javi expect me to do here? To agree with him? To joke with him about the man I'm marrying tomorrow morning? There is no universe in which this wedding isn't happening. Maybe the old Marisol would have considered it. But the adult version knows what's good for her. And it's time to tell him so. "Javi, this isn't cute anymore."

He draws back. "What isn't cute?"

"This"—I wave a hand between us—"*thing* you're doing. Trying to prove Alex isn't right for me."

"He isn't—"

"No," I say, holding up my hand. "It's no longer your job to approve the person I decide to be with. I gave you that privilege, and I'm withdrawing it—effective immediately. Alex *chose* me. You didn't. You *never* did. Not when I wanted to date you in college. Not when I wanted us to stay in touch after we graduated. Not even when I wanted us to explore a relationship when we reconnected. You always held back. You *always* had a reason for rejecting me. For *dumping* me. And now that I've found someone who wants to be with me, who doesn't view me as a burden, you're scrambling to upend everything."

He stares ahead, his jaw clenched. I know he's listening. A blink of an eye here. A deep breath and a drop of his shoulders there. I hope it's sinking in. Javi's one of the best men I know, but even good men can hurt the ones they claim to love.

I take his hand and squeeze it. "I am prepared to cherish you until the day I die, but as a friend and nothing else. I'm marrying Alex tomorrow. That's my choice, and you're going to have to live with it. Can you do that?"

A tear slips down his cheek, and he angrily swipes it away. "Of course. I can do whatever you need. But can I say one thing?"

"Sure."

He meets my eyes, his gaze piercing mine. "I never, and I mean *never*, considered you a burden. I was always worried *I'd* be a burden to *you*. Not that it's some big revelation or anything. I mean, look at you. And well, look at me. Or how I used to be. But yeah"—he shrugs—"I just think it's important for you to know that. It's important to our friendship."

I lean into him. As usual, he knows exactly what to say. "Thanks for saying that. It means the world. And it explains a lot. You thought I would only love you if you reached some pinnacle of success, but I always loved you for who you are. Still do." I rise and put out my hand; he takes it, and I pull him to standing. "I've got your back, and you've got mine, right?"

He draws me into his arms. "Para siempre."

I close my eyes as he presses his lips to my temple. "Para sempre."

He walks me to the door, where I turn to him. "Make sure you get something to eat. I hear the restaurant in the main building serves a killer steak."

"I'll keep that in mind," he says, opening the door and leaning on the frame.

"See you tomorrow," I say softly.

"See you tomorrow," he says, a tremor in his voice.

But I ignore it. I have to. Because it's time to get to know my future mother-in-law.

* * *

I need to pee before I return to this dinner, but the line for the ladies' room is two miles deep, the guests from tonight's wedding standing single file, their bodies packed in a row like sardines.

Shit, shit, shit. I don't know Alex's family very well, but his mother seems to be overly concerned with social niceties, so if I'm not back at the table within minutes, she'll probably think I'm blowing her off.

This dinner has certainly been enlightening, though. Mirna and Danila's apparent animosity isn't even about me; they're upset with the situation—namely, their mother told them not to be in the wedding party because she worried they would steal the spotlight from Alex. I'm flabbergasted but also tossing that revelation in the "problems for another day" bin. At the moment, the most pressing problem is my bladder.

A man exits the men's room, his fingers still fiddling with his zipper. First of all, gross. Second of all, score. There's no good reason I shouldn't be able to use either restroom; this venue should know better by now. I make a mental note to tell them so, then push the swinging door open and listen for any hint that someone's in here. I certainly don't want to surprise anyone—or be surprised myself. A toilet flushes. Dammit. But then I hear voices, both of them familiar, both of them agitated. And my stomach drops, because I have a sinking feeling that I'm not going to like what I'm about to discover.

CHAPTER 43

Javi

Now

I grip the bathroom counter, bow my head, and take in a deep breath. The steak was delicious, yet my stomach's churning. Not because of the food, but because I'm barreling toward the inevitable.

There's only one day to go, and although I definitely think Alex is an asshole, he's done nothing disqualifying. Would I choose him for Mari? No. But that's not groundbreaking. I wouldn't choose *anyone* for Mari—except myself. Is that reason enough to blow up this wedding? Of course not. Besides, Mari's told me in no uncertain terms that she doesn't want me to.

I lift my head and stare at my reflection in the mirror. I'm a decent guy, and big things are on the horizon for me, I can *feel* it. My friendship with Mari will endure, whether Alex likes it or not. That's got to be enough.

A flush in one of the stalls draws my gaze to the person leaving it.

Christ. Not now.

Luiz nods at me, then silently washes his hands.

When he finally speaks, his voice is low, his tone sharp: "I thought we had an understanding. But you're here, insinuating yourself into everything and trying to make trouble."

I could attempt to argue my case, explain that Alex is the true source of much of this weekend's sabotage, but what would be the point? Luiz doesn't like me, and nothing I say will appease him. *I'm* the one who doesn't fit into his carefully constructed world. *I'm* the interloper.

"Mari asked me to be here, and if you need to be reminded, this weekend is all about her, about them."

"So, what are you going to do next?" he asks, his eyes shooting sparks. "Raise your hand when the officiant asks for any objections?"

"I hadn't planned on it," I say. Wanting to annoy him, I shrug and add, "But one never knows what can happen at a wedding." In truth, I'd never do anything to mess up Mari's big day. This is important to her, so it's important to me. Sure, I wanted to find a reason why Alex wasn't her match, but I'm man enough to step aside.

My throwaway remark has incensed Luiz, however. He grabs my arm and spins me toward him, then raises his finger in front of my face. "Me escute, filho da puta!"

I back away and throw up my hands. "Luiz, relax. I was *joking*. Jesus. I would never—"

"You better be joking," he says, turning to the mirror and straightening his blazer. "This wedding isn't just about Mari and Alex. It's about our *family*. My *legacy*."

"Legacy? Do you even know if Mari wants children?"

He meets my gaze in the reflection and rolls his eyes. "Not that kind of legacy. The firm. Her future. Alex's future. Those two are going to run that firm together one day. He'll temper her softheartedness. Make the hard decisions. He'll do what I would have done. She *needs* him. And when Mari's ready to have children, Alex will run the place. It's how it should be. How I planned it."

I frown at him. "Does Mari know any of this? That you have her life mapped out for her? That you're planning to give the firm to her husband? That you expect her to give up her career for the kids she may or may not want?"

"She'll know soon enough. It's what her mother did."

"And look how that worked out," I mutter.

He grimaces. "Don't pretend you know anything about me or my ex-wife. You don't. What matters right now is that Alex knows his role, knows what's at stake. I've been preparing him for years."

Christ, this is all kinds of fucked up. But would Mari see it that way? Would she be satisfied with the crumbs her father is apparently intending to give her? She's poured her whole life into the firm. Has plans for its expansion. Wants to make it a place where small-business owners can thrive too. Is that mission even on Luiz's radar?

He turns to me again. "Let me give you some advice: If you want to be in my daughter's life, shut your mouth and smile tomorrow. This is much bigger than you or whatever fairy tale is in that lazy head of yours."

"Is that a threat?" I ask through narrowed eyes. "What happens if I tell Mari everything?"

"It would break her heart, and you know it," he replies blandly. "Do you really want to do that? And besides, if this wedding doesn't happen, guess who'll get the firm eventually anyway?"

Jesus. I hate this man at the molecular level. "You'd let Alex run it."

"It only makes sense. He's the future, and he understands the big picture."

"So why the marriage?"

"Don't you worry about that," he bellows. "I'm not some foolish villain here to spill all my secrets."

"And yet . . ."

He glares at me, his jaw clenched. "You know what? If you had listened to me all those years ago and stayed out of Mari's life like I asked, you wouldn't even be here. So be happy you're a guest and get out of my way."

With my hands fisted at my sides, I don't hesitate to get up in his face. "I shouldn't have listened to you then, and I shouldn't listen to you now. You've always thought I wasn't good enough for Mari, but you're wrong. I *am* good enough for her. You know why? Because her happiness will *always* come first for me. *Always.* Can you say the same?"

The tension between us is a bow bending in the seconds before it snaps apart. We stare at each other in silence, until we're startled by the restroom door swinging open, followed by the sounds of people talking in the hall. Luiz recovers quickly, plastering on a fake-ass smile. Yet no one comes in.

God, if Mari knew what her father's been up to, she'd be distraught, heartbroken, disillusioned. Her world would never be the same. If she wants to marry Alex, and Alex wants to marry her, though, how can I interfere? How can I shatter her dreams? I'm not the guy I was eight years ago when Luiz cornered me in that lobby. No, I'd fight for Mari this time. But would she want me to? Would she resent me for it? I don't know what to think, what to do. I'm stuck. Which, I suppose, is *exactly* what Luiz wants.

"Do we understand each other?" Luiz asks.

I'm once again on the spot, warring with myself to choose between what is best for the one person in the world I'd do anything for and what would make me happy. In the end, it's always been her. It's always been *about* her. After a long moment of silence, I nod. "Yeah, we do."

Luiz stomps away, leaving me staring at my reflection and wondering if I'm doing the right thing. Damn, this anguish is going to eat me up inside. And I should know. That's what happened last time.

CHAPTER 44

Javi

Eight Years and Five Months Before the Wedding

As the apartment building's elevator descends to the lobby, I touch my lips, as if I can recapture the feeling of Mari's mouth on mine. Last night was both a fever dream and a nightmare. I kissed Mari. And it was everything I ever wanted distilled to its essence.

A moment of absolute clarity.

A moment when nothing but the two of us mattered.

A moment when all the doubts I carry like an overstuffed backpack faded away.

Maybe Mari saw the panic in my eyes. Perhaps she was panicking herself. Because the next thing I knew she was laughing at the bar with a guy who was plainly into her, that mind-blowing moment between us long forgotten. Good thing I'm leaving today. The distance will help us get back on track. She'll be busy being a stellar law student, and I'll be busy . . . trying to find a damn job.

I hoist my travel bag onto my shoulder and stride through the lobby, dodging a delivery person struggling to carry several takeout bags in his hands. I double back to ask him if he needs help, but he says he's okay and pushes through. I'm so caught up in his saga that I bump into someone else.

"Apologies," I say, my eyes still on the delivery guy, who's now trying to call the elevator.

"Javier," the person says. "Fancy meeting you here."

I shake my head when my eyes land on Mari's father. "Luiz?"

Of course it's him. My brain just isn't computing that he's in front of me.

I glance around. "What are you doing here?"

He removes his sunglasses and peers at me. "I wanted to speak with Mari."

"At nine a.m. on a Sunday morning," I say, unable to filter the suspicion from my tone.

"Yes, that's right," he says, his hands folded over his chest as if he's bracing for a challenge.

"Well, uh, okay. But she's meeting with her study group, so she isn't home, and I need to head to the airport."

"Hang on, Javi. Since I have you, why don't we . . . talk."

Right. Because I know he didn't come here at this early hour to speak with his daughter.

This is Mari's father. You don't have to like him. You only have to tolerate him.

We drift over to a set of chairs arranged for conversation and sit down opposite each other. I nudge my bag out of the way with my foot and lean forward. "So, what did you want to talk about?"

"Look, Javier, this isn't anything personal. You seem like a decent guy."

I raise an eyebrow. "But?"

"But we both know you aren't on Mari's level, and I'm a little worried that you're going to drag her down. I don't think you'll mean to. It'll just happen. You're not doing anything. Not going anywhere. And Mari has her whole life ahead of her. She needs to focus right now. No distractions. No boys. No trips to New York to see her friends. You understand what I'm saying?"

"I understand that you're threatened by me for some reason."

"Threatened? No. Concerned? Yes. You know, when Mari's mother decided to move to Brazil, I kept Mari here. Because I knew she could do big things with my guidance. And it's working. Don't undermine that. Give her the space she needs. This . . . friendship, it was a college thing, right? You'll eventually lose touch anyway. Why not cut it off now? Save everyone the headache?"

I smooth my hands over my thighs, pick up my bag, and jump to my feet. "With respect, I think you're an asshole, and I wish you cared about your daughter half as much as you care about yourself."

He sighs and rises as well. "I'm sorry you think so. Just know this: She will *never* choose you over me. That's a fact."

"What are you talking about?" I say, slapping my baseball cap on, my shoulders more tense than they've ever been. "She shouldn't have to."

He nods repeatedly. As if we've finally made a breakthrough. "Exactly."

I blow out a disbelieving breath. Fuck this guy. "Have a nice life, Luiz."

"You too, Javier."

He absolutely means it as a final send-off. Considering I don't have a job to return to or anything else going on in my life, maybe it should be.

CHAPTER 45

Mari

Now

With my leaky eyes downcast, I bolt to my bridal suite, a million thoughts crashing around in my brain like bumper cars. When I get there, I shut myself inside and lean against the door. I gulp in several breaths as I survey the room. The space, decorated in celebration of the impending nuptials, mocks me at every turn. Sparkling-clean champagne glasses sit atop a gleaming silver tray. A vibrant basket of fruit covered in clear cellophane rests on the counter. My wedding dress, still in its double-lined garment bag, hangs from the wardrobe. All this pomp and circumstance. It's the icing on an underbaked cake. The glitter on a fast fashion outfit. A catchy tune sung by an off-key singer. Surface with no depth. If I'm being honest, I knew it from the outset. And still I went along with the charade because I thought it would be easier. Go to law school, join my father at the firm, get married to a well-respected person who could further my dreams. The end. All of this would make my father happy. All of this would align with what everyone expects of me. All of this would prove that my father's sacrifices were worth it. But *none* of this is real. Well, except my degree—that can never be taken away from me.

Oh God, what do I do now? I'm not even sure I've processed everything I overheard. At the very least, I'm not going to sit around a table with my groom's family pretending everything's okay. So I shoot Alex a text. Despite my chaotic thoughts, I manage to hide my distress: *Hey, sweetheart. So sorry, but I'm not feeling well. Going to skip out on the rest of dinner. Please pass along my regrets.*

He responds immediately: *Don't apologize. Tomorrow's a big day. We're almost done anyway. Do you need me to get you anything?*

"Yeah," I mutter to myself, "an enema so I can stick it up your ass."

To Alex, I reply: *I'm fine for now. Come see me when you're done.*

Because I need to look this man in the eye and find out what he knows. For now, I leave open the possibility that he's just as much of a pawn in my father's machinations as I am. But I'm steeling myself for the probability that he's very much an accomplice in this whole sordid fiasco.

* * *

Someone knocks on the door, and I freeze. I'm not ready to face anyone, so I remain silent, hoping whoever's there assumes the suite is empty and moves on.

"Mari," a trio of voices sings. "Let us in."

Sasha, Brittany, and Chloe are some of the most persistent people I know. There's no point in trying to avoid them, and I'm not sure I want to.

I trudge across the room and let them in.

"There you are," Brittany says, her hair covered with a scarf. "See? I told you she's fine."

Sasha, wearing a clay face mask and a fluffy robe, barges in and drops onto an armchair. "Alex texted to say you're not feeling well. We thought it might be pre-wedding jitters."

I scoff. "Hardly."

Sasha's eyes bulge. Chloe and Brittany tip their heads in my direction and wait for an explanation.

"Hang on," I say. "I need to get out of these clothes." As I walk to the bedroom, I unzip the sensible sheath dress that seemed perfect for dinner with my future mother-in-law but now feels all wrong. "Back in a sec."

When I return, I'm wearing an oversize T-shirt and slouchy sweatpants.

"What's the opposite of a glow-up?" Sasha asks.

"A dull-down," I say before lobbing a throw pillow at her head.

She laughs, dodging it with ease.

"Tell us what's going on," Chloe says, bouncing her crossed leg. "Something's not right."

"That's a cute short set," I tell her.

Chloe's eyebrows shoot up. "Are you high?"

I scrunch up my face. Honestly, I don't know whether to laugh or cry.

"Sweetie," Sasha says softly, "everything's going to be all right. Talk to us."

It's the encouragement I needed; after that, the floodgates open. I pick at my cuticles as I recount what I overheard in the men's bathroom, pausing to answer their clarifying questions. Sasha misses the point completely and fixates on what I was doing in the men's room in the first place.

"Sash, focus." I drop my head into my hands and groan. "Why is this happening?"

"This is the universe telling you that you shouldn't marry that man," Brittany says.

"You think?"

"I know," she says, nodding decisively. "We all do."

I look at all three of them. They're staring back at me with somber expressions. "Why didn't you say anything?"

"We did," Chloe offers. "Together and separately." She tilts her head back and forth, then adds, "Not outright, but we questioned why you were rushing to get married. Asked if you were certain. You assured us you knew what you were doing. I mean, after a certain point, we decided to trust your judgment."

"Why don't you think Alex is right for me?"

Sasha throws up her hands and chops them in the air. "Because. Javi's. Right. There."

Oh God. Javi. I've kept my feelings about his role in all of this in a locked box. Every time I consider unlocking it, I get overwhelmed. But Sasha's observation is spot-on. I cover my mouth and let out a muffled sob. "He's been here the whole time."

My girls are staring at me, nodding vigorously.

"We've been circling each other for years," I say, "but I finally resigned myself to the fact that he would never choose me, that he'd always erect roadblocks in our relationship. In his own way, though, Javi's been choosing me from day one."

"Hallelujah, a breakthrough," Sasha shouts, waving both hands in the air as if she's listening to a Sunday sermon.

I swallow and hold a hand against my chest. It's all coming together in my head. "In college, he chose our friendship over a relationship neither of us was ready for. And when I thought he'd abandoned me carelessly in my first year of law school, he was actually experiencing a rough patch and my father had pressured him to walk away."

Even now, on the eve of my wedding, Javi's prepared to let me go because he thinks the firm is my reason for being. And why would he think otherwise? I've never told him how I feel. Never given him an inkling that I care for him as much as he apparently cares for me. All this time, I've been too scared. Of rejection. Of not being chosen. I can't possibly marry Alex when the truth is staring me in the face.

"I love Javier," I say, my eyes flooding with tears.

"We know," they say in unison.

"Even if Alex isn't aware of my father's plans, I have to break up with him."

Sasha leans over from her spot on the armchair and squeezes my hand. "You do."

We all turn at the sound of someone knocking on the door.

Brittany jumps up, looks through the peephole, and lets out a long breath. "It's Alex."

We exchange worried glances.

"This is it," I say, lifting myself off the couch. "I know what I need to do. I'll check in with you guys later."

They gather their phones and key cards, then head to the door. Sasha turns back and points to a bottle of wine. "Can we take this? You won't be needing it, right?"

I give her a flat stare. She damn well knows she shouldn't be drinking wine.

"What about that fruit over there, then?" she says, glumly. "I can suck on the grapes and pretend it's the good stuff."

"The fruit's all yours," I say on a laugh while opening the door to usher Alex inside.

My friends slink past him without acknowledging his presence;

Sasha's the last to leave, the basket pressed against her chest and her nose in the air.

Alex raises a brow at their failure to greet him but quickly turns his attention to me. "Glad to see they checked on you. I came as fast as I could." He wraps me in his arms. "How are you feeling?"

"I'm fine," I say, easing out of his embrace. "But we need to talk."

"Okay." He ambles over to the couch, the confidence in his demeanor irking me because I highly doubt it's warranted.

I take the armchair Sasha was sitting in and inhale the faint scent of cocoa body lotion still lingering in the air. Alex and I simply stare at each other for several awkward beats. He blinks first, and I smile on the inside, appreciating this small but potent reminder that I'm in control of this conversation.

"Why did you ask me out last October?"

My question hangs in the air, and Alex's eyes go wide and unfocused. It's a split second of panic that vanishes just as quickly as it appeared. And in that moment, *I know*, I *absolutely know*, that Alex pursued me at my father's suggestion.

"I've always been interested in you, Marisol," he says, his voice calm and controlled. "Where is this coming from, babe?"

Ugh, *babe*. He's never called me *that* before. It's always princesa this, sweetheart that. I'm not a fan of either endearment, but *babe* is a decided step down from them both. It feels fitting. As if Alex's mask is slipping in increments as I discover more about him.

I roll my shoulders and take a deep breath. "I'm just going to say it. I heard an unfortunate conversation between my father and someone and it revealed things about us, about the reason for this marriage, about my future."

He peers at me, his face revealing nothing. "Who's the someone?"

I wave away the question. "Doesn't matter. The point is, my father has some very specific ideas about the implications of our marriage."

"Well, shouldn't you be talking to your father, then?"

"Oh, don't worry, I will. But in the meantime, I'm talking to you."

He shoves a hand through his hair, then cracks his knuckles. "What do you want me to say, Marisol?"

"I want you to tell me the truth. I deserve that much. I'm going to be your *wife*."

That false declaration seems to galvanize him. His eyes search my face as he recalibrates. He rises to his feet, then bends at the knee in front of me, taking my hand in his. He's a beautiful man, but he isn't meant for me.

"I *do* love you," he says, affection glowing in his eyes.

I nod and fill in the blanks for him. "But let me guess: It's a love founded on fondness and respect. It's not that soul-deep love. It doesn't upend your world."

He swallows, sadness clouding his features. "That's kind of the point, Marisol. I don't want my world upended."

"I thought I was looking for the same thing," I admit. "I guess I was afraid. Afraid of the kind of love that reaches the very core of you and risks destroying your soul if it's snatched away. I wanted a person I could rely on. Someone safe to share a life with. Now I see I went about this the wrong way." I take his chin and lift it. "Where does my father fit into this?"

Alex sighs, falls back on his haunches, and returns to his spot on the couch. "Three years or so after I joined the firm, your father took an interest in me, became my mentor. He started to make promises. That I would be his right-hand man. That I would run the firm one day. About a year ago I asked him how you would feel about that. You're obviously a force in your own right, and I expected that you'd be a part of the firm's future too. He said you would understand eventually, but that the entire transition would go more smoothly if you were satisfied that the firm would always remain in the family. He didn't say the words outright, but the implication was unmistakable."

"And that's when you asked me out."

He has the decency to look away. "Yeah."

It's the confirmation I didn't want yet sorely needed. The indisputable proof that my father has been stringing me along for years. I'm an unwitting participant in an arranged marriage. Except . . . I'm thirty years old. I have plenty of money. A fuckton of prospects. And I'm no damn burden to anyone. I *refuse* to be frightened by an unknown future.

I suppose I should have been suspicious of Alex's motivations, but if I'm being honest, he made his move at a time when I desperately wanted to sever my emotional connection with Javi. The fact that Alex was my father's protégé only made him more appealing. Because I've always been that little girl who wants to show her dad that she isn't an inconvenience, that she could add value to his life. I've been so preoccupied with not accepting crumbs from the men I've dated that I couldn't even recognize when I was accepting crumbs from my own father. Well, no more.

"I'm not going to marry you, Alex," I say softly.

He lets out a slow breath, then meets my gaze. "I figured as much."

"But I do need a favor from you."

He throws both hands over his heart. "You're killing me."

I narrow my eyes and give him a sinister smile. "Consider this: If people knew the real reason we aren't getting married, you'd end up looking much worse than you would in the narrative I'm contemplating."

"Jesus, you're merciless . . . but I'm listening."

"Good. Here's what I have in mind . . ."

CHAPTER 46

Javi

Now

"Bartender! Another!"

I raise my glass to get my new best friend's attention.

He throws a towel over his shoulder and glides over. "What's up?"

"I asked you to keep 'em coming."

"That's your fourth drink. Maybe you should slow it down."

"The love . . . of my heart . . . no, life, yeah, life . . . is marrying someone else tomorrow."

"Damn. Sorry, man." He sighs. "Are you staying on the property?"

"Yeah," I say, leaning back on my stool and rubbing my chest.

"One more," he says, lifting a single finger to underscore his point. "And then I'm going to have to cut you off, existential crisis or not."

"Fine," I grumble.

We fist-bump. "I'm Xavier."

"Javier."

"That's quite a coincidence."

"Your name sounds way"—I burp—"cooler."

"I have to agree."

"Make the last glass extra long, okay?"

"Tall, you mean?"

"Yeah. That."

He clucks his tongue and saunters off, leaving me alone with my muddled thoughts.

Not long after, loud, unintelligible voices pierce my bubble of melancholy, and I wince.

"Yo, this place is *unreal*," someone says in an awestruck tone.

"Worth the trip, for sure," another adds.

I *must* be drunk because these guys sound a lot like my brothers. They'd never travel here in a million years, though; that would be random as hell.

A hand slaps me on my back. "What's up, bro?"

I whip my head around and nearly topple off the stool. My older brothers are in California. I blink several times, tilting my head from side to side as I stare up at them. "What the fuck are you two doing here?"

"We're here for Marisol's wedding," Manny says.

I rub my eyes, then blink some more. "Why?"

"We're performing," Leandro explains.

They stare back at me, wearing gummy smiles and reeking of too much cologne. They're in the same uniform: black T-shirt, black belt, black jeans. They look like they're auditioning for roles as T-birds in *Grease*.

"Marisol said nothing would make her happier than having us sing at her wedding," Manny says, "so here we are."

"Marisol arranged for you to be here?" I ask slowly, trying to piece together what's happening.

"Yeah," Leandro says. "Only weird thing is, she wants us to perform 'Macarena' at the reception. That's kind of played out, right?"

Oh, this is diabolical. And perfect. And so damn Mari. She knew what this would mean to me. It's not the documentary chronicling my brothers' rise and eventual downfall, but it's pretty damn close. If I weren't already in love with her, this would be the moment I fall.

I chuckle, then full-out laugh my ass off.

Brows furrowed, my brothers exchange a glance, which only ratchets up my enjoyment.

Xavier returns with my drink and taps the bar counter. "What's up, fellas?"

"Meet Rico and Suave," I tell him. "My brothers."

Manny clips the back of my head. "Watch it. We can still put you in a headlock."

Xavier smirks. "Can I get you guys anything?"

"Corona if you have it," Leandro says.

Xavier nods. "I do. Be right back."

"Where's the third in your trio?" I ask. "Busy replacing an unsuspecting family member in another band, perhaps?"

"Damn, J," Manny says, climbing onto the stool next to mine. "You're still bitter about that?"

"No," I mutter. "I couldn't care less."

Which isn't true. My therapist tells me that experience made me question my worth, made me think I was deadweight in my own family. Ever since, I've lived with this fear that I'll be cast aside. Deemed unworthy. It's led to some remarkably poor decisions on my part, especially where Mari's concerned. That's heavy stuff to unpack, and I'm still processing it, but it's out of the box, which is a good start.

Leandro takes the seat on the other side of me. "Look, we probably didn't go about it the right way, but I think everything worked out for the best. You would have hated every second in the band."

I shouldn't even engage. This is only going to enrage me, and I don't have all of my faculties as it is. But this is some bullshit. "You're gaslighting me."

"Gaslighting?" Leandro asks, frowning. "Fuck does that mean?"

"It means you're trying to rewrite what happened. Trying to make me think that how I remember things isn't what happened at all. But I was there. *I* was the one who came up with the idea of the Triborough Boys. *I* was the one who searched for gigs. Y'all just went along with it because it would help you pull girls. And then when that record company started talking about money and what you would have to do to make it, you threw me away like yesterday's trash."

"You're right," Leandro says, his face flushing. "What we did was wrong, J. But we were young too, and we thought this was our way out. A way to make sure Mom and Pops didn't have to work until they took their last breath."

Manny clears his throat. "And if it's time for being honest and shit, we were jealous of you. *You* were the true talent. With your straight As and your ability to teach yourself piano and your fucking ridiculous vocabulary. You didn't need the Triborough Boys. We did."

"Perhaps you felt that way," I say, "but in the end, you screwed me."

"We're not denying that," Leandro says. "But we're older now. Wiser. Maybe it's time for us to be brothers. *Real* brothers."

I wish they'd said something like this years ago. Then again, I wasn't ready to listen. I'm not closing off the possibility that we could move past the band drama and how they treated me afterward, but I'm also not going to pretend all is forgiven. "Maybe" is what I manage to say.

Xavier reappears with a slip in his hands, presumably for my tab. "I'm comping you tonight," he says to me. "Can't have a man with a broken heart paying for his own drinks."

Manny draws back. "Broken heart? Who?" He points at me. "This guy?"

Xavier nods. "Says the love of his life is marrying someone else tomorrow."

My brothers' jaws drop, and their eyebrows lift in surprise.

"Oh damn, this is like those telenovelas Mami watches," Manny says.

"Tell us everything, man," Leandro says.

Which is how I end up recounting the entire mess to my brothers, starting with what happened that fateful weekend I visited Mari in L.A. eight years ago. When I'm done, my brothers peer at each other, their eyes sparking with mischief.

"Let's kidnap the fiancé," Manny suggests.

I roll my eyes. "That's a felony." Not that I didn't consider it for a millisecond.

"Or you could just tell Mari the truth," Leandro offers, his head tilted as if I'm ignoring the most obvious answer.

"I can't," I say. "It would break her heart to learn what her father's up to. And she'd never forgive him. Which means Alex gets what he wants anyway, and she loses her dad. If I keep my mouth shut, Mari gets the chance to run the firm with him. She's brilliant. A badass to the nth degree. Maybe her father will bend when he sees how well suited she is to the task."

"So you're just going to let the woman you love marry someone else?"

The question strikes at the very heart of me, breaks my spirit too. "Yeah, that's exactly what I'm going to do."

* * *

"Motherfucker!"

I'm staring at my reflection in the floor-length mirror in the cottage and trying not to lose my shit. And because I can't hold my liquor, I overslept and now have only twenty-seven minutes to get ready for the ceremony.

Leandro jerks awake and sits bolt upright in my bed. "What? What's wrong? What?"

The squatter crashed in my room last night, claiming he was too drunk to drive back to his offsite hotel; Manny disappeared with a woman he met at the bar. But I can't worry about these knuckleheads because I have an actual emergency on my hands.

"What the hell are you wearing?" Leandro asks, rubbing the sleep from his eyes.

I turn sideways, inspecting my profile. "The groom's idea of a joke, obviously."

"You look like Bo Peep."

Unfortunately, I immediately see the resemblance. Alex has arranged for me to wear a baby-blue suit with tiered ruffles on the cropped pant legs and a silver dress shirt with coordinating tiers down the front. He claimed the laundry valet was getting it cleaned and steamed, which is why I didn't see it until it was delivered moments ago.

Leandro snorts. "Actually, maybe it's a trend, like Jermaine Dupri at the Super Bowl."

"Fuck does that mean?"

Leandro grabs his phone, types in a few words, then holds the screen out so I can see it.

I groan. "If it's a trend, it shouldn't be, and I want no part of it."

Leandro climbs out of the bed, his boxers hanging off his hips. "What are you going to do about"—he points at my ridiculous getup—"that."

"I have the dress pants from yesterday and a regular button-down. Both still wet and reeking of alcohol." I scrub a hand across the back of my head. "Maybe I can get away with that?"

"Mari's going to be disappointed when she sees you. Or smells you, I should say."

I throw my head back and sigh. "She will be. Do you have time to—"

Someone knocks on the door, and we both whip our heads in the direction of the sound.

"Expecting anyone?" Leandro asks.

"No," I say, striding to the door. When I open it, Manny's standing there in a black suit and tie, a garment bag in his left hand.

"Wake up, pendejos!" he says, waltzing inside. "We have a wedding to attend!"

He looks me up and down and grimaces. "Why are you dressed like an elf?"

"Alex set me up, the asshole."

"Whoa. I guess he knows you're in love with Mari. Personally, I would have sent you room service and put a laxative in your coffee."

I shove him away from me. "You're *not* helping."

"Chill," he says, laughing.

I shove him again. "Now's not the time to be making jokes."

"Push me one more time," he says, fisting his hands.

"Or what?"

"Guys," Leandro interjects, "simmer down."

But it's too late, because Manny rushes me, then contorts my body until I'm trapped in a headlock. Soon after, we're tumbling around the room as if we have no home training.

Eventually, Leandro pulls us apart. Manny and I glare at each other, chests heaving.

Leandro breaks the silence by bleating like a sheep.

I narrow my gaze on him.

He throws up a hand, his eyes leaking with tears of amusement. "Sorry, man, but you really do look like a shepherd."

Manny snorts, and within seconds, I'm doubled over in laughter.

"It's good to have someone else Manny can beat up on," Leandro says. "He never picks on anyone his own size."

Manny and I stare at Leandro, and then we exchange a knowing glance.

Leandro's gaze swings between us. "What?"

"Lend me your suit," I plead.

"No way, I'm not performing in that costume," he says, backing up with his hands high in the air.

I fall at his feet. "You can get another suit during the wedding. No need for you to be there."

Leandro shakes his head. "Except she asked us to sing for the processional, so there's no time."

"But we can perform off to the side for now," Manny says. "No one really needs to see us until the reception."

Leandro mouths *Mind your business* to Manny.

"Please, Leandro," I beg from my position on my knees. "If you really want to make up for your treachery, this is a good place to start."

He sighs. "Give me the damn suit."

I jump up and discard the jacket in seconds. The pants are next. Leandro sneers at the various articles of clothing, holds them far from his body, and heads to the bathroom. Manny unzips the garment bag and presents the suit with a flourish.

He watches me as I get dressed. When I'm done, I survey my reflection in the mirror, confident that I look a thousand times better than Alex intended.

"Damn," Manny says, "that guy really doesn't like you."

"What gave it away?"

"He's willing to fuck up his own wedding to embarrass you."

Manny doesn't know that I've given Alex plenty of reasons to be vindictive. Still, he has a point. Shouldn't Alex and Mari's wedding day be off-limits to these kinds of games? If his only concern was to ensure that Mari was happy on their big day, he wouldn't have pulled this stunt. It occurs to me then: Whether or not he knew about Luiz's gambit, Alex isn't prepared to make Mari his number one priority.

And that's a big ol' red flag I can't ignore.

CHAPTER 47

Javi

The Wedding

I'm in awe of the picturesque landscape Mari and Alex have chosen as the backdrop for their ceremony. Nestled amid Crystal Canyon Farm's rolling vineyards, the meticulously groomed lawn stands apart from its surroundings, a slice of order within a natural oasis that refuses to be tamed. Behind the wedding arbor, a huge oak tree that's likely been here since time immemorial cloaks the space in shade and adds a majestic touch.

It's a beautiful place for someone to get their heart broken.

I refuse to let it be mine.

Alex cuts an imposing figure as he stands under the arbor and smiles at the guests. His cousin, Joel, and his uncle, Ramón, flank him like expressionless bodyguards. Joel's wearing sunglasses, for fuck's sake.

Beside me, Sasha smooths the skirt of her dress before taking my arm. She leans in close. "Hold on to that leash real tight. Mari will kill you if anything happens to that dog."

Thanks to Jeremy, Chocolicious looks sharper than I do in his silver bow tie and matching leash, and he's blissfully unaware of the drama that's about to unfold. If I could request one favor of him, I'd ask for a sudden need to pee right at Alex's feet.

Sasha looks up at me. "Ready?"

"Yes," I say, garbling the word.

"No regrets?" she whispers.

I sigh. "So many."

"It isn't too late to do something about it," she says, side-eyeing me with a pointed stare.

"Believe me, I'm well aware."

Her eyes widen and she shimmies her shoulders. "Okay, Javi, I see you." She wrinkles her nose. "But why is your brother wearing culottes?"

I bark out a laugh and shrug. "He's a strange bird" is all I permit myself to say.

To the right of us—and conspicuous enough to piss off Leandro—the Triborough Boys, accompanied by a guitarist, perform Luis Fonsi and Juan Luis Guerra's "Llegaste Tú." The lyrics are romantic, perfect for a wedding, but the narrator talks about being fortunate, about their role as the person who knows every line of their lover's hand, about walking by their side. Is that who Alex is to Mari? I suspect not. I knew that six weeks ago just as surely as I know it now.

Sasha tugs on my arm. "It's our turn."

I focus on the view in front of me, surprised that Chloe and Brittany are already several rows ahead of us.

Sasha and I glide forward, walking with a light step as instructed, and as I pass Alex on my left, we eye each other long enough for me to see a flicker of unease pass over his features. He licks his lips, then dabs the back of his neck with a kerchief. After a long, deep breath, he turns his gaze to the space Sasha and I just occupied. An instrumental interlude begins, and the guests stand as Mari and her father make their entrance, the soft murmur of oohs and aahs interspersing with audible gasps from the crowd.

I know she hates that Alex always calls her a princess, but in this moment she absolutely is. Her hair is pulled into a high ponytail, and a cascade of curls adorned with tiny iridescent pearls flows from the top of her crown. Her dress molds to her figure, a simple style that accentuates her shapeliness. Skin glowing, glossy lips parted, she radiates elegance and strength. It's a fucking sight to behold. The only thing that would improve her look is if she didn't have Luiz clutching her hand. He has no idea how precious she is, yet he still gets to walk her down the aisle.

I clock her every movement. She turns slightly, her eyes widening when her gaze snags on Leandro's ridiculous suit. Alex unwittingly gave me the gift that will never stop giving. She holds in a smile, then peers at me.

I swallow the lump in my throat, cuddle Chocolicious in my arms, and stare at my shoes. I'm here. I'm suppressing the urge to tackle Alex to the ground. She can't possibly expect me to watch her make her way to him. That's the very last thing in the world I want to see.

How long before we get to the vows anyway? Even a second more of this travesty would be too long.

Mari

I squeeze my father's hand, then present my bouquet to my mother, who's sitting in the front row. Her mouth gapes when I bend and kiss her forehead.

"Obrigada, Mãe. Por tudo."

I don't think I've ever thanked her for letting me stay in America with my dad. I've focused so much on my father's supposed sacrifice that I've discounted the gift she gave me, one she bestowed with a heavy heart but also with my best interests in mind.

She caresses my cheek. "I love you."

We exchange a smile, and then I turn back to Alex, whose eyes regard me with practiced affection.

"Hi," I say to him, my stomach overrun with butterflies.

"You look beautiful," he says. "Are you ready for this?"

I nod. "More than ready."

Teddy, the wedding officiant, chuckles. "The bride and groom are eager to get on with it," he says jovially, "so let us begin." His expression sobers, and then he says, "We are here today to witness the joining of two souls, Marisol Luzia Machado Campos and Alejandro Juan Carlos Flores Cordero . . ."

Am I really doing this?

I think I am.

Is this the most outrageous thing I've ever done in my life?

It is.

Will Javi even want this much attention on him?

Probably not.

Oh God, maybe I shouldn't put him on the spot.

Maybe it's the kind of gesture that will make him realize there's no one else for me.

I take quick, shallow breaths to calm my nerves. Oh Jesus, it's time.

"Marisol, are you ready to recite your vows?" Teddy asks.

I shake my head, unable to understand his question. "What?"

He leans over and whispers, "Your vows, dear. It's your turn to say them."

"Uh, but aren't you going to ask if anyone has an objection?"

Teddy squishes his eyebrows together and taps the book in his hand on his thigh. "That's not part of the ceremony anymore, dear."

I let out a sigh. "But—"

"What my fiancée is trying to get at," Alex whispers, "is that she'd *really* like you to ask if there's any objection."

Teddy looks between Alex and me, then nods. "Ah, I see." He scratches his head. "I think."

"Just wing it," I tell him. "*Please.*"

Teddy gives me a weak smile, then addresses the guests: "Friends and loved ones, Marisol and Alejandro—"

"Alex is fine," my fake fiancé says.

Teddy nods. "Oh yes. Sure. Uh, friends and loved ones, Marisol and Alex would like to go into this marriage with confidence that they have the full support of everyone in attendance. And as the wedding officiant, I have a vested interest in knowing there are no impediments to this marriage. So, if there is anyone who knows of any reason why the bride and groom should not be joined in matrimony, speak now or forever hold your peace."

I sway on my feet as the murmur of the crowd reaches my ears, and then I gather the strength to say what's in my heart: "I object!" It's so loud that the words echo in my ears.

"It's about damn time," Sasha mutters.

People gasp; others laugh; there's a "¡Madre de Dios!" in there as well. But everyone's looking past me, their attention trained on—I look over my shoulder—Javi?

Alex leans forward and whispers, "He objected too."

I whirl around, my hand pressed to my chest, and gape at my best friend. "What's going on?"

Javi meets my gaze as he rushes toward me. "I'm sorry. I

promised myself I wouldn't do this. But then—" His brow furrows. "Did you just object to your own wedding?"

I nod vigorously, my eyes wet with tears of laughter. "I did."

His mouth twitches, and it's the most beautiful sight I've ever seen. "Must you *always* have the last word? Always?"

I snort. "Oh my God, I can't believe this is my life right now."

I dart a glance at my father, who's frozen, his jaw on the floor.

Alex's mom jumps up from her chair and raises her index finger in the air. "¡Qué grosero! ¡Qué maleducado! ¡Así no es como se trata a alguien!" And then she marches off, her daughters trailing after her.

Well, Señora Cordero has a point, but she also has no idea that her son isn't blameless here and that I'm extending him more grace than he deserves.

A few steps of angry stomping later, Alex's mother spins around. "¡Alejandro! ¡Vámanos!"

Alex bares his teeth sheepishly, then grabs my hand. "I need to play the part of the aggrieved groom. We'll talk, yeah?"

I nod my assent, though I barely spare him a glance because I can't take my eyes off Javi.

"Can we talk?" Javi asks, handing off Chocolicious to Jeremy, who moonwalks out of the way. "In private?"

Teddy, the officiant, clears his throat. "Um, Ms. Campos, am I done here?"

I wince, then grimace apologetically. "Sorry, Teddy. Yes, we won't be needing you anymore."

"And that's a good thing?" he asks.

I throw my arms around him. "That's a *great* thing."

He pats me on the back. "Well, all right."

"Marisol!" my father calls out in an irate voice. "What is the meaning of all this?"

I release Teddy from our awkward hug and face my father head-on. "Javi and I need to talk. I'll find you later."

"*Later*," he says, gesticulating wildly. "You blow up the wedding that I paid a fortune for, and you'll talk to me *later*? Que diabos é isso?"

The front of Javi's body brushes mine as he positions himself behind me. That show of support means everything. It tells me that I'm not alone, that he'll stand by me no matter how I decide to handle the situation. I reach back and clutch his hand, then address my father. "You and I will talk when I'm ready. In the meantime, you should probably check in with your successor. He's the future of the firm, isn't he?"

My father's eyes blaze with contempt when his gaze lands on Javi. "Whatever he told you is a lie."

"*He* didn't tell me anything," I say, shaking my head. "I *heard* you. In the restroom. I heard all about your big plans. Just know that I will no longer be a part of them, so do with that what you will."

He points a finger at me. "You—"

"Fica quieto, Luiz," my mother snaps. "Você já disse o suficiente!" He clenches his jaw, looks between Javi and me, and then stomps off.

My mother mimics his blustery departure, drawing a few laughs from my friends. Her expression quickly sobers when she looks at me, her gaze softening as she squeezes my hand. "Go. Focus on you." She winks at Javi. "And him."

I glance around the garden. A dozen or so guests linger in the aisle; a few remain in their seats. To them, I say, "I'm so sorry, everyone." I consider explaining why I wrecked my own wedding, but I need to explain it to Javi first, so instead I say, "There's a lovely brunch waiting for you in the great room. Please enjoy yourselves."

Then I gather up the skirt of my dress and wave my bouquet around, unsure what to do with it.

"I'll take it," Brittany says, reaching for my free hand. "You got this."

"Thanks," I say, sniffling.

Sasha walks up. "Do you want me to . . . ?" She points to the hair comb holding my veil in place.

"Oh. Yeah," I say, rolling my eyes. "I won't be needing it anymore."

She smiles as she removes the veil, then says, "Much better." She wraps me in her arms. "You did good today. Remember, we'll always be here for you."

"I know," I say, squeezing her tight. "Love you."

"I love you too," she says. "Now go climb that man and get yourself some vitamin D."

I snort into her neck. When Sasha and I separate, I take a deep, cleansing breath and thread my fingers through Javi's. "Ready?" I ask him.

"Absolutely."

There's still so much to discuss, but it's the word I needed to hear. His assurance. His conviction. Because I've never been more certain that this man belongs in my future. Now I just need to know once and for all whether he's ready to take the leap with me.

CHAPTER 48

Javi

Now

As Mari and I wander the property, I clench and unclench my fists, trying to stop my hands from shaking. I've never felt more off-kilter in my life.

Mari isn't marrying Alex. Today or *any* day, apparently. And I don't know what this means for us, or whether it means *anything* for us, even, but I'm going to say my piece and accept the consequences.

She points to a low retaining wall that separates the main building from the cottages, the edges of the sunlit vineyards just in sight.

"This works," I say.

Mari raises the skirt of her wedding gown and tries to hoist her butt onto the stone cap, but she isn't tall enough to reach it.

"Here, let me help you," I say, lifting her by the waist.

Once she's situated, I settle next to her.

We sit together in silence for a long moment, until she raises her shoulders and lets out a long sigh. "I don't know where to begin."

I angle my body in her direction, eager to see every single expression on her face. "I don't know where to begin either. There's so much to say, but I'm worried I'll frighten you off."

She laughs. "Javi, I just called off my wedding. I'm made of sturdy stuff."

"Fair point, fair point," I say, rolling my shoulders, then stretching my neck. *Okay, you can do this, Javi.*

"Are you about to run a race?" Mari asks with an impish smile. "Need me to help you loosen your—"

"I love you," I say, unable to hold back the words any longer. "And it feels so damn good to finally say it out loud. Properly. Without reservation. That's the most important thing I need to tell you today."

Her smile slips just as her eyes widen, and then she draws in a steadying breath. "Go on."

I take her hand with every intention of saying all the things I regrettably left unsaid over the years. "I've fucked this up—this, *us*—for so long, and I don't want another second to pass without you knowing that, for me, it's you, it's *always* been you, it could never be anyone *but* you. It's taken more time than I want to admit for my brain to catch up with my heart. For too long, I made excuses for why we couldn't be together, why I didn't deserve you, why I'd never be enough for you. I let my fears and insecurities get in the way of fighting for the one thing I want most in this world."

"What do you want most in the world?" she whispers cautiously.

I don't want her to wonder what she means to me. I don't want her to guess how much I care. So I bring my forehead to hers, needing to be as close to her as possible when I say this: "What I want most in the world is your love in return."

She caresses my cheek, her sweet breath tickling my skin. "Oh, meu amor, you have it."

That simple declaration stitches itself onto my heart, and now it'll be with me wherever I go. Those few but mighty words give me the courage to tell her everything: the hang-ups, the doubts, the voices in my head that convinced me our friendship was all I could hope for. I finally tell her about her father. About the way his malicious words wormed themselves into my brain and settled there. I tell her, too, how much and how long I've adored her. "There wasn't a moment in all the years since I've known you that I wasn't in love with you. I pushed you away, at first because I wanted to protect you, and then because I wanted to protect myself. I'm so fucking sorry I let my fears get in our way." She listens intently, her gaze never leaving my face. When I'm done, I squeeze my eyes shut, then open them, drawing back so I can peer at her. "Tell me you love me. Say it out loud. Please."

"I love you, Javi," she says, her eyes steady and bright. "It's been a journey to get here, it really has, but you are the love of my life. Always have been. You're the person who knows me best. The person who's always looked out for me—even when I didn't realize I needed you to. The person who knew I deserved more when I couldn't see that on my own. We don't just fit. We're unique and interlocking pieces, with curves and edges that make it impossible for us to fit together with anyone else."

I'm overwhelmed by her words. They reveal so much more than I'd ever imagined for us. "You're incredible."

"And don't you forget it," she says with a wink. But then her smile fades much too soon. "There's something else, though."

"What?" I ask, an empty feeling settling in the pit of my stomach.

"I know you want to slay dragons in my honor, but you can't protect me from the ugliness of the world. If we're going to be partners, you need to trust that I can handle whatever life throws at us. When there's a problem, we need to tackle it *together*."

I nod so hard my head hurts. "Together. From this point on."

"Together," she agrees, her eyes glistening. "I like the sound of that."

Mari's absolutely the one. Always will be. I'm so fucking happy I feel weightless. Unstoppable but also utterly weak for her. I rest my finger under her chin and lean in for a kiss. She meets me halfway, fluttering her eyes closed and sighing happily when our lips touch. My heart thumps as I worship her lips, kissing them softly, reverently. Mari is mine, and I am hers. It's just that simple.

When we separate, I push a curl off her face and stare at her in wonder. "I can't believe any of this is real."

"It's not just real," she says, stroking my jaw, "it's forever."

Forever.

Para siempre.

Para sempre.

That's been our promise for so long. Now we're finally making good on it.

EPILOGUE

Mari

Two Years After the (Canceled) Wedding

A finger trailing across my hip wakes me from a restful sleep. The sun's just barely in the sky, but I can already hear Manhattan stirring outside our Soho apartment.

I peek under the coverlet to find Javi positioned between my legs, the breadth of his shoulders taking up much of the view. "May I help you?"

He looks up at me, waggles his unruly eyebrows, and licks his lips. "Yes, indeed. I'd like a table for one, please."

I throw an arm over my eyes and giggle. "Certainly, sir. We've reserved a special seating just for you." I gesture at the length of my body. "Right this way."

"Excellent," he says, his mouth tilted up in a saucy grin, his pupils blown wide. "I'm ravenous."

"May I interest you in the all-you-can-eat buffet, then?"

His mouth twitches. "You may."

Javi kisses a path across my belly, then nibbles on the skin at the juncture of my thighs. I let out a low moan and raise my arms over my head. My stomach contracts with each brush of his lips, each nip. I'm so damn warm, a steady throb in my ears matching the thump of my heart. This is what he does to me. Every time. I'm feverish with lust within seconds, desperate to have his hands all over me, desperate for us to rock into each other.

He lowers himself farther down the bed so I can widen my legs and wrap them around his torso, and then his fingers ghost over me as he sucks on the inside of my thighs.

"You're such a tease," I groan, writhing on the bed, my hands gripping the sheet.

"Is there something you need?" he asks, playfully taunting me.

I grab the back of his head, my thumbs pressed against his temples so he understands the urgency of my request. "I need your fingers in me and your mouth on my clit. For starters."

Javi's eyes gloss over. "What a coincidence. I was just about to get to that." And he does, his fingers splaying me open as he inhales my scent, hums his approval, and then laps at my nub.

I arch like a bow, heat radiating through my limbs when he strokes his tongue against my pussy, the tip flicking my clit and a single digit sliding inside to revel in my wetness. He groans against me when I grab his shoulders, when I dig my fingers into the skin of his back, the muscles there flexing under my needy touch.

"Oh God, come up here," I beg. "Please, I need you inside me."

We waste no time aligning our bodies, the coverlet thrown to the floor. Javi looms over me, his rigid cock in hand, his chest heaving. The sight of him makes me fuzzy, my brain dulling from the overload of sensation sweeping through my body. It's the anticipation, the exhilaration, the certainty that he will fill me to the hilt and drive me to the brink before backing off and building me up over and over again.

In the time we've been together, we've learned what brings us pleasure, what drives us wild. He knows that a breath against my ear inflames me. I know that he loves it if I grab his ass when he's driving into me. We've learned each other's love languages and added some new words of our own.

Javi positions himself at my center and pushes inside.

"Oh God, that's *so* good," I groan out.

He covers my body with his and grinds into me, his gaze never leaving mine. "It's always so damn good."

And it is. Because we've finally figured out that love isn't about being in the right place or finding the right time. It's about making a connection with the right person. Once that happens, everything else eventually falls into place.

* * *

Chocolicious whines outside our bedroom, bursting our post-sex bubble.

Javi lets out a heavy exhale. "I'll take him out. I need the fresh air anyway."

He starts to rise, but I pull him back under the covers. "Hang on a sec. I heard that sigh, so why don't you tell me what's *really* going on."

"I'm nervous about tonight," he says after a pause, his voice barely above a whisper.

I snuggle into him, tracing circles on his chest. "Oh, my love. I'd be nervous if you *weren't* nervous. But you've done everything possible to make *The Mailroom* a success. You've put your ego aside and found people to help you. You listened to the folks with more experience than you while never letting anyone alter the core of your vision. I'm no theater expert, but I've read the script, listened to the songs. It's phenomenal and others are going to feel the same."

"Doesn't matter what others think as long as you enjoy it."

"Well, let's not overstate the value of my opinion," I quip.

He lifts my chin and peers down at me. "I'm not joking. This is one of the scariest things I've ever done in my life, and if it bombs, it bombs. As long as it moves you, I'll be satisfied."

"But it'll be nice if everyone else loves it too, right?"

He smiles sheepishly. "Of course. But no one else matters. You told me so yourself."

I draw back. "What? I never said any such thing."

"You did," he says. "I'll show you." He reaches for his wallet on the bedside table, pulls out what looks like a laminated Post-it, and hands it to me.

I sit up in bed and scan the note—in *my* handwriting. My eyes bulge when the significance of the message sinks in. "This was from the night before graduation." I gape at him, my eyes blurring with tears. "You kept it? All these years?"

"I did," he says, nodding, his eyes glowing with warmth. "Now read it out loud."

I clear my throat. "'Javier Báez's untitled musical is an absolute masterpiece. Báez is the librettist of our generation.'" I turn the laminated note over. "'Marisol Campos, the only critic who matters.'"

I pull him to sit up with me and straddle his thighs, wrapping him in an embrace so fierce my limbs shake. "Just when I think I couldn't love you more . . ."

Javi

Daniel Romero sings the final verse of "What If" to a packed crowd at the tiny but mighty Public Theater. Danny's portrayal of Sid, a man who's come to terms with the choices he's made in his life and who has no regrets, is both tender and triumphant.

Sid reminds me of myself. Reminds me of the person who finally believed in his worth and got out of his own way. Beside me, Mari's fighting back tears, her hand squeezing mine. We're backstage, both of us too keyed up to have spent a second in the audience for the premiere.

Sid picks up the banker's box filled with his personal effects and walks away, refusing to look back at his coworkers. As he steps onto an elevator and faces the spectators, he sings the closing lyrics:

There's no point in wondering what if anymore
I want to know what my future holds
I want to grab it in my hands
I decide who I'll be
Never again will life make a fool of me

The stage fades to black, and then the house lights come on. After a heart-stopping pause, the audience breaks out into thunderous applause, a sound and sentiment that I will never forget. Within seconds, I'm being hugged by Mari, jostled by Jeremy, patted on the back by Arnie, the lead stage technician. Mari's mother, who's visiting for the summer for the second year in a row, presses a kiss to my forehead. Brittany congratulates me, Chloe high-fives me, Sasha tells me she wants to kick my ass for waiting so long to finish the script.

Everything that follows is a blur: an appearance onstage with the full cast; an interview with a reporter from Broadway.com that probably made no sense; a speech among countless speeches thanking everyone involved for not only bringing my vision to life but also making immeasurable improvements to it; a text from my agent telling me he's already fielding calls about the possibility of taking *The Mailroom* to Broadway; a quick chat with Stephen Lautner, the director, to discuss what needs to be changed for the remaining shows.

Through it all, Mari's always within arm's reach. I spy her chatting with my parents, although in typical fashion, my dad appears more interested in the hors d'oeuvres being passed around, and my mother's rearranging the dessert display. Then I see Mari chatting with my brothers, who probably don't understand that although she runs her own entertainment law firm now, she isn't actually responsible for getting jobs for the talent she represents. I seek her out in the crowd at every opportunity. Her presence fuels me. Gives me peace. Brings me more genuine happiness than I ever thought possible.

Which is why, even though I can't see her face, I sense that she's in distress a few minutes later: Her shoulders are squared, one hand is wrapped around a wineglass, the other hand is balled into a fist.

"Excuse me," I say to one of the show's investors. I don't bother to offer an explanation, and I instantly appear at Mari's side. It's then that I realize she's seeing her father in person for the first time since the weekend of her aborted wedding.

"What are you doing here?" she asks, her voice shaking.

"I bought a ticket like everyone else," Luiz Campos says. "I didn't tell you because I didn't think you'd listen to what I had to say."

Her face hardens. "You chose one of the most important nights of Javier's life to show up unannounced. How did you think this would go?"

I wrap my arm around her waist and pull her close. I'd never tell her how to handle this situation. Whatever she wants, whatever she needs in this moment, that's what I'll give her.

"Can I talk to you in private?" he begs. "Just give me five minutes."

Mari looks up at me. "Is there somewhere . . . ?"

"Of course," I say, nodding. "Use the rehearsal room."

"Thanks," she says, though she seems to be operating in a daze, barely aware of her surroundings.

"Do you need me to go with you?" I ask, bending so I can meet her gaze head-on.

She smiles and squeezes my arm. "No, I've got this."

I have zero doubt that she does.

A few minutes later, she returns and slips her hand into mine. I look down at her, searching her face for any signs of distress, but there are none.

"Everything okay?" I ask.

She caresses my jaw, her expression serene. "I'm here with you, so everything's good."

"What was all that about?" I say, jerking a thumb behind us.

"Long story short, he apologized. Says he wants a chance to be the father he never was. Said he knows he can't fix things between us overnight, but he wants to try."

"And you're willing to do that? Try?"

"We'll see," she says, raising a shoulder. "I suspect he has more work to do if he thought this was the right time to reach out. But I don't have to decide anything tonight. We're here to celebrate you."

"We're here to celebrate us too."

"I like the sound of that: us."

"It'll always be us, Mari."

"Always," she agrees.

The air around us is charged with electricity and excitement, everyone riding the high of a wildly successful night, but it's my connection with Mari that makes me feel invincible, that makes me want to take on another day and tackle whatever challenge it presents. Because, in her eyes, I can see the man I want to be. Because we push each other to be the best versions of ourselves. Because when I'm in her arms, there's nowhere else I'd rather be.

"Ready to sneak out of here?" I ask.

"With you?" she says, her eyes blazing with affection and a dash of heat. "Absolutely."

While the cast is stagedooring out back, we slip through a side exit to avoid the chaos. There's a car waiting out front, and thankfully, no one's paying us any mind. Before we climb in, Mari looks up at the theater's marquee. "That's your name up there," she says, pointing at the sign. "Can't wait to see it on Broadway too."

I pull her into my arms. "I was thinking, if it gets to Broadway—"

"*When*," she insists.

"Right. I was thinking, *when* it gets to Broadway, I'd like my name on the marquee to read Javier Campos-Báez. Thoughts? Suggestions? Counterproposals?"

Her eyes go wide as saucers, and her mouth falls open, but she recovers quickly and straightens her shoulders. "You'd be taking on my dad's name, though. You realize that, right?"

"I'd be taking on part of your name, and that's all that matters."

"Well, then I think you're a brilliant man. No notes."

We seal our next chapter with a kiss. And it's magic. As if the seed that was planted so long ago has finally come into bloom.

"I love you, Marisol."

"I love you too, Javier."

"Para siempre," I say.

She gazes at me tenderly, her eyes glowing with the same soul-stirring love I feel for her. "Para sempre."

- The End -

ACKNOWLEDGMENTS

That was fun, wasn't it?

Thank you, dear reader, for opening your heart and mind to Javi and Mari's story. I'm truly honored that you spent some of your precious time in my fictional world. I hope it brought you a bit of joy, made you laugh, and kept you turning the pages to see how these two would finally figure out that they're meant to be together.

As you can probably imagine, *When Javi Dumped Mari* (*WJDM* for short) could not have been published without the help of dozens of folks; here is where I get to express my deep gratitude for their part in getting *WJDM* into your hands.

To Kate Dresser, my editor extraordinaire: From the beginning, I had a hunch that our partnership would thrive, and I'm thrilled that my instincts were spot-on. You took the word salad I gave you and helped me turn it into an honest-to-goodness book. What a feat! Your ability to see the big picture and distill it to its essence was invaluable, and your guidance centered me in those moments when I questioned what I was doing. Thank you for honoring my vision and being such an encouraging presence throughout the editorial process.

To Sarah Elizabeth Younger, my agent and GIF master: Before we started working together almost a decade ago, you told me you

ACKNOWLEDGMENTS

wanted to be my champion and support me over the course of a long career. You've done that and more. I can't imagine navigating the publishing gauntlet with anyone but you at my side. Sending you so much love.

To Tarini Sipahimalani: Is there anything you can't do? I'm in awe of your ability to tackle any situation with kindness and professionalism. Putnam is very lucky to have you, and I'm doubly lucky to work with you.

To Lindsay Sagnette, Regina Andreoni, Katie McKee, Jazmin Miller, Brittany Bergman, and the rest of the Putnam team working behind the scenes to get *WJDM* into the world: It's been such a pleasure! You have welcomed me into the family with open arms, and I am honored to be the beneficiary of your efforts and expertise.

To Sanny Chiu: I bow down to you! The *WJDM* cover is a thing of beauty, and I am in awe of your design prowess.

To Julia Jacob: You are a rock star, and I can't thank you enough for illustrating the characters of my dreams.

To my beta readers, Ana Coqui and Denia R. Martinez, and my trusted early reader, Tracey Livesay: Your eagle eyes and respect for the craft of writing shone through in your feedback, and *WJDM* is all the better for it. Let's do this again, please.

To Zoraida Córdova, Alexis Daria, Adriana Herrera, and Tracey Livesay: This was a scary endeavor, and you ladies helped me through it. You're all brilliant and witty, and I aspire to be an amalgamation of each of your best traits. Thanks for the big hugs, the sound advice, and the countless laughs.

To my cousin Fernanda Santos-Shaw, who answered a dozen questions about the Portuguese phrases in *WJDM* and was always willing to help out at a moment's notice: Obrigada, prima. Beijos!

To Victoria Colotta of VMC Art & Design and Shelbe Renè: I'm

ACKNOWLEDGMENTS

so lucky to have you both in my corner. Now I can *really* step away from Canva.

To Kristin Dwyer and Molly Mitchell of LEO PR: Thank you for sprinkling a bit of your PR magic to help this book shine.

To the many author friends who make the romance community a special place, particularly Olivia Dade, the #BatSignal crew, and the #LatinxExcellence collective: I love that we're doing this thing together, and I'm rooting for all of us.

To the booksellers, librarians, book influencers, book reviewers, and book lovers who shout their love of romance books from the rooftops: I wish you endless TBRs filled with fantastic books that feed your souls and warm your hearts.

To my girls: I am immensely proud to be your mother. Thanks for helping me brainstorm, thanks for listening, thanks for being you. I couldn't love you two more. Truly.

To my mother: No, I'm not *still* working on the book; I'm working on the next one. Thanks for always being there and being more than enough. Te amo.

To my husband, the person who knows me best: I'm so glad you took that leap all those years ago. You are my constant, my lodestar, my everything. You're always patient, kind, and thoughtful. How fortunate am I that the man of my dreams is also the man of my waking hours? But please don't let any of this go to your head; I'm a great catch too. ☺

DISCUSSION GUIDE

1. This novel's title in some ways pays homage to the classic romantic comedy *When Harry Met Sally,* but with a twist. Discuss how author Mia Sosa uses the title both to set and upend your expectations about Javi and Mari's journey.

2. The story opens with an on-edge Javi eager to declare his feelings for Mari. Of course, nothing goes as planned. What would you do if you were in Javi's position? Based on their story, discuss to what extent a romantic relationship that starts off as a friendship has a seamless path forward.

3. From the get-go, we are primed with Javi and Mari's complicated history. Still, Alex is introduced to readers alongside Javi in the very first chapter. What were your initial impressions of Javi and Alex, respectively? Discuss how, if at all, Sosa signals to readers where our allegiance should lie.

4. Young Javi and Mari find their way to a pact, which allows them to decide who the other can or cannot date. What did you initially make of this pact? Did you think it was fair? In which

DISCUSSION GUIDE

ways do we already carry out the essence of such a pact in our closest relationships?

5. In the first few chapters, Mari thinks, "Contrary to whatever Javi might believe, this engagement isn't an impulse or a rebound. It's a manifestation of the mature love I've always dreamed of. Steady. Dependable. *Grown*." What do you think drives Mari's quest for "mature love"? To what extent is this a universal pursuit? How does the idea of "mature love" interact with "true love" if the timing might not be right? Do you believe in "right person, wrong time"?

6. When Javi first meets Mari's dad, Luiz, it's clear Luiz doesn't deem Javi suitable. Why do you think Mari's dad is so difficult to please? To what extent should one factor in family when it comes to making decisions in love?

7. *When Javi Dumped Mari* is set on two coasts. Discuss whether distance played a role in Javi and Mari's mismatched timing before the point at which the story opens.

8. Mari keeps a Post-it at her desk reminding her of this: "You are allowed to be both a masterpiece and a work in progress, simultaneously." Discuss what this might look like in the context of a relationship.

9. Throughout the story, Javi considers himself a work in progress. How does this self-assessment affect his openness to a relationship with Mari? Discuss whether his concerns were well-founded.

DISCUSSION GUIDE

10. Sosa intentionally denotes any non-English phrases in roman. Discuss how else Sosa takes care to prioritize and promote cultural diversity in *When Javi Dumped Mari*.

11. The book plays with narrative structure, whether it's through flashbacks directed by Javi and Mari's present-day recounting, Mari and Javi's text messages, or the voice memos from Mari's mother. How did the story's structure enhance the read?

12. Mari's mother, Patrícia, no longer lives in the United States, yet she manages to maintain a close relationship with her daughter despite the physical distance between them. Discuss how Sosa depicts this unique mother-daughter relationship and the unresolved tensions that sometimes arose as a result of Patrícia's decision to return to Brazil.

13. What was your favorite scene in the novel, and why?

14. What do you see next for Javi and Mari?

Keep reading for an exciting excerpt from

The Starter Ex

by Mia Sosa

PROLOGUE

Vanessa

It started out as a joke. In my junior year of college.

Red flags: 2. Vanessa: 0.

My roommate at Penn's International House, Elena Fernández, a well-off Spaniard who was fluent in two languages but skilled at cussing in five, complained that she'd been unable to snag the attention of her latest boy crush. He seemed mildly interested, she explained, and they'd gone on a few dates, but she couldn't close the deal (her words, not mine). What she wanted was a boyfriend. What *he* wanted wasn't entirely clear.

One evening, Elena and I sat at the table in the living room of our two-bedroom campus-adjacent apartment, noshing on jamón, albóndigas, and patatas bravas. Elena was an excellent cook; many of the international students were. Indeed, the high probability that I could sponge off their scraps factored heavily into my decision to select International House as my top choice in the school's emergency housing lottery.

Minutes into stuffing our faces, Elena ventured into uncommon territory: asking for someone else's opinion. "What would you do if you were me, Vanessa?"

I took a sip of water before I spoke. "Honestly? I'd find another crush."

I didn't understand why this was such a big issue. College boys back then were as interchangeable and as ubiquitous as off-brand iPhone chargers.

"But I like *him*," she said, her eyes pleading with me to devise a solution.

"The thing is," I said in between bites, "he needs a push in your direction."

"Get him jealous, you mean?" she asked, her eyes wide and creepily unblinking.

"Nah, that's not something you want to encourage."

"So what do you suggest?"

I thought about it for a second and casually dropped this gem: "You know what would be downright Machiavellian? If you could manufacture the world's worst girlfriend to date him for a while. Then, when she's made his life miserable and he's hit rock bottom, you can swoop in and save the day. Be the breath of fresh air he so desperately needs."

Blissfully unaware of the wheels turning in Elena's brain, I chomped on fried potatoes while she picked at her food.

Suddenly she straightened in her chair and set her plate aside. "It's a brilliant idea, actually."

"What?" I asked, my eyebrows snapping together. "No, it isn't. I was *joking*."

"Joking or not, I think you're absolutely right. And I want *you* to be the girlfriend."

I cackled. I wheezed. My eyes welled up with tears. Until I realized Elena wasn't joining in on my amusement. "Oh shit. You're serious?"

"Very."

I scoffed as I brought my dirty dish to the sink, the ratty sweatpants I adored sitting on my curvy hips. "Absolutely not."

"I'll pay you."

Insert the proverbial record scratch.

I'm ashamed to say the prospect of getting paid made me pause. After all, I was a scholarship student living off work-study hours I'd been fitting into a jam-packed schedule of classes and frequent weekend trips to New York to help my overworked parents run a bodega in East Harlem.

Not that Elena knew any of this.

Making sure to mask any eagerness in my voice, I asked, "How much are we talking about?"

She shrugged. "For two to three weeks of your time? Does a thousand dollars per week sound fair? We can see where we stand after that."

My heart galloped in my chest. Three thousand dollars. With the possibility of extra cash if the assignment proved to be more challenging than expected. Damn, I could do *so* much with that money. Buy books for next semester. Send most of it to my family. Not kiss my roommate's ass in order to eat a decent meal, at least for a month or two. Which reminded me: "Kissing?"

She narrowed her eyes. "If you must. No fooling around, though, and *definitely* no sex."

"Oh, you don't have to worry about that."

But teasing was fair game, it seemed. And hey, I could be coy. I certainly could be a bitch. Someone's worst nightmare? Sin duda. These were my personality traits in a nutshell, so the assignment wouldn't be a stretch by any means. In fact, this would be a cinch.

Well, that's what my overconfident and underdeveloped twenty-year-old brain reasoned, at least. So Elena and I shook hands, and thus began my lucrative college side gig.

By the time I graduated with a degree in business from Wharton, I'd served as the starter ex for ten struggling-to-solidify relationships. Bonus? I never had to explain why I wasn't interested in dating anyone—because I *was* dating. Sort of.

Yes, I should have kept this highly problematic venture firmly in my past. But I didn't. And now I'm screwed. What follows is my pathetic story. You're going to want to grab some popcorn for this one.

Side note (in case you were wondering): A few years ago, Elena and her boy crush got married in a lavish waterfront ceremony at Penn's Landing. They didn't invite me to the wedding.

CHAPTER 1

Vanessa

Present Day

Let's get this out of the way: I'm a terrible person. No, I'm not being self-deprecating in an effort to gain your sympathy; I truly am a terrible person. If you trust me on this now, whatever happens next will make a whole lot more sense. That said, I believe in seeking redemption, so after working as a financial planner in Chicago for eight years and accepting a job transfer over unemployment in a limp economy, I'm back in New York licking my wounds and trying to make amends for my past transgressions. Judging by my younger sister's flat expression as she studies the restaurant menu in her hands, I have my work cut out for me.

We're sitting in Grenadine's Café on the Upper East Side of Manhattan. My treat, my choice. I may have miscalculated on that front. Admittedly, it's a bad habit of mine—miscalculating things, that is.

"Is this supposed to be appealing?" Lisa asks, her dark brown eyes narrowing in confusion. "Pea foam and carrot purée? And how the hell does one deconstruct bread?" She sighs and tosses the menu on the table, a huff of breath ruffling her curly bangs. "Get the hell out of here with this."

For as long as I can remember, this has been my life: straddling two worlds, the haves and the haves-not-enough, neither of which fully embraced me. Or I suppose it's more accurate to say I never fully embraced them.

Jesus. It's as if the overwrought prose in my brain just writes itself.

Get it together, Vanessa. You're here to atone for your mistakes.

"This isn't what I usually eat, but the place is close to the new office, and I'm trying to find lunch options so I'll be ready to entertain clients once we start accepting them."

She dismisses my explanation with a wave. "Ah, this is research. How convenient . . . for you."

Oof. Lisa's not in the mood for my bullshit. And I don't blame her. Still, it's hard to square the person in front of me with the fifteen-year-old who worshipped the ground I walked on when I left home for college more than a decade ago. Since then, she's always been polite whenever our paths cross, which, granted, hasn't been often, but civility between siblings is an embarrassingly low bar, and her attitude this afternoon suggests she's no longer interested in meeting even that. There's a bite to her personality I'm not used to, and it only underscores how far we've grown apart.

Promising to return for our orders "in a jiff," the server sets down our glasses of water and rushes off.

"I'll let you choose next time," I say, leaning over to take Lisa's hand.

She dodges my effort and sits up straight. "Why am I here?"

I roll my shoulders and compose myself. This isn't going to be easy, but I want to lessen the tension between us—once and for all. "I'm sorry."

The blanket apology snags her attention. She stares at me, and for the first time since we sat down, the furrow between her eyebrows disappears. "For what exactly?"

"For everything, Lisa. For leaving New York and never looking back. For saddling you with the job of looking out for Mami and Papi on the daily. For missing out on some really important moments in your life: Prom. High school graduation. The celebration dinner when you got your master's degree. Hell, for limiting your opportunities because you felt you had to be the one to stick around and watch over our parents."

I didn't *want* to miss any of those milestones, but I couldn't face my family back then. Not Lisa. And certainly not my mother and father. So I pretended I was too busy managing other people's money and made myself scarce at home. In the end, I only managed to become even more estranged from the people who truly matter.

Her lips thin as she studies me, and then she says, "So you've decided that my job as a school counselor is a direct result of the supposedly limited opportunities I had because I stayed in New York to keep an eye on Mom and Dad. Wow." She pulls in a so-help-me breath, then blows it out slowly. "You're a piece of work, sis."

See? Terrible.

"That sounded different in my head, Lili." I press on despite the side-eye she's giving me for resurrecting a nickname I lost the right to use years ago. "In my mind, it was ten times less condescending and a thousand times more gracious."

She sighs wearily. "Look, I'm not trying to be difficult. I appreciate that you want to reconnect. It's just . . . I don't know you anymore, Vanessa. You want to pick up where we left off, but that's not going to happen overnight."

"I get it. I do. All I'm asking is that you let me in. Even if it's only a teeny bit. Now that I'm here, I'd like to spend time with you. Remember what Mami used to tell us? 'You two need to have each other's backs. It's you two against the world.'"

A hint of a smile battles the rest of her cloudy features, and for the first time since we sat down at the table, a sense of hope takes root in my chest. Lisa's smile tells me the door to her heart is still open. Not *wide* open, mind you, but if a crack is all she'll give me, I'll gladly take it.

"We used to make fun of her when she told us that," she says, her expression wistful, as if she's remembering us giggling and sneakily rolling our eyes while Mami lectured us on the importance of sisterhood.

"We sure did."

Back then, Lisa and I were know-it-alls. Now, I'm perfectly comfortable acknowledging I don't know shit about anything. Well, that's not entirely true. I know *a lot* about what makes men tick. As to everything else? Zip.

Lisa twists her lips, then angles her head. "Tell me about Chicago. Why'd you leave? What happened?"

My boss, David Warner, happened, I think to myself. For six months, I was happily dating a man who never asked me for more. Figuring we were on the same page about the obvious limits of our relationship, I foolishly overshared parts of me I'd never shared with anyone. Stuff about my goals and dreams, my strengths and weaknesses. My strained relationship with my family and my fears about returning home someday. And then I continued to disregard everything I know about men and did the unthinkable: I rejected his attempts to take us to, as he put it, "the next level." Worse, I told him I couldn't see myself being serious with anyone, let alone my boss.

In a tale as old as time, he lashed out when I rejected him, accusing me of using him to climb the work ladder. As if my disinterest in a lasting commitment couldn't possibly be genuine and had to be part of an elaborate ploy. He wouldn't be duped, he said, so he recommended me for the team that would help build the New York office. A relocation would be good for my career, he suggested—in the middle of a staff meeting. Wow, message received.

David Warner taught me another lesson: Give men what they claim to want, and they'll *still* find a way to screw you over.

Frankly, I wanted to shove that transfer up his ass. But I didn't have that luxury. Not when my parents are struggling to keep their business afloat until they can sell it. Not when my sister's working sixty hours a week and helping my parents at the store on weekends. How selfish would I be to put my needs before theirs? *Especially* after I cast them aside so easily years ago. No, the only answer was to grin and bear it.

"An opportunity to return to the city presented itself," I tell Lisa. "A promotion of sorts."

I'm not sharing the particulars with my sister. They're unimportant.

"So you're here for the foreseeable future?" she asks.

"Yeah."

"Then I'd like you to help us offload the store," she says, picking at the sourdough carcass that passes for bread at Grenadine's. "Mami and Papi are procrastinating, but they need to slow down. Like yesterday. They're exhausted. And they haven't taken a vacation in God knows how long. It's time."

La Flor Superette is my parents' bodega in East Harlem. Well, that's the name in the official paperwork, but to the neighborhood, it's the corner store. One of hundreds in the city. As to La Flor, though, my parents' blood, sweat, and tears are built into its foundation. Their life's work situated at the intersection of 106th Street and Second Avenue. Getting them to give it up won't be easy.

"Whatever you need, I'll do it. And I'd like to talk to them about their retirement funds too. I can help them make some strategic decisions. Do you happen to know if—"

"Vanessa?" a high-pitched voice behind me says, interrupting my inevitable train of bulldozing questions. "Is that you?"

I twist around in my seat and see an old college acquaintance—and former client. Yes, I'm using the term loosely here, but still. *Shit*.

"Charlotte," I singsong, recovering quickly and jumping to my feet. Unfortunately, she's not alone. The woman beside her could be her twin, though. "It's *so* good to see you."

"Get over here, woman." She steps forward and pulls me into a light hug. "It's totally bizarre that I'm seeing you after all these years. And today of all days."

"Oh, is it a special occasion?"

She swings her blond bob around and raises a thick, legal-sized accordion envelope in the air. "Receipts. The divorce is officially final."

"Oh no, you and Ian split up?"

I remember him well: Last name Thompson. White guy. A third-year economics major from California. Straitlaced and serious. Biggest pet peeve: untidy people. Hence, the name of the assignment: Operation Messy. That one was fun.

THE STARTER EX

"Sweetie, this is a *good* thing. I was in love with him. Truly. Then I discovered Ian doesn't have a loyal bone in his body. Short story: He's loaded. He cheated. No prenup. Cha-ching. We're visiting my parents to celebrate. In fact, I'd clink glasses with you if I had any champagne handy." Charlotte glances at her companion and furrows her brow. "Goodness, sorry. Julia, this is Vanessa Cordero. Vanessa, this is my bestie, Julia." Turning to Julia, she says, "Vanessa and I went to college together. She's the starter ex I told you about. The one who helped me land *the asshole* in the first place."

In the beginning, I'd considered asking my clients to sign a nondisclosure agreement, then felt mildly embarrassed at the thought of taking what I was doing so seriously. In this moment, however, I have regrets. Many, many regrets.

Her companion's eyes grow wide as saucers. "Oh-em-gee, *this* is the genius who tortures men for a living?"

My face warms under her blunt appraisal. "That's not an accurate description of what I did. And anyway, it's all in the past." I wave away my and Charlotte's connection as if it's no big deal. "Misguided college stuff." Damn, it's hot in here. Is the restaurant's ventilation system on the fritz?

"Well, past or not, I bow down to you, *girlfriend*."

Still seated at the table, Lisa clears her throat. Or maybe that's a snort. Yeah, considering this stranger unironically called me *girlfriend*, Lisa definitely just snorted.

I spin around as if my sister's appeared from nowhere. "Oh, right. Charlotte, this is Lisa. My younger sister. We were just heading out—"

"No, we weren't," my traitorous sister says. "We haven't even ordered." She motions to the empty chair next to hers. "Want to join us? I'd love to hear more about this torturing business from someone who has firsthand experience seeing my sister in action." Lisa pins me with a frosty stare, as if to say, *You have a lot of explaining to do, pendeja.*

I drop onto my chair and rub my temples. Damn, this is going to be painful.

Photograph of the author © Ginny Filer Photography

Mia Sosa is a *USA Today* bestselling author of romantic comedies and contemporary romances that celebrate our multicultural world. She has received praise from *The Washington Post*, *Bustle*, NPR, *Entertainment Weekly*, *PopSugar*, *BuzzFeed*, *Oprah Daily*, and many more. A New York City native, she now lives in Maryland with her college sweetheart, their two book-obsessed daughters, a gentle Cavalier King Charles spaniel, and one adorable rescue cat that rules them all.

CONNECT WITH MIA SOSA ONLINE

MiaSosaRomance
MiaSosaAuthor
MiaSosa.Author